Great-Grandpa's Tree

Diane Moyna Ross

From little acorns grow mighty oaks.

GREAT-GRANDPA'S TREE
Diane Moyna Ross

Edited and produced by Graham Bathgate

ISBN: 978-0-473-54498-0

A 2020 publication of Fine Line Press

www.finelinepress.co.nz

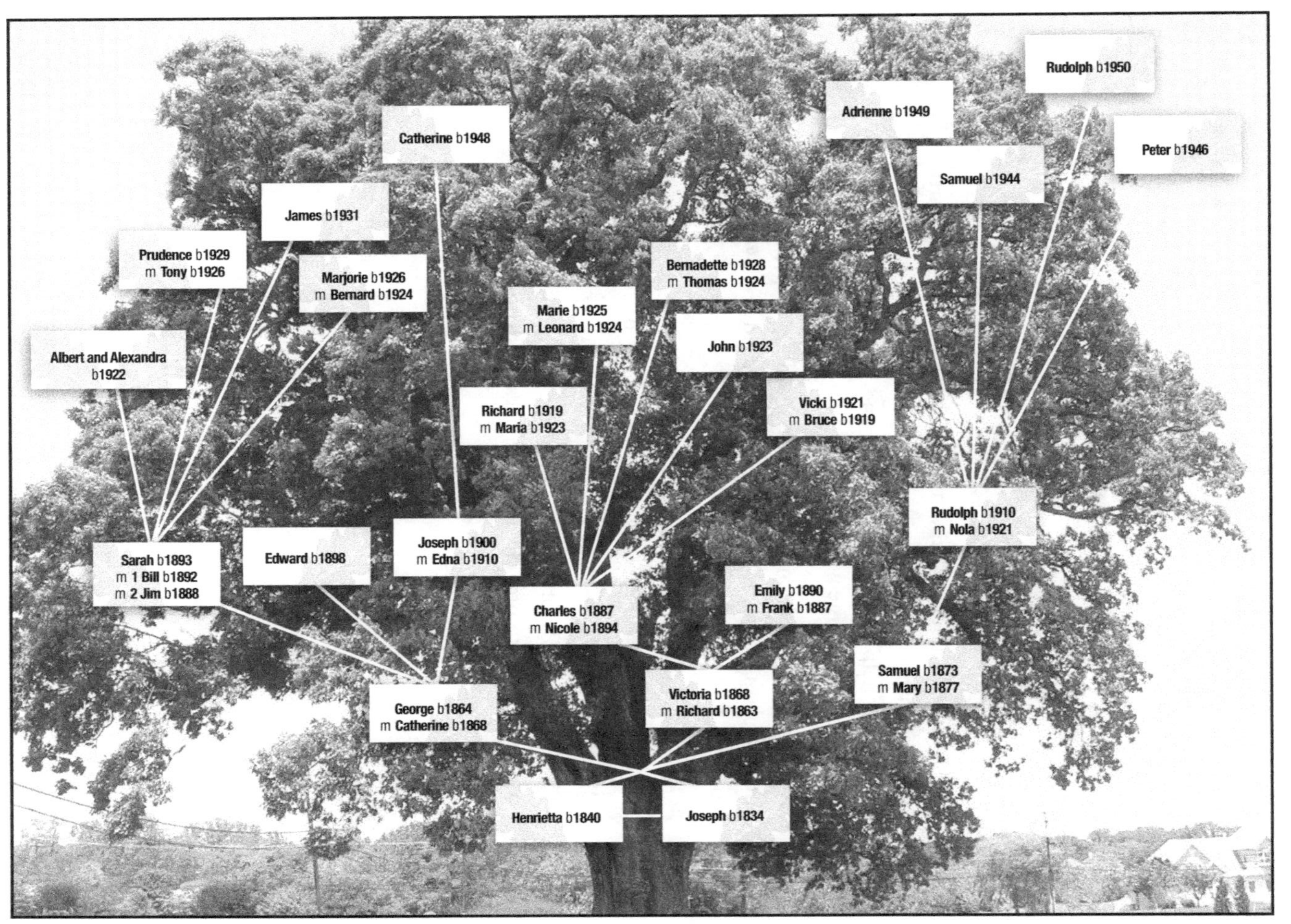

HAMILTON FAMILY TREE
Rudolph b1950
Adrienne b1949
Peter b1946
Catherine b1948
Samuel b1944
James b1931
Prudence b1929
m Tony b1926
Bernadette b1928
m Thomas b1924
Marjorie b1926
m Bernard b1924
Marie b1925
m Leonard b1924
John b1923
Albert and Alexandra
b1922
Vicki b1921
m Bruce b1919
Richard b1919
m Maria b1923
Rudolph b1910
m Nola b1921
Sarah b1893
m 1 Bill b1892
m 2 Jim b1888
Edward b1898
Joseph b1900
m Edna b1910
Charles b1887
m Nicole b1894
Emily b1890
m Frank b1887
Samuel b1873
m Mary b1877
George b1864
m Catherine b1868
Victoria b1868
m Richard b1863
Henrietta b1840
Joseph b1834

ACKNOWLEDGMENTS

My gratitude goes to Ian, my patient husband, for putting years of love and support into this project. There was also his invaluable help with the family tree and provision of computer expertise where mine was lacking.

My thanks to Graham Bathgate for his diligent proofreading, insightful suggestions, encouragement and advice over several months.

Special thanks to Jo Aitken, whose creativity, patience and expertise as a designer have transformed my basic ideas into a charming reality.

Thanks go to Ralph Bolton for using his photographic and computer skills to provide quality images for the book.

DEDICATION

To my cousin Anne: her gentle enquiries and enthusiasm over the years helped me to return to the task.

To my family: I hope that through this book, the story of a family not unlike ours, they will see not only an example of perseverance but also the value of family. The writing of it has taught me how much they mean to me, and I have tried to emphasise the importance of relationships between my characters.

Introduction

A keen reader of historical novels, I found very few set in New Zealand. At the age of thirty I decided to write one. The timing was not good – I was working and bringing up a young family, but I set out the scope of the novel and filled in some of the themes. A cousin and my mother prodded me from time to time, so I would manage to prioritise the book for a while.

In 1972 my husband and I started a love affair with Canada, living in British Columbia for a year and driving up to the Yukon Territory in the summer. In December, 1985 we flew to Whitehorse to experience the Yukon winter. In 1990 we spent a further year in Ontario. I saw a chance to draw on travel experiences in my writing and give expression to the bond I felt between New Zealand and Canada.

1975

Confident that I would eventually finish the book, I researched the historical events I planned to cover. I would be ready when I finally had time.

In 2011 we relocated following a period of trauma and upheaval. Our house was condemned and demolished after the Christchurch earthquakes. A new set of friendships and commitments was formed.

As my seventy-fifth birthday loomed up this year I made the decision and the effort to complete my tale, managing to write "The End" four days before the birthday. "Great-Grandpa's Tree" has been forty-five years in the making – I hope you enjoy the result.

PART I

CHAPTER 1

Arrival

As the 'Cressida' crept closer to the still distant land, tossing a little on the choppy water, Joseph turned his thoughts to those who had arrived 18 years before, on the first four ships to bring settlers to this coast. A second-cousin had voyaged on the 'Charlotte Jane', but had died within a year. Fortunately he was not a married man. What must it have been like, to look upon an empty land, with beautiful bays and coves, and try to envisage a prosperous future? What misgivings had they felt about their decision to make the voyage?

Joseph had no misgivings, just a slow-burning enthusiasm to begin this new life. He felt as if he stood on the crest of a hill, looking back towards England and the known but unfulfilling life, and forward to New Zealand, with all the promises for him there. Henrietta should be with him, but she was in the cabin caring for little George and his baby sister, Victoria, named after the queen who was now so far away. Could this land really be a part of her Empire? It was some comfort to know that, after months at sea, where all was strange and new, there would be this one tie with England, although every sight and sound in the new land might be different.

Henrietta simply must come up on deck to view the land of her future. It was not far to the cabin. As Joseph stooped to clear the six-foot doorway, she motioned him to silence. Victoria had dozed off in the tiny crib and George was industriously drawing a Christmas tree on his slate. Henrietta looked tired.

"Come up on deck, I have something to show you, my dear," whispered Joseph. "Victoria will sleep for a while now, I am sure. Come, George."

They made a striking sight. Joseph was so tall and straight, managing to appear impeccably dressed in the far-from-luxurious conditions on board, his ginger moustache neatly clipped and his blonde hair plastered into place against the stiff breeze. Henrietta was short, dark-haired, rather plump, and feeling heartily sick of the once-attractive dress she was wearing. Little George, aged four, a perfect blend of his parents in appearance, dark and solid like his mother, but long-legged; he would be tall like his father some day. He walked between them, accentuating the contrast in their heights.

By now the coast was clearly visible, with a large peninsula jutting out on the starboard side. It might even be an island, Joseph mused, and he felt a surge of excitement now that he could actually see his future homeland.

"It looks dry, hard land, Joseph," declared Henrietta soberly.

"Yes, but it is high summer and they've evidently not had the rain we endured through the tropics," replied Joseph.

Henrietta lacked her husband's enthusiasm. She had been less discontented with life in England and so had not dreamed, as he had, of a magic place across the world where every man could be his own master and land was there for the taking, for a nominal sum. She foresaw all manner of difficulties raising children in an uncivilised place, with unpredictable savages living nearby. However she said nothing of her feelings, not wanting to dull the light she had seen in his eyes these past months.

"We shall be landing in an hour, sir," announced a ship's officer, who still managed a smile after making the same announcement some thirty times. "Would you please take your family below to prepare for disembarkation? Please check that your papers are in order."

There was little delay when the ship berthed. These were all legal immigrants: no stowaways and no-one who had not paid his passage in full or been thoroughly approved for an assisted passage before leaving England. "Hamilton, Joseph James, age 34; Hamilton, Henrietta Martha, age 28; Hamilton, George Edward, age 4; Hamilton, Victoria Louise, age 9 months. All correct. Proceed, please."

"Where do we go from here, Joseph?"

"We will be met by a gentleman who will tell us where we may buy our plot of land. I understand the land for sale is on the other side of those hills you see ahead, in a small town that has been named Christchurch. Ah, that will be the man, there, where you see people gathering. Come along!"

The man gave advice as to the location of the land sales office, but his news of how to reach Christchurch was disturbing. "There is no road yet; you must follow that path to the top of the hills you see there and then take what we call the Bridle Path down the other side. You would be advised to purchase food for the journey before you leave, for there is nothing on the way." Henrietta's heart sank, her unvoiced fears firmly founded. Joseph was undaunted.

"Courage, my dear, it will not take us long. Let us see what food we can find at that stall. George must walk as far as he can and then I shall carry him. Until then I shall take Victoria if you will carry the food. We shall leave the trunks here for now and take only the cabin baggage. Can you manage the smaller grip? Good! Let's be on our way!"

It was almost 11.00 on Joseph's pocket-watch. The sun was still climbing, but it was already warm as they set out. Others leaving at the same time accompanied the Hamiltons and this cheered Henrietta somewhat. The other women looked no happier than she felt – except one, younger than the rest and obviously a recent bride, who saw beauty in the countryside which the others found dry and drab, and who had enough energy to hold a conversation as well as gather up her skirts and trudge upwards through the tussock and bracken. She carried Victoria for a time and took George's little hand when he stumbled.

It was a tired, bedraggled group that reached Christchurch late that December afternoon, a group no different, however, than established settlers had seen several times before, and by now there was a reception routine established. They were met on the outskirts of the little town and each family was given the name and address of a home where they would be accommodated for a few nights for a small charge. Henrietta was greatly relieved, for this had been worrying her all day, whereas Joseph, she assumed, was more concerned with being among the first to visit the land sales office.

The Hamiltons' hosts, the Andersons, lived in Worcester Street, just off Latimer Square. The familiarity of the street names made Joseph feel that this was indeed a corner of Queen Victoria's Empire, although this Christchurch was a far cry from an English town. The hospitality was as warm as the weather, and soon a nourishing meal had raised their spirits.

The Andersons had arrived on the 'Seymour' in 1850, and so considered themselves veterans, having been here for eighteen years now. They answered all questions fully, but did not offer unwanted advice, believing that true pioneers learned best from experience. Mr Anderson had a nephew working at the land sales office, so it was arranged that this young man would call for Joseph on his way to work next morning. There could be no favours, but at least Joseph would be among the first there.

At 6.45a.m. there was a knock at the back door. Joseph was ready and with a quick glance at his wife, who smiled her encouragement, he was gone. As the morning wore on Henrietta tried to do a few domestic duties, but she was weary and unsettled. She was glad when Mrs Anderson said, "Leave the children with our Mary and we'll have a look at the town. Nothing energetic," she added hastily, "just a quiet little stroll. I'll show you the shops. You will not want to spend any money until your husband is established, but it will do no harm to look in the windows."

Changing her house slippers for street shoes and putting on a bonnet, Henrietta joined Mrs Anderson for her first glimpse of this town which would be home for the rest of her life. After cautioning George to be good, she stepped out into the warmth of the late morning, sensing at once that she was going to love her new home. The trees in the square were already large enough to offer chequered shade from the summer sun. How tall would these oaks stand a hundred years from now, she mused. There were not many houses in the street yet and Henrietta tried to imagine which site Joseph was negotiating to buy at this moment. She had been content to leave this to him, since it was to be not only their home but Joseph's business site also.

As they walked Mrs Anderson had left Henrietta absorbed with her thoughts, and she was surprised to find they had reached the centre of the town. Mrs Anderson began to point out the established shops, greeting acquaintances as they passed but declining to stop and introduce her new charge. She well remembered how overpowering her first weeks in this country had been. Taking in the names of the businesses they passed, Henrietta tried to memorise them. At first she saw them clearly: Mrs Pope's, children's clothes; G. Tombs, stationer; E. Reece, ironmonger; G. Coates, clockmaker; A J White, furniture; but soon they whirled through her head, the only ones standing out being the larger stores facing each other across the street, one bearing the name of Beath & Co., the other Ballantyne's.

Watching her carefully, Mrs Anderson could see that this was enough for now. Steering Henrietta towards the pretty stream which wandered peacefully along some way from the shops, she led her along its bank until they reached Market Square. It was not quite on their way home, but she wanted to show Henrietta the immigration barracks, the official temporary accommodation for arriving families and single people.

"We regard this as a harsh introduction to a new life. That is why we set up the reception committee," she stated simply. Henrietta's heart warmed to this kind woman, who had wanted to offer new families more than the type of living quarters she had experienced on her arrival. Here was her first New Zealand friend, she was sure.

Joseph returned just before midday, jubilant.

"Just what I wanted, Henrietta! An acre of land, only a short distance from here. And at a good price too. We'll build the shop across the front and the house behind, with a yard where the children may play. By the time I left the office the land on each side had been sold, but I feel sure we made the best purchase." Henrietta had never seen him so excited.

"Oh, and who do you think I saw at the Land Sales office this morning? He was just arriving as I was coming away."

Someone we know, Joseph? Someone from the ship, then?"

"Indeed. None other than young Gainsborough! And he was looking as keen as a man in a gold rush. I was quite surprised."

Henrietta thought back to the tragedy the young man had suffered on the voyage to New Zealand. If he was settling nearby they would invite him for a meal once they had their own home.

That afternoon Joseph sat down and drew up plans to show her how their new home would look, before they inspected the piece of land together. Henrietta was glad of this, for it was difficult to envisage this empty space as a built-up street with shops and houses along each side.

Within a matter of days the house was under construction. Although Joseph would have preferred to establish his drapery business first, the more urgent need was undoubtedly a home for his family. The Andersons were kind-hearted, but it was not easy for any family to have four extra people in their house for long. As soon as the new house was habitable he would move Henrietta, George and little Victoria into it and complete the building around them. Joseph was doing much of the work himself but one of the Anderson boys, Charles, was a carpenter by trade and he gave advice and assistance on the more detailed matters.

Christmas came, and was shared with the Anderson family. It was fortunate that the children were easily satisfied – a gift or two, a tree and some carols sufficed – and they were too young to feel the strangeness of a summer Christmas. No snow, no sleighs, no boots and muffs, just a glorious day when turkey and plum pudding seemed inappropriate, but the settlers had brought their traditions with them when much had needed to be left behind, and the Andersons were no exception.

After the festivities Henrietta recalled the many Christmas Days spent with her father, now separated from her not only by distance but by death. It was hard to conjure a picture of him in her mind, with so many new sights and sounds around her. She forced herself to think of the loneliness and suffering her father had endured from the very day of her birth. Yet she had always felt sure he loved her, as a treasured memento of the mother she had never known. Allowing herself the leisure to reminisce before embarking on her new rôle as a pioneer woman, Henrietta withdrew into herself to wrap and seal the package of her old life. There would be times to unwrap parts of it in the future, but the next years promised to be too full for glancing over her shoulder into the past.

CHAPTER 2
Henrietta Martha Baker

In a darkened room, the blinds half-drawn to keep out the bright morning sun, Martha lay waiting for the next racking spasm. It was always a darkish room anyway, she reflected, letting her eyes wander from the windows to the black fire-surround, topped by a walnut mantel shelf. Even the clock, which chimed the half-hour as she was looking at it, was dark-stained. Moving on, her eyes found her pride and joy in the furthest corner of the room. Her parents had given her the box ottoman as a gift on her sixteenth birthday, so that she might have somewhere to store the trousseau she must collect. Quilted and studded with stones that sparkled in the faintest light, it winked back at her as she smiled.

The pain came on suddenly, sharp and lasting. She cried out involuntarily and the midwife bustled in.

"There, there, Mrs Baker, just try to relax, dear. You've a while to go yet, I'm afraid." Mopping her patient's brow she added, "Try to catch some sleep between the pains, for you'll need your strength when the child decides to come."

Martha Baker, at forty-four years of age, had been married twenty-three years. It had been a happy marriage, marred only by the disappointment of having no children. Eventually she and her husband George had resigned themselves to this situation, but both had been overjoyed to discover last year that they were, after all, to be blessed with a child. Martha hoped, from the start, for a son, imagining that this was what George would want, but at forty-eight years of age, George was so overwhelmed at this miracle that he wished for no more than a healthy child.

It was late afternoon before the doctor was summoned. Martha's strength was barely equal to the task. It had been a long and difficult labour, dragging on for two days and a night, and at times it seemed poor Martha would collapse completely. George had been shocked at how old and tired she had appeared when he was permitted to see her. Where was the joy they had shared six months ago? He stayed only a few minutes, as instructed, and left feeling dejected.

He went to dine that evening with his neighbours, the Chestertons. They had been kind these past few weeks and George was grateful. He was not a man who had had to look after himself and he had no idea of how to do "women's work". Mrs

Chesterton's offer to keep an eye on the house, and on George, had therefore been deeply appreciated by Martha, while she had been obliged to stay in bed or rest on it most of the day these past weeks.

A small man, George Baker was nonetheless a good eater, and he had thoroughly enjoyed the meal of roast beef and Yorkshire pudding, as well as the delicious apple pie Mrs. Chesterton had made for the occasion. Settling back to enjoy a pipe with Mr Chesterton, George had just struck the match when a piercing shriek jerked him to his feet. He dropped the match, which fell into the hearth unnoticed, as another scream, and yet another, paralysed him where he stood.

"That's my Martha! I must go home." Sarah Chesterton took his arm, guiding him gently back to the armchair.

"If you will just wait a few minutes, Mr Baker, you will probably be able to meet your child. You have your pipe first, now."

Unconvinced, but aware that he would probably not be allowed near his poor dear Martha anyway, George sat puffing agitatedly at his pipe, which went out twice in protest at his vehemence. With a gesture to her husband, Mrs Chesterton slipped out through the back door and scurried to the Bakers' house. As she entered she caught the wail of a newborn baby. Reaching the upstairs room she asked Dr White in a whisper if Mr Baker might come home, as he was quite alarmed. Still busy, the doctor nodded and Mrs Chesterton crept back the way she had come.

She found George Baker perched on the edge of the chair, his pipe finished and back in his pocket, but he could not leave because Mr Chesterton was regaling him with the story of Palmerston's recent negotiations with Turkey and the new treaty signed just a few days ago with Russia, Austria and Prussia. Both men rose to their feet, equally relieved, as the flustered lady made her entrance.

Since there was no longer any need to keep George from his wife, the Chestertons bade him goodnight and he thanked them for their hospitality. Like a schoolboy he rushed home, took the stairs up to the bedroom two at a time, and stood panting sheepishly in the doorway, looking questioningly at Dr White.

"Well, Mr Baker, I am pleased to tell you that you have a bonny daughter. However I must also tell you that your wife is exhausted. You must understand that at her age …" George blushed, and the doctor continued, "Whether she will be able to nurse the infant we must wait and see. I shall arrange for a young woman to be available if need be. Your wife is sleeping now. Let her rest as long as she needs. It was quite an ordeal for her, you know. Mrs Carter will stay tonight to help you, but I think you may have to engage a servant. It will be some time before Mrs Baker will be on her feet again."

Thanking Dr White for his services, George tip-toed over to the cradle to meet the tiny person who had brought Martha such pain and exhaustion. All he could see was a head that would fit in his hand. It was thatched with black hair, but the face was unmistakably Martha's. It was uncanny, as if Martha had been reduced to this size. Strangely moved, he crossed to the bed and kissed his wife gently on the forehead. He had not meant to wake her but was rewarded with a saintly smile and Martha saying softly, "We have a daughter, George." Tears welled in his eyes as he whispered hoarsely, "Thank you." Her eyes closed and she drifted back to sleep.

George slept downstairs on the sofa so that he would not disturb Martha's rest. He was worried about her pallor, for she had always been a rosy-cheeked, plump, jolly woman. Now she looked drained and ashen. Mrs Carter, the midwife, slept during the early part of the evening, taking over from George at midnight. He had really had nothing to do. Some hours later Mrs Carter shook him awake, a note of urgency in her voice.

"Mr Baker, Mr Baker, come quickly. She's slipped away, I think."

Torn from a sound sleep George stammered, "Away … how can she? She is too weak to go anywhere. What do you mean, woman?"

"Sir, I think she has … died!"

"Died? My Martha dead? She can't be!" It was unthinkable that he would never see her smile again, never hear her say his name. George raced once more up the stairs, calling her name, softly at first, then almost shouting, to make her hear him. There was not a flicker of life. He lifted her hand to his lips. Although still warm it slid back onto the counterpane when he released it. Mrs Carter pulled back the covers, revealing a blood-soaked sheet where Martha lay.

"Loss of blood, the poor dear. She has haemorrhaged to death. I'll fetch Dr White. Come away now, Mr Baker, there is no more you can do."

In a daze George let himself be led back down the stairs to the sofa in the sitting-room. He wished it were the child that was dead, the one that was the cause of all this. How could he ever love her, when she had killed her mother? He did not voice his thoughts to Mrs Carter when she brought him a cup of sweet tea, nor did she confide in him. She would have to go herself for Dr White, yet she did not want to leave Mr Baker alone. She decided to wake Mrs Chesterton and ask her to sit with him.

It was Mr Chesterton who opened the door to Mrs Carter's urgent hammering. Still tying the cord of his dressing-gown, he frowned at the unknown woman who stood before him. Before he had a chance to speak however, she blurted out the story and asked if one of them would sit with Mr Baker. To Robert Chesterton there seemed no need to wake his wife: he would go for Dr White, leaving Mrs Carter in the house. She would have more idea of what to do than either he or Sarah. Passing on the address and expressing her gratitude, Mrs Carter made her way back to the house.

When she entered the Baker home, an inconspicuous dwelling like so many others in industrial cities like Birmingham, it was utterly quiet. Although she had not expected to hear a noise there was a quality to the silence that made Mrs Carter uneasy. Mr Baker was not in the sitting-room or the kitchen. He must be upstairs, she thought. No doubt he had wandered back to his wife, trying to grasp the reality of her death.

Entering the bedroom as noiselessly as she had climbed the stairs, she stiffened. He was not there! Had he gone out into the night? In his state that could be dangerous. Then the sudden awareness of a presence in the room made her turn to the darker corner, and there, bending over his baby's crib, was George Baker. In the lamplight his face wore the strangest expression, hatred and anger battling with the grudging love he felt for this little being which had cost his adored Martha her life. No, he could not hate her – there was too much of Martha in the face. And Martha had been so proud and happy to give him this daughter. George hoped that she had died happy. Henrietta, that was the name Martha had wanted if she gave birth to a girl.

George slumped on to the end of the ottoman, his shoulders drooping. The struggle was over. So much to do but so tired. Although Mrs Carter had been in the room for several minutes, it was only now that he noticed her.

"What are we going to do when the child wakes, Mrs Carter?" George asked wearily.

"Dr White will be here soon, Mr Baker, and he will take care of everything. When he comes we must get you off to bed too. There will be arrangements to be made tomorrow."

"Yes, for both Martha and Henrietta."

"So you have named her then, sir? A pretty name too."

"It was the name Martha chose, but I want her to have Martha as a second name, in memory of her mother."

Mrs Carter was relieved to see that, in spite of his grief and tiredness, Mr Baker was beginning to think kindly towards the child. The little mite would bring him a lot of comfort in the years ahead. Thank Heaven he had too much sense to blame her for his wife's death. She had seen it in his eyes a few minutes before, but any ill-will had melted away as his weariness took over.

Dr White duly administered a sleeping draught to George and he was tucked up on the sofa before both doctor and midwife attended to Martha. It was not the first time that Mrs Carter had helped lay out a body. This sort of thing happened too often for her liking. She would be glad when more was known about the complications arising in childbirth.

The next day Dr White summoned to the house a young woman whose first baby had died just two days earlier. Inconsolable with grief, she had dried her tears at the thought of mothering a baby. Lucy Stanton had been married barely a year when her son was born. Her husband, John, was as thrilled as she was at the child's birth, but the baby was sickly and soon developed a chest ailment, which carried him off in less than a week. At Dr White's suggestion that both she and her husband might live in at the Baker home, should Mr Baker find her suitable, Lucy dressed carefully and made her way through the streets to Birch Grove.

She paused outside number 15 to survey the house before knocking on the front door. It was not an attractive house, but it was free-standing, unlike the rented tenement house in which she lived with John. Built of brick, which the murky city air had dulled to brown, it was a two-storeyed building, appearing to have three bedrooms. The small flower beds at the front of the house were rather unkempt, but showed signs of having been carefully tended until recent months.

Gathering her courage Lucy knocked at the door. It was opened by a short man of about fifty, whom Lucy knew to be George Baker by the set of his face. Listlessly he ushered her into the sitting-room, offered her a chair and sat down in another. He only half registered a plump, healthy-looking young woman of hardly 20, with thick auburn hair cascading from under her simple bonnet. Neatly, though modestly, dressed she was a pleasing sight. He tried to throw off the weight over his heart, so that he might talk to her. He saw pity in her eyes as he tried to marshal his thoughts.

"Mr Baker, I … I want to tell you I think I understand how you are feeling," she murmured hesitantly.

'Yes, perhaps you do, Mrs Stanton. You too have suffered a great loss, I am told. I am sorry to have brought you out so soon afterwards, but we must act quickly, for Henrietta's sake. Would you care to see her?"

"Oh yes, Mr Baker. My arms ache to hold a baby again."

George led the way upstairs to the second bedroom, where Mrs Carter was trying unsuccessfully to feed Henrietta with a bottle of milk. The child was rejecting the teat and squealing with frustration.

"Oh, the poor little lamb! She wants a mother, not a bottle. Mr Baker, I have plenty of milk still, would you allow me to …?"

George nodded dumbly. This was what they had hoped, he and Dr White. While Lucy took the screaming infant, he left the room hastily, on the pretext of making a cup of tea. As he put the kettle on Sarah Chesterton poked her head around the kitchen door with a "Yoo-hoo Mr Baker!" Finding him there she came in with a basket of warm scones and buns.

"How are things turning out, Mr Baker? Will you be able to manage with the baby? We have three of our own, as you know, but if you need help …"

"I think we have just solved the problem of Henrietta, Mrs Chesterton," replied George with a smile. It was such a relief to see him smile, thought Sarah. He proceeded to recount how he would offer Lucy Stanton a job as a live-in housekeeper and nanny to Henrietta, and Lucy's husband could live there too and go to work from Birch Grove each morning. If they had a family of their own in the future so much the better – Henrietta would have some playmates. This satisfactory arrangement worked out well.

Lucy and John, released from the burden of paying rent, gave up their cramped tenement quarters and moved their few possessions into 15 Birch Grove that same evening. John and George (who insisted they both address him thus) took an instant liking to each other, and Lucy was more than happy looking after little Henrietta. After Martha's funeral George returned to his job as foreman at the textile mill, as happy as any man could be who had just lost his dear wife. It seemed weeks already since Martha had died, for so many things had changed in such a short time.

As Henrietta grew into a chubby, lovable child, able to crawl and pull herself upright, Lucy saw to it that George always felt the child was really his. She would excuse herself from the room sometimes, leaving him alone with his little daughter. On her return she would find George holding her affectionately on his knee, while Henrietta gurgled contentedly; or the child would be standing clutching his leg, grinning triumphantly up at him. These were moments both would treasure, and Lucy knew by instinct how important they were.

Just before Henrietta's first birthday Lucy was safely delivered of a daughter. This did nothing to diminish her love for Henrietta, who was too young to be jealous. She would never have to suffer the loneliness of the only child. The following year Lucy produced a bonny boy, and the next another girl.

By now the house was far too small for seven people, with little doubt of more to come, but George had grown devoted to his adopted family so he would not ask them to leave. Instead he and John set about adding two rooms to the back of the house. The brood continued to increase until, by the time Henrietta was ten years old, Lucy had six of her own to care for. George insisted that Henrietta help in the house and with the younger children, and be treated in the same way they were, although she knew that Lucy and John were not her parents.

In recent years John had become more discontented with his work. For a man trying to keep a wife and six children, being a builder's labourer was not rewarding enough. He was not a greedy man, but where would they be without George's help? A man had his pride, after all.

George sat back and watched John tussle with his thoughts at home, while at work he kept his ears open for any opportunities that might suit him. Finally, when he had something up his sleeve, he broached the subject over a pipe one evening, when the children were all in bed and Lucy was ironing in the sitting-room with the men, as was their custom. He gave John the chance to voice his feelings and then said quietly,

"There is a job at the mill that I think would suit you well. It is a skilled job eventually, but you could be trained to it soon enough."

John's eyes lit up, but dulled with disappointment when George explained that a man was wanted to service the new machinery recently installed at the mill.

"But you need an engineer. I am a builder! Why are you mentioning this to me?"

"Because you are mechanically minded and it is a job with a good future. If you learn a skill like this you will be able to command a place in any mill in England. There are so few men with this knowledge, and one of ours is leaving soon. We want him to have time to train a replacement before he leaves."

"But why not take on an apprentice boy?"

"It would take too long to train a lad. We need a man with a keen brain and nimble fingers, and you have both. You would be paid almost twice what you earn now."

Hearing Lucy clear her throat, John turned to her with an inquiring look. "Well Lucy, what do you think?"

"I think you will be sick tomorrow and go to work with George to have a look at what is expected in the job."

"Well … I don't know …"

"Look, John Stanton, you have been unhappy for a long while with your work. Now you are being offered a chance to improve your lot, and that by a person who knows both your abilities and your weaknesses. If George has faith in you then you must take the chance!"

"You are right, of course, Lucy. I'll go with George in the morning. But you know I never miss a day's work …"

"It will be worth your while, John."

CHAPTER 3

Joseph Hamilton

While Henrietta had been growing up amidst a happy, loving family, with a father ever more amazed at her likeness to her mother and the Stanton children idolising her as a big sister, a young man was making his way, with some trepidation, towards Birmingham. His had been a very different life so far.

Joseph Hamilton was born on the 16th April, 1834, the fourth child of a middle-class family. His parents had been drowned, along with his younger sister, when their carriage was swept away in a raging flood as they crossed the wooden bridge near their home. The carriage and horses had added just enough weight to snap the weakened bridge piles. It had been a wild, stormy night, not a night for venturing out, and the other four children had been left in the care of the servants while Mr and Mrs Hamilton rushed little Amelia to the doctor.

At just six years of age then, Joseph began a new life. He was taken, with one of his brothers, to live with the bachelor uncle after whom he was named. The other two children went to their mother's sister.

Joseph Hamilton the elder took his duties as god-father and guardian seriously. Although fond of the boys, David and Joseph, he lived by the maxim of 'Spare the rod and spoil the child', so they were no strangers to vigorous beatings for minor misdemeanours. He sent them to the village school, where they were encouraged to play with working-class children and to think themselves no better than anyone else. When David was thirteen his uncle found him a place as an apprentice in a cotton mill in Manchester. This meant leaving his second home and journeying alone to Manchester, to be met there by a family who had agreed to furnish his board and lodging. Uncle Joseph had made all the arrangements and would pay his expenses, but it was a lonely boy who hugged his eight-year-old brother, for the last time in many years, before boarding the coach for yet another new life.

Left alone with his uncle, upon whom he had always looked with some awe, Joseph discovered that either the old chap had mellowed or he could manage better with just one charge. Whatever the reason, his manner changed towards Joseph and they became firm friends. An intelligent boy, quick to master new things taught to him, Joseph was surprised at his uncle's interest in him. He learned all sorts of card games during the long winter evenings as they sat in front of the blazing fire, and his uncle introduced to him many brain-teasers in the form of wooden puzzles and optical illusions. There developed between them a strong bond, broken only by the old man's death many years later.

Keen to please his uncle, Joseph shone at school and his teachers considered that he should continue his education. Convincing his uncle proved quite a task, for the latter saw trade as the future of the nation. However, he allowed the boy to stay on at school until he was fifteen. Then, through his numerous trading contacts, he found him a position in the largest textile mill in Birmingham. Since Joseph's maternal aunt lived in that city, it was logical that he should board with her, reuniting with his sister Anna. Now seventeen, she had last seen Joseph just after the death of their parents. His other brother, Donald, also brought up by Aunt Margaret, had left home several years before to work in Wales.

As the coach rattled south towards Birmingham, Joseph wondered if he had been right to reject his uncle's surprising offer to accompany him. He had felt so grown up, but now, as the miles dragged by, he was feeling less sure of himself. Tall for his age, he felt gangly and awkward in the cramped coach; his gold-blond hair was thick with dust, since he had removed his cap. He was unaware that the very ladies for whom he had removed it found him most appealing. They chattered and giggled, being younger than they cared to show. Joseph kept his thoughts to himself.

It was not because of his aunt that he felt nervous. He remembered her as a tall, graceful lady, like his mother in looks, always kind to the children and never flustered. She had hair that had reminded him of the rust around the base of the old pump in the yard of their home. He smiled, thinking it was not very complimentary, but it was surprising what comparisons you made at the age of six. At his smile the girls opposite burst into renewed chatter, so that he glanced at them involuntarily. He had had little contact with girls of his own age, for there had been few girls in his school, and none had stayed beyond the age of eleven or twelve. He guessed these girls were about his age, although they were dressed in similar fashion to the lady accompanying them. They were such foreign creatures to him so he gave up contemplating them and returned to the more urgent matter of the source of his tension.

If it was not the prospect of living with Aunt Margaret and meeting his sister Anna again (he wondered briefly if she would be as giggly as these two girls), then it must be the thought of his employment. Because of his age and schooling he would not start as an apprentice, but would train as a manager. He would need to learn the rudiments of the whole trade. Could he do it? Would he let Uncle Joseph down? He was only fifteen, after all.

Joseph decided to concentrate on the new foliage on the oaks that lined the road and the daffodils growing in wild abundance beneath the large protecting trees. The many shades of green fascinated him as they blended into each other, creating a rich fabric interwoven with the dotted yellow of the spring blooms. Fabric – yes, for a moment he *had* forgotten that his life would be woven into fabric from tomorrow. The letter he had received from Mr Baker had been kind and understanding: the fact that it had been enclosed with the reply to Uncle Joseph's told him something about his foreman, so perhaps he was worrying about nothing.

For a moment he relaxed, suddenly sensing the prying eyes of the two girls on him again. He supposed they had been watching him all the time, but he had been so engrossed in his own thoughts that he had forgotten them. Their companion murmured something to them and they began to fuss with gloves, handkerchiefs and parasols. Soon the coach came to a halt and Joseph was relieved to see all three alight and rush into the arms of a gentleman waiting for them. Now he would be able to pursue his thoughts uninterrupted.

Two new passengers joined him for the last few miles, a man and a boy. Joseph wondered fleetingly if the boy were in a similar position to his own, but soon forgot them as neither spoke much during the journey, the boy, looking miserable keeping his eyes on the floor most of the way, speaking only when his father spoke to him.

Joseph was hungry by the time the coach pulled into the depot in Birmingham. Although it was spring, the evenings were still short and dusk was falling. However, he recognised Aunt Margaret with no trouble, despite the threads of grey in her beautiful hair. But could that slender, elegant young woman beside her really be Anna? He had calculated that she must be seventeen years old by now, but could she really be so grown up? She had been a freckle-nosed little girl of eight when he had last seen her! He hesitated, not knowing if he should kiss her or shake her hand, but she solved his dilemma by rushing forward and throwing her arms around his neck, exclaiming how he had grown and how good it was to see him. There was evidently some girlishness left in her. Aunt Margaret hustled the young ones out to her waiting carriage, while she collected Joseph's luggage. Supper would be ready when they reached home, and there was a chill in the air. The sooner they were inside the better; besides, the children were waiting to meet their cousin.

Joseph was impressed by the family's contentment on that first evening in Birmingham. It revived long-buried memories of the years before the tragedy that had torn apart his own family's happiness. They had all been kindly treated since then, but it was only now that Joseph realised how much he and Anna and his brothers had missed as they grew up. It was no-one's fault, and they were lucky to have been cared for by relatives rather than sent to an orphanage or workhouse, but if ever he married and had a family he would do his utmost to see that they were raised with a strong family spirit.

Uncle Matthew, a burly, hearty man, observing that the boy was retreating into himself, said, "Come, Joseph, you and I must have a small brandy to celebrate the occasion!"

"Well, I …"

"I don't expect you are accustomed to drinking it, but if you are old enough to make your way in the world I think you could manage a small one. I shan't offer you a cigar, as I don't hold with encouraging others to take up the habit. Wish I'd never done so myself. Come through to my den."

Anna and Aunt Margaret exchanged a look of pleasure and relief that Uncle Matthew had taken a liking to Joseph, as indeed had his little cousins. Joseph had slipped unobtrusively into the family pond without causing so much as a ripple.

It was still dark when Joseph awoke next morning. He had slept well and felt refreshed, but as he became aware of his surroundings his stomach lurched with nervousness. Pulling up the blind to catch the sunrise, he reached for the pocket-watch Uncle Joseph had given him as a parting gift. Good old Uncle! For a moment Joseph wished he were back in the familiar world he had known for nine years. Six o'clock. He had exactly two hours to be at Rathbone's Textile Mill for his appointment with Mr Baker. Best to get up now, as he did not want to keep Uncle Matthew waiting. Joseph had been touched by his uncle's offer to accompany him to the mill. Over his first-ever brandy, which Matthew had taught him to savour and to sip gently, they had discussed the huge step Joseph would be taking today. This time he would not reject the offer of support as he had, to his regret, on the coach journey yesterday.

They were ready with time to spare, so Matthew took his nephew to the stables. They would take the gig, since the ladies were not travelling with them. It was lighter than the carriage and more manoeuvrable in the heavy traffic they would meet this morning. With four horses the Barclays had a pair for the carriage, one for the gig and one in reserve in case of sickness or injury. All of the horses could be ridden, Matthew pointed out, and Joseph would discover that his sister was no mean horsewoman. There was a love of horses on both sides of the family, and even as a little girl Anna had often been found in the stables, watching the groom at work or caressing a horse's muzzle. Joseph shuddered as he recalled those very horses, sleek and beautiful, plunging into the swollen river, carrying his beloved parents and little Amelia to their deaths. It was a fleeting memory, now it was time to bid the women and children good-bye.

The journey across the city intrigued and fascinated Joseph. He felt like Gulliver in Lilliput, seeing all these people hurrying and scurrying in every direction. He felt so far apart from them that he did not see himself as belonging to the bustle. They were like field mice, when the thresher disturbed their nests, fleeing desperately for their lives; or like slaters, when their sheltering brick or stone was tossed aside, revealing the harsh light of day, which forced them to trudge purposefully away to a new corner. Some of the people they passed appeared in danger of being late for their destination – these Joseph saw as the field mice, with their sense of urgency and their furrowed brows, even though some were quite young children. How lucky he had been, to stay at school, instead of having to help support an ever-growing family at such an early age. Many of these little mice looked no more than seven or eight years old! The slaters moved more slowly, plodding, as they had done for perhaps twenty or thirty years, to the same job in the same mill, factory or shop, treading the same cobbles morning and night every day of their lives. They looked weary even before starting their long workday. Would he see them stumbling home this evening as he himself found his way back to his new home at the Barclays'?

Suddenly aware that he had not been taking account of the route they were following, Joseph gave a start. Uncle Matthew smiled.

"A bit over-awed, aren't you, lad? You've a bit to learn about how other folks live. You and I have it easy, and don't you forget it. Keep your eyes open when you get to that mill and you'll see what I mean. Now, as regards tonight, I think I'll come and collect you – just this once, mind. I don't think we'd be seeing you till midnight if I didn't, and I'd have those women at me!"

"Thank you, sir. I meant to keep an eye on the streets we took, but it was all so interesting."

"You have the makings of a man who cares about his fellows, Joseph. You'll be a good employer, if you get that far, and your workers will respect you for your fairness. This man Baker at the mill has the name for it too – doesn't try to squeeze the last ounce of energy out of his millhands. He knows they are done long before the end of their shift. There are some in other mills who think him soft, but he's never had a hand collapse and die like that fellow Wilstrom over at Johnson's Mill."

"But was the man ill, Uncle?"

"Could hardly put one foot before the other to get to work for a month before, but with eight children to feed what could he do but keep working? And that old devil just told him if he missed a day he would give his place to someone in the queue that waits at the gate every morning. Anyway, you'll find all these things out for yourself, without me filling your head before you start."

As his uncle finished speaking, they came to a halt outside a dark, hulking building, its chimneys already belching filthy smoke into the greying sky. An air of dinginess and drabness hung over the whole building and even the name plate of Rathbone's Textile Company needed a coat of paint. Joseph's spirits sank.

Six o'clock. The whole Baker-Stanton household was awake and breakfast over. Lucy had been up at 4.30 to attend to the baby and by the time he was fed it was time to prepare breakfast for John and the other children. Henrietta rose at five o'clock, never needing a call. She dressed the little ones, laid the breakfast table and even helped to feed the younger ones. Lucy's eldest, Helen, was also obliging in this way and Lucy often wondered how she would manage without these two, who had also become close friends. Henrietta always ate breakfast with her father, after the others had eaten. This was the only way in which she was treated any differently, but Lucy had always considered it important that Mr Baker should be given the opportunity to have his daughter to himself at times.

While the three eldest Stanton children prepared for school John packed his lunch into his knapsack, ready to set off at 6.30. George Baker sat down to breakfast with little Henrietta. As always he marvelled at her likeness to his dear Martha, dead these nine years almost. The child would be nine in July – how time went by! Martha would have been proud of her, with her dark ringlets and her happy, rosy little face. Henrietta was quite accustomed to the way her father sometimes gazed at her without speaking, then a far-off look would come into his eyes. She knew not to interrupt his thoughts then. When she had asked Lucy a year ago what it meant, Lucy had replied, "When he looks at you he sometimes sees your dear mother." Not really understanding, Henrietta had accepted this statement, but now she was beginning to realise what a mixture of sadness and happiness it must bring her father to contemplate her.

George roused himself, telling her, as he always did, what the day held in store for him. It did the child no harm to have some understanding of a man's life and work.

It would probably make her a better wife some day.

"I have a new boy to meet this morning, Henrietta. He has come all the way from the Coventry area to work here in Birmingham. Do you know where Coventry is?"

"No, Father. What is his name?"

"Joseph Hamilton. He has been living with his uncle, who has the same name."

"How funny, two people with the same name living together! But it is a nice name, isn't it?"

"Er, yes, I suppose so."

"Is this Joseph a new apprentice, Father? How old is he? What does he look like?"

"Now just a moment, one thing at a time. No, he is not an apprentice, but he will be trained to do a job like mine one day. He is fifteen years old, and as to what he looks like, I have no idea, but I will meet him at eight o'clock this morning. If you wish, I shall tell you about him this evening."

"Oh yes, Father, please do!"

Surprised at her interest, George resolved to take note of the boy's appearance. That evening he duly regaled his daughter with every detail: Joseph was tall and quite thin, with fair hair and hazel eyes. He was tidily dressed and spoke with respect. Henrietta was glad that she could picture him now.

Although John and George worked at the same mill their hours were different, so they did not walk together to their work. John would not have walked with George Baker in any case, for George was a foreman and John a technician, a new class of worker in this machine age, who had not yet found his niche in the social strata of the mill.

George Baker relished his walk to work each morning, although he did not always enjoy the sights around him. The spectacle of sooty-faced little mites, no bigger than Henrietta, scuttling to and from their work – and they worked longer hours than he did himself – always sickened him, but he had the solace of knowing that Rathbone's did not traffick in such wickedness. No child under thirteen years of age was taken on, and no-one worked more than ten hours a day. The mill was closed on Sundays, unlike some, and this gave all God-fearing men, no matter how poor, the chance to take their families to church, without the dread of losing their places to someone less Christian. Not a self-righteous, nor a religious, man, George Baker felt he treated his workers as well as anyone did, and better than most.

As he neared the mill a mournful wail filled the air. Checking his pocket-watch, he smiled with satisfaction. Only 7.30. He would have plenty of time to clear up the matters from yesterday before showing the new lad over the factory at eight. George found himself looking forward to meeting this boy. The uncle's letter had been full of praise for him, and George had written to his school for an impartial view. The headmaster had used words like 'outstanding', 'promise' and 'exceptional' in his reply, which made it seem that this was the young man the directors were looking for. His age was right: in eight to ten years he would be ready for the foreman's job and he was well-educated, so must be intelligent. He would need to be, to cope with this new age of industrialisation. George wondered fleetingly if the boy realised what an opportunity his uncle had procured for him by biding his time and knowing people in high places.

He arrived at the mill gates, where workers stepped aside with a gruff "Mornin' Mr Baker" to him. He still had twenty minutes till the boy's appointment, but George felt sure that Joseph Hamilton would be on time.

They were ushered into an anteroom with box seats along the wall opposite the narrow window. The grime had not penetrated as far as this, but it was an uninteresting room, except for the two sketches on the whitewashed walls. One showed a huge machine, like a loom, suspended from the roof of a large shed and standing three feet from the floor. Half-way across the stretched threads was a wooden frame which seemed to be towing a thread from one side to the other. A woman stood with an arm outstretched, waiting for this carriage to reach her side. Joseph was shocked how little he knew of this life he was taking up. The other picture, framed to match the first, was labelled "Arkwright's Loom". It fascinated the boy, although he had no idea how it functioned.

Uncle Matthew stood up suddenly, interrupting Joseph's thoughts. A gentleman was approaching from the office, stretching out his hand in introduction. He was a little man – Joseph was already taller than him – with a kindly face, and he was smiling broadly as if it were a genuine pleasure to be meeting them.

"Mr Barclay, Master Hamilton, I am really glad to meet you." What a tall boy for his age! He must be five foot ten already, and with a couple of years still to grow! George Baker was trying to take in the boy's appearance, although it was not natural for him to notice such details. He was tidily clad, soberly enough, but the cloth was of good quality he could tell by nature and training, and his blond hair was neatly slicked down. He held his cap in his hands, fidgeting with it, but this was the only betrayal of nervousness.

"Please be seated. We have some things to discuss and then we will tour the factory for a good part of the day. Will you join us, Mr Barclay?"

"No sir, I shall not, if you will excuse me. Joseph is more than able to fend for himself in all respects, that is except getting himself through the traffic of Birmingham. I shall fetch him myself this evening, if you can give me an idea of when he'll be finished for the day."

"Well, from tomorrow his hours will be eight in the morning to six at night, like mine. But for the first day I think we'll let him go home at four. How does that sound, Master Hamilton?"

"Please sir, I'd much prefer it if you called me Joseph. And that sounds most generous. I am sure my head will be spinning with all I have to learn, sir."

"And a right good metaphor you've chosen too, lad. All right then, Mr Barclay, I shall deliver him into your hands at four o'clock."

Watching his uncle leave, Joseph was aware that the last prop of his childhood was being taken away, and that he was now expected to stand alone, to think and act as a man. Uncle Joseph had made it clear to him that this was no ordinary job he had found for him, that he would be trained to take his place at the top end of the labour force, but that he would have to know the workings of every part of the mill before he was ready for that.

"Now then, Joseph – yes, I do prefer to call you by your Christian name, for I believe you and I are going to be friends – let us make a start." George Baker was eager to begin working with this new employee, so like a bale of raw cotton which would arrive at the mill to be worked and processed until it was finally woven into a fine fabric, of a quality unrivalled in the industry.

Following an hour spent in the office, where Mr Baker had had a second, smaller, desk installed adjacent to his own imposing bureau, they set off around the various departments of the factory. Beginning where the incoming bales arrived, they observed the cleansing process, the combing, spinning into thread, the threading of the large mules, and the actual weaving of the material, before visiting the dyeing room and the vast drying shed. Finally Joseph was taken to the packaging and dispatch department, where men lifted huge packages, with the help of pulleys, onto waiting wagons for delivery to warehouses or the docks.

George Baker, who had escorted the boy on the whole tour, had been impressed by the fact that, although all that he had seen was new to him, Joseph had not been over-awed by the size of the factory. They had covered miles by the end of the tour, but he was still asking intelligent questions as they returned to the office at three-thirty. There was a maturity and a quiet self-confidence about him that marked him out for a successful career.

Summer passed, after months of long, suffocating days at the mill. In the hot months the drink breaks were increased to a ten-minute recess every two hours, a generous allowance by the standards of most factories. Mainly because of this, there were only isolated cases of people fainting at their work, and there was usually some other explanation. Walking about in some of the more enclosed workrooms, Joseph wondered why there was not more ventilation provided. If blowers could be used to dry the yarn, why could they not be used to blow cool air in, and even reversed to suck out the fetid air which hung over the workers? To his surprise Mr Baker suggested he put his ideas into a sketch, and the Board would see how practicable this would be.

Joseph spent many hours perfecting the sketches, labeling the parts and drawing them all to scale, before handing them to Mr Baker. Hiding his amazement with a perfunctory nod, the foreman accepted the drawings and changed the subject. Joseph was not to know for years that those sketches were exhibited at the next meeting of the Board of Directors, where heads nodded sagely and Mr Rathbone himself expressed an inclination to meet this new rising star. Nothing was said to Joseph, and nothing done about the extractors. He stifled his impatience by telling himself he was, after all, only a small fish in this great ocean.

When the Chairman of the Board of Directors visited the office one morning it was no real surprise to Joseph. He had heard that Mr Rathbone took a personal interest in the running of the family's mill, unlike his father, a dour man with little fellow-feeling for his workers. In old Mr Rathbone's day, thirty or forty years ago, there had been little children of six or seven working from three o'clock in the morning till ten at night, according to Mr Baker. That was in the brisk time, but their normal hours were from six in the morning till eight-thirty at night, and all for a shilling a week. Their growing bodies soon bent under the strain, and while some grew bow-legged the backs of others were permanently hunched or their feet splayed. The next Mr Rathbone had sworn to have none of this in *his* mill, and there were none. Even before Lord Shaftesbury had forced the ten-hour day through Parliament a couple of years ago, Rathbone's mill had reduced its hours of work and provided safety fences around its dangerous machines.

Rising to be introduced to the man in whose hands lay his future, Joseph felt small and insignificant, despite the fact that he stood as tall as the gaffer. What a chasm lay between them, and what a long road he had to travel! It was like a cabin-boy dreaming of becoming the ship's captain. Would he, Joseph Hamilton, ever have his own mill, with hundreds, or maybe over a thousand, hands working for him? It was possible, anything was possible at this age. At the age of fifteen one's life is a series of unfolding dreams, interspersed at times with nightmares.

It was almost seven years before Henrietta met Joseph. By then she was fifteen and Joseph twenty-two. Her father had often talked about him in such glowing terms that she had a clear picture of him, almost like a Greek god with the qualities she had given him. Would she be disappointed?

George Baker had invited Joseph to dine with them a year earlier, but the invitation had to be cancelled on account of the cholera epidemic which had swept through the city at that time. It would be too much of a risk crossing the town, even at night when fewer people were about. As long as nothing was done about the filthy courtyards and alleys, and the price of clean water, the poor would continue to spread these dreadful diseases. Now, a year later, the epidemic had passed, the town councillors had regained their apathy concerning open drains and foul living conditions.

Making his way across the city in Uncle Matthew's gig, Joseph reflected on the first time he had ridden in it. It would soon be seven years since he had arrived in this city which, for all its evils, he had come to love. The Barclay family had made their house his home, even after Anna's marriage two years ago. He wondered briefly how she would be enjoying the highlands of Scotland at this moment on a foggy February night. His situation had changed dramatically since those days when, as a gangly lad of fifteen, he had not yet learnt the art of controlling his height. Now he saw it as an advantage, and he carried himself straight, with pride but not with arrogance. His was the pride of knowing that he did his job well and that he was well equipped to do it, having spent six years in training before rising to the rank of deputy-foreman. Now he was pleased to be addressed as "Sir" by the labourers, but he considered himself no better than them, only luckier.

He had skirted the poorly-lit slum area, where the fog, not yet too thick, had trapped the rank odours that always emanated from this part of the town. Joseph had never given much thought to how or where the poor lived in Birmingham. A glimpse at his pocket-watch told him he had plenty of time yet. He turned the horse towards this dingy section of the city and drove across one corner of it. Although nauseated by what he saw, he was so fascinated that he resolved to return by day. His departure was hastened by a gang of urchins who swore at him in oaths the likes of which he had never heard and began to hurl missiles at both him and his horse.

Re-orienting himself, he found his way to Birch Grove, noting with pleasure as he drew nearer how the houses here were detached; there were even trees, a small common and gardens around many of the houses. Filling his lungs with the cleaner air, Joseph turned his thoughts to George Baker's daughter. How old must she be now? Should he really be dining with his superior because of the whim, albeit oft-repeated, of the daughter? Probably an over-indulged, precocious little miss, he thought, as he brought the gig to a halt in front of Number 15.

Joseph's heart was thumping, as he threw the covers over the horse, patted him reassuringly and strode up to the front door. As he rang the bell the grandfather clock in the hall sounded seven deep gongs and there was a great deal of scurrying before the door was opened by a dark-haired, pretty young woman who asked him in. Without a word Joseph was led into the parlour. Could this be Mr. Baker's daughter? This was no little girl, she was grown-up and – comely! George Baker rose to greet him.

"Ah, so you have met then. But let me introduce you properly. My daughter, Henrietta, this is Joseph Hamilton."

"Mr Hamilton."

"Miss Baker."

It was stiff and formal. Henrietta began to chuckle in such an infectious way that Joseph found himself smiling in reply.

"Oh Papa, do I *have* to call him 'Mister'? And I hate being 'Miss Baker'! It sounds like a maiden aunt, and I am only fifteen-and-a-half!"

"Well, my dear, we must see what Joseph thinks about that. We should at least *start* by observing the proprieties, but I confess I don't hold much with them myself."

Joseph's smile widened as he totally agreed. He recalled saying much the same thing, at the same age, when he first met George Baker at the mill.

Lucy Stanton, the housekeeper, served them their meal, but did not dine with them, having already eaten with her husband and family. John would be tucking the smaller children into bed, while the two eldest had charge of the middle ones. It was quite a job with eight children, especially when Lucy was needed in the kitchen and dining-room. John did not complain: they had fallen on their feet when old Dr White had asked Lucy to suckle George Baker's new-born daughter. What sort of a home would he have been able to provide for a wife and eight children? They would have ended up in the slums and half of them would have died of the cholera last year.

The evening passed quickly, see-sawing between serious discussions on new developments in industry and more light-hearted chatter with Henrietta. However Joseph noticed that the girl made some startling observations during their business conversations. She was obviously no fool.

When he came to leave Joseph discovered that the fog was thick, but he would not hear of staying the night with his hosts. His Aunt Margaret would worry – no, he would press on home, but in no haste. Chilled by the damp cold, the horse stamped his foot to be off. Removing one cover and fastening the other securely, Joseph set off slowly into the night, with Henrietta's words drifting after him: "Do take care, Joseph!"

It was a hazardous journey, although only a few miles. When he could not see in front of the horse he climbed down and led him until visibility increased. Both man and beast were cold, despite their exercise, when they reached home two hours later. Joseph would always think of it as a memorable evening. In later years he would see it as a life-changing experience for him.

CHAPTER 4

New Horizons

Henrietta sat musing, absently smoothing the wrinkles in her black dress. It was a time for thinking back to her childhood, to her first meeting with Joseph (could it really be eleven years ago?), to her father's unfailing love and kindness towards her over so many years. She could not feel sad for him, only for herself. He had tried to be both mother and father to her in the twenty-seven years since her mother had died. Now at last he would be reunited with his beloved Martha, whose name she bore but whom she had never known. Her own sense of loss was more acute than she had imagined it would be. Even since her marriage to Joseph four years ago her father had played a large part in her life, and when little George was born George Baker had almost burst with pride at being a grandfather.

Since retiring from the mill in 1862 George Baker had felt rather lost. For the first time in his life he felt the Stantons had taken over his home. Although they were good children there were so many of them that there was always noise. Now that he was at home during the day this irritated him. Understanding his feelings Henrietta often took the children out to play or just for a walk to give him the quiet he needed. When a man was seventy he was entitled to a peaceful home. After her marriage to Joseph in August 1863 Henrietta had suggested her father live with them, but George would not hear of it. What would happen to John and Lucy Stanton? They would never allow him to *give* the house to them, and he, for his part, would never turn them out after all they had done for him. No, he would stay there with them, and when he died the house would be theirs, as stated in his will. There could be no argument that way.

During the past months George had spent more time in his den, either reading or reflecting on his life. He was not ill, but he was aware that his life had almost run its course. It was good that Henrietta, his reason for living these past twenty-seven years, was happily married and had survived the birth of her son. George could not have chosen a better husband for her than Joseph. A bright future awaited them, he was sure.

Death, which he did not fear, had taken him quickly. He had gone inside to rest, after working in the vegetable garden, and enjoyed the cup of tea Lucy had brought him. As she walked from the room she heard a clatter. Rushing back into the room,

Lucy found him lying on the floor.

The funeral was held, the eulogies delivered, and the earth thrown on the casket. It was all over. Her father was dead and buried, Henrietta told herself again, trying to grasp the finality of it; but each time she said it to herself a feeling of vagueness enfolded her as if in a cosy blanket, insulating her from the harsh reality of her loss.

Joseph had been reluctant to leave her this morning, but she knew there were many demands on him at the mill. Accordingly she had put on a cheerful face, but dropped the mask as he strode away from the house. Little George had stopped her brooding several times, with demands or questions or the crises of a small child. It was not that she was grieving greatly, but her thoughts kept returning to her father. Surely that was the least she owed him.

He could not be serious! He must be jesting! Give up all he had worked for years to learn? From the bottom to the top? She tried to smile, but did not succeed.

"I shall make the tea," she said abruptly, rising hastily to avoid his eyes.

Alone in the parlour Joseph realised that he had not prepared Henrietta for the cannon shot he had just fired at her. Only a month ago she had told him that their second child was to be born next March, and here he was, talking about giving up everything that was known and accepted as a part of their lives, and setting off on a hundred-day voyage across the world, to a land where only a few hardy souls had thus far dared to go. It was no wonder that her eyes had filled with tears at the mention of it. Joseph reproved himself for letting his own enthusiasm make him blind. As Henrietta returned with the tea trolley, he said gently, "My dear, I really must apologise for upsetting you. No, please leave the tea a moment." Stepping over to her he put his arms around her tenderly, murmuring, "You know, I would be nobody without you, Henrietta. You give me strength." He had to release her to stoop and kiss her, and now she could smile up at him. "Oh Joseph, don't be foolish! I am just a silly woman who weeps when she doesn't understand what her husband is trying to say. Let us discuss this sensibly over a nice cup of tea. Mrs. Pearson has taken George to feed the ducks."

As he was to feel many times before the end of his life, Joseph was amazed at the practical common-sense of his wife. Much of this down-to-earth trait she had inherited from her father, as Joseph had learnt in his long association with George Baker. The rest had been instilled in her by Lucy Stanton, who had been her nanny and surrogate mother from birth.

Henrietta knew little about emigration. As a child she had heard of the scandal of the Lloyds, but had not understood what it was about. She knew only that many children had taken ill and died on the ship to New Zealand, and that the voyage had taken five months. She listened attentively now as Joseph recounted the details he had learnt: how the voyage now took three months; how land was almost given away in new towns being established in New Zealand; how business was there for anyone who had the initiative to set up a shop or workplace.

"But what would you *do* there, Joseph? They would not need mills in an untamed country."

Joseph's eyes lit up. "I would realise my dream, my dear. Since I first came to Birmingham as a boy I have wanted to be my own master, to deal with cloths and textiles, yes, but not in a factory. I would open a shop!"

"A shop? But how would you stock it?"

"I should take as much as the shipping company would allow me to carry, and leave orders with Rathbone's to send a shipment with every subsequent vessel making the voyage." The answer came so promptly that Henrietta realised Joseph had already calculated the details. This meant he intended to go ahead with the scheme, or he would not be using precious time gathering all the necessary information. There would be no dissuading him. He had told her nothing of his plans until he was ready. Frustration at her powerlessness vied with her curiosity to hear more of this outlandish scheme.

He explained that the New Zealand government was offering free passages for those men who would work the land or labour to build roads and railways in the new country, or for young women who would work as servants, cooks or dairy-maids. These people needed to pay only twenty shillings per adult, for the provision of mattresses, bedclothes, soap and utensils on the voyage. Seeing her look, Joseph said they would *not* travel to New Zealand like that. They would pay their fares and be beholden to no-one. Joseph answered Henrietta's many questions, and then outlined his plans.

His enquiries had established that there was a sailing in early October, 1868, a year hence, which should suit them, giving them ample time for preparation, as well as allowing for their expected child to be six or seven months old. George would be four years old and probably quite helpful on the voyage. He would perhaps be old enough to have some understanding of the magnitude of what they were undertaking. Each vessel carried a strict quota of assisted passengers, who were housed in the lower decks and who had little to do with the paying passengers. Joseph had been assured that the voyage would cause his family no hardship or discomfort, except for the weather, over which mere mortals had no control. Indeed, they would look back in later years with nostalgia on their adventure. Since this was what Joseph already believed, he was easily convinced by the emigration officer.

"And did you actually make a reservation for us, Joseph?"

"I was tempted, Henrietta, I really was!" He sounded so boyish in his eagerness. "But it would not have been fair to rush ahead without consulting you first. After all, my love, I am asking you to leave everything and everyone familiar to you, to tear up all your roots. We shall have only each other and the children. It is a lot to ask, I know. Do you think you can do it?"

There was a charged silence as Henrietta sipped the last of her tea. Placing her cup and saucer carefully back on the tea-trolley, she murmured, more to herself than to Joseph, "So, we are to be pioneers, are we?"

Every day Joseph came home with more news of ships, climate, clothing they must take, prices of goods in New Zealand, even the revelation that there were nine million sheep in the country. Gradually, Henrietta built up a picture in her mind of their new home. There would be sheep grazing at the door, and natives living nearby. She always willed herself to think of them as friendly, as any other thought filled her with dread. Joseph would be busy in his little shop and she would have the children to occupy her. But in the evening, when the shop was closed, they would have several hours to themselves, not knowing anyone else. She hid her misgivings about several aspects of this venture, not wanting to see the animation die in Joseph's eyes.

Today, when he returned from his office, he handed her a letter as he swept George into the air for their customary play. The envelope bore the return address of:

W.N. Twelvetrees,
Local Agent for New Zealand
Grove Road, via Bow Road
London, E.

Slipping the letter out, she read, as Joseph had done several hours before:

Dear Mr. Hamilton,

Thank you for your letter of 12th inst., in which you ask for particulars and detailed conditions regarding emigrant ships to New Zealand, and further regarding life in that colony. I must state at the outset that the lists set out below are especially for the use of assisted emigrants and that for passengers in your position they may be taken simply as a guide.

Clothing

Males	**Females**	**Children**
6 Shirts	*6 Chemises*	*7 Shirts or Chemises*
6 Pairs Stockings	*2 Warm Strong Flannel Petticoats*	*4 Warm Flannel Waistcoats*
2 Warm Flannel or Guernsey Shirts	*6 Pairs Stockings*	*1 Warm Cloak or*
2 Pairs New Shoes	*2 Pairs Strong Shoes*	*Outside Coat*
2 Complete Suits of Exterior Clothing	*2 Strong Gowns (1 must be warm)*	*2 Suits of Exterior Clothing*
		2 Pairs Strong Shoes

Emigrants are further expected to provide their own towels and all other requisites except those pertaining to bedding and meal utensils.

I trust, Sir, that this information will be of some use to you. I append a list of prices of basic commodities, and some facts regarding the colony of New Zealand.

Bread (4lb loaf)	*1/6 to 1/7*
Beef (per lb.)	*1/2½d to 1/4¼d*
Mutton (per lb.)	*1/2½d to 1/4¼d*
Butter (per lb.)	*1/- to 1/3*
Tea (per lb.)	*2/1 to 3/2*
Sugar (per lb.)	*4½d to 6d*
Coffee (per lb.)	*1/3 to 1/6*
Potatoes (per lb.)	*½d*

Although New Zealand is larger than England, Wales and Scotland united its European population numbers only 250,000.

The climate is temperate and healthy.

Most of the land is well adapted for agricultural and pastoral purposes.

A standard day's work for mechanics and labourers is 8 hours.

Clothing is sold at 20–30% over English prices.

The letter ended with an indecipherable signature. Henrietta was grateful to this unknown person for giving her the facts she had wanted. Now she could get to work, assembling the clothing they would need. Although it was a year to departure she could not bear to be idle when there were things to be done. It was far too soon to be packing anything, but for some time she had been mentally cataloguing household items as "go" or "stay". Those on the stay list would be sold, of course, and here her common sense had often to do battle with her sentimentality. The lists were becoming clearer, however, which meant she was making progress.

Joseph had always liked to spend the last hours of the old year looking back over what the year had meant to him, and the first of the new year straining, like an eager dog on a leash, to see into the future. This year, above all, he wished he could see ahead.

The magnificent old grandfather clock they had inherited from Henrietta's father struck three. So, the first three hours of 1868 had gone by already? His thoughts had been interrupted several times by people out first footing. It was not how he liked to see the New Year in, but Joseph considered himself a tolerant man, and so he turned no-one away. Henrietta had retired hours ago, feeling tired, as she so often did these nights. It was only two months until her confinement and she was so busy all day that Joseph was not surprised she felt weary in the evenings. Yet he could not go to bed, for he was just beginning his look at the new year. Deciding the time was right for a cup of tea, he stoked the fire and put the kettle on the hob, settling back into his armchair to give his mind to this momentous year just beginning.

First of all there would be Victoria (Henrietta was adamant that this child was a daughter, and had not even considered a boy's name) in March. Joseph knew that his wife would go through the same anxiety that she had suffered before George was born. They would talk about it all again and she would agree that just because her own mother had died in childbirth, this did not mean it would happen to *her*. He knew, however, that when the time came all the fear would rise again, and they would not let him near to try and comfort her.

The kettle boiled and he made his tea, buttering a scone and spreading it with jam as other thoughts jostled in his mind.

The other important event of this year would be their departure. He felt a thrill of excitement at the prospect. Never one for a display of feelings, he allowed himself to grin at the flickering fire, which in turn painted his face with light and shadow, giving him a gnomish look. How would little George stand up to the rigours of the voyage? And was it wise to travel with a newborn infant? Was he being irresponsible? Joseph had heard more about the emigrant ships than he chose to share with his wife. It was no use alarming her. She had a good constitution and George kept good health. They would have to take chances if they were to start a new life.

On one of his regular visits to the office of Mr Twelvetrees, Joseph met a gentleman who reminded him of himself. A tall man, striking in appearance, with jet-black hair and mutton-chop whiskers, he was addressed as "Mr Gainsborough" by the clerk. Joseph found himself eavesdropping on the exchange between them. The Gainsborough family had had to change bookings because of the recent birth of their first child. The clerk pointed out that, if they gave up this reservation, there was no assurance of another placing inside of nine or ten months. There was a well-mannered coolness between the two as Mr Gainsborough, a man of about thirty, agreed to have his name added to the passenger list of the Cressida, sailing in September.

As Mr. Gainsborough turned away from the desk, Joseph stepped up to him.

"Excuse me, I could not help overhearing the name of the ship you are to travel on. My family and I are on that passenger list. Perhaps we should become better acquainted?"

Taken aback, Mr Gainsborough stammered, "Er, well …" before suddenly thrusting out his hand. "Yes, of course, quite right sir." Joseph introduced himself and invited his new acquaintance to accompany him home, quite forgetting what trivial excuse had taken him to the office.

Henrietta looked up with consternation as the two men stepped into the entrance hall. With only a matter of weeks until the baby was due, did Joseph really have to bring someone home with him? What was more, someone she had never met. But Joseph's face told her this was no ordinary visitor. Who on earth could it be? Joseph looked so lively and boyish!

"Mr Gainsborough, this is my wife Henrietta. Henrietta, Mr Gainsborough, whom I met at the agent's office. His family is to sail with us on the Cressida!"

"Ah well, you two gentlemen will surely want to put your heads together. George and I will leave you undisturbed. I shall bring you some tea in half an hour."

Joseph led his new-found friend into the parlour, almost as surprised at himself as Mr Gainsborough seemed to be. His instant liking for the chap was unusual for him, as he normally weighed a person up before offering his friendship. Frederick Gainsborough, for his part, felt himself caught up in a current. Far from fearing that he would drown, however, he was enjoying drifting along. He considered himself enough of a judge of character – as a banker this was part of his training – to recognise that Joseph Hamilton was guided simply by the desire to become acquainted with a future fellow passenger.

They talked honestly and openly about their hopes and dreams for their new life in the colony. Before long it became clear that Mrs Gainsborough was an unwilling partner in the venture and that, following the birth of their daughter last November, she had refused point-blank to leave until the child was close to a year old. Nothing Frederick could do would change her mind. They were to have sailed in June and would have reached New Zealand by early October. He had been bitterly disappointed at her stubbornness but was not the sort of husband who overrode his wife's wishes. Hence his visit to the office today.

As Henrietta brought the tea into the parlour she heard Mr Gainsborough saying he was glad now that his wife had been so determined, for he felt sure the two families would become close friends.

Two days later a message arrived inviting the Hamilton family to dine with the Gainsboroughs on Saturday evening. Henrietta, feeling very cumbersome, was reluctant, but Joseph was so looking forward to forming a close friendship with the family that she relented.

It was a pleasant evening. The two women discovered that they shared many small fears and worries, which would have been dismissed as silly and trivial by their husbands. Henrietta felt a mixture of admiration and pity for Anne Gainsborough. Not much more than a girl, tall, slender, pretty and rather delicate, she undoubtedly had spirit, but because her family lived a hundred miles from Birmingham, she had no-one with whom to discuss this voyage. Frederick, she complained, would hear nothing of difficulties on the voyage, barbarous natives in the colony or wild animals that could devour a child. She was only twenty-one years old, and she filled her empty hours with nightmarish thoughts about the new life, fears she dared not share with Frederick. Henrietta invited her to visit soon with little Jessica, so they could continue their conversation.

On the drive home Henrietta thanked Joseph for insisting that they make the visit. Poor Anne had herself so tied up in knots, just as well she could untangle some of them. Smiling in the darkness Joseph murmured, "Insisted? Who insisted?" and he leaned across to kiss her on the cheek.

The return visit was made and the two women grew closer to each other as a result. Soon after, Victoria Louise entered the world, in such a hurry that her mother had no time to think of death. On March 4th, during the night, Henrietta had wakened Joseph who dispatched a sleepy Mrs Pearson, the housekeeper, to bring the midwife and doctor. By breakfast time on the 5th they had a bonny daughter, named after the Queen, as a talisman for the future.

A healthy child from the start, Victoria soon won all their hearts. George would perform all sorts of antics just to be rewarded with one of her smiles, and Joseph was delighted with his daughter. Henrietta was quietly content that all had gone well and everyone was happy.

By mid-summer their plans were well advanced. With two months to the sailing date most of their heavy goods were crated ready to be delivered to the dock when the Cressida arrived in early September. Their crates would leave Birmingham for London in late August, along with the Gainsboroughs' crates. The family would live, in the meantime, with the possessions to be sold, disposing of these as the time was right. Then, at the end of August, when the house was, hopefully, sold and all the contents dispersed, they would travel to London to spend their last two weeks of life in England at a hotel. Henrietta had misgivings about this part of the plan, but Joseph insisted that it was better to be near the port in case the sailing schedule should change, rather than remaining in Birmingham until the last minute. Further, he insisted she was to have as many creature comforts as possible until they were on the ship. She felt some apprehension, wondering if Joseph was withholding some details about the emigrant ships.

August was sultry and hot. The heavy industrial air outside brought no freshness, choking rather than reviving. More factories were being built, to pour more filth into the air. Last year's Factory Act had improved conditions for workers, cutting back the hours employers could demand of them and raising the age of children they could engage, but nothing was done to filter the cloggy, thick smoke that belched all day and all night from some of the chimneys. Too many children in the city were developing a harsh cough, like little Jessica Gainsborough. Her cough had started a week ago and it seemed nothing could shift it. Henrietta was glad neither of her children had caught it. Joseph had been wise to buy a house on the outskirts of the town. He had said he had seen too much evidence of what the mills could inflict on innocent children. At the time she had thought he meant in the factories – only now did she understand the full meaning of his words.

The last weeks were crowded. Henrietta would look back on them many times in years to come, marvelling at how they managed it all. The days went so quickly, with the departure date creeping up stealthily on them all the while. Mercifully, little Jessica's health improved, although she never entirely lost the cough. Anne was plainly unhappy to be leaving England and her family, and, far from thinking that the sea air would be beneficial to Jessica, she held a morbid, irrational fear that the child would not survive the voyage. To Frederick Gainsborough this was how it seemed, he having no respect for unsubstantiated evidence. Little George's excitement mounted daily at the prospect of sailing in a huge ship, and his father was equally impatient for the date to arrive. There were many arrangements to be finalised, however, and these he attacked with an energy that exhausted those around him, delivering furniture, seeing that their immigration papers were in order, selling the house and settling all the details himself. Fortunately, the baby was thriving, allowing Henrietta to help with the preparations for the voyage.

At last the day came for them to leave Birmingham. There were storm clouds looming and it would rain before long. Thunder growled, as if in warning, and a couple of flashes of lightning lit up the sky, but the impending storm had not yet gathered its forces for the attack. Henrietta glanced anxiously at the angry sky as they left the house for the last time. She could not look back. The house was sold and tomorrow another family would begin life there. She and Joseph and the children would have no home. They would exist from day to day until the Cressida came in. Beyond that she dared not think. It was something she had to do. There was no point in questioning the inevitable.

CHAPTER 5

Farewell

There she lay at anchor with little wind-blown waves lapping at her sides, the sails tightly lashed in place, her sleek bow glinting in the autumn sun and her proud name ornately painted in bold lettering. Joseph and George had watched her come up the harbour yesterday, with her mighty sails unfurled, an awesome sight with a grandeur of its own. How had man learned to tame the wind for his use, to create and stitch sheets of canvas to utilise this power for himself? One day, Joseph was sure, those engines driving the machines at Rathbone's would be adapted to power sailing ships. John Stanton flashed across his mind, as he compared how much more serene the ship under sail looked than one belching smoke and fumes like those mill chimneys.

As Joseph had speculated, their departure date had been brought forward, to September 8th. With favourable winds the Cressida had made good time on the last part of her homeward voyage. She would take on a fresh crew and leave in four days. With little to offload, the colony still needing much and supplying little, they would be ready tomorrow to begin loading cargo and baggage for the next voyage to New Zealand.

There was nothing more to be done. The Gainsboroughs had arrived at the Excelsior two days ago, as arranged. Henrietta was putting up a brave front in an attempt to convince Anne that their husbands' dreams would become realities when they reached the colony. However, Anne was tearful at the prospect of leaving her family for ever, and Henrietta wondered how she would have felt had her father been still alive, too old to travel with them, yet very much alone if they had gone without him. Anne's feelings, though, were for herself. She would miss her mother especially. Although they had lived many miles apart for two years, it was not the same as knowing that she would never see her mother again. Frederick had quite lost patience with her, leaving her to her self-pity, as he called it, and taking frequent walks, with or without Joseph, to the waterfront. It was not that he did not love his wife. At the time of their marriage he had been the happiest man alive, he assured Henrietta, but he was disappointed that Anne could not see what an opportunity this was to be free of the ties that British society imposed on them. He could be managing a bank by the time he was 35! What chance would there be of such a thing in England? Henrietta listened carefully to each side of the argument, trying to say a little on behalf of the absent partner, to smooth the way for peace. They were like a pair of unco-operative Clydesdales pulling a dray, heavy-footed on each other's feelings, the blinkers they wore not permitting them to see the other properly and just not understanding that if they pulled together the whole load would be lighter.

The Cressida was to sail with the afternoon tide on the 8th. They were to embark from 10 o'clock that morning. When she awoke at six, Henrietta found Joseph up and dressed, and George about to dress with the help of his father.

"We shall be the first on board, Joseph!" she exclaimed.

"And what would be wrong with that? I do not want any confusion about accommodation, so I intend to be there early."

"Is excitement driving you, Joseph? You look as eager as a boy this morning."

With a sheepish grin he turned back to George, while Henrietta too arose and dressed. Victoria was still asleep, waking only when it was time to descend for breakfast. By then Joseph had delivered all but the smallest bags to the wharf. If he had had his way, thought Henrietta wryly, they would all have been on board at dawn!

They decided to leave the hotel at nine-thirty and walk to the dock. The Gainsboroughs agreed this was likely to be their last real walk for three months or more, so they all set out together, and a striking sight they made. The men, both tall, led the way, Joseph's blond hair gleaming in the sunlight, Frederick's dark curls bobbing as he walked. Little George struggled valiantly to keep up with their long strides, while the ladies, smiling at their husbands' eagerness, each carried her daughter to meet whatever the future had in store for them.

When they reached the dock the men attached themselves to a short queue of others waiting to board, leaving the ladies and children free to sit or walk about for the remaining time. Joseph and Frederick would locate their cabins and check that the cabin baggage had been correctly delivered. At exactly ten o'clock the gangway was lowered into place and the men went on board. Anne glanced at Henrietta for reassurance. In a few minutes they would know what their living quarters were to be for the next three months.

Henrietta's first surprise came when she saw their cabin. Her vision had been of a tiny space, with a low ceiling crowding in on them, no room to turn around and a certainty that claustrophobia would attack her. How wrong she had been! Joseph caught the pleasure in her eyes as she surveyed the cabin: the three bunks and tiny crib, the latticed window (for they were above the water line) and the wardrobe space. There was room beneath the bunks to store their bags, and George declared at once that this was an ideal place for pirates to hide out. Perhaps the voyage would not be so unpleasant after all, thought Henrietta. Anne would surely be relieved, too. Voicing this thought, Henrietta received her second shock.

Joseph had been wondering how to tell her that the Gainsboroughs' cabin was cramped, dark and damp. Frederick had paid the basic fare, without enquiring what sort of accommodation this gave him. Joseph had learned that the comforts gained by paying considerably more greatly outweighed the expense. Both he and Henrietta would need their strength and energy for the time when they were establishing a home and a business, putting down roots into the colonial soil. He felt obliged to give her some inkling before they paid the Gainsboroughs a visit.

Henrietta listened without comment as Joseph explained why he had paid more for their passage. She knew she should be glad that he deemed their comfort so important, and in a way she was. She worried the contrast would make Anne all the more despondent. She could not say this to Joseph, however, and simply nodded to show she understood what he was saying.

It was necessary to descend two stairways to reach the Gainsboroughs' cabin. The first was wide, with polished brass railings, for this staircase led from the first-class cabins to the saloon, a huge room some 130 feet long and the full width of the ship. The second, leading down to the second and third class quarters, was just wide enough for two people to pass, provided both were not corpulent. During the voyage Henrietta would never venture lower in the ship, although Joseph would have reason to do so.

As they went down the second stairway Henrietta prepared herself for the scene she knew would confront her. Anne would be close to tears, Frederick would be impatient with her, and Jessica would be crying and unsettled. It was worse. She heard them from the bottom of the stairs, Anne sobbing and Frederick shouting that he was sick of her childish nonsense and that she had better start behaving with the dignity to be expected of a married woman. Just as Joseph raised his hand to knock, the door burst open and Frederick crashed into Joseph. In the confusion of the apologies that followed, Henrietta slipped past the men and seated herself on the bunk where Anne lay face down, her body shaking with sobs. Jessica lay in her crib, alternately crying and coughing. The cough was not deep but it sounded enough like the one that had plagued her in Birmingham for Henrietta to understand that this was a part of Anne's grief.

Joseph suggested to Frederick that they go up on deck, to watch the preparations being made by the crew for their departure. No persuasion was needed, and George, confused by all the shouting and weeping, seized his father's hand, eager to be out in the rising stiff breeze.

Laying Victoria on the empty bunk and tucking a blanket around her to prevent her falling off the bed, Henrietta took the younger woman in her arms, comforting her and soothing her until the sobs subsided. Jessica, exhausted, fell asleep and all was quiet. Now Henrietta could look around at the tiny space that would be Anne's home for one hundred days. There was no storage, one bed being low to the floor and the other bunk above it. Jessica's crib took up a third of the whole floor space. They would have to put it and their luggage on the beds when they wanted to walk about in the cabin. There was, of course, no porthole, for they were amidships. Candles were required all day – no wonder Anne was in tears. Men could be so thoughtless, thought Henrietta hotly. But they could also be kind and considerate, as her Joseph had been.

Anne had tired herself so much from weeping that Henrietta persuaded her to lie and sleep for a time. Almost as soon as she was covered with the blanket Anne was asleep. Taking her baby Henrietta tip-toed out of the cabin and made her way upstairs to her own, feeling guilty that she would be so much more comfortable. Lying back on the bunk, with Victoria nestled in the crook of her arm, she drifted off to sleep.

As the tide came in quite a crowd had gathered at the dock. There were those who had relatives on board, but many were people, from all classes, who loved the sight of billowing sails and enjoyed hearing the barked commands to the crew as they made ready to cast off. Yet others, who stood watching as the Cressida slipped her moorings and sailed gracefully down the harbour towards the Atlantic Ocean, dreamed of making this voyage themselves. One day some of them would join these folk in the colony half a world away, but others would have to content themselves with dreams. For some, like Frederick Gainsborough, it might have been better to have left the dream untouched. No-one knew exactly what lay ahead.

They had been at sea exactly five weeks. Anne had marked off each week on the calendar, like a prisoner awaiting the longed-for day of release. Not only did she feel imprisoned, but Jessica was ill and Anne's worry was turning to fear. Other children had died already and been buried at sea, with all the ceremony of a proper funeral and a beautiful polished casket. Was her darling Jessica to be one of them?

The possibility was looming ever larger in Anne's distraught mind. Frederick was also anxious, having seen how the child was weakening, how she coughed until she vomited after every meal, and then slept until the next coughing fit. The ship's doctor diagnosed the illness as bronchitis with respiratory complications and said there was little to be done but to let Nature take her course.

Henrietta did her best to help, sending the Gainsboroughs up on deck for fresh air and a change while she sat in the fetid cabin with the child. She never took her own children with her on these visits, for there had been an outbreak of thrush on the lower decks two weeks ago which had carried off several children. Joseph stayed with the children or took them out on deck if the wind was not too cold. There was always wind – where would they be without it? When it gusted strongly Henrietta felt restless. She preferred to be below rather than walking about where men were working sails and ropes. In the Gainsboroughs' cabin she could not hear the howling of the wind, drowned out as it was by the noises of children and the adjacent cabins.

It was October 20th - six weeks in the Atlantic. The weather was good until two days ago, when sudden downpours began. They were warned to expect torrential rain and sticky heat in the tropics. However, in a week or so they would round the Cape of Good Hope, and then they would *really* be on their way towards New Zealand. Joseph had explained to Henrietta and George how they had sailed south right down the middle of the huge Atlantic Ocean, which was why they had not seen a sign of human habitation. As they neared the Cape, they would see land, and after that – well, his knowledge ran out after Africa, although he did know that the great southern continent of Australia lay somewhere near their path.

"I shall be learning with you from then on, George. I could not find any books on the southern … " An urgent knocking on the cabin door interrupted Joseph. It was Frederick, white-faced and panting.

"Henrietta … quickly, please … Jessica …Anne," he gasped.

With a glance at Joseph, Henrietta snatched up a shawl and hurried from the cabin. It seemed a mile to the Gainsboroughs' cabin. Frederick's arm steadied her on the stairs, but he was too breathless and overwrought to elaborate on the crisis. As they reached the cabin they heard the doctor's voice saying soothingly,

"I am sorry, Mrs Gainsborough, but she is slipping away. She is beyond help now. She cannot last more than a few hours. I have given her a sedative. We can only hope that the little lass goes in her sleep. Ah, Mr Gainsborough, I was just telling your wife …"

Thank you, Doctor, but I heard you. Is there *nothing* to be done? It seems criminal to just let her die!"

At this Anne began to croon softly, "My baby, my baby," rocking Jessica gently in her arms. Henrietta, feeling more helpless than she had ever felt in her life, looked on this scene in silent pity. What could she say? They were in the presence of Death, and its power rendered them all dumb.

Henrietta stayed with the couple until the end came. It was towards nightfall, when Frederick, drawn closer to his wife by these weeks of trial, noticed a change in her expression. Anne had sat holding the child all afternoon, refusing to give her to either Frederick or Henrietta for even a moment. She had rocked the child slowly back and forth in her arms for hours, murmuring endearments to her and smoothing her tangled curls now and then. Suddenly she stopped rocking, just for an instant, shot a furtive look at Henrietta and Frederick and then began the crooning and rocking again. Frederick, who had caught the look, understood that Jessica had died, but the glance from his wife had defied him to take the baby away from her. Henrietta had missed the moment as she was arranging the wrappings in the crib to try and persuade Anne to give herself a rest and let the child sleep.

Lost for a second, Frederick waited until Anne bent her head over Jessica before whispering to Henrietta, "She is gone, I am sure." Together they tried to press Anne into relinquishing the baby, but the very suggestion set her shrieking hysterically. Frederick had no idea what to do, so Henrietta sent him to fetch the doctor, tell him what had happened, and ask him to bring a sedative with him. While he was gone she tried again to persuade Anne to give her the child, but again Anne refused.

"She is *my* baby and *I* must look after her," was all she would say. Henrietta decided to change her tactic. She pointed out that after all the rocking little Jessica would be more comfortable stretched out in her crib, where she could move about. Anne thought for a moment and a childlike smile crossed her face.

'Yes, I *shall* put her to bed, but you are not to help me. I can care for her." So saying, she laid the still-warm infant in her tiny bed and fussed over her as though all was normal.

By the time Frederick returned with the doctor, Henrietta was urging Anne to have a little rest before the baby awoke again. Anne fell asleep immediately having taken the sedative. There would be another crisis when she awoke, but the doctor was sure they had at least twelve hours until then. Henrietta left the men to make funeral arrangements, returning to her own little nest. George, full of questions, was silenced by his father, and Victoria, mercifully, was asleep. Henrietta sank gratefully onto the soft bed.

Frederick decided to hold the service the next morning, without his wife being present. No purpose would be served by her being there and, moreover, the doctor advised against it. Any further upheaval could tip Anne over the brink into insanity, he said. She was to be kept partially sedated with sleeping draughts for at least a week, but these were not to be left where she could find them, to avoid her doing herself a mischief.

A small group gathered for the service. Joseph, Henrietta and their children joined the families whose cabins were adjacent to the Gainsboroughs', a sprinkling of crew, who were obliged to send representatives to all shipboard funerals, and the captain, who read the lesson and intoned the prayers. It was all over quickly, the tiny white coffin lowered over the side and gently released by Frederick into the great calm ocean. Lapping softly against the ship it enfolded the little man-made box of wood like a large, loving mother hugging to her a crying child.

Two weeks passed and on November 1st they rounded the Cape, so aptly named. There was hope among the passengers now: this was the final stage of the voyage. They were past halfway, and, in most cases, those who had survived the outbreaks of illness could expect to reach their destination. They had left the wintry fogs of the North, and the tropical rains; here it was warm and sunny, with the twilight growing daily longer. Henrietta spent long periods, with Anne and the children, on deck. Victoria loved the motion of the ship, and when its roll tipped her off balance as she sat or crawled about, she would chuckle with glee. George had suffered with seasickness at first, but now that the weather was better and the seas less rough he was happier. He could find his way from their cabin to the usual spot they occupied on deck, and to the saloon where Joseph and Frederick so often played cards, the one trying to keep the other from drowning his sorrows in whisky.

Frederick saw his dreams of a promised land falling in tatters at his feet. He had accepted Jessica's death as an act of God, which was not to say that he had not loved the child. They could begin again when they had settled in Christchurch: they were young, and they could put this all behind them. They would not forget their first-born but, he tried to tell Anne, the wound would heal, if she let it. There would always be a scar, but they still had a future. Anne, on the other hand, could not forgive her husband: neither for bringing her and the baby on this voyage, nor for the living conditions he had imposed on them – conditions, she was sure, which had helped to cause Jessica's death – and then the final blow of holding of the funeral service while she was ill.

Constant brooding on all these things warped Anne's mind, twisting them out of proportion and bringing her to the point where she could hardly bear to set eyes on her husband, let alone allow him to touch her or speak to her. She became quite immersed in herself, until even Henrietta found it difficult to rouse her. Not only was she sliding into insanity, but the girl would not eat and so was getting physically weaker. Henrietta racked her brains for ideas, but she had tried all she knew. As two weeks became three there was one incident which did arouse Anne for a short time because it caused such anger among the passengers.

Each week the ship was fumigated, with the portholes closed and cabin doors propped open. All passengers were ordered to remain on deck while this was done, for the fumes were lethal enough to cause suffocation. It was the job of the duty steward to check that all quarters were empty, before placing three buckets of Stockholm tar on a grating and lighting a coal fire beneath them, so that the tar boiled for an hour. On this particular morning the steward had been delayed and black clouds on the horizon signalled rain. So he made only a hasty inspection of the lower quarters of the ship before lighting the fire.

Joseph and Frederick, standing on deck with their wives and Joseph's children, became aware of a disturbance quite near them. A young woman with five children clustered around her skirts was becoming very agitated. Joseph could watch no longer. Striding over to her, he enquired what was troubling her.

"I cannot find my Ben," she replied. "I think he is still below!"

The fire was beginning to catch and the steward was adding the first coals to it.

"Wait!" ordered Joseph. "There is a child below!"

There was a gasp from the passengers.

"There is nothing of the kind, sir. I have looked in every cabin." The woman was pulling at Joseph's sleeve. "Not a child, sir, my husband. 'E was up much of the night with our youngest and I think 'e must 'ave been asleep when they called us."

"Now look, madam, I have told you, I looked in every cabin. He must be elsewhere on the deck." So saying, the steward shovelled more coal on to the glowing fire. The tar was showing the first signs of smoking. Joseph knew there was no time to lose. Turning again to the woman he asked, "Which cabin?" and when she gave him the number he caught Frederick by the arm. "I shall need help. Will you come? We may have to carry him."

Pulling their handkerchiefs from their pockets as they ran, the two men scurried past surprised crewmen and down the nearest stairway, feeling the effect of the fumes already.

"Won't be so bad down below yet. This way!" called Joseph over his shoulder. The cabin number they had been given was in the bowels of the ship. Here only canvas separated one family from the next. The steward had probably looked into one or two cubicles and decided all were empty.

"Ben! Ben!" called both men, through the masks they had made from their handkerchiefs. They had never met Ben but this was no time for formalities. The acrid fumes were overtaking them and Joseph placed his sleeve across his mouth.

"Have to find him soon," spluttered Frederick, snatching a towel from a cubicle they were passing.

"Here, this is the number." Although Joseph shouted, his voice was so muffled that Frederick did not hear him at first. "Frederick!"

The man lay on his back, mouth open, gulping for fresh air but inhaling only the smoke and fumes wafting into the cabin. Realising that these men had come to save him, he scrambled to his feet, only to fall back onto the bed. "We shall have to carry him," muttered Frederick through the towel. Binding a cloth around the man's head they picked him up between them and hurried from the room into a wall of dark grey smoke. With half-closed eyes streaming they blundered up the narrow stairwell. Ben was jostled about as one carried his feet and the other held him under the arms. It seemed an eternity till they caught sight of the daylight that told them they were almost on deck. Joseph wondered if they'd make it, not daring to speak now as all his strength was needed. He could hear Frederick's feet dragging. Only one more set of stairs!

Stumbling out into the daylight the men dropped their burden and sprawled beside him. A great cheer from the crowd went unheard by the rescuers. Three wives rushed forward, kneeling before the inert forms of their husbands. Ben's wife put an ear to his heart before deftly unwrapping the cloth from his head. Anne, forgetting her resentment, laid her husband's head on her lap, smoothing back the dark curls and waiting patiently until Frederick's eyes should open. Henrietta, passing Victoria to someone beside her, knelt beside Joseph, relieved to see that this was nothing more than exhaustion.

The crowd had hushed, but as the steward moved to stoke the almost-dead fire again, angry shouts broke out and someone took a swing at him. It was a wild punch which merely knocked the steward off balance and made him stagger a little. He did not hit back as he would have enough trouble to face when the captain heard of this, without inciting a crowd to violence as well. He bent again to add more coal to the fire. The captain arrived on the scene to investigate the disturbance. Several of the immigrants accosted him with their version of the incident, sparing no detail of the steward's culpability. The captain strode through the hostile crowd, selecting three men and taking them with him to his cabin, where he could listen to a coherent account. Passing by the three prostrate men on the deck, he called over his shoulder,

"Please see that these men come to me when they regain consciousness."

It would be another hour until the passengers could return below. Despite the steward's strong words, he had let the fire die down from the time Joseph and Frederick had gone below. As the men opened their eyes the flame of anger in the crowd was gradually snuffed. No lasting harm had been done, but what *might* have happened incensed them.

As the excitement died down the curtains closed in Anne's mind again. With Frederick restored to her, she withdrew into herself once more. By the time it was safe to return to their cabin she returned to the remote, wild-eyed woman who had come up on deck an hour and a half ago. Both Frederick and Henrietta could see it happening and their hearts sank. She had looked so alert a few minutes ago that they had both hoped for a miracle, but there was to be no miracle.

In the following days Anne grew steadily worse, until not even Henrietta could elicit a response from her. The hallucinations became regular and frequent. During one of them she snatched another woman's baby, almost crushing it to death in her fervour. Finally the ship's doctor said that she must be kept under constant sedation. There was no "until", Frederick noted, no light at the end of this darkness. What did it mean? Could she really die? Did people actually die of a broken heart? What was happening to his dream of a new life? Must he start again, alone? At the thought of losing Anne, as well as his only child Frederick's heart contracted. He knew he had not been a good husband, but in his way he had loved her. Was she now to be kept in a drugged state, not recognising anyone, until she died? "For the safety of others," the doctor said. Gentle Anne, who could never even crush an insect, a danger to others! This sacrifice was too much. If there was a benevolent God why did He demand such a price? Frederick worried day and night. By day the sight of her, so pretty and fragile, tore at his heart. At night he tossed in his bunk, while his wife slept soundly, unaware of his torment.

The ship was far enough south now for summer weather. There was always just enough wind to keep her moving – how frustrating it must be to lie becalmed, thought Henrietta – and the distant views of Western Australia encouraged the passengers. Soon they would sail close to the island of Tasmania, and then the next land to be sighted would be New Zealand, their destination! Only Frederick could feel no enthusiasm as all his dreams turned to dust.

They sighted Tasmania soon after, and Joseph did his best to describe to George how Abel Janzoon Tasman had charted these waters over two hundred years ago, using the stars and the few instruments known at that time to make what had proved to be quite accurate charts of the southern seas. Joseph's own knowledge of this part of the world was scant, but he felt no shame. Apart from ships' crews who else made the return voyage to England to pass on the information gained? What man would subject his family to this ordeal twice? Joseph's thoughts turned to the Gainsboroughs, for whom this voyage was an ordeal. Henrietta was with them now, although there was little that could be done. It was a tragedy, with only one possible outcome now.

For Ben Harper and his family the fumigation incident was also a memorable event in their lives. The family's gratitude to Joseph and Frederick for rescuing their husband and father was touching. Their poverty had kept them a close family, and it was plain that all the children loved and respected their father. A carpenter by trade, Ben Harper had never been idle for so long – his only work on the ship had been the making of coffins – but his children were keeping him occupied. One, a frail little girl, had died early in the voyage, thus starting him in his coffin-building trade, and now the baby was ill, but the other four were healthy and active, enjoying the rigours of shipboard life.

Ben was aware that his next coffin could be for the wife of one of his saviours. Supplies of wood were running low, but he would see to it that she had the best that was available. How else could a poor man thank gentry?

On December 4th, only two weeks out from Lyttelton, the port for Christchurch, it happened. Frederick had left her apparently sleeping; he had quietly placed the sleeping potions in the compartment above his own bunk and tip-toed from the cabin to join Joseph for a stroll on deck. A few minutes later, Henrietta slipped down, leaving Victoria asleep and George drawing his own map of New Zealand, to see how she was. The sight which greeted her would remain with her for ever. In the moment it took for her to knock and push open the door, Anne snatched the bottle and drank the whole phial of liquid. She stood staring at Henrietta for an instant, and fell back as Henrietta forced herself to move forward. The phial crashed to the floor, Henrietta screamed and then, to her embarrassment later, she fainted on the floor at Anne's feet.

Frederick sensed, rather than heard, the scream, his mind tuned to an imminent crisis for days now. In a daze he stood up and rushed from the saloon, leaving Joseph uncertain whether to follow or not. He decided to return to his cabin, to find the children alone. With a quick comment he admired George's map, noted that Victoria was still sleeping, and set off for the Gainsboroughs' cabin, pushing his way through curious by-standers as he neared it. Frederick was using smelling-salts on Henrietta when Joseph burst into the cabin. The doctor was on his way, but it was clear that Anne was beyond human help.

Angry at the morbid curiosity of the people outside the door, Joseph shouted at them to get out of the way. He called them "ghouls" and said there was little enough privacy on the ship without having people blocking up the narrow passageways for no good reason. Since he had become something of a hero following the rescue of Ben Harper, they listened to him and dispersed to their own quarters.

Seeing Henrietta revived, Joseph sought out Ben, but he was not with his family. Mrs Harper told him he was in the toolroom, next to the crew's quarters. Joseph made his way there and discovered, to his amazement, that Ben was working on a coffin. Ben pointed to the initials 'A.G.' he had engraved intricately on the lid.

"Been workin' for a while on this one I 'ave, sir. 'Ave you come to tell me she be ready for it?"

Joseph nodded, deeply moved by this man's dedication to repaying a debt of gratitude in the only way he could. It was a magnificent coffin. Ben had somehow found stain and polish which had given simple pine a finish like mahogany. Joseph hoped that Frederick, in his grief, would notice it. Nothing more to do now but return to his cabin and take care of his children until Henrietta was able to do so.

"Land ahoy to starboard!" The call from the crow's nest brought a flurry of activity, uncharacteristic of the December afternoons. This was the first sighting of their future homeland! From now on they could think of themselves as settlers and no longer as immigrants. The thought gave Joseph a feeling of belonging to this new land. He knew already that he would love this country. He was eager to see as much as he could while they kept the coast in sight. How varied was the scenery! There were glistening sandy beaches, breakers crashing against sheer cliffs, rocky outcrops protruding from deep-tinted water. It was no wonder that the ship kept her distance from the unpredictable shoreline. One of the stewards had told Joseph that they would view some two-thirds of the east coast before landing. It was like sailing from Thurso to London, reflected Joseph, smiling wryly to himself at the thought that he had never made that trip.

They were two days sailing along the coast. Henrietta came up on deck when she could, but Victoria, cutting teeth profusely, was irritable and restless, requiring far more attention than usual. George had been fascinated since his first view of the land and asked incessant questions, most of which did not require an answer. His seasickness was forgotten. He was soon going to be able to play on a floor that did not move, to kick a ball where it would not be forever lost in water, to see people he had never seen before.

On the third morning an announcement was made that they were through the Heads and would dock at about ten o'clock. There was final packing to attend to and the time passed quickly. The cabin, their home for three months, looked warm and inviting, compared with the unknown which lay ahead. Henrietta wondered where they would be sleeping that night.

Joseph was as excited as a child on Christmas Eve, heading out to view the land, returning with a glowing report, and then rushing off again. Henrietta smiled to herself, glad to see that he was still so eager. They would need plenty of enthusiasm to see them through the next few months.

CHAPTER 6

Establishment

The debt was paid. Henrietta had strolled mentally back through her life, and was ready to put it behind her now, thinking only of todays and tomorrows as she and Joseph built a new life for their family. She had no inkling that they would establish a dynasty in the new land where they had chosen to make a home.

Joseph, with a sound business head, had come a long way since having his trunks, loaded with fabrics and haberdashery, hauled over the Port Hills to set up his little shop. Hamilton's Drapery was well known now and well-respected in Christchurch. He had left room for expansion when he built and before long he would need to extend the frontage of the building, for business was especially brisk with spring coming on. The ladies' minds all turned to pretty materials for cooler dresses on summer days with warm nor'westerlies.

Henrietta's mind was on dresses also, since none of hers was comfortable now. She was expecting her third child in March and was choosing fabrics carefully – not the bright floral one Mrs. Jamieson had chosen for her twelve-year-old daughter; they would be shocked at this use of it. And not the rest of the bolt selected by Mrs. Adams – she too would be offended at sharing it with a woman in that condition. Joseph came to her rescue by unwrapping several new bolts that had just arrived from England. They were muslins and cottons, most suitable for a warm Christchurch summer.

"This way you have first choice. Anyone who chooses them after you cannot be put out, or, if she is, can hardly blame you, my dear."

Although both Joseph and Henrietta were delighted at the thought of having a New Zealand-born child, they were aware that in a small town people could be easily upset, and that was bad for business.

The summer was kind to Henrietta that year, at least until February, when the nor'west wind drove across the Canterbury Plains and Henrietta longed for the change to the cool easterly wind each evening. By March she wanted nothing more than to be safely delivered of the heavy child she was carrying.

Samuel James was born without incident, with the able assistance of Mrs Anderson, on March 6th, 1873. George, now approaching nine, and Victoria, who had just celebrated her fifth birthday, were fascinated by this pink bundle that only slept or screamed. Although it would have been hard to explain that Samuel crowned the success of their giving up everything to immigrate to New Zealand, the children sensed that he meant something special to their parents. Joseph and Henrietta had considered naming the child after their friend Frederick Gainsborough, but there was so much sadness surrounding the man that they felt it would be wrong. Frederick had tried to make a success of life in New Zealand, but he was unable to overcome the tragedies that had dogged him on the voyage, and last year, on the urging of his parents, he returned to England to make his peace with Anne's family. They had heard nothing from him since then.

From the age of six George had been attending the little school run by Miss Rolls. Next year Victoria would join him there for her father was adamant that she too was to be not only literate but well-educated. Miss Rolls, a plump, rosy woman, liked children but did not believe it was good for the children to know this. Thus her discipline was rigid and many a child whimpered in the corner for not knowing that 4 x 6 = 24, or that "thistle" had a silent "t". Fortunately George was an able scholar, when it suited him, and when he saw the colour rising in Miss Rolls's cheeks he would show sudden flashes of genius. He had a charm which Miss Rolls could not resist and so was seldom punished for his misdemeanours.

At home George had taken over the responsibility of nurturing the six little oak trees he and his father had potted as acorns when they were staying with the Andersons on their arrival five years ago. It was time to move them to larger pots. Three looked very healthy, but the others were not thriving. Joseph and George decided to repot only the three sturdy ones. Henrietta suggested they keep the strongest one and donate the other two to the Christchurch Botanic Gardens, established ten years ago when an English oak had been planted to commemorate Queen Victoria's son Albert's marriage to Princess Alexandra of Denmark.

Victoria, at five, was a delightful child. Old enough to do many things for the baby, she was a great help to her mother. With blonde curls tumbling onto her shoulders and striking hazel eyes, she attracted much attention in her father's shop. For this reason Henrietta saw to it that she was always well dressed. Other mothers were influenced by what they saw the child wearing.

Henrietta liked to help Joseph in the shop. From her father she had gained a sound knowledge of the fabric industry, never realising at the time how valuable this would be. Now she was thankful that he had passed on some of his knowledge to her. From Lucy Stanton, who had raised her in her father's home, she had learned to sew, and Lucy had never accepted inferior work. Henrietta herself had become an expert seamstress, and when she was not helping Joseph in the shop or attending to the baby's needs she could be found measuring or stitching a dress for one of the many ladies who sought her out for her skills. There were few women in the town that could make clothes of the quality they had known in their homeland.

It was Samuel's third birthday and just past the date of Victoria's eighth. Joseph and Henrietta had decided to hold a combined gathering for them. Henrietta had some reservations about how five three-year-old boys and six eight-year-old girls would mix, but George had promised to help entertain the little boys and Henrietta thought that she could amuse the girls for the afternoon.

George, tall for his age at thirteen, towered over his little brother and the young guests as they played ball in the backyard. He had to restrain himself often from laughing at their antics as they attacked the game, and at times each other. He spent so much time untangling small bodies with flailing appendages that he never managed to explain the game to them. No matter, he was keeping his promise to his mother, which was important to him, and leaving her free to manage Victoria's friends.

The girls were competing all this time to see who could make the best little rag doll in the fastest time. There was to be a prize for the best as well as the first finished, and if one person achieved both then she would deserve both prizes. Henrietta was musing on the range of ability in the group and wondering if she should set up a sewing class for young girls in the town when George's voice reached her, shouting frantically,

"Mother, come quickly! It's Samuel!"

Startled, Henrietta ran to meet him. "What has happened, George?"

"They were rolling about in a heap on the ball, so I separated them and off they went. Then I saw Samuel still lying on the ground. He won't get up, just keeps saying 'Mummy'," he gasped.

They had crossed the yard and were approaching Samuel, who was bravely stifling his sobs as the others crowded around him. It took only an instant for Henrietta to see that his left leg lay at the wrong angle from the knee down.

"George, we must fetch Dr Macfarlane. Will you go please?"

Feeling partly responsible for the accident, George was only too pleased to do something to help. He sprinted away as Henrietta explained to Samuel that the doctor was coming soon.

Joseph had heard the commotion but had put it down to high spirits being checked by Henrietta, until George dashed past the front windows of the shop. Alerted by George's urgency he hurried towards the little crowd of children on the grass, much to the relief of Henrietta. Victoria, who had followed her mother, was sent to attend to the shop, Joseph staying with Samuel, and Henrietta leading the birthday party guests into the house to enjoy the feast without any Hamilton children present. The festive spirit had gone out of the afternoon, but the children's appetites were unaffected by the accident. They enjoyed the spread while Dr Macfarlane set Samuel's leg where he lay in the yard.

That evening Samuel ate his birthday cake lying on the settee in the sitting room with his leg in a splint. His day had been ruined and his leg ached, but it was a story he would enjoy recounting through the years. Sitting with him as he fell asleep Henrietta and Joseph were filled with pride and love for all three of their children.

George had just begun high school, at a time when there were many changes being brought about in education. Schools were now less religion oriented, and this was a relief to Joseph. He had never been a regular churchgoer and had found it difficult to answer some of the questions George brought home from his scripture classes. Joseph felt the emphasis was now better placed on academic achievement. George, he felt, would do well – he was intelligent and alert, sensitive to criticism, but in a way that spurred him to improve his results. Joseph nursed the hope of seeing his son a partner in the business in a few years, with the possibility of a second branch of Hamilton's Drapery in his care in another town; however he kept these thoughts to himself, for he would not force his son in any direction he did not choose for himself.

Victoria showed signs of having inherited her mother's sewing skill. As Henrietta picked up the abandoned, half-completed rag dolls on the evening of Samuel's birthday it was easy to see that Victoria's would have won both prizes. Henrietta was pleased to see this for, combined with Miss Rolls's recent declaration that Victoria was quite the ideal pupil, being polite, well-spoken, quick-witted and gifted, it promised well for her future.

It was early days to wonder about Samuel, but it was obvious he had little in common with either of his siblings. His was a more straightforward character, which met a challenge head on and solved it by brute force or not at all. When he was angry everyone knew; when he was hurt or sad he did not hide it. Whereas George suffered silently and had to be asked what was wrong, Samuel brought the cut or bruise to his mother with a full explanation and a demand for sympathy. Tact and shrewdness were completely lacking in him, although his mother still hoped that he would develop a measure of each. With a shock of ginger curls, inherited, apparently like his temperament, from Grandfather Hamilton, he bore little immediate resemblance to either Victoria or George, but there was a likeness in their features, despite the extraordinary variety in their hair colour. Henrietta would muse on how they managed one dark, one blonde and one ginger.

It was not often that Henrietta had the chance to daydream like this and she felt a little guilty for wasting valuable time as she hastily stacked the dolls in a box, to be given to the mothers or the girls next time they came to the shop. As a birthday party it had been a fiasco and the children had been sent home early, but a little note to each mother would explain everything.

Placing the neatly printed notice on the shop counter, she surveyed it critically before deciding the best position to catch the eye of the customers. Now she would wait patiently to see whether or not her idea would become a reality.

Within three days there were ten names on the list and Mrs Hamilton's Sewing Class for Girls was ready to commence. It was to be held on Mondays and Thursdays, once the girls had been home from school to collect their sewing requirements. They arrived in ones and twos, but all were present by 3.45 p.m. Henrietta had placed no restriction on the age of the girls eligible for the class, but most were between eight and thirteen years old.

Before long, word spread and there was a waiting list. Henrietta started another class on Tuesdays and Fridays. Now she had twenty girls learning the rudiments of dressmaking. Pleasing as the response was, she could take no more girls. She decided that if more mothers approached her she would visit Miss Rolls to suggest that sewing be taught in the upper classes of the school. The outcome of her chat with the schoolteacher was that Henrietta found herself employed two mornings a week at the school. She taught the girls the elements of dressmaking as well as embroidery, and was surprised to find how much pleasure she gained from her association with the girls. For their part they looked forward to Mrs Hamilton's visits, for she was less severe than Miss Rolls, and she soon had them making garments they could wear beneath their school smocks and show off to the other girls during the lunch break.

Joseph applauded his wife's new enterprise, because he knew she liked to be busy, but also because he saw in her venture a future clientele for his business. Women, he reasoned, would always want new dresses, and the more skilled hands there were in the town to make them the more dress materials he would sell.

CHAPTER 7

1880

Joseph had felt it imprudent to remove George from school at the end of the previous year, as he did not like the economic outlook of the country. Business was still steady, he had no reason for alarm there, but he felt uneasy. In the last year unemployment had become too common and he considered it better that George should gain the best education before venturing into the business world. The boy was assured of a job, which gave him an advantage over many of his contemporaries, but at the same time Joseph could not be extravagant paying another wage when there was no bright future. He would wait until the end of 1880 before making the final decision. He knew George was eager to join the business, but his motives showed how immature he was. Joseph could see that he wanted to show his school friends, many of whose fathers had lost their own jobs, that he had a secure position to go to. His youthful arrogance concerned Joseph, but he hoped the boy's attitude also showed pride in his father's achievement. It mattered greatly to Joseph what George thought of him, as a businessman, as a father and, above all, as a man. Yet he often felt that George's deepest affection was reserved for his mother. Although this disappointed him it was also reassuring, for he knew that if he left Henrietta a widow George would take good care of her.

As Henrietta and Victoria turned their minds towards preparations for Christmas Joseph decided late in November that it was time to have a chat with George about his future. As a result George left school before Christmas, just before his seventeenth birthday, and joined his father in Hamilton's Drapery. Joseph intended that the boy would spend three or four years learning every aspect of the trade, from the raw materials that went to the factories to the finished product sold over the counter, as well as all the technicalities of importing goods from the textile centres of England. At the end of that time, whenever Joseph thought he was ready for it, he would take George into the business as a full partner. This would be timed to coincide with George's coming-of-age in January, 1885 if all went well.

Henrietta decided to make many of the Christmas presents this year, having been advised all year by Joseph that some curbs now might mean less discomfort later, if the worst came to the worst. She and Victoria therefore spent little money and much time on gifts for Joseph, George and Samuel. Victoria was making a beautiful waistcoat for her father, a cravat for George, and a shirt for Samuel. All were a challenge to her at the age of twelve, but with her mother to help her at home and the new sewing teacher at school she knew that she would get them all finished. She hoped her father would be proud of his plum-coloured waistcoat, and that George would be glad to wear the cravat when he was working in the shop. She did not expect much in the way of thanks from Samuel, whose clothes suffered a short, brutal life. For her mother she was making an apron, which was almost completed, and which she kept at school. She had taken special care with her stitching, since she knew her mother would appreciate the straight rows of tiny, barely visible stitches laboured on through many sewing lessons. She longed to tell her mother of Mrs Adamson's praise, but it would have to wait until Christmas morning.

Henrietta was also busy with her sewing. It seemed that every time she picked up Samuel's new jacket to add a stitch to it, he would appear from nowhere, usually asking for something to eat or drink. He did not notice that she hastily reached for the same pair of trousers or stockings each time. Henrietta was making Joseph and George a suit each, but was glad that Mr Dick, the tailor, was only a few doors away, for she needed his advice often. This was the first time she had attempted to make men's clothing and she was not really enjoying the task. She was determined to persevere, having persuaded Mr Dick to buy the material from Joseph on her behalf. She was trying to complete Joseph's suit first because, if time ran out, George's could be a birthday present in January. This was a likely scenario, as it was already mid-December. Thank goodness the dress for Victoria was ready.

George was to begin work in the shop on the second Monday before Christmas. In his quiet way he was excited as he prepared for bed on the Sunday night.

"What time would you like me to be up in the morning, Father?"

"Well, we open at eight o'clock and I think we should be in the shop ten minutes before, so do you think perhaps six-thirty?"

Having lain awake since 5.00 George was up and dressed by 6.00. He had made his bed and set out the breakfast by the time his father appeared in the dining room at 7.00. Joseph was warmed at this show of enthusiasm but thought it unwise to show what pleasure it gave him. He would not tease the boy, for fear of making a fool of him. They sat down together to their meal and had almost finished when the rest of the family arrived.

At 7.45 Joseph took the shop key down from the wall of the kitchen and handed it to George. "You go on ahead. I'll be along in a few minutes. Take the key, but do not open the front door until the little clock on the counter shows exactly eight o'clock. It is a matter of principle to me to be neither early nor late."

At 8.00 Joseph was still not in sight, so a nervous George picked up the key from beside the clock and strode through the shop to the front door. As he did so Joseph crept through the back door and was proud to witness this symbolic act. He felt a load lifted from his shoulders, and as George returned from opening the door Joseph stepped forward to shake his hand, without a word.

As well as sewing requisites, Joseph stocked some ready-made garments and novelty articles, many of which were Henrietta's work. He knew from now until Christmas they would be in demand. He would put George in charge of this corner, leaving himself free to wait on customers who needed his advice on less straightforward purchases.

It was a busy morning for both and Joseph made a point of introducing his son to any of his customers whom he did not already know. By lunchtime George felt befuddled but not despondent, having enjoyed his first morning's work. Joseph always closed the shop between 12.00 and 1.00 as he liked to sit down to a proper meal with his family. George was hoping for some sort of appraisal of his progress but when Henrietta asked how the morning had gone, Joseph had little to say, and nothing concerning George. She smiled encouragingly at George. If Joseph had nothing to relate then he was satisfied with his son's work.

Victoria and Samuel were also at home for lunch. This was their last week of school for the year and for Victoria a time of mixed feelings, as she would be leaving primary school this week. Samuel's feelings were, as usual, unmixed. He did not like school and made little effort to give his teacher a peaceful existence. Constantly in trouble, he seemed to spend a part of each school day explaining his actions to the headmaster. The resulting punishments made little impression. At lunch he kept up a string of cheerful chatter while eating several times more than his sister. Victoria was bursting to show her mother the completed waistcoat, but this must wait until Father had gone back to the shop. As he passed the coat rack in the hall, Joseph called,

"What is this package, Henrietta?" and a flustered Victoria rushed to claim it.

"It is mine, Father."

"Then don't leave it here, my dear. I thought it was to go into the shop."

"Oh no, Father – it's your Christmas present! You didn't look at it, did you?"

"No Victoria, I did not, although I am curious now."

"Well, only a few more days, Father. Goodbye." As she stretched up to kiss her tall father, she could picture him with his waistcoat on. "Oh, I do hope you'll like it."

"I'm sure I shall," replied Joseph. "But now I must hurry. I can't have George being back at work before me. Goodbye."

Joseph gave a moment's thought to the contents of the parcel, before reaching the shop doorway. Victoria hurried back to the dining room. Samuel and George had gone, she was relieved to see.

"Here it is, Mother!" She laid the waistcoat on the dining table. It was well made, and the black edging looked striking against the rich plum colour of the velvet. When she had cut out the pattern for her daughter, Henrietta had hoped it would look just like this.

"Do you think he will like it?"

"You have made it beautifully, dear, and he will be proud to be seen wearing it." Henrietta turned it inside out and exclaimed, "You know, Victoria, he could wear it this way, too!" The child flushed with pleasure, knowing that Henrietta placed as much value on the finish to the inside of a garment as the outside.

At this moment the mantel clock chimed and Henrietta gasped, "That's one o'clock. You must run now, you are late for school. Tell Miss Rolls it was my fault. I'll put the waistcoat away in your room. Wherever is Samuel?"

"George sent him back to school, I think. Goodbye, Mother!"

Unable to find Samuel in the house or garden, Henrietta assumed that he had indeed returned to school. Mr Henderson would have been relieved if he had not. It was a worry to Joseph and Henrietta that he seemed unable to settle at school. In two years he had had time to realise that he had to go there each day, whether he liked it or not. Yet he still rebelled and made life a misery for his teacher. Joseph felt there was time to worry when he was older, but Henrietta was sure he was forming bad habits which would lead to a shiftless life. A worrier by nature, she tried not to think too much about it. Better to guide him where she could and leave the rest to time. She tried to take heart from his forthrightness and good nature, qualities which would develop as his character was formed.

Henrietta had cleared the table and washed up the lunch dishes while she had been preoccupied with these thoughts. Now she was free to spend the afternoon putting the finishing touches to Joseph's suit and Samuel's jacket.

The suit was hanging behind the door, ready to be pressed, and Henrietta had just sewn one sleeve into Samuel's jacket when George came through the house calling her. There was no urgency in his tone as there had been on that day four years ago, when Samuel had broken his leg, and Henrietta simply called back. "In the sewing room, George."

"Father asks if you could help in the shop for a time, please. We are very busy and …"

"And what, George?"

"Well … I just don't feel I'm being much help to him. I keep interrupting him to ask prices and other questions."

"Has your father complained about that?"

"No, Mother."

"Then don't worry, George. You must be doing well. Go back and tell your father I shall be there in a few minutes. Are you enjoying the work?"

"Oh yes, Mother, more than I expected to, but I don't want to be a hindrance to Father. I want him to be glad he has taken me into the business."

"You won't let him down, George, as long as you have your heart in your work. But this is not a time to stand talking. I'll come now." She had hoped to put the other sleeve into the jacket, but had now spent those minutes talking instead.

They found Joseph apologising politely to waiting customers as he attended to Mrs Thurley, and looking anxiously over his shoulder in search of his reinforcements. Henrietta took in the situation at a glance. Mrs Thurley was a lady who could not be hurried, nor would she be left alone to make a choice. As soon as a shop assistant turned away to help another customer she would ask a question regarding the fabric or garment in front of her. Henrietta had made a dress for her once, and had vowed never again after the final, long-drawn-out sitting. Now she and George separated and in a few minutes all the customers were being shown what they wished to see. It was some time, however, before Henrietta had a chance to speak to Joseph.

"Which one did Mrs Thurley take?"

"She took a sample of each – she could not make up her mind – and she says she will return tomorrow to make her final choice. Can you imagine it, after wasting half an hour of my time!"

"Well, dear, it is always a good sale when she does make up her mind. She is a well-built lady and she likes her dresses full!"

"Yes, but one day she will cost me three or four other sales while she dithers! Luckily most of the local people know her well enough not to blame me."

Henrietta stayed for an hour or so before returning to her sewing. Samuel's jacket required only a few stitches when Henrietta put it aside to prepare the evening meal.

The shop closed at 6.00 and Joseph again gave this task to George. As the two returned to the house Henrietta smiled to see George pull off his shoes and draw up a footstool as he sank into an armchair. He felt a new respect for his father as tiredness flowed over him. He would be early to bed this evening.

When George had gone off to his room soon after 8.00 Henrietta brought out her sewing and sat down in the armchair opposite Joseph's.

"How was your new apprentice on his first day, Joseph?"

"He shows great promise, although of course there are many gaps in his knowledge which will have to be filled. His manner with the customers pleased me, though – that will be his strength, I feel. He has far more patience with the more difficult ladies than I have."

"What will be the next step in his training?"

"After Christmas I shall arrange for him to spend a month at the mill. A few days in each department should give him a clear picture of the whole process."

"Will he need to go out there each day? It is almost fifteen miles, isn't it?"

"I should think the manager would accommodate him. After all, we are good customers of theirs, and we will offer to pay for his keep, of course. I'll see to the arrangements as soon as the Christmas holiday is over."

The gifts were ready, but not without several long evenings of work on Henrietta's part. Mr Dick, the tailor, had pressed the suits for her and had complimented her on the finished garments (purely out of politeness, Henrietta was sure, but it was kind of him). Tomorrow was Christmas Day and, as always, she thought back to their first Christmas in New Zealand, twelve years ago. How strange it had all been, yet now it took an effort to picture the wintry scene in England at Christmas time. Then she had only looked forward, not daring to think back to her known world, but now, having just celebrated her fortieth birthday, she liked to cast her mind back to the life she had known in England and the great step she and her husband had taken in starting afresh. She had never regretted it and somehow it seemed linked with the hope of Christmas and the New Year.

Samuel was the first up next morning, and the whole family was awake within moments as he went from room to room to share his exuberance. A sleepy glance at the clock told Victoria that it was not yet 6.00, and she turned over to go back to sleep. As she did so something pink and white behind the door caught her eye.

She said to Samuel, "Yes, yes, a lovely jacket – glad you like the shirt – we will have fun with the playthings – why don't you show them to George?"

Samuel, unsuspecting, took the hint and Victoria carefully closed the door behind him. Now she could see the new dress, and she gazed at it in awe. However did her mother make that, leaving not a scrap of material to give the secret away? There were other presents at the foot of the bed, but they were overshadowed by the dress. The special thing was that for the first time it was not a little girl's dress, but more the style that her mother wore. The pink material and white sleeves with pink wristbands made it too young-looking for her mother though. She would wear it today, but not until after breakfast.

Samuel went to George's room. An early riser like himself, George was awake and opening his presents. Samuel noticed something on the back of the door.

"Where'd the suit come from, George?"

"It's from Mother and Father, the card says. Do you think Mother might have made it?"

"No, I bet Mr Dick made it. It's just like that one of Father's that Mr Dick made ages ago. It's nice though, not saying this one looks old or anything."

"No Sam, that's all right. I like it anyway. What have you got there?" George was genuinely interested. He and Samuel had always been on good terms, despite the nine years between them. George envied Samuel his courage to do things he had never dared to do, and Samuel admired George because he was more grown up now that he worked for Father. Out came the presents and they spent half an hour together before making a pot of tea and joining Victoria and their parents in the master bedroom. This was a family tradition by now, and it gave the children a chance to thank everyone for their gifts, as well as bringing their presents for Joseph and Henrietta. Joseph was already wearing a magnificent waistcoat over his nightshirt.

There was always a time of tumult as everyone said "Thank you" at the same time, followed by a lull as everyone examined the other presents. Henrietta always thought of all the work that had gone into making these minutes so happy, and each year she decided it was definitely worth the trouble.

The rest of the day was spent as usual, with the traditional meal and a few visitors in the afternoon. It was a pleasant day, but Henrietta was weary by the evening and glad to sit with her feet on a footstool. Christmas, with all its bustle, was over for 1880.

George spent his 17th birthday away from home, but his parents took Victoria and Samuel to visit him that evening. It was to be a surprise for George, although Joseph had made the necessary arrangements with the mill manager. It would be a good chance to discuss the boy's progress over a cigar in the sitting room.

It was the first time the children had driven along the road north of the town. On a warm summer evening such as this they delighted in the wind through their hair as the horses cantered ahead of them. For an hour they passed green fields dotted with small farm cottages and, every few miles, a grand homestead. Tall trees lined the narrow road, at times forming an umbrella above them, before parting to reveal the evening sunshine again. Victoria was captivated by the furry-trunked tree ferns, which she imagined to be the homes of fairies and elves, so delicate were their unfurling leaves. Samuel preferred the tall, husky pines, stretching upwards with spiky arms, yet leaving beneath them a soft bed of brown needles in which he would have loved to romp. Silver poplars, some planted by early settlers, others sown by the winds, caught the late sun and the light breeze lifted the shaggy arms of the willows as they crossed the rivers threading their way over the wide Canterbury Plains. It was a perfect night for an outing, and Joseph was glad to see his family all taking pleasure in this land he had come to love.

The reunion was a happy one, especially for George. He had never been away from his family for so long and it had given him a chance to look at them more objectively. He had reached the conclusion after two weeks that he was lucky to have understanding parents and a brother and sister with whom he could live in harmony. The Donahue family, where he was staying, had provided just the contrast needed to show him how fortunate he was. The four children, aged between eighteen and twelve, argued constantly, the parents seemed to disagree on every issue, and the children lacked respect for them. Only fear of punishment made them do as they were told. George missed the warmth he was accustomed to in his own home.

Mr Donahue, an efficient businessman, whose greatest error had been to try to run his family in the same way as his business, had nothing but praise for George when Joseph enquired how the three weeks had passed.

"Your son has a naturally tidy mind – wish I could say that of any of mine – and a basic understanding of the process, which he must have picked up from you. He has taken his own notes and has asked me to check them each week to see that they are correct. Be careful, Joseph, or the lad will have you out of a job in five years!"

"I'll not give up easily, Henry, but thanks for the warning. George seems to have inherited my love for this trade."

On the way home that night Joseph passed on this information to Henrietta. George had given her his opinion of the Donahue family, which she recounted to Joseph in return. They enjoyed a quiet chuckle together, but both felt more pride than amusement.

CHAPTER 8

Partnership

Among George's friends at school were several whose fathers were farmers in the area to the north and west of Christchurch, within easy reach of the rapidly expanding town, but distant enough to own large tracts of land. When George had been at high school, these boys had talked eagerly of returning to help their fathers on the farm. He had spent a weekend at the Davis farm, about twenty miles inland, experiencing a life so different from his family's that he was quite amazed. It was the lavish meals that staggered him, and the sumptuous morning and afternoon teas. He felt he had spent the whole weekend eating. The Davis boys took it for granted and George wondered how they existed on the meals at boarding school. When he saw them at work with their father in the paddocks however, he understood how they could eat so much. He went home on the Sunday evening, feeling he would not need to eat for a week.

Now, six years later, the Davis brothers were farming the land, following their father's sudden death a year ago. Richard was almost the same age as George – he would come of age just before Christmas – and his brother Alex would be nineteen in November. It was a great responsibility for these young men, but they had competent legal advisors and their mother saw to it that they made a good job of running the farm. They must have had cash to spare, for in these depressing times they had decided to throw a barn dance for their young friends.

George had kept in contact with Richard Davis over the years – Richard called on him at Hamilton's whenever he was in town, sometimes staying for lunch with George's family. George was not surprised to receive an invitation to the dance, but was mystified by the meaning of a barn dance. His mother was equally puzzled, suggesting he ask the first farming customer to come into the drapery, as the replies had to be sent within a week.

Several evenings later, at dinner, George revealed that it was a modern idea, the dance being held in a barn, seating was bales of hay, and the guests should dress as farm labourers. Henrietta was shocked, Victoria was fascinated, Joseph uninterested, and Samuel, off in a world of his own, oblivious to the conversation.

"But George, will gentlemen and young ladies be seen going out in such outfits?"

"It does not start until dark, Mother."

"Who will accompany you if you go?"

"I have someone in mind, Mother, but I have not yet asked her."

Henrietta was taken aback, because George was painfully shy with young ladies. At twenty he still blushed if he waited on any lady under forty!

"And do you think she will still want to go with you when she learns the dance is being held in a hay barn?"

"If you were her mother, would you say 'No'?" asked George innocently.

"Well, I would think twice about it."

"And what would you decide?"

"I would probably say, 'Yes', but you know I am not a typical mother."

"That's all I need to know, Mother – you see, it's Victoria I am going to take! Richard seems to have taken quite a fancy to her; he enclosed a letter asking me to be sure to bring my charming sister."

Victoria was delighted and surprised to hear this, delighted at the thought of the dance, and surprised, first at George's wish to take her, and second, at the thought that Richard Davis had noticed her on his visits to the Hamiltons' for lunch.

The evening of the dance was warm and still. George and Victoria did not set out until 8.30, and no-one would have guessed that they were going to a dance. George wore a pair of old pants frayed at the calves, red braces and an old tattered shirt with no collar. He had conjured up a well-used straw hat which was perched on the back of his head. Hoping to meet several old school friends, he had made up his mind to enter into the spirit of the occasion. Victoria's outfit was less authentic, but more romantic. Her mother had made her a full blue skirt trimmed with braid and she wore a white peasant blouse with matching braid. Through her blonde hair she had woven a length of the braid, and for once her hair hung loose down to her waist. Excitement had given a sparkle to her hazel eyes, and George suddenly realised his sixteen-year-old sister was growing up.

When they reached the farm it was not difficult to find the hay barn. Lanterns hung from hooks to light the way, and several gigs were tied up near the barn. Victoria felt suddenly nervous.

"George, you will stay with me, won't you? I won't know anyone there."

"Yes, but I think Richard will look after you, once he finds you."

Richard met them at the door with a warm welcome. Fair-haired like Victoria, he was well-tanned from his work on the farm. He was wearing his oldest clothes and chewing a piece of straw. He was a handsome young man, and Victoria felt honoured to think he had requested her company. He was unable to join them until he had welcomed all his guests, but it was not long before George saw him approaching. Accompanying him was a girl, about Victoria's age, who bore a close resemblance to Richard. As Richard led Victoria on to the dance floor, George was left to converse with Catherine Davis. For a little while they watched the dancers in silence, each feeling more tongue-tied than the other, until George finally made an effort to break the heavy silence. Since the only thing they had in common was their connection to Richard, they talked of him, George soon learning the girl hero worshipped her older brother. It was easy to relieve her shyness by means of this topic, and they were quite absorbed in their conversation when the others rejoined them.

The evening passed quickly and both Victoria and George went home tired but happy shortly after midnight, already invited to the Davis home for dinner the following week. They had little to say to each other on the way home, both engrossed in their own thoughts.

Henrietta observed that Richard Davis's visits to town became more frequent, as did his invitations to lunch. She reached the conclusion that between George and Victoria there was a conspiracy going on, and she passed on her view to Joseph, who merely grunted and said, "She could do a lot worse for a husband."

At this stage Henrietta was unaware of the friendship developing between George and Catherine. She assumed that George's only interest was in helping to further the relationship between his sister and Richard Davis. Henrietta had no objection to Richard – he was well-mannered, wealthy and obviously becoming devoted to Victoria – except that she thought Victoria rather young for a serious romance. The girl had just left school. She should mix more widely before choosing a husband.

With this in mind, Henrietta allowed Victoria to attend most of the social functions for young people that year. Each time she had a different escort, thanks to her mother's connivance with other protective parents. Outgoing by nature, Victoria enjoyed these evenings and gained a certain poise from them, but she gave a warm welcome to Richard Davis when he called at the shop.

Christmas, 1884 held the usual excitement and air of festivity, but these were outshone for the Davis and Hamilton families by the announcement of Richard and Victoria's engagement at New Year. It was no real surprise – George had seen the writing on the wall a year ago, and Richard had, of course, asked Joseph and Henrietta's consent some time ago – but this did nothing to diminish the gaiety and happiness of the occasion. Richard had dined with his future in-laws, while his mother, brother and sister had arrived for the little celebration later in the evening. Sam was the only one who had not noticed anything special until the announcement, but to him, at eleven, marriage was a necessary evil. He could see no reason for anyone to actually *want* to be married.

Because Victoria was so young, Henrietta had insisted on a long engagement. There were still many things to be learnt about running a house, and a farm house at that. Richard had agreed to wait until March, 1886, when his bride would be eighteen years old. He was content to know that no-one else could snatch his beautiful prize away.

For George there was a poignancy to the evening. Catherine was there, of course, and he would have liked to mention his hopes for the future, but his plans held too many uncertainties. Next month he and his father would travel south by train to Dunedin, where arrangements had been made to open a second branch of Hamilton's, now to be called "J. J. Hamilton & Son". With George's twenty-first birthday only a matter of weeks away, Joseph had told him that he would become a full partner in the business on that day. If all went well in Dunedin in February, Joseph would return within a few days, leaving George as manager of the new shop. It would be years before he could hope to feel secure enough to marry, and he told himself repeatedly that he could not expect Catherine to sit at home and wait for him during that time. It was better to say nothing that might raise her hopes.

Catherine spent the evening smiling bravely, hoping she would get home before she burst into tears. Nothing had been said on the subject, but she had dreamed of a double celebration and had wondered throughout the party whether George might suddenly surprise everyone by proposing to her in front of them all. It was a silly dream, for that was not George's way of doing things. Knowing now that he was going away indefinitely, she felt unsure of his feelings towards her. Only her genuine happiness for Richard and Victoria helped her through the night.

The sun, appearing around the edges of the blinds, woke Victoria. She smiled. God had granted her a fine day. There was much to do, and she could hear her mother already busy in the house. For a few minutes she gazed at the wedding dress, made by her mother and hanging behind the closed door. Her thoughts went back to the pink dress which had hung there one Christmas morning. She remembered how thrilled she had been that day, afraid to put the dress on until breakfast was over, for fear of damaging it.

Looking at the masterpiece her mother had created, she felt the same apprehension now. With only one daughter, her mother had taken the chance to use all her skill to make the most magnificent wedding dress. The off-white silk was the colour of Victoria's hair – Henrietta was adamant that a blonde bride should not wear white – and hung to the calf, where a frill took the dress to the ankles. The bodice was trimmed with bands of a soft tangerine coloured silk, tapered in a way which accentuated her slender waist. An insert of ivory lace, decorated with tiny orange glass beads, rose to the throat. Victoria knew that it added to the elegance of the dress but hoped that it would not be too hot – please don't let it be a nor'wester today, she prayed. She had baulked at long sleeves, insisting on puffed sleeves to the elbow, with matching lace hanging loose from there. Henrietta had trimmed the sleeves and the frill with the tangerine silk and the little beads, so that there was a harmony to the dress. Victoria knew, with a warm glow, that Richard would catch his breath at the sight of her.

Mrs Pearson, that dear kind lady, had offered to make a hat to match the dress and complete the outfit for the big occasion. Henrietta had given her pieces of the fabrics she had used, and Mrs Pearson had set her imagination to work. The result was a brimmed hat, high enough at the crown to accommodate Victoria's hair piled up. It was ivory with tangerine trim, decorated with small flowers, and even a little orange artificial bird nestling in the foliage around the flowers. It was extraordinary, lying on the spare bed, with the cream silken shoes neatly arranged on the floor beneath it.

How different life was going to be from today! Catherine, her bridesmaid, would become her sister. Dear Catherine, who longed for nothing more than to be with George, would leave the church on his arm today, because George was to be Richard's best man. They would make a striking couple, she in her tangerine dress, with flowers in her dark hair, and George dressed, like Richard, in striped trousers, a high-necked white shirt and a waistcoat of the tangerine silk, topped off with a long black jacket and top hat. Both of the men would wear orange roses in their button-holes.

A knock on the door stirred her from this delicious rêverie. It was her mother coming to ask if the bride had managed enough sleep to see her through her big day. With a hug that spoke of all the love she felt for her mother, Victoria was ready to start the preparations.

Cathedral Square resounded to the pealing of the church bells as the carriage drew to a halt at the door of the beautiful new cathedral, built only five years ago, and not yet completed. Joseph stepped down and reached for the hand of the beautiful young lady who had sat beside him a moment ago. Could this really be his little Victoria, who had been but a babe in arms when they had arrived at Lyttelton? And now he was giving her into the care of another man for the rest of her life. There would be babies and the cycle of life would go on.

As they entered the majestic nave the organ music swelled to enfold them and to announce that this woman had indeed come to be united with this man, until death them should part. Hearts were full and throats constricted with emotion. There were gasps and whispers as Victoria passed by their guests on the way to the altar, where Richard and George waited. As they turned to greet the bride and her father, Henrietta saw the loving look in Richard's eyes, and knew that she and Joseph need have no qualms about this marriage.

"Joseph, hadn't you better be changing your clothes? They'll be here in a few minutes. Do we have enough chairs for the visitors tomorrow?"

"Plenty, my dear – remember this is not our daughter's wedding, but our son's. We are not the most important guests this time, you know. Do calm yourself, or you will never enjoy seeing the grandchildren when they arrive. I'll go and change – you sit and relax now."

Sam met his father in the doorway, almost spilling over him the tray of tea he was carrying. Excusing himself, Joseph took his cup to the bedroom while Sam handed the second cup of tea to his grateful mother. He was the most considerate of her three children and perhaps her favourite, but she could not have said why. Now seventeen and tall like his father, Sam had lost much of his reckless exuberance, and Henrietta had only his lack of perseverance to worry about. His attitude to young ladies had changed of late. They found his dark auburn curls and freckled, friendly face irresistible, and he was always to be found at the centre of a group of them. It was he who had organised a group of volunteers last year when an earthquake had toppled the spire from the cathedral. While others bemoaned the damage, thirty-five feet of it scattered on the ground, Sam had rounded up his friends and they had worked hard for a day to clear the rubble. He had a good heart, young Sam.

Henrietta was savouring these thoughts when she heard a little voice calling, "Grandmama, Grandmama!" It was always a shock to hear herself addressed in this way, but she had just celebrated her fiftieth birthday and knew she must resign herself to the passing of the years.

Little Charles Joseph hurtled into the room, followed by his mother. Victoria held in her arms her new daughter, born just three months ago. Eager as she was to admire little Emily Catherine, whom she had seen only once, Henrietta knew that her first task was to welcome her three-year-old grandson. Extricating herself from his smothering embrace, she asked him,

"Have you anything to show me, Charles? Something new, perhaps?"

"Yes, I have a new suit to wear for Uncle George and Aunt Catherine's wedding, but Mama has that in the suitcase. Oh, there's our new baby – is *she* a surprise?"

"She is indeed. May I have a look at her?"

Henrietta turned to the tiny Emily and saw a replica of Victoria as she was when they stepped off the Cressida at Lyttelton twenty-two years ago. At any other time this would have set her reminiscing, but there was too much excitement in the air for this. She took her grand-daughter, who was not yet shy, to an armchair where she might examine her at leisure. Charles had turned his attention to his uncle and was now perched on Sam's shoulders, which gave him a commanding view of the room. Victoria managed to squeeze a greeting to Sam between exclamations of, "Look at me, Mama!" and "I'm taller than you, Grandmama!"

Joseph's entrance created just the diversion needed. Charles scrambled down from Sam, who immediately took second place to Grandpa, and wrapped his arms around Joseph's legs. Victoria, now able to remove her light coat and converse without too many distractions, settled on the sofa with her younger brother to hear about George's state of mind on the eve of his marriage.

"I'm so glad he finally made up his mind to marry Catherine, Sam. She has been so patient. It must have broken her heart to see us married four years ago. And Richard says his mother has had the greatest difficulty in persuading her to attend any social functions in that time."

"I don't think George needed to make up his mind. It was just that he wanted to be able to buy his own home. Now that he has done that …"

"But Catherine said only yesterday that that was a headache they had to face as soon as they returned from their wedding tour."

Sam lowered his voice to a hoarse whisper. "Well, I knew you could keep a secret. George told me just last night that he has found a very suitable house within walking distance of the shop. There's a steep hill between them, but he says at least it is downhill in the mornings, which should help if he is running late! He wants it to be a surprise for Catherine. She thinks they will have to live in a hotel when they return."

"What a wonderful idea, so typical of George! No doubt he has Mrs Barrett making curtains for his house, when she is not busy serving his customers during his absence. And Catherine had no real thoughts on what sort of a home she wanted, as long as George shared it with her, so she will not care if she had no choice in it."

"How's Dick managing on the farm when we are supposed to be in a depression?"

"You know, Sam, you and Alex are the only men I know who insist on calling him 'Dick'."

"Well, it's much more down-to-earth, sounds more like a farmer's name. Anyway, don't evade the question! Doesn't he feel guilty, living so well when so many others have to give up land for next to nothing?"

"It's the small farmer who had the real problem. Richard and Alex have enough experience and knowledge to stay away from the more doubtful ventures, as well as still being able to draw on the advice of the men who helped them when their father died. Richard says another three or four years will see the country back on its feet, and we have lost so much of our surplus labour to Australia in the last few years that things can only improve. What about you, Sam? Where do you go from here, now that you have left school?"

"I'm going to try the student life to get some qualifications for when I make up my mind what to do. I can't stand the thought of being cooped up in the shop with dusty bolts of material and featherbrained women who want advice on what would best cover their bulging figures."

Wincing at his turn of phrase, Victoria asked, "Has Father asked you to work for him permanently? Mother says you have been helping there since school finished."

"Yes, I've been in there, but I don't think I've been very helpful. Father sends me out on all the errands, to collect and post the mail, deliver orders, that sort of thing. No, he hasn't mentioned the shop when we have talked of my future."

"Well, that is not luck, Sam, that is Father. He has never pushed any of us, the way so many other parents organise their children's careers. I have appreciated this only since being married and living away from home."

"I have no wish to marry, but I do want to travel. However, I'll complete my degree and then spend a couple of years working at something to save enough money for the boat trip to England or America. It's vague at present, but the *Wanderlust* is definitely there."

Emily had been gradually making her presence felt and now, thoroughly frustrated, she began to scream, in spite of all Henrietta's efforts to soothe her. Victoria reclaimed the baby, and the crying stopped immediately.

"There's one thing you cannot provide for her, Mother! Excuse me, I'll feed her in my old room. Do you want to come, Charles?" Charles, however, was receiving far more attention from his grandparents than he could hope for from his mother.

Henrietta had forgotten the tension she had felt before Victoria arrived. She had even forgotten, albeit temporarily, about the wedding, until George came into the sitting room. Obviously preoccupied, he managed to greet his nephew before announcing that he was going to pay Catherine a visit to finalise arrangements for tomorrow.

"Would you mind coming with me, Sam? You might think of something that has slipped my mind."

"Like the ring. Have you picked it up from Radford's yet?"

"There, you see, I'm as flighty as my worst customer today. We'll collect it on the way. Remind me!"

The wedding was to take place at 11.00, and the Davis household was a hive of activity at 6.30. Richard had not accompanied Victoria to town as he had the job of arranging the reception, which would be held at the homestead, as well as the honour of giving his sister away in marriage to George. In an attempt to take most of the burden from his mother's shoulders, he had a busy morning ahead of him. Whilst Mrs Davis was accustomed to large gatherings at her home, the mixed emotions she felt at seeing her youngest child, her only daughter, being married made her less efficient than usual. Instead she fussed over Catherine and her two bridesmaids until Richard suggested she make everyone a cup of tea just before they changed to leave for the church.

At the Hamiltons' home Henrietta was in much the same state. Joseph had persuaded her to stay in bed until half past seven, but only with the bribes of a cup of tea and a copy of "The Press". Once Victoria and the children were on the scene, however, there was no restraining her and Joseph hoped that they would keep her occupied enough to leave poor George in peace. It was best to keep mothers busy on wedding days, as he knew from his own day twenty-eight years ago, although in his case it had been his aunt. He didn't look back much, so would never have remembered how many years it was, had he not been reminded recently of their anniversary. Victoria had sent him a note to tell him about a dresser her mother had seen in town and would dearly love, pointing out that, quite by chance, it had appeared in the store just in time for their twenty-eighth anniversary next Thursday. Joseph was trapped by his own soft-heartedness. He had no regrets because Henrietta was a good woman and Victoria had turned out a nice lass.

George and Sam, accompanied by little Charles, who was to be a page boy for his uncle and aunt, left home at 10.00. This would make them early, but George wanted to allow time for any emergency en route. Victoria fed Emily and duly delivered her to Henrietta's eager neighbour, Mrs Fisher, promising to be back before her next feed at about 2.00.

"Don't worry about her, dear. As you well know, I've raised quite a brood of them and now they are bringing me their little ones. You go off and see your brother safely brought to the altar."

Victoria joined her parents in the carriage hired for the occasion. George, Sam and Alex were already sitting in the front pew, waiting none too patiently for the church clock to chime eleven. As it did so Catherine and Richard arrived in a brougham, the horses festooned with white ribbons and bows, the carriage with a fringe of white satin around the hood. They made an impressive sight as they swirled in through the gates and up the curved drive to the steps of the little country church.

Those not invited to attend the ceremony crowded about the door to see the bride, all observing the radiance shining through her nervous shyness. Charles was seated in the next carriage with the two bridesmaids, friends of Catherine, and her cousin's little daughter Annabelle, who was her flower girl. At seven Annabelle felt responsible for Charles. She offered him her posy if it would make him behave nicely in the church, but please, wouldn't he hold her hand, just until they reached the front? That was what Aunt Catherine had said they were to do. Charles was tiring of this business of being all dressed up and being told he looked "sweet" and "a darling". He had decided he would walk *behind* Annabelle, so that he could go as slowly as he liked and find his mother on the way.

The procession entered the church, turned right and made its way down the nave. At the turn Charles caught up with the others, managing to tread on the hem of Annabelle's muslin dress. Above the organ music no tearing sound was heard, and the little girl's wail might have been attributed to the organist's faulty fingering, but the seamstress couldn't possibly have miscalculated a hem by three or four inches. Annabelle's pink satin sash hid the gaping hole at the waist. Wearing an expression of martyrdom that would have done credit to Joan of Arc, she proceeded down the aisle, going past her distraught mother, who had witnessed the mishap, and rejoining the party as it reached the altar steps.

Turning to greet his bride George realised for the first time what a pretty girl she was. Looks did not matter much to him, but today he felt he could count the curls on her head, smell the roses outside the church and hear the finches in the trees. It was as if all his senses were primed to a peak.

Victoria was proud of Richard and was surprised to see that Charles looked better dressed than Annabelle. Something must have happened on the way to the church for the little girl's dress to be sagging like that. It was a miracle that Charles had not yet shed his jacket or bow tie – but why on earth was he carrying Annabelle's flowers? At least *he* could not be responsible for the dress, or she would hardly have given him the flowers. Richard, having given the bride away, rejoined his wife, who discovered with a shock that she had not yet heard a word of the service. Charles was now obscured from her view and she resolved to focus her attention on Catherine and George.

At the reception, held in an enormous marquee on the lawn of the Davis home, the men talked about the state of the country and the forthcoming election, now only two weeks away. The ladies extolled the virtues of their children or grandchildren. The children, still in their Sunday clothes, ran off their bottled-up energy.

"John Ballance is the key to our future. If we want to be rid of this depression he's the man for the job."

"That's only because Atkinson has not been able to reach the public as freely. A man cannot help being ill, can he?"

"Well, is he the man we need, if he is ill? We need a man with strength, both physical and moral, at the helm, or we'll never be out of the doldrums."

"What about the Liberals' land policy? Do you want to see your land divided into smaller holdings?"

"Well, let's be realistic. Is it fair for about five hundred people to hold half the land in private ownership? Now that we can send refrigerated cargo to England, small farms would be an economic proposition."

Richard had joined the discussion, and these were his words. Although one of the landowners, he was a Liberal at heart. He could see the plight of many of his contemporaries – school friends in some cases – would be much improved if he and others in his position were to subdivide their land.

At this moment Victoria caught his eye and motioned him towards her.

"Richard, I really must return to town. Emily will be due for her feed soon, but you are still needed here, I can see. Mrs Fitzgerald has kindly offered to take me. Shall I leave Charles here to come back to Mother and Father's with you, or would it be best if I took him?"

"Leave him, he's having such fun. In any case I am not too sure where he is at the moment."

"I do hope Annabelle is not taking her revenge by ducking him in the horse trough!" Victoria said.

Richard agreed, saying, "She would be almost within her rights, after his clumsiness!"

A weary Richard arrived at the shop with his soundly sleeping son just in time for dinner that evening. Charles was put to bed, fully clothed, with buttons and studs loosened. It was eight o'clock next morning before he stirred. With his father he watched his Uncle George and Aunt Catherine depart on their wedding tour. His father saw to the dismantling of the marquee, but tiredness overcame Charles, so he crept into the waiting gig and curled up on the floor. Richard found him there after searching the house and barn. There were limits to a chap's endurance at the age of three, he thought, smiling tenderly as he covered his son with a rug for the journey to town.

CHAPTER 9

End of an Era

It was many years since Henrietta had been to Lyttelton, and each time she accompanied Joseph she thought inevitably of that trudge over the Bridle Path, now twenty-nine years ago. How ironic that it was Samuel they were bidding farewell today, the only member of the family not present on that unforgettable day. Or was it really so strange?

Sam had applied himself far more steadily to his studies than his parents had thought possible, and had been rewarded with a Bachelor of Arts degree at the graduation ceremony three years ago, in 1894, to the great delight of his whole family. He had helped on Richard and Victoria's farm, making and carting hay, harvesting crops and assisting with the milking, over the summer and autumn but after graduation, as the winter came on, he turned to industry and had spent the next three and a half years in a leather factory, earning good wages and gaining skills which he hoped would prove useful. In the direst of circumstances, he would at least be able to make himself a coat and a pair of boots.

Joseph had been puzzled to learn of Sam's desire to leave the land he had chosen for his family. He felt hurt that his son should reject it when he found it so much better to live in than England, where Sam was now going. Sam could not understand why his father should be so against his desire to see the world. It was natural for an educated man to feel confined in a country, no matter how beautiful or free, which lay thousands of miles from its nearest neighbour. Only by comparing it with other places could he truly assess what New Zealand meant to him.

With his business thriving after several rather lean years, George had written to say he was unable to leave Dunedin at this time, but that Catherine and little Sarah would come by train to see Sam before his departure. Sam read between the lines that this first meeting with his niece was perhaps of more importance to George than a handshake between the brothers. With the less said the better concerning the business, there had always been news of Sarah's latest achievements to fill the pages.

Of all the family Victoria understood best how Sam felt and why he must leave the security his parents had provided for him. As well as inheriting the very pioneering instinct which had brought their father to New Zealand, Sam had to prove that he could stand alone, without the pillars of his parents to support him. Only Victoria knew that his destination was not England but the Far North of Canada, if he heard the same tales of gold discoveries in England as here. It was as well that their parents had no inkling of this as the horses rounded the final bend before Lyttelton.

Henrietta had not felt such a wrench when George or Victoria had married and left home because they would be within reach in any crisis. There was something physically painful in this parting. She felt heavy and tired as she climbed down from the buggy. Sam had always had a special place in his mother's affections and he knew that she had championed his cause with Joseph because of this, not through any desire to see him leave home.

The partings were brief. Sam restrained his excitement, Henrietta her tears. Joseph had little to say, except a word or two about money being available if an emergency arose, and it was left to Victoria to fill the silences. Sam had preferred that they part before the boat sailed, and so it was from a vantage point on the Port Hills Road that they watched the vessel leave her berth and sail out towards the Godley Heads.

Knowing it would be months before they would hear any news of Sam, Henrietta was grateful when Catherine wrote, only a few days after his departure, that Sarah was to have a little brother or sister in June of next year. She had delayed passing on this news so that Henrietta could look forward to an event closer than Sam's return. This was just the diversion Henrietta needed and in the remaining six months she steadily knitted, sewed and crocheted for the new baby. Neither woman ever doubted that this would be a boy, and little Edward George did not disappoint them.

Two weeks before the baby was due Henrietta packed her bags and Joseph took her to the station in the morning to catch the express train to Dunedin. As they admired the cloistered walk along the platform Henrietta voiced again her reluctance to leave Joseph, but he was adamant, saying, "Of course I shall be all right. You have so many people keeping an eye on me that I shan't be able to move without tripping over someone."

"Well, you keep warm, Joseph. You know how I have always to remind you to put a coat on when you step out to collect the mail or go across to see Mr. Dick. I do wish there was some way to persuade you to come with me."

"Now, Henrietta, it is far too late for that, and you know that as well as I. George needs you as a housekeeper and a nanny at present and you are to stay there until Catherine is able to run the house as usual. And that will be an end to it."

As she sat for hours on the steadily plodding train, unable to knit or sew because of the soot belching from the engine, Henrietta's mind was free to wander. As always in these rare times of idleness it turned first to her family. Where was Sam now? It would be early summer in England – a pretty time, May – but was he still there? He was far too restless for England to hold him long. He was probably tramping about Europe delving into living history. But was there enough excitement in that? She had sensed in Sam a desperate need to throw off the shackles of everything he knew and plunge into something wild, even dangerous: the old recklessness had never entirely disappeared. Just what he could find to satisfy this urge his mother could not imagine, but she knew he would not return till he had burnt it out of his soul.

Henrietta sat nibbling without enjoying her sandwiches. She had made them herself because she wanted to avoid the human scramble at the cafeteria at Timaru. Joseph's face appeared in her mind. He was ageing, as she was herself – after all, they were sixty-three and fifty-eight now – but Henrietta felt she was not showing her age as Joseph was. Always tall, he now stooped a little, and was gaunt rather than slim. Short bouts of illness had given him a bad start to this winter, and she was anxious at the thought of leaving him for up to a month. If the train had stopped at that precise moment, a little stout woman might well have been seen scurrying to the booking office to buy a ticket for Christchurch, but there was no such divine intervention, so Henrietta forced her thoughts towards George's home in Dunedin.

George himself might be unable to meet her, in which case she would hire a cab. Catherine and Sarah, the latter greatly excited at the thought of a real baby in the house, would surely be at home and the welcome would be warm. Henrietta often rejoiced at the affection between her daughter-in-law and herself. Not every mother-in-law was called upon at times such as these. With Catherine's mother bedridden for the past three years, she turned willingly to Henrietta for support. It was many years since Catherine had made her appearance in the Hamilton fold, at first as the fourth person in the group led by Richard and Victoria. Lacking the assurance Victoria had always shown, she had been happy to walk in the shadows as long as George was in the party.

There was no need to worry about Victoria who had always known her own mind and her early marriage had been no ignorant blunder. At thirty she had a son of eleven and a daughter of eight, a fine figure and a fond husband. Henrietta could see her happiness, there was never any need to ask banal questions.

Back, full circle, to Sam. This time her mind spun faster – Joseph, George, Catherine, Victoria, Richard, the grandchildren. Too much leisure – not used to this – think of something more general – Joseph, unwell. There now, it's raining – Oamaru, stop – buy a newspaper? Too cold, warm in here – doze for a time, Joseph …

Henrietta awoke to the sensation of rocking. The young man beside her, seeing her eyes open, apologised: "Do excuse me, Madam, but I see that your seat is reserved until Dunedin. We are pulling into the station now. May I help you with your bags?" As the fog cleared in her mind Henrietta realised her head must have fallen on the man's shoulder. Years ago she would have blushed at the discovery but now she merely smiled and hoped she had not caused him too much discomfort.

As his mother had anticipated, George was unable to meet the train, but he had arranged transport for her and before long she was warming herself in front of the fire at his home. Sarah was delighted to see her grandmother, a rare pleasure, given the 250 miles separating their homes. She showed Henrietta to her room upstairs, Catherine being only too willing to forgo the honour.

For four days Henrietta busied herself in the house, keeping little Sarah occupied, a task in itself, for she was an intelligent and active child with a vivid imagination. Catherine rested in the afternoons. Then came George's knock on her door, well after midnight. There was no fuss. Sarah remained asleep and by morning her grandmother announced to her that baby Edward had arrived.

Within two weeks of the birth Henrietta was sitting again in the train. Catherine could sense that this had not been a good time to take her mother-in-law away from Christchurch, although Henrietta had hardly mentioned her ever-increasing concern for Joseph. She had helped in every possible way, and Catherine would miss her greatly, but she had persuaded Henrietta to leave them and return home.

The trip seemed endless. She had written to Joseph so that he would be there to meet her when the train arrived in mid-afternoon. He would not hear of her taking a cab to save him the trouble. It was with a sinking heart, therefore, that she saw Victoria coming towards her as she crossed the platform, greatly relieved to be home.

"Mother, how lovely to have you home! Father wanted to come, but I persuaded him not to on such a cold afternoon."

"How is he? Have you been with him long? I have been so worried about him. Is it his chest?"

"Yes, Mother, and the doctor is not happy with his progress. I know you will want me to be truthful with you. It was Dr Macfarlane who asked me to come on Monday."

"Oh dear, I knew I shouldn't have left him at this time, but he would not consider going with me, and Catherine did need help."

"How is the new babe, Mother? Who is he like?"

"Like his father, and like his grandfather too. Little Sarah is thrilled with him, and has been allowed to hold him, as long as she sits still in an armchair. She loves to fetch and carry for her mother, which saved my old legs on the stairs. I would stand at the bottom and Catherine at the top, and Sarah would do the running between us. She is a real little mother."

On her arrival home Henrietta found an unopened letter from Sam propped against the vase of flowers on the hall table. Her joy at receiving this first news of her younger son was clouded by the thought that Joseph was too ill to have it read to him. She felt close to panic as she turned the knob of the bedroom door.

Dr Macfarlane stepped forward to greet her.

"Mrs. Hamilton, I trust you travelled comfortably?" But Henrietta barely heard him and answered mechanically, her eyes unable to leave Joseph, so old and tired looking. His face had creased into a wan smile at the sight of her, but he was too weak to do any more than take her hand. Dr Macfarlane withdrew, leaving them together.

Sitting on the bed, holding and stroking Joseph's hand, Henrietta did her best to be cheerful, bringing Joseph up to date with the news of the family in Dunedin. He seemed interested at first, but within a few minutes his hand loosened in her grasp and his eyes gradually closed. Tip-toeing from the room Henrietta joined Victoria and the doctor in the sitting room, where Victoria had prepared some tea.

"He has aged over five years in the last month, Doctor."

"He is a stubborn man, Mrs. Hamilton. If he had come to me a couple of weeks earlier I might have been able to help him more. As it is, he has now contracted pneumonia and I may have to transfer him to hospital if he gets worse. It's the business of exposing him to the cold that prevents me moving him now. We've another two months of winter at least. I don't know what's for the best, but you must not hesitate to call me if he worsens – the telephone is a wonderful invention, and it has already saved many lives. Well, I'll be going, now that you are here. Your daughter has the necessary draughts for him and will explain them as well as I could. She would have made a darned fine nurse, had she not been in such a hurry to marry that husband of hers! Good day to you both."

Pneumonia was worrying, and Joseph was sixty-four years of age, in midwinter, and a cold, bleak winter too. With a sense of despair Henrietta looked down at her hands, to find she was still holding Sam's letter. Putting on her spectacles she studied the envelope. The letter had been posted early in March, so he must have caught a sailing immediately for it to arrive so soon. So soon? He had been away six months already. Perhaps now they would learn what he planned for the next year or so.

Dear Mother and Father,

It is now six weeks since I left you all and I have been enjoying the leisure of the voyage after the years of preparation for it. The Achilles is a comfortable ship, but I am glad to have saved enough extra pounds for a berth on one of the upper decks, as you advised. I have met several young men whose cabins are well below mine and they tell me the comfort diminishes steadily as one descends the stairways. I try to invite them to spend time with me, as they are beginning to show the effects of interrupted sleep and upset stomachs. They will be glad to reach the port of London.

Let me tell you my plans once I reach England. I think you, Mother, suspected that I do not really intend to stay there. I want to go to the Yukon Territory in the north of Canada. If I find in England that the stories of gold being discovered up there have any truth to them, then I shall sail as soon as possible for Canada. When the spring thaw takes place that will be the busiest part of the world."

Henrietta took off her spectacles and sat gazing at nothing for several minutes, as the import of Sam's words penetrated her mind. The Frozen North, wild bears, and desperate, drunken, ruined men as companions. The Arctic cold. Oh Sam, she thought, thank Heaven it is too late for me to stop you! By now you will have been there a month or more. At least it will be summer now.

"By the time you read this letter I shall be there, along with thousands of others, equally hopeful of riches. I shall not be going alone – at least, not on the overland section. I am told groups are formed at the little port of Skagway, in Alaska. The route from there crosses a narrow pass and reaches the headwaters of the Yukon River, where the men build rafts or boats to navigate the river right to the goldfields. If I find all this information to be correct, that is the route I shall take, for I see no point in trying to take horses thousands of miles overland when the greater part of the journey can be done by boat.

It will not be possible for me to send you regular letters, so please do not be alarmed if there is no news from me for a year or two. If you wish, you may address mail to me at Dawson City, Yukon Territory, Canada, but I may never receive it. I cannot imagine men undergoing the rigours of this trek just to carry mail to glassy-eyed prospectors.

My love to you all. You will not see me until I can return as a wealthy man.

Your loving son,

Samuel

She shuddered at the implication of words like "rigours" and "glassy-eyed prospectors". It was almost forty years since men had thrown up everything they owned or loved and rushed to the goldfields of Otago, but Henrietta could remember the stories they had heard when they first arrived in Christchurch. So many of them had returned broken men, and a few had not returned at all. And this in a land they knew, not a country covered in ice and snow for most of the year. She knew he was not as confident as he was trying to sound. She also knew that Joseph was in no condition to know of this letter, unless Victoria had already told him about it..

Looking up from her reverie, Henrietta was surprised to see Victoria sitting in the armchair opposite her.

"Mother," she said gently, "it is time for Father's draught. Would you like me to take it to him, or would you prefer to go yourself?"

"My dear, how long have you been there? I was thousands of miles away."

"I came in as you put your spectacles on and picked up the letter from your lap. Did it not make pleasant reading?"

"I shall leave you to read it while I take Joseph his medicine. Must I waken him for it?"

"Dr Macfarlane said it was important to keep strictly to the four-hourly dosages for the next three days. Yes, we must waken him, but he will be sleeping lightly."

Joseph was asleep, so soundly and peacefully that Henrietta fearfully touched his forehead. The warmth of his skin reassured her and she gently shook him awake. He was surprised to see her, unaware that it was her presence in the house which had given him a more restful sleep.

"Good to have you home, my dear."

She wanted to scold him for not calling her home sooner, but it would serve no purpose. Instead she replied, "And I am very glad to be here. The young ones are managing well. They knew I was fretting to be with you. Catherine practically banished me from their house in her efforts to send me home!"

"A fine girl. George is lucky. How is he?"

"He says business has never been better than in these last three years since the slump. There's a real dearth of drapers in Dunedin, and by keeping up the quality of his fabrics and the workmanship of his seamstresses he has attracted much of the wealthier clientele."

Henrietta chattered on about their family until Joseph dropped off to sleep again. The sedative she had given him acted quickly on his tired body. She returned to the sitting room where Victoria was writing a letter.

"Oh Mother, I am writing a note to Richard. Would you mind if I were to go home tomorrow? It's difficult for him to manage collecting the children from school and keeping an eye on his mother too. She should not be left for long at a time, and Alex has done more than his share to help in these last few days."

"Of course, my dear, you must go home to your family. The children will be missing you, although an absence of a few days does them no harm. They will appreciate your apple pies and roast beef all the more after their father's efforts. If it suits you better why don't you telephone him now and he could come for you tonight?"

"Well, I shall telephone, but tomorrow would be better. Father is more restless at night, and you are tired from your journey. Richard will make a business trip of it if he comes in the daytime. I'll go and make the call now."

Joseph made a steady improvement, and Henrietta was encouraged to find him eager to talk several days later. Dr Macfarlane was cautious in his choice of words when she asked if Joseph was out of danger, but today she felt a great relief. Richard and Victoria were bringing the children to see him this afternoon. Thank goodness he was so much brighter.

"Henrietta, come and sit by the bed. I want to discuss my will with you."

"Oh Joseph, why should you want to do that now? You are so much improved, you will be able to go and see Mr. Harrison yourself in a couple of weeks."

"Nevertheless, there are things on my mind which I want to tell you. The first is about Sam. I was deeply offended when he told me he was leaving New Zealand, and I hit back at him by cutting down his legacy. Now I realise that I was being bigoted and foolish. I want you to know that I intend to reinstate Sam. Then there is our new grandson. I have set aside a sum for each of our grandchildren, and we must add baby Edward to the list. If there should be others after I am gone …"

"Joseph, don't you talk like that! It's all very well to plan for the future, but I won't listen to that gloomy talk."

"Yes, you'll listen, my dear wife. I need only a good attack of coughing and I'll be gone in a minute. Now, where was I? Ah yes, if there are more grandchildren please make sure they each receive the sum I have arranged for these four. It is a thousand pounds for the boys and five hundred pounds for the girls. You may add what you wish, for most of my estate will be yours. When is Dr Macfarlane to call on me today?"

"Quite soon. Do stay awake if you can, you have tired yourself with all this talk. I'll go and brew some tea. It will soothe your throat and keep you awake until the doctor arrives."

As the water boiled she heard him start to cough. "A good attack of coughing", she recalled. Must take the tea to him. There's the doorbell, thank Heaven. "Come in, Doctor". Now there are two of us to help him, she thought with relief.

However, it was Dr Macfarlane and Mrs Hamilton who sat down to the tea, and the doctor, in pouring it, had added a sedative to Henrietta's. He made a call to summon Victoria, this time to help her mother. They were unable to save Joseph, who had sensed he was slipping away when he had insisted on talking about his will. In a daze Henrietta tried to come to grips with everything, but it was all too difficult. A rest would help, and Victoria would be here soon. Another farewell in the family , this time to the love of her life, the man who had brought her across the world to start a new life for their family. This parting was much harder than kissing Sam and wishing him well at the Lyttelton dock last year.

PART II

JOSEPH AND SAMUEL

1898 – 1926

ADVENTURERS

CHAPTER 1

The Klondike!

It was a long voyage from England, but Sam met some helpful people on the way, gleaning useful information mixed with less credible rumour about his destination. Jim Henderson and his friend Frank Browning had the same goal, as did many others on board the ship, and the three men pooled their ideas.

They discussed the different routes to the goldfields, sharing the knowledge they had each gained, both in England and on the ship. The easiest route was the longest, through St Michael's and then by steamer down the Yukon River, but this was a roundabout and expensive route. By common consent it was rejected. Frank had heard of a route known as the Dalton Trail, which joined the river further north than most of the overland routes, but none of the men could see any advantage in trekking overland when they could be sailing downstream. There was also the long route in from Edmonton, but this included far from navigable water, and casualties were said to be high.

No, it seemed their best approach was to cross Canada first by train, from east to west,giving them a chance to make acquaintance with this huge country destined to become either their friend or foe, and then take a steamer up the rugged coast of British Columbia to Skagway in Alaska. At that point they could decide on the merits of the two passes between the coast and Lake Bennett, launching point for the Yukon River Trail.

Crossing Canada they took pleasure in the signs of spring, ever more advanced as they travelled westwards. Purple crocuses dotted the last snow in the East, daffodils and prairie flowers laid a carpet further west, and all the conifers were sprouting their tufts of tiny bright green needles in the Rockies. There was some warmth in the sun in Vancouver, but the sea voyage north taught them the winter was not yet over in those parts .It was late May when they reached Skagway.

Now they must be on their mettle. They must gamble on taking enough supplies to cover emergencies, but not enough to give them unnecessary weight. They must be prepared to take risks, but not be foolhardy. They had chosen the Chilkoot route, not the easiest, but one they all felt they could conquer. First, they must get to Dyea, then eighteen miles to the summit of the Chilkoot Pass.

Setting off in high spirits and under a feeble sun, Sam, Frank and Jim made good time on the first leg. Before long they reached Dyea, where they bought food rather than raid their precious rations. They camped that night at Canyon City, along with many others. The night was bitter, a warning that summer was still far off in this land. They rose early and were on the trail before their campmates had stirred. Passing Sheep Camp mid-afternoon, they decided that they could cover more than the accepted distance in a day, and followed the course of the Taiya River, as directed. Now the going became steeper and they had to call a halt at the foot of the Chilkoot Pass. Tomorrow they would make their assault on it.

Sam's sleep that night was filled with vivid dreams in which all that he had heard about the Yukon whirled in an ever faster spinning kaleidoscope of patterns in front of him, never quite forming a picture before shattering into fragments, which began to form a new shape, building into something which almost made sense and then, in a flash, it was gone again. He saw men trudging in single file up the steps to the summit, but then came an image of lengths of wood and men arguing about building a boat, which fell apart, with the horses tumbling from it and landing in the snow. Frank and Jim were there in the dream, one cheerful, the other with hollow eyes and a mask of death. Sam awoke with relief, shivering. It was daylight, but then most of the night had been light. Better to leave the others sleeping as long as they could. It would be a long day.

Someone else was awake, stirring up a fire with a stick. The temptation was too great – Sam shuffled past sleeping men to join him. John Fleming had left Skagway the day before Sam and his friends, but had kept to the recognised stops, as he knew no-one and had only a hazy idea of where he was going. An Englishman, he had been on the same ship which had brought Frank, Jim and Sam to Canada. He had seen them together, but, being reserved by nature, had not liked to push his way into their group. Sam was impressed by his honest looks and air of decency. He would ask the others if John might join them in their venture.

After treating themselves to a hearty breakfast in preparation for a testing day, the four men set out to conquer the 3,739 foot pass. From the bottom of the steep slope there were steps cut into the packed ice, but the climb was unending and the loads heavy. The sled which they had congratulated themselves on buying proved unworkable on this gradient. Not only did they have to unload their stores from it and carry these in relays, but they also had to carry the sled. However, there was no alternative. They knew that if they arrived at the police depot on the summit with less than 1150 lbs of food per man, the Mounties would send them back to make up the provisions. And all this in addition to the weight of tents, cooking utensils, prospectors' equipment and carpenters' tools. It looked an impossible task. Yet thousands of hopeful prospectors like Sam and Jim, Frank and John had succeeded in reaching the Klondike by this route – they told each other they must not lose heart.

A watery sun gave an illusion of warmth. They could think of nothing but the next few steps. It would be easy to give up, but to go back now would be as difficult as to push onwards, and the humiliation would cut a man down faster than any frostbite or blizzard. Only three weeks ago, they learned, an avalanche had wiped out this part of the route, taking with it sixty men's lives. Every few paces there lay evidence of shattered dreams – a broken wheel, a rotting saddlebag, even the carcass of a horse, preserved in the snow. As morbid thoughts assailed him, Sam was glad of the company of the ever-cheerful Frank, and Jim gave encouragement in his quiet way, although he looked unwell and his breath came in gasps. John brought up the rear, as yet unsure of his place in the group.

It was the longest, most arduous day for any of them. They trekked on upwards long after others had stopped to make camp and cook a much-needed supper, but their reward came in reaching the summit, where the police detachment gave them assistance. Some erected the tent, while others cooked their meal for them as the four men thawed out in front of a fire. The Mounties admired these determined men, recognising the kind of courage they needed in their work every day.

The fire and the food revived them, but the policemen knew it would be only temporary. They had no sooner led the four men to their tent than they collapsed into bed. Dreamless, snoring sleep overtook them instantly.

Nothing in future would be as gruelling as the ascent to the Chilkoot Pass, around which there formed an aura of unreality. Had they really gone through that day of Hell, or was it all a part of Sam's dream? Waking late the next morning to see a long line of dark dots forming far below them on the steep incline, they knew it was no dream. The aching backs, the jolting knees, the tight calf muscles, the frozen hands that would not grasp – it all came back as they stretched their stiff bodies. But there was no time for sitting about. From here it was downhill, and in most places they would be able to pull the sled with little trouble, or so the Mounties told them. In fact, they would have to hold it back.

On the fourth day after leaving the summit, the men sighted Lake Bennett, with its town clustered in disarray on the shore. It was a scene of feverish activity. Shoulder to shoulder, in silence, men were constructing rafts and scows of every design, using whatever materials they could buy or scavenge. Everywhere there was a sense of urgency about the operations, as if any delay meant life itself slipping away. Some flung their contraptions together in haste, while others, still working rapidly, gave more thought to the six-hundred-mile waterway ahead of them, preferring to put in a life-saving hour now. As the party of newcomers drew closer one gallant adventurer bade his fellows a rousing farewell, leapt aboard his makeshift raft, loaded with his copious provisions, and was pushed on his way by his neighbouring builders. He had covered no more than twenty yards when the raft capsized, throwing him into the icy water. Despite the air of comedy about the scene, no-one descended to scornful laughter as he was hauled from the water to begin all over again.

Learning from this tragicomic scene, Sam and his friends spent three precious days on the building of their scow, felling the timber themselves for the base – there was just enough left around the lake now. They purchased the timber they needed, at highly inflated prices, from those fortunate enough to have it. It took time to see that the ballast was right, and to construct a cabin – was it really necessary? Time was important, since much of the Klondike area must already have been staked, but all of the men valued their lives too greatly to go plunging recklessly down an unknown river without proper preparation and protection.

Only when they had tested the boat and declared her fit and ready, did the four set off down the lake to the birthplace of the Yukon River. On the lake, with no current to disturb her, she sailed perfectly, but the true test would come on the river. They had rigged a small sail to help them along, but each man also held a long, sturdy paddle for rowing, steering, and fending off logs or other debris. Their aim was to cover thirty miles each day, but they could only guess at a figure. At that rate it would take them almost three weeks to reach Dawson City and the goldfield. They simply could not spare any longer – they would *have* to achieve this pace.

The infant river was placid as it flowed out of Lake Bennett, and the pace it set was unhurried. They were surrounded by majestic spruce along the banks providing playhouses for lively chipmunks and wide-eyed, serious squirrels watching the strange craft pass by. The bells of the fireweed were just breaking out their first pink blooms beneath the canopy of blue-green trees. Accustomed to pine, with its bottle-green needles, Sam was intrigued by the smoky haze that seemed to linger over the spruce forests. As the men drank in the peacefulness of the scene, a swooping hawk set a dozen gophers piping their warnings before scampering to the safety of their burrows. Fascinating little creatures, they were back out, standing upright again, and sounding the all-clear, the moment the hawk was gone.

In contrast to the movement of the animals, the smooth flow of the water mesmerised and relaxed the four men. The future promised well: they were safe, they had food, it was sunny, and the land about them was of great grandeur. Suddenly a shout from Jim broke the spell.

"Look!"

"Where?"

"Over there, where that creek comes down."

It was the remains of a raft, caught up in a tangle of logs and rocks where the current of the stream met that of the wide river, but the wood was rotting and the canvas torn. It was no use looking for that prospector, he would never reach any goldfield.

Sobered in their sorrow at the sight, the men paid more attention to their own craft. They would be ready when they approached Miles Canyon – that surging, racing gorge would not claim them. If it broke their backs they would manhandle their scow along the bank of the five-mile section of river that comprised the Canyon, the Squaw Rapids and the White Horse Rapids. Too many men had taken the chance and lost.

They beached the boat where the current grew more rapid, and where they could see ahead the basalt cliffs of the Canyon. Carrying her was heavy work and they stopped frequently to rest, but also to wonder at the power of the mighty river, here compressed to only a third of its width. What treachery lay beneath those foaming, swirling masses of water? Rocks, currents, whirlpools, all had caused the destruction of countless craft now lying strewn along the banks where the river spilled out of the chasm. It had been a wise decision to portage for a short time.

What a river! Sam thought of the rivers he had grown up to know and love in Canterbury. The Avon was a picturesque little stream fringed with young weeping willows, adding character to his hometown with its neatly trimmed lawns and dignified buildings along the banks. But nowhere was it more than two or three feet deep. The Waimakariri was another fine river, where he and his father had fished often. With a vast stony riverbed, it never ran bank to bank, even when it raged in flood. Yet in places it had this same blue icy colour to it. He loved those rivers at home and for a moment he longed to be there, but this river beneath him had an exhilarating thrust of power. If they never found any gold the trudge up to that summit would be worth it just for the wonder of this river voyage.

Jim was looking better after a few days on the river. The breeze had whipped some colour into his cheeks, and the sun had cheered him. His eyes still held a hollow look but the others decided not to quiz him, to let him be. He had chosen to come. Far be it from any of them to tell him he should have stayed at home.

Through the first half of June they made good progress, the long sunny days warming and tanning them. They even swam in the river to wash themselves briefly. It seemed they led a charmed existence, in which nothing could go wrong. Suddenly there was an electrical storm, with pelting rain. They took turns, in shifts of two, standing in the driving rain, trying to see into the murky grey afternoon. They had just changed teams, and Sam and Frank were trying to make themselves a warm drink in the cabin, when John let out a shout: "Oh no!" There was a sharp crack and the boat rose from the water, then dived like a pelican, hit a submerged rock, and floated to the surface, upside down. Men, paddles, provisions, equipment were scattered across the river. The scow kept floating on for fifty feet before graunching aground in the shallows. Calling to each other, the men were relieved that no-one had drowned. That was something, as the irrepressible Frank was quick to remark, and they still had their boat. But where was all their food? Almost two tons of it! They had tied some to the boat in case of an accident like this, but other food would be at the bottom of the river, and it was too grey to see much today.

All they could do was right the boat and drag her ashore for the night, lighting a fire with wet wood, and trying to dry and warm themselves between the intermittent downpours threatening to douse the fire. The rain eased as the evening wore on, and a stiff breeze came up to dry them as they sat around the fire, discussing tomorrow's task. It promised to be a better day, which would mean clearer water. Sam and Frank, the strongest swimmers, would dive to search for their possessions, while Jim and John would stay on the bank, cleaning out the scow, drying their bedding and repacking the stores they had already salvaged. It would mean a day's delay, but everything they had brought was crucial, as they had whittled everything down to just a fifth of their possessions for this trip.

The weather was glorious next morning, as if in apology for driving them onto the rocks. Daylight revealed that the infamous Five Finger Rapids had swallowed them, but again they had been luckier than some. In their diving Frank and Sam had come across a submerged craft with two men trapped in it. John and Jim buried these hapless voyagers.

By evening they had retrieved all that was left of their provisions, plus some from the submerged boat. They decided to rise early and put in a long, careful day's sailing to try to make up for the time lost. By their calculations they would reach Dawson in the last week of June. They must not be any later.

Whether because of extra caution or just luck, the rest of their river voyage passed without incident. On June 25th, 1898 they raised a ragged cheer as they rounded a bend in the river and sighted Dawson City, nestled between a domed mountain and this great river. To Sam, accustomed to life in an orderly town, where local pride had always demanded high standards of cleanliness, the view caused him little excitement. Tied up at every possible point along the river bank was the strangest collection of river-going conveyances, some of which he recognised from the boatyard at Lake Bennett. Pitched on the bank, right alongside, were all kinds of tents, surrounded by the greatest jumble of half-made hut frames, salvaged wrecks of boats and other bits and pieces treasured by men who were struggling to survive until they could get up to their claim and strike it rich. The overall picture was one of squalor and clutter which made his heart sink, but he said nothing to spoil his companions' pleasure.

Frank was jubilant, unable to decide which should come first: a visit to the nearest restaurant or to the registrar of claims. Jim, hungry but a little nervous, cast his vote for the meal since the claims office didn't close for hours. John pointed out that having a meal would give them a chance to find out where the office was situated.

With their trusty little boat tied to a rough but sturdy jetty on the Klondike River, just a few yards upstream from where it joined the now mighty Yukon, the men sauntered as casually as they could downtown. They had no desire to be conspicuous, least of all as novice prospectors, who knew nothing. They knew that the sooner they adapted to this new way of life the better their chances. To find their bearings they walked back along the waterfront, for in passing on the river they had thought the centre of the city lay back towards the scarred mountain that rose behind it. They paused to admire the steamer they had sighted less than an hour ago. Moored between King and Queen Streets the "A.J.Goddard" was a magnificent sight.

"Must be two hundred feet long at least!"

"A floating palace!"

"How on earth does a thing like that get through the Canyon, and over those rapids?"

"Oh, she doesn't have to come through Miles Canyon." said a knowledgeable voice behind them. "We are just establishing a steamer service from Lake Bennett to the head of the Canyon, and another from the foot of the White Horse Rapids to Dawson. There will shortly be a tramway along the banks of Miles Canyon."

They turned to see a dapper little man, a starched collar and bowler hat complementing his English public school accent.

"You mean that there is no longer any need to sail down the Yukon by raft or scow?" sighed Jim.

"Certainly not in the next few weeks," replied the little man.

"Come on," said Sam gruffly, seeing Jim's crestfallen face, "I wouldn't have missed that ride for the world!"

"Nor I!" chorused John and Frank. Jim was silent as they wandered on.

The presence of the steamer assured them of a good meal, since large quantities of stores could now be brought in. Over heaped plates of food such as they had not seen in months, they checked the plans they had made during the long days on the river. It was Frank who spoke first.

"We want a four-way partnership if possible, but we would share with up to four others if we had to. Right?"

"We'll have to be prepared to pay, but we must have enough to live on for a few months. There's no leaving till next May if we stay past October," threw in Jim.

"We're staying," muttered Sam. "We didn't come all this way to turn tail."

"Well," added John, "the best step now is to go straight to the claims office and find out what is still available."

After an hour of discussions and with a kindly clerk's help, they negotiated to buy a claim on Eldorado Creek. Most of Bonanza Creek, where the original find had been made, was staked, and the small pockets remaining aroused suspicion. Frank was all for setting out immediately to view the claim but, since it was several miles out of town, Sam saw more sense in buying up what they needed and trying to find a horse – a rare commodity. John supported this move. The search for a horse proved hopeless, and the prices for their other purchases were exorbitant, a warning of what they could expect in the winter, when no steamers would come. Loading the goods onto their boat they paddled as far up the Klondike as they could and made camp for the night. Only Sam's old watch, in his waterproof document pouch, told them it was 10.30 at night, for it was quite light when they bedded down, content with their lot. In fact the sun merely dipped below the horizon that night before reappearing, but the four sound sleepers on the bank of the Klondike River knew nothing of that.

On a warm, sunny morning, under a sky streaked with threads of cloud, it was difficult to think back to the frozen Chilkoot Pass just a few weeks ago. But where was the sense in looking back? They had staked their future, quite literally, in the

Klondike soil, and in about an hour they would reach their claim. Frank wanted to dismantle the boat and carry the materials it gave them to their site, to construct a crude hut as a temporary measure. The others, less impulsive, preferred to see first whether it might still be of some use for transport to and from Dawson.

It was further than they had anticipated and they alternately trudged and paddled ten miles by the time they reached the fork of Bonanza Creek. Having kept close to the creek they had seen many prospectors at work. Most had given them a friendly welcome, looking up from their work to greet the new fellows. Those who were bitter about their own failure said nothing, working on without raising their heads. A group of Australians invited them to share a frugal meal, which they accepted gladly, contributing a loaf of the fresh bread from the town.

Advised that they had another two or three miles to cover, they left just before two o'clock, having spent some time observing their new friends sluicing, digging and panning. Sam was keen to peg out their claim and establish where the hut, or boat, would best be situated before they sat down to their evening meal. This would give them time to inspect their boundaries and prepare their implements during the long evening, ready for a start next morning.

CHAPTER 2

Bonanza

The team of Hamilton, Browning, Henderson and Fleming had been working its claim for three months, with just enough success to frustrate them. They were sure the gold was there – all they had to do was locate it! Each month one of them went into town to buy necessary items like fresh bread, a real treat, and the usually available half-fresh produce was better than preserved food. However, mostly they were still eating what they had carried over the Pass with them, food bought far away in Vancouver or Dyea. They also needed nails and new mesh for one of the gold pans. There was quite a list.

It was Sam's turn to go into town this October morning. The owner of one of the claims further downstream had sold up his share and was pulling out, so that he could catch a steamer home to California before the winter. Sam had negotiated to buy the man's ten-year-old horse, named Joe. In a fit of patriotism Sam renamed the horse Zealandia, although no-one else took the name seriously, including the horse. Now Sam was riding it into town in time to farewell its former master. "Going home in style, not the way I came!" he had called in parting.

Sam was one of many buying the last of the "fresh" food they would see for seven months. This was the last steamer for the year. He was loading up the saddlebags when he heard the first plaintive whistle of the departing boat as she headed back up the Yukon River.

There was mail to be collected from this steamer too. Sam did not really expect a reply from his mother – she would have had to write almost immediately – but it was worth enquiring. There could also be mail for his partners, so he called at the counter. There was a letter for Frank, which he tucked safely into his jacket and one for him, from his mother. This he tore open, surprised at his own eagerness.

"My dear son," he read, "I am indeed sorry to be writing to you on such an occasion, but I know that you will have the strength and courage to bear the news I must send you. Only a matter of hours ago your dear father passed away, having been ill these last few weeks with pneumonia …"

The last haunting hoot of the paddleboat's whistle resounded through the hills behind Dawson as Sam instinctively turned his horse towards Midnight Dome. If he hurried he might catch a last glimpse of the ship from the summit to try to stave off the heavy feeling of isolation creeping over him. The road leading up to Midnight Dome was winding and it took him a good half -hour to reach the top. As he strained his eyes to see the steamer that had brought him this letter, he was glad of the solitude. This was his thinking place. He fancied he could see a puff of smoke rising now and then from a little dot on the water. He took the saddlebags off Zealandia and left him to graze while he finished reading the long letter.

His mother wrote of the change to his father's will, and said she understood he would have mixed feelings on hearing of his father's death. She knew there had been bitterness in Joseph's heart when Sam was leaving, but it was best forgotten now, she assured him. Forgotten! He could not so easily forget the way he had seethed for a week, not wishing to say more since it seemed better to part with at least some semblance of respect. So now there was no chance to show his father what he would make of himself. Yes, he acknowledged, there was shock at the finality of the news, but the only pain he felt was for his mother. There was no way of sending word to her now, unless there was an overland mail sled leaving soon. It was about a month till the real freeze, but he did not know what he wanted to say, and she had said at the end of the letter that she did not know if it would ever reach him, so he decided to leave it until the spring thaw.

A glance at his pocket watch told him he had been sitting musing for over an hour. There were still a few purchases to make, and the boys would be expecting him back for supper, so he must hurry. Calling Zealandia, who came only when he added, "Well, Joe then", he rode down past the cemetery and the few houses on the outskirts of the town, into King Street, completed his business quickly, and was soon back on the road to Bonanza Creek.

Along with the letter for Frank he handed over the statement of their joint bank account. They were making a modest income from their claim, although all four partners were waiting for the big strike. Their Australian friends down at the Forks were confident that they were also on the brink of a great discovery, while there was a strong rumour that McPherson's death last week upstream on Bonanza Creek was suicide. Sam was quite satisfied to be in the middle, neither strained to breaking point like poor McPherson, who now lay in the cemetery on the hill, nor subjected to the grasping of false friends at the moment of success.

They worked the claim through the winter, but progress was slow and the weather unbelievably cold. In a co-operative move with several others on the Eldorado, they installed a steam engine, from which steam could be fed through a reinforced hose rammed into the frozen bank. In this way, by heating the gravel for up to twelve hours, they could loosen three cubic yards at a time. The gravel was piled up ready to be cleaned when the spring thaw came. This was safer than lighting underground fires, where more than one miner had been asphyxiated in the past year.

By the time the thaw came, they were only three. In the depth of the cruel winter Jim succumbed to the strange illness that had stalked him from his home to the goldfield. All the men knew he was mortally ill, but he never wanted to talk about it and they respected his privacy. He suffered terribly in his last week or so, yet never once did his quiet courage fail him. He had set a standard of endurance for them all to follow. So hard was the ground when he died that the first use of the new steam engine had been to prepare the place for his burial. With heavy hearts the three men laid their brave friend to rest on their plot of land, and gave the remainder of the day over to his memory. Jim's death added an incentive to their work, however, and the announcement from the Records office soon after his death, that the Klondike goldfield had yielded over ten million dollars worth of gold, made them renew their efforts.

Through the summer of 1899 they slogged, sometimes sharing equipment with those on neighbouring claims, always with Jim in the back of their minds. They had bought a second horse, which Frank had dubbed Victoria. He and John went into town every week, but Sam went only when necessary. Although he disliked the ugliness and squalor of the mining camps, where greed and lust tempted men to senseless acts, the town was no better, and he wanted to work at the challenge they had set themselves.

They had worked on, completing the section where they had been sluicing and panning for weeks, with little result. After Jim's death Sam suggested moving higher up the hillside, to follow up on his hunch. One day last year, as they had boiled up the kettle for their tea, and before he had become too ill to work with them, he had said suddenly, "I've been thinking." Nobody was really listening, but he proceeded, "If the present course of all these streams is bringing down so much gold, who's to say that earlier courses, a million years ago maybe, did not carry gold too?"

"Good thinking, Jim," said Sam. "We must have a look higher some day. But right now let's finish the section we are on."

Sam cringed with shame now at his patronising words, as he blasted away the gravel around a shiny rock face. Frank and John had gone into town. Was he imagining the sight in front of him? The sunshine was giving the rock face a golden sheen. He wiped his hand across the surface and rubbed his eyes. Jim had been right! They could have saved themselves months of winter work, if only they had acted on that one remark. What's more, Sam thought, Jim would have been here to see what he was looking at now.

Sam chipped and watered, chiseled and coaxed the big rock until he finally dislodged it from the face. Packing the two-cubic-foot hole with gravel, he carried his treasure back to the hut to await the return of his partners. He could hardly contain himself, but was determined to give nothing away until they arrived.

They had had a few drinks, he could tell, as they came singing up the valley in the early evening. Good luck to them! He had enjoyed a drink too, until he saw what booze and gold fever could do to a man. He felt a surge of excitement as he considered how to tell them the news. They swayed as they came through the door, and Sam hoped they were not too drunk. But no, they had just been clowning about. They were merry, but they would be even merrier in a few minutes.

"Well, did you bring back a bottle with you?" he asked.

"What for" queried Frank suspiciously.

"Oh, I just thought a drink might be nice," said Sam nonchalantly.

"Hmmph, well, as it happens, I did buy a spare bottle. Which saddlebag is it in, John?"

"Joe – er, Zealandia's, Frank. I'll get it for you."

Frank looked quizzically at Sam. "You're up to something, aren't you? I've been with you too long not to know when you are hiding something. Now, what is it?"

"Oh John, good man! Here's to whatever I'm hiding!" And Sam took a generous draught of the whisky, letting it burn its way down his throat, before he opened his eyes.

"Now come on Sam, what *is* it?" Frank was consumed with suspense.

"Well, if you both sit there at the table, with your eyes closed, I will bring it to you."

"But Sam – "

"Do you want to see it or not?" The suppressed urgency in his voice made them play along with the childish game. Sam went into the bunk room, returning a moment later on tip-toe, and placed a cloth-wrapped object on the table.

"Open!"

John removed the wrapping, exposing the rock with its golden centre. The sheer beauty of the sight left both men speechless. Frank recovered first. Leaping up, he grabbed Sam, dancing him around the small room, shouting cowboy "Yee-has" at the top of his voice. John joined them and they cavorted about until the drink took its toll, whereupon they collapsed on the floor against the wall. There they sat, drinking to Jim, to the gold, to the Klondike, even to the Chilkoot Pass until the bottle was empty and they lay in a heap on the bare boards, the rock of gold glinting over their heads in the early twilight.

Between their groans and aching heads next morning they tried to take in what this discovery meant to them. Until the rock was chipped away and the gold assayed they could not put a value on it. They appointed Sam to take charge of that, but he would have to wait until his head had cleared. To help this along they all went to examine the site where he had found the rock. Dragging out the loose gravel he had stuffed into the hole, Sam showed them the exact location. There was more gold there, glistening in the midday sun. John and Frank were eager to work on it, and Sam now felt able to tackle the delicate job of extricating the gold nugget from the slab of rock. Headaches were forgotten.

In three days they had exhausted the streak that followed the line of the prehistoric stream as it had cascaded down from the four thousand foot Dome of King Solomon, birthplace of all these gold-bearing creeks. They deputised Sam to take it all into town for valuing. With only two horses they could not all go. John and Frank, who had been absent when the gold was first discovered, agreed to share the agony of waiting until Sam returned. They had settled on a four-way equal distribution of the money. Jim, knowing he was dying, had left his wife and children so that they should not see him suffer. After his death they had found a note of his wishes. Now his family would receive his quarter share, whatever it might be.

From the assayer's office Sam turned Zealandia again towards Midnight Dome. There he could think, without the sights and sounds of the lust for gold around him. The others could wait another hour to know. Up on the hill, looking back along the silken river towards all that was known to him, Sam knew the time had come to return home. He turned to gaze over the Klondike River and his heart tightened. It would not be easy; he loved this place, as he loved the men who had shared it with him. They had been luckier than most, thanks to Jim. They had all answered the cry for adventure, and each would take home 100,000 pounds as his share. Jim's young widow and children would be comfortably off.

Four hundred thousand pounds! The other two men were stunned. They had not dreamed of such a figure! Where would they go from here? Surely the world was at their feet. They were shocked to learn that Sam was leaving them as he had always been their leader.

John said to Frank, "How does England sound to you, with a hundred thousand in your pocket?"

"I would say a fine place to go to. And perhaps we could visit Mrs. Henderson on our arrival, John?"

"An excellent idea, my friend!"

They would stay until sale of the claim was settled, but with such a recent big find there would be plenty of offers. They decided that, even if they sold immediately, they would stay to join in the annual Discovery Day celebrations. Held on August 17th these festivities relived the day, only three years ago, when George Carmack and his Indian wife's brothers, Tagish Charlie and Skookum Jim, had accidentally discovered gold in Rabbit Creek, which they renamed "Bonanza Creek".

"Without them we would never have come here!" exclaimed Frank.

"Any regrets?" Sam asked both of his partners.

"Only Jim," they replied, as one.

The show was to be held in the aptly-named Palace Grand theatre, and promised to be a night to remember. They already had so many memories to take away with them from this fascinating place. Not just that they had found their bonanza, but the magic of characters like Diamond Tooth Gertie and Klondike Kate, and places like Skagway, Whitehorse, Dawson and Midnight Dome, Sam's place of quiet. These names would tumble over each other in his mind when he was thousands of miles from here.

He too would leave in style, by steamer to Lake Bennett and then on the brand new White Pass and Yukon Railway to Skagway. He would not even dirty his boots this time. John and Frank wanted to stay till the last steamer left for the season, but Sam, now that he had made his decision, was impatient to be off. It was an emotional parting from such trusty friends, and a brief visit to the grave of Jim, where he checked that the little gold nugget lay secure in its niche beneath his name. He boarded the August paddle boat. Having watched many a steamer puffing up that stretch of river, Sam found it strange to be the one on board.

For the rest of his long life Samuel Hamilton never lost the feeling of leaving a part of himself in the Yukon Territory. A mere mention of the place would bring memories flooding back, none more pleasing than the news that John had married Jim's widow and would be a father to his children.

CHAPTER 3

Return

Sam's letter reached her early in January 1900, and Henrietta had not been so excited for many years. Since Joseph's death eighteen months before life had been rather dull, apart from brief visits to Victoria and her family, and the calls they made on her when they were in town. George and his family had come to stay for a fortnight, but that was a year ago, so she was more than ready for the joyous reunion of Sam's return.

He had posted the letter from Seattle, on his way to California. His plans were vague. He just said that he would try to be home for her birthday in June. It was an affectionate letter, and she could sense his desire to be home. He would be ready to settle down now. Whether he would work, or just live on the interest of his fortune Henrietta could not say, but he would soon be home with her, to share this large, empty house.

The intervening months passed surprisingly quickly with Catherine's news that she was expecting her third child in September, and Victoria's regular telephone calls. Charles was at boarding school in town, and Henrietta usually had a visit from him on shorter exeats. It was good to be able to tell Victoria that the boy was settling in well, in spite of bouts of homesickness at first.

Now there was a further letter, posted from some port she had never heard of, announcing his date of arrival. He was spending two weeks at this place to await the next ship bound for New Zealand, hoping for one with better service than the first. His letter had caught the mail and been carried ahead on that ship, so it must be only two weeks till his arrival.

Henrietta had made this deduction by the time she had read the first paragraph. To savour the remainder of the precious epistle she put it down while making a cup of tea. This allowed her a few minutes to take in the thought that her dear Samuel would be home soon, no doubt a different young man from the one who had left his family two years ago. With her cup of tea in one hand and the letter in the other she headed for an armchair to enjoy the rest of the letter.

The ship was due at Wellington on September 9th, and it would take him another three days to reach Christchurch. On no account was she to try to meet him. He wanted the pleasure of opening the back door and finding her there, with her apron on and her hair dishevelled. He had obviously given his homecoming much thought, and of course she would accede to his wishes. Today was August 28th – now where did she put that calendar?

There was no warning, no voice thanking the driver, no sound of a step on the gravel. The door burst open and he swept her up in a bear hug that squeezed the breath out of her. There were tears in his eyes as he put her down gently and wiped hers from her cheeks.

"Now, stand back and let me look at you, Samuel."

"And I'll do the same. You haven't changed, Mother. A couple more grey hairs perhaps, but nothing else."

"I can't say the same for you, my lad. You've lost that timid look that made me fear for you when you left here. And you have a few lines here and there, no doubt gained from a harder way of life but you look good. You've fared well."

"Better than many, Mother. I have seen sights I'd rather not have seen, but they teach a man how to handle life. I have some thinking to do now I'm home. All my thoughts have led only to this point."

"You have time for that, Sam. There is no need to hurry. You know that I want you to stay here with me as long as you can. I shall understand when the time comes for you to leave, when you know where it is you want to go. And now, would you like a nice cup of tea and some of my scones?"

"Mother, I don't know how I've survived without your scones and cakes."

It was midnight when they finally went to bed, a very late night for Henrietta. She had felt almost afraid to let him out of her sight, in case she was only dreaming and he would vanish. Silly and childish, she told herself, but still she sat there, revelling in his company. Sam had set aside this first evening for his mother. He could not explain it to her, but it seemed to compensate for his absence at the time of his father's death. He made no attempt to contact anyone else: there would be time for that later. He was tired, lacking the energy he needed to build a new life in New Zealand.

Henrietta left him undisturbed next morning and was not surprised that he slept until noon. She had been quite shocked at his appearance. He looked thin, weary and strained, and much older than his 27 years. He looked more like George now, having closed the gap in their ages. It worried her, but no doubt a good rest would bring him back to himself. With spring coming on now he could only improve.

It was ten days later when George telephoned from Dunedin to say that Catherine had just presented him with his second son, and that, with Henrietta's approval, they would like to name him Joseph. He would possibly be the only grandchild not born in the lifetime of Joseph Senior, so it seemed fitting that he should carry on the name. Henrietta was touched at the thought, and that she had been consulted. She had never seen herself in the role of matriarch in this widening family circle. George assured her that there was no need to make the long journey to Dunedin this time, as they had a young friend, Mary Daniells, the daughter of a middle-aged couple they knew well, to care for the other two children. Henrietta knew, of course, that Sarah was at school now, and did not doubt that this young lady, although unmarried, would manage well for a week or two.

When she told Sam the news he replied promptly, "I think I'll take the train down and visit George. You don't think it a bad time, do you Mother?"

"Not at all. You will have him to yourself, apart from the times when he visits Catherine in the hospital. It is an excellent idea!"

Henrietta was delighted. Sam was evidently feeling ready to stretch his wings. He looked healthier now, thanks to the pampering of a fond mother. The change of air would do him good.

George was pleased to see his brother. It was years since they had met, and Sam had been just a boy. Their only news of each other had been through their mother. Returning from work the evening after the telephone call George found Sam waiting for him in the sitting room. He would be glad of company once the children were in bed. Mary had bathed and fed them, and prepared a meal for George and Sam, before leaving to go home.

Little Edward took a liking to his tall bearded uncle, and was happy to sit placidly on his knee while Sarah recounted her day to George. Sam felt out of place in this domestic scene. He had no particular desire to marry, and there had been few women in his life these past years, but he liked children, and he was not shy with young ladies. Perhaps if he met the right one he would view marriage differently.

Early next morning Mary Daniells arrived to help George with breakfast and to remain with Edward when George took Sarah to school on his way to the shop. They walked, since neither was more than a few hundred yards from home. George saw no point in awakening his brother, and it was after ten o'clock when Sam emerged from his room. He found Mary dusting the sitting room. She did this not as a servant but in the manner of one brought up in a genteel home. He watched her for a few moments without her knowing, admiring the gracefulness of her movements and the abundance of her pretty hair, before retiring discreetly and making a more obvious entrance.

"Oh good morning, Mr. Hamilton, did you spend a comfortable night?"

"I certainly did, thank you, and a good part of the morning also. Having arisen at five o'clock for more than a year I am surprised that I can now sleep until nine or ten in the morning."

"Being so close to the sea may be a part of the reason. You must be hungry too. If you'll come through to the kitchen I have everything ready, and I must also see what Edward is up to in the yard."

Sam felt he was putting her to a lot of trouble, but she was so natural and self-possessed that he became tongue tied at the thought of telling her that he could manage for himself. If she only knew how rough his meals had been in Dawson.

"I shall be taking Edward along to the park later in the morning, since it is such a mild day. He likes to feed the ducks there. Would you care to join us for the walk?"

"Well, yes I would. It *is* such a beautiful spring morning." Sam was irritated that a young woman could make him blush and stammer, at his age. Was it proper to be strolling with a girl he hardly knew and on her invitation too, without George's knowledge? Mary was unaware of his confusion, or gave every appearance of being so. Having served him his breakfast she returned to the sitting room as Edward bounced in through the kitchen door to show her what he had found.

"Hello, young man," said Sam. "What have you got there?"

"Me find a pittilar," was the reply.

"A what? Show me."

A grubby little fist opened to reveal a fat green caterpillar on a screwed-up leaf.

"He is beautiful! You must go and show him to Miss Daniells. She is in there."

As Edward scurried off to find Mary, Sam silently opened the servery slide to see her reaction. He was intrigued to see whether this would shake her composure. Recoiling initially she bravely admired the caterpillar then finally persuaded Edward that it would be happier outside.

It was a spring morning, the sun and the light breeze announcing that winter had gone. The park was a vibrant green and in its carefully laid-out garden plots the brilliant lavender of crocuses gave way to the massed scent of freesias as the three wandered towards the duck pond. On an island in the middle of the large pond several willows were beginning to show their new foliage, while around their sturdy trunks grew a profusion of daffodils. This was the wild corner of the park. With the only access to the island being by boat Nature could run riot. The gardeners' visits were rare, and the ducks had taken over the island. Many people, including Mary, loved to come and sit here, losing themselves in the feeling of belonging to this little wonderland, and several benches had been placed around the pond. Mary headed for one of these, letting Sam know it was her favourite spot. Edward, armed with a large crust of bread and instructions not to give it all to one duck, set off at speed to feed the ever-increasing number of ducks.

Sam, too self-conscious to sit down with this young woman whom he had met only last evening, and quite sure that he would be called upon at any instant to pluck the adventurous little Edward from the duck pond, paced about as casually as he could. He was on edge, unable to settle, and he wondered if Mary could sense this. An occasional glance at her did nothing to help, since she did not take her eyes from her charge for a second. As Sam grew more and more wretched she became aware of his discomfort, and when he finally flopped down on the other end of the bench in utter confusion and dejection, she turned slowly to face him, giving him an angelic smile.

There was a sudden splash and a frantic squawking of terrified ducks. Sam was instantly in the water up to his knees, clutching at a sodden little boy. Through a mouthful of stagnant pond water, he spluttered,

"More bread for ducks?"

"It was time to be going back anyway," said Mary, as she wiped Edward down and removed weed from his hair. "It must be almost noon, and that is Edward's lunch time. Then he has a sleep and we go to meet Sarah."

Taking out his old friend, his pocket watch, Sam declared that it was indeed just after twelve.

"I fear we shall attract some curious glances on the way home, Miss Daniells. If you would feel happier, I shall escort Edward back and you might walk alone. In our present state neither of us does you much credit."

"Mr. Hamilton, had you not been with us, it is I who should have been wet to the knees, and a far worse sight too. I am most grateful to you, and not in the least embarrassed to be seen with you."

Delighted at her spirit, but unconvinced by her argument, Sam hailed a passing cab as they reached the street, and they travelled back to George's home in comparative comfort. When Sam recounted the story to his brother that evening, after Sarah and Edward were asleep in their beds, he knew this tale would join his store of anecdotes. It would be aired on appropriate occasions and then packed away for future use. How often he would tell the tale he didn't know, for the future was very vague in his mind.

On the evening before Catherine was to bring the new baby home, Sam said he would catch the next morning's train back to Christchurch, and so be out of the way. George would not hear of this. Catherine had told him plainly that she wanted to see Sam before he left. Mary would continue to come in daily until Catherine had re-established her routines, and he would be no trouble to anyone. Sam was easily swayed, in need of something to do before returning to stay with his mother.

He stayed a further week, and in that time he found a ready listener in Mary. Not a talkative person, she was content to let him talk himself out before she offered an opinion. He told her things he would normally have thought over alone, discovering that at times she understood him perfectly. She was sure he could not live the leisurely life of a gentleman, even though he could afford to, if he invested wisely. She suggested he look for a post as a school master and by the end of that week she knew more of his thoughts than anyone, Sam realised how much he owed her, and how much he would miss her company.

"Mary, I have talked so much about myself and I know so little about you. I know you are younger than I, but you are so much wiser. I have bared my soul to you – please tell me a little about yourself."

Mary told him she was an only child, aged twenty-three, that she had wanted to study for a university degree but that her parents had not thought it seemly for their daughter, and that she read widely. "But I am not a very interesting person. I have done nothing exciting, as you have."

"Do you like to write letters, Mary?"

"It is my favourite pastime. It fills in many empty hours."

"Then will you please write to me? I warn you though, I am a very bad correspondent, as my mother would attest to, but I do not want to lose contact with you." A blush crept up her neck, and she stammered that it would be an honour indeed.

When he left her this was all she had to cling to, this half-promise and a brief touch of the hand. Would he really remember her once he was busy arranging his future?

One week was not long to find a place in his heart, yet the tightness she felt when he was gone told her that Sam Hamilton had found a place in hers.

Henrietta was pleased to see Sam looking much more like his former self. He was seldom home these days as he contacted school and university friends, spent a couple of days at Victoria's, and sorted out his affairs in town. George had asked him about joining the business, but Sam had no interest in this. George wanted to return to Christchurch, but saw problems with the family home. He did not want his mother to feel she must have them all there with her, nor that he was pushing her out. On the other hand, the house was part of the business and it was only because the present manager was a bachelor, who had no need for a house, that Henrietta was able to remain in it. Sam had promised to try to arrange something for his mother, hence his visit to Victoria.

Victoria proved willing to offer her mother a place in her home, but was it a favour or a disservice to uproot her at the age of sixty? The problem was Henrietta would go along with her family's wishes even if it made her miserable. Victoria saw the need to be discreet in mentioning the subject.

With this in mind Sam next went in search of a small house, not too far from Hamilton & Son's shop. He found just what he wanted and was now ready to broach the subject with his mother. He felt there were enough alternatives for Henrietta to be able to make her own choice. The matter proved simpler than either he or Victoria had feared, for Henrietta had already thought about it. She had read into George's letters that he would like to take over the parent branch. Far be it from her to do anything that would stop her son and grandchildren from living closer to her. She had hoped that Victoria would offer her a place in her home, but was prepared to buy a cottage in town if this did not come about. A reserved person, she had not made a wide circle of friends, her interests lying rather with her family. She was relieved to know that Victoria would take care of her in her old age. She would not leave this house without regret, knowing what it had meant to dear Joseph and what memories it held for her, but Henrietta was a practical woman. It was too big for her, her memories would travel with her, and it was not going out of the family. She would visit for family occasions.

The move was accomplished towards the end of the year, when the weather was more settled. It was not easy to move into smaller quarters at the age of sixty, but Henrietta was determined not to clutter Victoria's home with her useless keepsakes, and so had sold much of her furniture, leaving in the house only those items George had expressly requested. She was glad that these included the dresser and the hallstand which Joseph had commissioned on their arrival, as well as the magnificent settee he had bought several years later. Upon her death these three pieces of furniture would be divided among her three children, and George understood that he would just be temporary custodian of them. Her other treasures were smaller, and she had allowed herself some sentimentality with them. They would be of comfort to her as she grew older, and she hoped that her grandchildren would be interested in the letters and trinkets she was packing into a leather suitcase, itself a relic these days.

For George it was not as easy to move house. There were business affairs to arrange, the transfer of the Dunedin house they had outgrown to the new manager exchanging positions with George, and then the upheaval of moving with small children. In this respect they were glad of an offer from Mary Daniells to accompany them and remain for a week to care for the children until the family was settled. George and Catherine were surprised at the offer, but discreet enquiries revealed that the suggestion had been made to Mary in a letter from Sam.

It was late January when George retraced, with his family, the steps he had taken alone in 1885, as a young man being given the responsibility of a new branch of the family business. It seemed an eternity ago. Now, because of their ageing mothers, both he and his wife felt the time was right to return. They were looking forward to regular family gatherings as an unaccustomed pleasure, after fifteen years of rare meetings and partings. George was particularly keen to see how the family oak tree had grown.

Sam appointed himself temporary concierge when his mother moved to Victoria and Richard's home on the farm. He would be taking up a post in February at the high school in a small town 60 miles from Christchurch, but until then he would remain in the family home, at first alone and then for a week after George, his family and Mary arrived.

It was four months since Sam had returned from Dunedin, four months since he had seen Mary. She had written to him regularly and he valued her letters, even though he had not always replied to them. He had always intended to, but his efforts seemed too clumsy to send to someone who reminded him of Dresden china. Instead he would sit with pen poised and picture her slender figure, her pretty face with its high cheekbones and the crown of chestnut-coloured hair that she could never quite tame, as its curls escaped the pins she tried to capture it with. The longer he thought of her the harder it became to write a letter, and he would throw his stumbling efforts away in disgust. She must be disappointed in him, for which reason he desperately wanted to see her again. He would have to find a way to tell her she had been in his thoughts every waking hour.

As he watched the express approach the long wooden station buildings Sam knew he would have to go through the motions of greeting his brother, as well as Catherine and the children, and so be distracted from his purpose, but as long as he could read Mary's expression first he could wait an hour, if needs be, to talk with her. The train came to a halt, disgorging a horde of passengers. George was tall enough to stand out in the crowd, and with Edward on his shoulders, even more conspicuous. Catherine was partly obscured behind him, carrying the baby in her arms, but there was no sign of Mary. Panic came over him, but he fought it as he strode towards George. He could not ask immediately where she was, enquiring first about the journey. Then he asked as casually as possible,

"Did you not bring Mary with you, then?"

George looked puzzled. "Did you see her, Catherine?"

Was there a twinkle in her eye as Catherine replied, "Edward left his teddy bear on the seat and Mary has taken Sarah to retrieve it for him."

The relief almost made him laugh. He felt like a schoolboy caught hiding a peppermint under his desk lid. And he thought he was being so subtle.

Sam's visits to Dunedin, to stay with the Daniells family, and Mary's visits to Christchurch, where George and Catherine had said she was always welcome, formed a regular pattern. Sam would return to Christchurch after school on Friday, to spend the weekend either with Victoria, Richard and his mother at the farm or with George and Catherine in the family home in town. The weekends without Mary were so dreary for him that the family wondered how long it would be before he plucked up the courage to propose to her. Or was it rather that Sam didn't realise the solution lay with him, that the poor girl's heart was breaking at every parting?

During a winter weekend at the farm Victoria came upon him sitting in a corner of the drawing room, gazing, unseeing, through the book on his knee.

"Good book?"

"Uh? Oh, the book ... I wasn't really reading it."

Forthright like her mother, Victoria asked, "Why on earth don't you ask her to marry you?"

"What?"

"You do intend to marry the her, don't you? If you don't, then you've encouraged her to think you do."

"Yes, of course I do. But it's just …"

"Go on."

"Well, marriage is such a binding thing, it scares me."

"But you do love Mary, don't you?"

"I think so. But Victoria, how do you know when you love someone enough to marry them?"

Her expression softened as she realised his dilemma. "That is one of the hardest questions in life, and I am no philosopher. This may not work for a man, but I always asked myself whether I would have liked that boy to be the father of my children. Can you picture Mary holding your baby in her arms?"

"Yes, I think I can."

"You know, Sam, you have kept her waiting for over two years now, and she will not allow anyone else to call on her. You are lifeless when she is not here. Only you can change it."

"I have been selfish, I suppose. I hadn't thought of her side of it. Next weekend I am going to Dunedin, so I shall give it some thought this week."

Exasperated again, Victoria retorted, "Give it some thought? Do you ever give anything else a thought? I think your mind has been made up for a long time, Samuel Hamilton – you just needed me to give you a good push!"

Over a cup of tea that afternoon Victoria and her mother discussed the conversation.

"She is a lovely girl, Victoria, but even she will not wait forever. Do you think he will take your advice?"

"Yes, by next weekend he will be wondering why he did not do it a year ago."

"Do you think they would accept the diamond ring I used to wear? I have no use for it, and it would remain in the family."

"Why don't you ask Sam? I think he would be delighted. He could take it with him when he goes next Friday."

A week later it was all settled. On his arrival at the Daniells' Sam had a very brief chat with Mary's father, who showed genuine relief that the constant strain on his daughter's emotions would soon be over. As Mr. Daniells hustled his bemused wife out of the room, Sam opened the small box in front of Mary, revealing the lovely old ring with its solitaire diamond atop a wide gold band. Dropping onto one knee, he asked if she would do him the honour of becoming his wife.

He was taken aback when Mary burst into tears. Was this what every young woman did? Had he done it all wrong? She soon recovered her composure, however, and, after a whispered "Yes", allowed him to place the ring on her finger. As if summoned, Mr. and Mrs. Daniells came back into the room, to hug their daughter and share the joy.

The rest of the weekend was spent discussing all the plans, thoughts and dreams Mary had kept to herself for years. It was now August, and it would be sensible to be married when Sam had his holidays, but that left little time for preparations. Sam had no preference, other than as soon as possible, leaving it to Mary and her mother to make those decisions. Seeking out Mr Daniells in his study, Sam asked if there were any financial matters to be discussed. Mr. Daniells was aware that his daughter was marrying a wealthy man and would want for nothing, so their conversation was lighthearted. When they rejoined the ladies the two men were surprised at the ground already covered. Mary had no doubt been dreaming of this occasion for some time.

The date was set for the second Saturday in January, and the number of attendants would be six, subject to Sam's approval. Mary hoped that Sam's nieces Emily and Sarah might be included in the wedding party, and little Edward, in whose company their romance had begun, would be their page boy, along with Joseph, without whose arrival they might never have met. Sam felt it was biassed towards his side of the family, but since Mary was an only child and this was what she wanted, he offered no resistance. She had one dear friend, Jane Brownlie, on whom she had leaned heavily during this past year, who must be her chief maid. For his part Sam wanted only George in attendance, unless he had to provide escorts for Emily and Sarah. So the discussions continued, until Sam lost much of the elation he had felt when Mary had accepted his proposal. Must it be so complex? He seemed to be only a necessary trapping to make the wedding possible, rather than a key figure. He was glad to escape on the Sunday train.

Sam changed his mind about travelling to Christchurch the following weekend. Mary and her mother would be at George's, where he knew they would be discussing the merits of Maltese lace and zibeline, velvet and cashmere. He preferred to be missed by one rather than be ignored by all. It was the first time that he had spent the weekend in the village, and he was lonely, but he had to show Mary that he felt excluded and he wanted to avoid a scene in front of the family.

Mary spent a wretched Saturday. He had not written to tell her he could not come. He could have telephoned if some obstacle had arisen last night. He must be upset and felt it better to stay away. How could she put right what was worrying him if she could not see him? She could not bear the thought of returning to Dunedin without resolving the problem. She made up her mind to visit him on Sunday and if there was no way to return that evening she would stay at the hotel and come back on Monday.

Mrs. Daniells was not pleased at the idea, but she well knew her daughter's determination and she too had noted Sam's absence with surprise. She would return on the night train on Sunday, leaving Mary to make her own way. There was also good sense in Mary having a chance to see where she would be living next year.

It was approaching noon by the time the cab from the station dropped Mary outside the school headmaster's home, Sam's address. She wondered how he would receive her. Was she intruding on his solitude? Walking hesitantly towards the front door, she saw him gazing out of the window at the few remaining leaves on the fruit trees. Then, as she raised her hand to the knocker, he wrenched the door open and enfolded her in his arms

"Is it really you, my love? I was trying to make you suffer, but I was hoist with my own petard! Oh Mary, how childish I was! I am sorry."

Seated in the drawing room where she could warm herself by the cheerful fire, Mary felt her spirits revive as her cold feet thawed. She saw how selfish she had been since they had announced their engagement, only a week ago, but it was almost worth it, to be received with such loving warmth as Sam now showed her. They had never spent more than a day or two together before being forced apart, and this time would be no different, but nestling her head on his shoulder she imagined having him all to herself every evening – and night. She was a little nervous about the nights, but a chat with Catherine on the subject would certainly help. She was afraid Sam would not understand her naiveté.

They had settled into a companionable silence, enjoying their togetherness, when the headmaster and his wife returned from church. Mr. White's greeting was warm.

"It is indeed a pleasure to meet you, Miss Daniells. We were quite despairing how to rouse this young man from his self-pity. You will stay and dine with us, having made such a long journey? And if you plan to spend a day or two in our little town you would be more than welcome to share our home, would she not, my dear?"

As his wife concurred Mary stammered, "Oh but I could not impose upon you in that way. There is a hotel in the main street, I believe?" Catching Sam's eye as she spoke she blushed at the expression she read there. He had really suffered this past week. Perhaps she should be as close as possible to him at this time? Seeing her hesitate, Sam gave her a reassuring smile, which melted the last of Mary's doubts. "Well, if it is no trouble …"

It was cold but clear for the first two days of her visit and Mary enjoyed exploring the shops in the main street. She was surprised to find more than a general store, and could see that even the smallest business had its loyal clientele. Although it was obvious she was a stranger, she was greeted cordially wherever she went.

On the second afternoon, when his lessons were over, Sam took her to see the schoolhouse, which would be their new home in January. It was occupied by a teacher whom Sam knew well, and they spent an hour in the house before Mary shyly asked if she might see the other rooms. She was eager to have a tangible place to picture in her mind during the ensuing weeks. Passing from room to room she was planning what furniture they would need, the colour of the drapes in each room and a hundred other details. She was glad of the little notebook and pencil she always carried with her. When she rejoined Sam her eyes were shining. Tomorrow morning she would be gone, her head full of housekeeping ideas and her heart full of happy memories from these three days.

CHAPTER 4

Looking Ahead

Victoria's daughter Emily was so excited she could hardly contain herself. It was not Christmas that was agitating her, although that was fast approaching. There would be the usual family gathering, with gifts, the tree, and an enormous meal for them all. This year everyone was coming to the farm, so Mama would need plenty of help. No, it was the events of January and February that were preoccupying her.

Emily was going to stay with her cousin Sarah after Christmas, so that their matching dresses for the wedding could be made at the same time by Catherine's dressmaker. Emily knew Mary would be a beautiful bride. She was so pretty, with her copper-coloured curls and her gentle features. Mary knew just what to wear, too, and never looked all bits and pieces, as Emily felt sometimes when she tried on skirts and blouses to go out. She wished she had a better dress sense, but perhaps it would come when she was older. She would never be as slender as Mary, but at least she could learn to dress with taste.

Consoling herself that all was not lost at the age of thirteen, she turned her thoughts to February. This always made her stomach lurch, for she was nervous about this new stage in her life. Her mother had decided that she was to attend a small school in town, really just a large house. Victoria had taken her daughter there to meet the principal and visit the school, with its long verandahs shaded by sweet-smelling creepers. It did not look like a school, but it seemed warm and homely. Emily was to be one of only eight boarders at the school, and the prospect thrilled her with excitement and fear. Although it was small in comparison with other high schools, there would be sixty girls, of all ages, and this was twice as many pupils as there had been at the country school she had attended until last Friday.

This was the first turning-point in Emily's short life. It was the first time she could stand on the hill crest and look back at her life, before turning to gaze into the more mysterious future with its untold possibilities. She had inherited from Joseph, her grandfather, that quality of seeing adventure in the unknown, but, unlike Uncle Sam, she was cautious by nature. Her emotions were in conflict. She wanted the next few weeks to rush by. But if time went too quickly to the start of the school term, then Christmas and the wedding would be over before she knew it. There was no satisfactory solution to the dilemma. With a sigh she resolved to enjoy each event as it came, thinking only about that one until it was past.

Mary had had a long chat with her future sister-in-law, Catherine answering all her questions with no embarrassment or derision. For this Mary was deeply grateful. Her mother had tried to talk to her about married life, but she had been so circumspect and ill-at-ease that Mary had changed the subject as soon as she could.

It was only a little over two weeks to the wedding day, and Mary was beginning to show signs of strain. She knew that Sam was impatient, and each time they met it was an effort not to disagree on some matter. Both had reached the point where they would gladly have married in secret the very next day, but they knew there would be an uproar in both families.

Sam had been busy until the end of the school year, but now time was hanging heavily on him. Christmas was imminent, although he had scarcely given it a thought this year. Why must they wait for one particular day? All the arrangements were in place. Now they just had to watch the calendar. All he wanted was Mary!

George and Catherine tried to keep Sam busy, helping with their business, and the week before Christmas passed quickly, as the shop was always full of people. He had not seen Mary for a week; both had thought this best. Now they were set to enjoy the festivities with the family and this year Mary's parents were invited to share a Hamilton Christmas at Henrietta's suggestion. She realised Mr and Mrs Daniells would be away from friends and relatives unless they undertook the journey home to Dunedin for a few days before the wedding. Mary, too, would be in a spot, there being too much for her to do in Christchurch, yet she should spend her last Christmas as their unmarried daughter with them. She felt a rush of warmth for her future mother-in-law.

It had come at last. Emily blinked several times to be sure she was awake. Sarah, aged ten, was still asleep. Mama had said not to wake her early, but it must be about seven o'clock.

"I'll wait until the next chime of the hall clock and then decide," she thought. Within a few minutes the old grandfather clock struck the quarter hour.

"Hmm, not a quarter past eight or everyone would be bustling about, and I don't usually wake up by a quarter past six …" Undecided, Emily slipped out of bed and crept out into the hall, almost shrieking as Mary, clad in a white nightgown and soft silent slippers, crossed the hall a few paces away going to the bathroom. Emily went back to bed, banishing all thought of the time or waking Sarah. She reflected on the vision she had just seen. Mary, thinking she would be alone, had not put on a robe, and the early light from the window at the end of the hall gave her an ethereal look, like an angel or a ghost. Emily preferred to think of her as an angel, since she had always admired Mary. She might have gone on to imagine her as a goddess had Sarah not opened her eyes, wide awake and asking the time. It was quarter past seven.

The morning flew by. The girls were bathed and pampered with perfume and talcum. Since both were young they would wear their hair loose, festooned with gold and yellow ribbons, and decorated with matching flowers. One fair, one dark, they both suited the colours. Then it was time for the dresses. Victoria and Catherine helped their daughters with the lemon chiffon dresses, adjusting the golden sashes at the waist. The dresses were ankle length, to show the ivory boots they wore. The large gold sashes on the back would be seen when the girls stood at the front of the church. Both mothers felt the puffed sleeves were just right for their no-longer little girls. There were tears as they stood back to admire them.

Mary and her maid were dressing too. Jane Brownlie wore a dress of similar material to the younger maids, but made in a more adult style like Mary's. Her hair was dressed on top of her head, and both she and Mary wore hats with feathers. Mary's dress was ivory silk with large sleeves and a square insert of lace at the throat. Simple but elegant, with a long train falling from the narrow waist. The little page boys would need to be kept away from this. Edward and Joseph, aged six and four, were a portent of disaster, but Mary would not consider leaving them out of the party. They were the very reason this wedding was coming about. The girls would keep an eye on them.

The morning had been glorious, but now the heat was intense. Henrietta felt a sense of unreality as she prepared for the occasion. Was it because her youngest was leaving the nest? When he had been away on the other side of the world she had not felt like this. She felt Joseph's presence beside her, could almost feel his touch. It was six years since he had succumbed to pneumonia. Dear Joseph, he had been the love of her life, and look at the dynasty they had founded. She had to get ready, George would arrive soon.

Seated in the front row of the church, Henrietta wished she could remove her gloves and stole, but although she had always rebelled against appearances, she felt she owed it to Mary to act properly today. Even at the age of sixty-three one was still not able to do as one pleased. Never one to attract attention to herself, Henrietta sat quietly in the stifling air of the church. She still felt strange, perhaps today a new phase was beginning in her life, looking ahead to the birth and growth of her grandchildren rather than back to the upbringing of her own children. Whispering Joseph's name she settled back into the pew.

The service proceeded smoothly. All the small attendants played their parts, with little Joseph determined to pass the ring to Uncle Sam. It was as if he knew that it was his birth which had brought Sam and Mary together. He would always be special to them.

At the conclusion of the ceremony, as the bride and groom left the church, George turned to offer his arm to Henrietta, still sitting as if in a dream.

"Well, Mother, how does it feel to have Sam safely off your hands at last?"

There was no reply, and as he patted her arm to rouse her, the smile was jerked from his face. The guests were leaving the church, he could not make a scene. Mary and Sam were still greeting people at the door. It was too late anyway, but he would not be able to hide it from them. How peacefully she had gone. How like her to slip away unobtrusively. He had heard her murmur his father's name during the wedding service, but he could not have guessed that she was saying softly, "I am coming, Joseph. Be there to greet me." He had squeezed her arm, now cold and lifeless.

Catherine, beside him, had realised what had happened. She whispered, "I will go out through the side door and bring Dr Macfarlane in. We must give Sam and Mary a few minutes of joy before we blight their day. Just sit with her a moment."

George struggled with his feelings as he sat looking at his mother. Small she might have been, but she had held their family together for many years, the hub of a wheel which widened as the grandchildren increased in number. She had provided the strength of the family, even before his father's death. Their lives would lack something without her.

Dr Macfarlane said it was a heart attack, and recalled how he had sat with her when Joseph died. The bridal party had left by now, and George knew he would have to make arrangements for another kind of service. Dr Macfarlane, their family doctor for so long, offered to help. Catherine could only rejoin the guests and say nothing for now. At the wedding reception George would make the sad announcement at the appropriate time, after having a word in private to the bride and groom.

As a result of Henrietta's death and the obligation to be present at the funeral two days after their marriage, Sam and Mary decided not to take a honeymoon. Their thoughts would be on Henrietta, their pleasure in each other's company thus spoilt. It was Mary who suggested that they move straight into the schoolhouse. It was a pity they must start their life together under a cloud of sadness, but Henrietta would not want them to mourn. An active person herself, she would be the first to say, "You have plenty to do in the house. Keep your mind and your hands busy and, if you must think of me, remember the happy times."

Sam tried to be positive. It could have happened while he was away; his father had died then. He had been shocked then, but this was worse. At their very wedding! How could they ever forget it? Mary had burst into tears on hearing the news – who ever saw a bride overcome by grief on her wedding day? But they must be thankful for her life, and not dwell on her death. So his thoughts see-sawed for several days, leaning one way, then tilting back, until he managed to busy himself with something that took his mind off his loss.

Henrietta was laid to rest beside Joseph at a simple ceremony. She had lived a simple life, in spite of being a mother of three and grandmother of five. A busy little woman, she had always found time for any who came to her. When her family spoke at the funeral service they expressed the hope that they and their children might have inherited some of the fine qualities they had seen in Henrietta.

CHAPTER 5

War

The newspapers were full of it. Inevitable now, they said. Only a matter of a spark to light the fuse. At George and Catherine's family gathering the men could talk of nothing else, while the women tried to think of *anything* else. George, Richard and Sam, leaning back in their armchairs to enjoy an after-dinner cigar, were thankful they were now too old to be called up, but their sons would be eligible, except for Rudolph.

Sam and Mary had been married for six years before Rudolph was born, and in that time Mary was sad that she was unable to bear a child. Sam had said nothing, but his joy at becoming a father and his great love for the boy, now aged four, showed how he had longed for a family. She had never questioned his choice of name for the child, even though it was a departure from all the traditions of the Hamilton family. Mary watched fondly as the little chap clambered onto his father's knee, turning to fire an imaginary gun at his big cousin, Joseph. Poor little Rudolph, there were no young cousins for him – even Joseph was ten years older, and all the others were grown-ups to him.

Sarah and Emily were in their twenties now, and Emily was to be married next year. Edward, George's older son, was a gangly lad of sixteen, trying hard to grow a moustache. Charles, having defeated his cousin at chess, pulled up a chair beside his father, Richard, and added vigour to the conversation by declaring that he would enlist for officer training. His mother shuddered at the thought, but her son was now twenty-six and completely independent, so any resistance from her would be useless. Catherine was relieved her boys were too young for service, and if there were a war, it should be over before they came of age. The men all said it would last less than six months. Still, she thought how impulsive Edward was, and she felt uneasy.

The coffee arrived and the ladies joined Emily and Sarah, who were discussing the upcoming wedding. Victoria found it hard to see herself in the role of the bride's mother. She would probably be a grandmother before she was fifty.

"Was not Frank to join us after dinner, Emily?"

"Yes, Mama, but as I mentioned to Aunt Catherine, he said not to wait for him. He may be quite late."

Emily and Frank's romance had been so like hers and Richard's that Victoria had watched it blossom with a nostalgic pleasure. There was one point of difference, however, since Frank was a town boy. It was he who had to travel to the country to see his love. Victoria recalled going to the barn dance with her brother George, travelling out from town to meet his farming friend Richard almost thirty years ago. Not comfortable with that thinking, she went back to Frank, remembering him as a boy the same age as Charles. Yet by the time she was twenty-six, Victoria had borne two children, and would not have appreciated being thought of as a child. "I *am* getting old," she thought. "That is surely one of the signs!"

Frank worked at the city bank, and had already been promoted twice. His career looked promising, Richard was pleased to see. Although willing to provide for his daughter beyond marriage if she married a man of little means, he preferred that a young couple chart their own course, and was glad that Frank was industrious and prudent. With such an uncertain future one needed security.

At last the wedding day dawned in March, 1915, and Emily floated through the day. She remembered Uncle Sam's and Aunt Mary's wedding, at which she and her cousin Sarah had been bridesmaids, as she was dressing for the ceremony. She recalled the horror of her little grandmother Hamilton's death on that day, but pushed it aside. This was not a time to think of the past, but rather of the future. Both she and Frank dreamed of a future filled with love, laughter and children.

After the wedding the young couple settled in Christchurch, in a little cottage. Frank talked of getting a house later, but was unwilling to invest more precious capital at this point. When this home became too small for them they would move. Emily loved the charm of the cottage, planting pretty flowers around it. A country girl, she tried to bring a rustic atmosphere to the little house, with hollyhocks and wallflowers, hyacinths, daffodils and roses. There were new strains of roses arriving from England and Emily ordered several to flank the path to their front door.

Frank was delighted to see her happy and settled. It was never easy to transplant a country girl into an urban setting, but Emily was contented with the help of her gardens. Their life was idyllic until, early in 1916, Emily carried into the house a brown envelope marked "O.H.M.S. Army business". Her heart sank. It would be hours until Frank arrived home, but nothing would induce her to open that letter. She was tempted to burn it, but that would be burying her head in the sand. There would be another. The afternoon was spent trying to adjust to the idea of living here without him, of waiting until he returned – *if* he returned. Thoughts tumbled about in her mind: "Frank is not a soldier, he is too gentle. He could not kill other men! He hates to watch Papa kill a sheep, even. And if he doesn't come back, what is left in life for me? He *is* my life. No children, hardly a chance to have any after so little time married, and I couldn't go back to living with Mama and Papa, like a girl again . . . ." She let that terrible thought go.

When he came home, Frank was tired. This war was creating havoc in the banking business. People were breaking investments, buying and selling property, doing irrational things as they needed their money, while the stock market plunged up and down. Emily's heart filled with pity for him as she handed him the mail with trembling hands. She could not look at him, and hurried to the kitchen to attend to the dinner, which was already cooking. In a moment he was behind her, with the letter still in his hand as he hugged her fiercely. There was a desperation in his embrace. He said nothing, releasing her and handing her the letter. He would leave in two weeks! Had she really expected it to be longer? How could they live under this cloud? It would be like living with a dying man.

Pulling herself together Emily decided they must make the most of every moment before he left, and she must give him as many happy memories as possible to take with him. She must not buckle under the strain – there would be time to weep when he was gone.

Frank worked for the first of the two weeks, finalizing the transfer of his files to a colleague, but he wanted to spend the final week before his departure with Emily. They spent every minute together, revelling in each other's company and refusing to look beyond the days they had left to them. They talked and wept together, and they laughed together when they could keep the pain beneath the surface. They spent two days with Richard and Victoria just before Frank left. It was a chance to leave his father-in-law in charge of his financial affairs, but also he begged Emily's parents to keep an eye on her, to see that no harm came to her. He would be dreaming of his homecoming, and everything must be just the same. Suddenly this wretched war, thousands of miles away, was right here in their home, their family, their hearts.

Then he was gone. A dull, hollow ache flowed through Emily. Was it better to conjure up happy thoughts of him or to push him out of her mind? By the end of the week she was assisting the nuns at the city orphanage several hours a day. She neither wanted nor needed money, she told the Mother Superior; she just needed to think about someone other than herself and Frank. Throwing herself into the work with enthusiasm, she read stories, built block towers, took children to the nearby park, sang to them and taught them songs. She was exhausted every evening, just as she hoped to be, but she could not control her dreams, and that was when Frank came to her. Every night he was there with the same gaunt, hollow-eyed look she had seen in his eyes as he had stepped on to the train.

Each Sunday Emily either went to the family farm or her parents visited her at the cottage. They alternated to share the inconvenience of travel and to give Emily some variety. Each time her parents saw her their anxiety increased. She was losing weight, the glow had gone from her cheeks and the lustre from her beautiful hair. She was suffering, but she put up such a façade of cheerfulness for them that they never knew whether to break it down or to continue humouring her. She never mentioned Frank, except to show them his letters, which were full of endearments, exhorting her to be brave, and telling her that it would not be long now. He never wrote of the horrors and bloodshed around him and he knew better than to mention the slight wound to his arm, even though it affected his writing a little.

He had been gone four months. On her next visit Emily had no letter to share. There had always been a letter every two weeks. Her façade was crumbling, and Victoria tried to reassure her by saying that the mail would not be regular from the battlefield, but Emily muttered darkly, "There was the dream too." She looked haggard today, with dark lines under her eyes. Reluctantly Victoria prompted her. "What was the dream, dear? Would you like to tell me about it?" Emily said she had always seen Frank the same way in her dreams, ever since he had left, but last night … . She faltered, looked at her mother, and burst into tears. Victoria let her cry, smoothing her hair, trying to give her distraught daughter comfort with her arm around her shoulders. At length Emily recovered enough to stammer, "He was covered in blood, on his face and his hands. He … he just kept saying my name, that special way he had of saying it. And … and then he was gone!"

"Oh, my poor girl! I do hope you are wrong. You must not place too much importance on a dream. Of course, you have been thinking of that, and your thoughts have returned in the dream."

"No, Mama, I feel sure there will be a telegram for me today or tomorrow."

"Emily, stay here with us."

"No, I must go home. I must *know*."

"Then let me come and stay with you. You should not be alone at such a time. Your father won't mind, in fact he would suggest it if he were here now."

"Thank you, Mama, but I really do want to be alone to deal with it. If it makes you feel better, telephone me in the morning before I leave for the orphanage. Let's say about nine o'clock?"

"Are you sure you will be all right alone, darling?"

"Yes, Mama, quite sure." Emily seemed oddly calm now, as though she had come to grips with herself, or reached a decision. Kissing her mother, she left early, without seeing her father, who was busy with farm work, as several of his workers were ill with influenza.

Left alone, Victoria could not rid herself of the image of Emily, so desperately unhappy, but then so coldly calm and almost detached as she had said she wanted to be alone. Fear gripped her and she decided to call George, but first she calmed herself as she did not want to alarm him. When she made the call she simply asked if he or Catherine would pay Emily a visit that evening as Emily's spirits seemed very low. She said nothing about the dream.

Emily reached home at five o'clock, cooked a meagre meal, not because she was hungry but for something to do, washed the few dishes, tidied up the room, and then, with a feeling of inevitability, sat and waited. Soon after six o'clock there was a knock at the front door. As if in a dream, propelled to the door, Emily opened it to a postman.

"Good evening, madam. May I come in, please? I have some news for you."

"Yes, I know. Please come in. I have been expecting you."

Frowning in bewilderment the postman entered and asked Emily to be seated. He had done this many times before. He took an envelope from his breast pocket and handed it to her. It swam before her eyes, but she managed to open it and force her eyes to read that Francis Grant Williams had died a brave death at Verdun on March 12th, 1916, and had been buried with honour in the military cemetery there.

The postman watched carefully for a reaction. He did not know the contents of the telegram, but he had a fair idea. She might faint, she might shriek or weep. He was trained to handle these things. But this young lady had a face as expressionless as a stone. "Shall I make you a nice cup of tea, ma'am?" Nothing. No response. He took a step in the direction of the kitchen. She stirred. "No. No, thank you. I shall be all right. There is no need for you to stay."

"Do you have a relative I could summon, ma'am?'

"I shall telephone my brother in a few minutes. Thank you, I feel quite composed."

"If you're sure, ma'am … I wouldn't stay against your wishes, of course, but …" The postman felt increasingly uncomfortable with this young woman's stoic reaction to the telegram. Something was not right.

Emily hastily ushered the fatherly postman to the door, her mind racing. I have to hurry now, before Mama comes or Uncle George rings up, or anything else interrupts me. Where is it? In the cupboard by the bed – wonder how long it takes – where is the photo?

Placing the telegram beside the photo of Frank, she kicked off her shoes and lay down on the bed. Smiling lovingly at the photo for a moment she thought of the love she had shared with Frank. Theirs had been a perfect partnership, filled with so much promise. Sighing, she reached for the two little capsules she had prepared. They looked so small and innocuous, but they would take her to Frank. She had filled them with rat poison at the farm. It would be agony, but no worse than her beloved had suffered, and on the other side they would be together. "Wait for me, my love!" were Emily's final words.

George was busy with stocktaking. "I'll call on Emily in the morning, I think. As long as I can tell Victoria she is all right by mid-morning it won't make much difference. I want to finish these estimates tonight." But Catherine had read between the lines of Victoria's concern. "If you have no time on a Sunday evening, George, you certainly will not find it on Monday morning. No, I shall pay her a visit after dinner."

It was seven-thirty when Catherine walked up the path to the cottage. The evenings were drawing in now, yet there was no light in the house. Perhaps Emily enjoyed sitting in the twilight, bringing Frank closer to her? She felt a great pity for Emily – only 26, and deprived for an indefinite time of the only man she had ever loved … maybe for ever. There was no reply to her knock, but the door was not locked. The sitting room was to one side of the central passage, and the bedroom to the other.

Ah, there she is, dozing on the bed. "Emily, it's Aunt Catherine. Emily?" The photo of Frank, turned towards his wife, smiled over a piece of paper. Lighting the candle on the dresser, Catherine crossed the room and picked up the telegram, scanning it quickly.

"Oh no! Poor little Emily. Wake up, dear girl!" Only then did the double tragedy strike her. Rushing to the telephone she gasped to George to come immediately, and to fetch the doctor on the way.

Doctor Macfarlane, nearing retirement after long and devoted service to his community, had been called on three times now on the death of a Hamilton. Shaking his head he said, "George, I was sorry to see both your parents go, but this is an utter tragedy. This was their grandchild, and a fine young woman she was too. She has done what she felt she must do, but what a waste of a promising life!"

More arrangements, another funeral. But George had a worse trial ahead. He must leave now for the farm, for he could not give his sister such news on the telephone. He had thirty minutes to decide how to phrase it, but on his arrival he was in a worse state than when he had left Christchurch. He now blamed himself for not acting more promptly on Victoria's request, even though the doctor had said he would still have been too late.

Victoria herself opened the door to him. He handed her the telegram, glad that he had snatched it up. Her only word was "Emily?" George choked. He had not cried since he was a little boy, but now he wept with his sister. Collecting herself, Victoria went to tell Richard, and both returned to sit with George. Charles burst in as George was telling them about the rat poison. Reading the telegram, he exclaimed, "Good God, poor old Frank!" When told about his sister, he was overwhelmed. They had always been close, although neither would have admitted it.

It was a sorry group that drove to town late that evening. They would stay with George and Catherine until the funeral was over.

A year had passed since the tragedy of Emily and Frank. Charles had enlisted in the army almost immediately in what Victoria saw as a show of loyalty to his sister. Young Edward also enlisted on his eighteenth birthday, and was now in the north of France, not far from Verdun. Charles had wanted to find Frank's grave, but he had been sent to Italy. There he had been wounded a month ago, and he was now in an improvised hospital on the Riviera. A wealthy Frenchwoman had offered her villa as a convalescent home, and from his letters Charles was enjoying himself immensely with the nurses. Victoria, who had aged dramatically since Emily's death, hoped and prayed that he would not be sent back to the front. She could not bear the thought of losing her son, too.

Charles saw more action, at Caporetto, where he was wounded again, more seriously this time, and hospitalised in Italy. When he was recovering he was able to pull strings for a transfer to the same villa near Nice, where he could renew friendships from his earlier stay. He had often thought about Nicole, one of the nurses, and now, when he saw her smile of welcome, he knew why. Part-Italian, part-French, she spoke halting English. She was olive-skinned, with thick shining black hair which he guessed must fall to her waist when not pinned up under her cap. He would love to see her when she was not working and ask her to wear it loose.

Without realising, he was filling his letters home with her. It was better than talking of war and asking if his mother still made apple pies. Victoria's letters to him were usually cheery, but she felt she must tell him that his cousin Edward had been killed recently, just a year after he had left home, and at the age of nineteen. Charles felt sick, not from fear for his own life – apart from the pain his death would cause his parents his life meant little to him – but sick at the thought of how many promising young lives were being thrown away. The war to end wars, they had said, only six months at the most, they had said – but it was three years now, and no end in sight. How many lives had been lost, regardless of which army they had belonged to? There was no difference between the way an Austrian or Turkish mother would feel and the way Aunt Catherine would be feeling now. So senseless!

It was Nicole's day off the following day, and Charles invited her to spend part of it with him. He could not walk far yet without becoming short of breath, but he wanted to be out in the sun, in an open space, not a building nor a soldier in sight. He told her of his young cousin Edward, of how futile this war was, of Frank and Emily and of his parents. She listened, smiling encouragement. Charles did not know how much she understood, for it had all tumbled out of his brain, and he must have talked too quickly for her. He paused for breath, reaching out to touch her arm. Would she do him one favour, please? Her smile wavered and she raised her eyebrows. "That depend what it is, my soldier."

"Oh, it is nothing bad. Don't misunderstand, please. Would you let your hair down loose for me, just for this afternoon?" She laughed, perhaps relieved that it was so easy to comply with his wish. "*You* undo it, then!"

He felt clumsy as he fumbled with the bow of the scarf that tied it back, but as the black waves tumbled over her shoulders and cascaded down her back he sat on the grass, six feet away from her, and gazed at her till she dropped her eyes.

"I am sorry, I am embarrassing you. You look very pretty like that. It's like looking at a different person. I feel I have not seen you before." She did not speak, and he noticed little tears on her cheeks. "Nicole, have I upset you? Have I said something wrong? Please tell me what it is!"

Quickly wiping her eyes she stammered, "I am sorry. How you say? ... I am not upset. I am happy that you see me not like a nurse. You see me a woman now."

Charles was so relieved that he threw his arms around her neck and buried his face in her beautiful hair. "Oh Nicole, if only I could hide in this darkness until this stupid war is over!"

They spent all of Nicole's days off together, and Charles wondered what his life would be like without her because sooner or later he would probably be posted to Ypres or Mons, or even back to Italy. But months went by and they seemed to have forgotten him. His respiratory trouble was much better and he felt guilty being so happy here when there was a war on.

At the beginning of December Nicole brought him a letter from the commander of his division. Opening it nervously, with his mind in a whirl, Charles was amazed to read that he was to be sent home in January, 1918. That was next month. Home! Good Heavens!

He looked at Nicole. There would be no joy for him in going home, except to know that his parents would rejoice to see their only remaining child safely returned to them. What could he say to Nicole? Could he expect her to give up her family and travel all the way to New Zealand with him? He observed her as he told her the news. She said sincerely, "That is wonderful for you, and more for your mother. She love you very much." Her eyes were glistening – could it be tears? She did not look as though she would cry.

"Nicole?'

"Oui?"

"Your family… they must be waiting for you to come home after the war?"

"Do not talk of my family. Six months ago, when you were very ill – so I did not tell you it then – they were died … killed, by a bomb from the Germans. My father, my mother, my young brother – *tous*. I have only one sister and she is married, not at home. I have no home."

"Where will you go when the war is over?"

"When the war is over I see."

Charles felt as if he was on an express train speeding past his stop. He needed to stop the train and get off. "Nicole, I am very sorry about your family – you know how I hate this damned war – but their tragedy lets me ask you a question I could not otherwise ask you." There it was again, that sparkle as she looked at him. Was it hope? Did he fully understand what he was about to do?

"Well, I know it is a lot to ask and I shall understand if you say 'No', but …"

"Yes, Charles?"

"Would you be prepared to come to New Zealand and marry me there?"

There was no sparkle now. She began to sob and threw herself into his arms, murmuring endearments in French. "I have thought of nothing else since two months, dear Charles.""You will? You have? Really? Oh Nicole, I love the French way you say my name. Don't ever say it in English, please."

"Non, cheri. I must teach you some French."

"Some day. But we have much to discuss and arrange. I did not plan all that has happened today. You do know that you will not be able to travel with me, because my ship will be a troop carrier? Tomorrow we will go into Nice. I have some business to do there. We shall find out about the first civilian sailing to New Zealand. You won't be afraid, travelling all that way by yourself?"

"When I know you will be waiting for me, I am afraid of nothing."

"You're a brave girl."

"Not brave, I am in love, and love brings courage, *n'est-ce pas?*"

The next morning they were able to travel into Nice in a Red Cross truck. It was not very comfortable but Charles no longer felt like an invalid, and they barely noticed the ruts and dust, so engrossed were they in their plans. The truck was to return from Nice at 4.30 pm, which gave them a good long day. Charles's first piece of business took them, not to the waterfront, as Nicole had expected, but into the main business centre. The town was quiet, perhaps because rain was threatening, and most of the town's visitors were sun seekers. He led Nicole into a little boutique and before she knew it, she was being shown beautiful sparkling rings, such as she had only ever seen on the fingers of wealthy ladies.

"But Charles, what is this? We are not married yet. And why the beautiful stones? I don't understand. In France we have a gold band for marriage, but not this."

"This is not a wedding ring, Nicole. It is an engagement ring, to tell everyone you are going to marry me. I don't want someone else to snatch you away before you reach me."

"Oh, you are funny!"

"Please choose the one you like best and I'll pay for it."

"But the prices, Charles…." A quick word with the shop assistant saw to the removal of all price tags.

"Is that the one?" Taking the ring from her finger and shooing her outside into the rain, Charles paid for the ring, had it boxed, and then added a little brooch made from butterfly wings. He stepped outside to rejoin Nicole, who was struggling with her tears. What emotional people these Europeans are, he thought. Not at all like New Zealanders, but Mama will love her, I am sure.

Finding a bench seat at the waterfront they sat under a dripping tree, where Charles passed the little package to Nicole. Before she opened it, he said, "I must propose to you properly." He knelt in front of her, on the wet pavement, and, lifting her chin until she looked at him, said very seriously, "Nicole, will you consent to be my wife?'

"Yes, my Charles."

"Then open the box, my darling." She opened it and he took out the ring with its blood-red ruby flanked by two diamonds, placing it tenderly on her finger. Still holding her hand in his, he raised her to his feet as he stood and there, with the rain seeping through the tree to drip on their oblivious heads, he kissed her as he had often wanted to but never dared. Only as they rescued the brooch, which had fallen unnoticed from the box to the pavement, and they sat holding hands afterwards, did they notice that it was raining.

"Now that you are really mine, we must book your passage to New Zealand."

"I have been yours since you first came to the villa since almost two years."

"Yes, but I did not see it till yesterday."

As they strolled along hand in hand, ignoring the drizzle, they chatted until they reached the shipping office. Charles was impatient and annoyed to find that it would be months until he could claim his bride.

"Well sir, there *is* a war on. We have to be careful. The first availability is April 20th , 1918. It reaches Wellington on May 27th , sir."

"But that is six months from now!"

"I am sorry, sir, that is the best we can do. Would you like to discuss it with your, er, fiancée?"

"Yes, just give us a few minutes, thank you."

"Charles, that is not so bad really. It will give me time to gather a trousseau. I have saved all my money since my family was died, and I will sail only three months after you. It *is* the best they can do."

"Oh, all right. I just want them to meet you, my love. Mama will love you, I know, and Papa too. He really misses having a daughter."

Back at the desk Charles paid the deposit. Nicole insisted that she would pay her own fare at a later date, telling Charles he did not have to buy his bride.

When Charles left for his ship in January, their parting was a wrench. They made promises to write, to be faithful, to count the days, and before she knew it he had boarded his ship.

Nicole was not lonely at first. There was so much to do. She spent all her free time embroidering and sewing for her trousseau, writing to Charles and visiting the dressmaker who was making her wedding gown. This had been Charles's suggestion. He had said he wanted to whisk her straight to the church when she arrived – no delays for a dressmaker to finish her work. She smiled as she thought of it. "I shall need him more than he needs me. I shall know no-one. He will be my whole life."

When thinking of Charles, she would look down at the beautiful ring she wore. She saw it differently now – one of the diamonds was Charles, the other herself. The ruby between them was the blood Charles had shed, which had brought them together and bound them in love. She often wore the brooch too, but it had no symbolism for her. It was, however, another reminder of his love for her. How full her life had become, whereas it had seemed so empty just a few months ago.

The months hurried by, filled with many soldiers' faces as the casualties flowed in. In each she saw something of Charles, and they loved her gentle manner, her sweet smile. She wore her ring on a chain around her neck, not being allowed to wear jewellery on her fingers, and there were times when she showed it to an overfriendly soldier to dissuade him from getting ideas. In mid-April Nicole left her colleagues, with their good wishes ringing in her ears, and headed for Marseilles, from where her ship would leave on April 20th. Now she was leaving everything familiar. The future was unknown, except for Charles. She must keep him in her mind. Although she had no photograph of him, she had been with him so long that she could easily conjure up his image.

At Marseilles station Nicole searched anxiously for a porter. Although she didn't have as much luggage as a rich lady, she had been busy dressmaking and she would need assistance with the trunk. She had even made some baby clothes, although she would not let Charles see these until they were required. She longed to have his children, but they had never discussed the subject. There was such a distance between them across the world that they could not think too far ahead.

Her trunk loaded onto a motorised taxi, Nicole took her seat inside and was driven to the dock. There she saw the "Veronica". How large she was! No-one could feel cramped on such a huge ship, surely. But six weeks was a long time. Nicole was glad she had been able to save enough for a cabin above the water line. She had brought some favourite books to read (where would she ever find French books again?), as well as an English phrase book, which she opened every day, practising the greetings she would need when she met Charles's parents. She knew of the tragic death of his sister Emily, and that she, Nicole, would become the new daughter in the family. She prayed that they would like her, and clung to the hope that Charles's parents must be fine people.

He had said that he would travel to Wellington to meet her – try and stop him, he wrote in his letter! She would be utterly lost if anything had happened, if he had changed his mind, if he had met someone else. When the ship finally docked there were so many reunions all about her on the wharf, she began to feel totally alone. In that moment of emptiness, there was a hand on her arm and he was embracing her right there in the middle of the dock. So much to say, but their hearts were too full to speak as he guided her into the port building. There would be formalities and some delay with her luggage, giving them time to talk. Taking their places in the immigration line, they could not take their eyes from each other, and Nicole felt Charles was going to take her in his arms again. At her little frown, he lifted her left hand to his lips and kissed her engagement ring. She could not hold back a giggle of sheer joy. Nicole was glad she had been studying English on the voyage. Charles was delighted with her progress. She had always been able to make herself understood, and he had found her errors quaint, but now she had learnt so much more. He was sure there would be no problems communicating with his parents.

That night they crossed to the South Island on the ferry and when they arrived at Lyttelton, the port for Christchurch, he told her the story of how his grandparents had trudged over the Port Hills ahead of them now, how they had carried his mother as a babe in arms, and Uncle George had had to walk, at the age of four. That was fifty years ago, but as part of the family's history it was as clear as if he had seen it with his own eyes.

Nicole was fascinated with the story and with everything she saw. They were to drive straight to the farm, on Victoria's instructions. Richard had lent his son his new motor car, which had been garaged at Lyttelton these past two nights. Now he and Nicole thrilled to the power of its engine, and the comfort, which contrasted with the truck that had taken them into Nice. Soon Nicole caught her first view of Christchurch nestling at the foot of the hills they were crossing, and the plains stretching away for miles towards the backdrop of the Southern Alps. In the early morning, with a nip of frost in the air, the mountains stood out sharply. Later, Charles told her, there would be some haze. She was seeing the view at its best. As they drove on, skirting the town and heading north, they laughed together over the most trivial things, until Charles said, "Almost there now. Only about five miles to go."

Nicole stiffened, realising how nervous she felt about this part of her new life. What if his parents didn't like her? They would pretend to, of course, but she would sense their disappointment. She could never replace their daughter, she was sure.

"You are very quiet, darling. Scared?"

"Scared? What is that?"

"It means afraid. You are afraid my parents won't like you, aren't you?"

"Yes, Charles, I am very afraid."

"Well, don't be. I have told them all about you and … ."

"That is just the trouble, Charles. You have told them I am an angel or something and now they will be disa- … what is that word?"

"Disappointed. No, they have learnt to take all the lover's glow out of my words and then work out what is left. They think you are a very pretty girl, which is true, rather shy… true I think, and nervous about meeting them. Here we are, anyway. They are going to love you – but not as much as I already do." With a quick kiss for reassurance, he squeezed the hooter, bringing his parents out on to the verandah of the big house. Victoria welcomed Nicole so warmly that all her worries were forgotten, and Richard, who had never quite recovered from the loss of his only daughter, greeted her as his new daughter. Hearing these words, Charles knew that his bride was accepted by both parents, and he felt a rush of love for them. Nicole was so different from Emily, but perhaps this would be an advantage.

True to his word, Charles had set the wedding date for three days after his bride's arrival. Nicole was glad the dress was ready. It was a quiet wedding, at which the relatives met the newest member of their family. Nicole could feel the love and acceptance of her new family, and particularly liked Sam's wife, Mary. She looked forward to visiting these new in-laws in the course of the wedding journey.

On his return from the war three months ago, Charles had told his father he would be happy to work on the farm, but Richard had made other plans. On hearing that their boy was to be married, he and Victoria had decided it was time for them to give up the big house. They had arranged for a charming little cottage, with views over the farmland, to be built for them. They would move into it while Charles and Nicole were on their honeymoon.

CHAPTER 6

Family

Sam, at 47, was a senior teacher in history at Otago Boys' High School. They had been living in Dunedin for five years. Mary had wanted to be nearer her father and mother, whose health was not good, and as they were Rudi's only grandparents there was not the same emotional tie with Christchurch. Two or three times a year they journeyed to Christchurch, staying either with George and Catherine, in town, or with Richard and Victoria, in their delightful cottage on the farm.

Nicole and Mary had kept in touch regularly since the newly-weds had visited two years ago. They had formed a bond of friendship, despite a difference of seventeen years in their ages. Mary felt sorry for the poor girl, facing so many strange people and experiences, and admired her for overcoming such obstacles to marry Charles. She was a brave girl. Nicole saw in Mary a woman who felt the same sort of love for her husband as she felt for Charles – a love which gave strength rather than leading to weakness.

Mary's greatest disappointment, after the birth of Rudolph, was her inability to bear more children. Rudi was ten now, and tall for his age. Somehow, with copper-haired parents, he had been born blonde. He had Mary's grace of movement, but Sam's impulsive nature. When other boys came home with jackets or pants torn, he would bring home wild tales of his exploits and adventures, but never a mark on his clothes. Imaginative and sensitive, he was a source of joy to his parents.

Nicole wondered how Mary would feel to find out she was expecting her second child. The first, Richard, was only eighteen months old. She was delighted, wanting to establish a brood around Charles and herself. She would write and tell Mary the news, before it became obvious at cousin Sarah's wedding.

Mary was glad for Nicole. Not a person who descended to petty jealousy, she had resigned herself to having only one child. She knew that Nicole wanted a large family, and understood how this made her feel more secure in her new homeland.

When they met at Sarah's wedding, Mary hurried over to congratulate Nicole and Charles, and to admire Richard who was tottering about grabbing at his mother's skirts when in danger of falling.

Catherine had wondered if her daughter Sarah would ever marry. She had been very fond of young Mark Wilson, and when he had been killed in the War, soon after her brother Edward, Sarah had grieved bitterly. Although Sarah had never told her as much, Catherine had guessed that they had been betrothed and would have married when he returned from the War.

Last year, however, Sarah had formed a friendship with another young man just back from France. Bill Houghton had not known Mark and was not at all like him. For this Catherine had been thankful – she would have felt uneasy to think that Sarah was marrying a substitute. Although Catherine and George did not care for the young man, they considered that at twenty-seven Sarah must know her own mind, and so they endured his brashness as best they could. Joseph, on the other hand, avoided Bill. A shy young man of twenty, he found the loudness and overconfidence of his new brother-in-law intolerable. He would be glad to know that he and his parents would have the house to themselves after the wedding without that fellow visiting every evening.

Joseph had found it difficult to accept the death of his older brother. Edward had always been the leader, he the follower. He had thought of volunteering for service, but by the time he had turned eighteen, the War was winding down – cousin Charles had even been sent home – and he knew it would have upset his mother. Now he was restless. He enjoyed working for his father, and he knew that as the only son he would inherit the business, but he would have to spread his wings before he could settle to building a nest.

It was 1922, and Sarah had just caused great excitement in the family by giving birth to twins. Everyone knew that Bill had a twin sister, but it was only in the latter months of Sarah's confinement that the doctor began to speak of twins. Catherine had longed to be a grandmother, especially since Victoria was always overflowing with news of Richard and his baby sister, whom Nicole insisted on naming Victoria.

Sarah and Bill's twins, Albert and Alexandra, were a wonderful excuse for Catherine to visit her daughter daily. Sarah did need assistance, especially after they learned to crawl. They would set off in opposite directions, and Sarah was run off her feet once they were walking. She was glad of the secure fences and gates on their property, but when Bill left for work in the morning, he would often leave the gate open and little Alex would totter off after Dada. Sarah learned to check the gate each time he went through. It was easier than trying to make Bill remember. He could not understand what all the fuss was about. His mother had managed to raise him and his sister, as well as three others, without anything drastic happening to them.

One who did understand was Nicole. Catherine took Sarah and the twins out to the farm regularly, and Victoria always called at the same time. The grandmothers sat crowing over their darlings while the mothers chatted together. Nicole's children were both older than Sarah's, but her Vicki loved babies, and having two to play with kept her busy. No sooner would she have one on its feet than the other would topple over, or Richard would push it down. At four he was a little boisterous to play with such young children, but he preferred their company to being alone outside.

Nicole would soon have a third child, but this did not worry her. She loved children and enjoyed Sarah's visits, mostly because of the children. Although she wanted several children Nicole had no desire for twins. She liked to enjoy the babyhood of each of her children – it did not last long. Vicki would be two and a half when her next baby was born.

Charles came in to tell Nicole he was off to pick up some hay from the neighbouring farm. "Want to come, young chap? We'll go and see your Grandpa while we are out, eh?" Richard was thrilled. He adored his father, and it was a real treat to go out with him.

With a kiss for his wife, Charles left. He always felt amazed at having Nicole here. He often thought back to the days at the villa in France. Who could have seen this in the future? Just reaching home again was an achievement, but now his life was filled with a richness that humbled him. He lifted his dark-haired son on to the dray and leapt up beside him. The War was so far away now. Occasionally he suffered shortness of breath or nausea, which brought it all back to him. He would remember the shells, the trenches, the gas, and the dead comrades around him. The only way to climb out of it was to recall Nicole's pretty face bending over him as he lay helpless in hospital. She understood him well enough to be there when she saw him in the grip of these dark thoughts. He would cling to her and bury his face in her luxuriant black hair. What if she had refused him? He would still be here and perhaps even be married to someone else by now. Hard to imagine . . .

"Hello, Grandpa. We're going to get the hay from Mr Wilkinson. I'm going to help my daddy put it on the dray. We've left all the ladies at home. They can't lift hay, can they?"

"No son, at least not as well as you and your dad. How are you, Charles? That boy will be taking over your job before you know it! Will you get the hay under cover before the rain?'

"Should do, Pa, it's just the one load. But we'd better get moving. I was dreaming. Doris and Fergus spotted you just now, but we'd have stopped in on our way back."

"A good horse never forgets her old master, do you, Doris? But I won't keep you, son. Give my love to the girls."

That night Nicole cried out to him. He thought it was a bad dream, but as he reached across to comfort her, he found she was bent double.

"The baby?"

"Yes – oh Charles, something is wrong. Would your mother come in the night?"

"I'll telephone her, I will not leave you." Feeling quite helpless, but deeply concerned, Charles called his mother.

"Go back to her, Charles. I will be there in a few minutes, dear." Victoria, too, was disturbed. The child was not due for several weeks yet. Could she deliver her own grandchild? Could she handle the complications her son's cherished wife must be suffering? As soon as she reached the homestead Victoria dispatched him in the car for Dr Anderson. Charles would be better fetching help, rather than a nuisance hovering about.

Nicole was in great pain. "I don't think he has turned, Maman. He will be born feet first. And quite soon, I fear."

"Calm yourself, my dear. If I must, I can deliver the child. But Dr Anderson will be here soon."

However, the baby was in a great hurry and it was Victoria who first held him in her arms. Nicole had been torn about and Victoria prayed for the doctor to arrive soon. Although small the infant had cried lustily enough, but his mother needed help.

There was a sound of wheels on the gravel. Charles dashed into the house and bounded up the stairs, followed at a more sedate pace by the older doctor. Charles did not notice his new son; he saw only his ashen-faced Nicole lying still in the bed.

"Mother, she's not …?"

"No, Charles, but she is not at all well. We must leave Dr Anderson to take care of her. Come with me. We must bathe your younger son and find him some clothes."

Reluctantly he followed his mother down the stairs and did everything she asked of him, but at the first step of the doctor on the stairs he rushed into the hall.

"Ssh, Charles, she is sleeping now. She has lost a lot of blood and is very weak."

"But Doctor, I can't even think it, let alone ask you …"

"She is a strong lass, Charles, and I am sure she will come through this. As for having any more children, that might be another story. I shall call again in the morning. Now, will you excuse me? My bed is calling." It was 3.30 a.m.

"I can't thank you enough, sir. If I were to lose her, I would have no will to live myself."

"Let me hear none of that talk, boy. You have three children to support now. Let me see that little lad before I go. Ah yes, small but he will be wiry. Keep you busy, that sort. Look at the trouble he's caused his mother already!"

"Good night, Doctor. I'll leave her asleep as long as she wishes." But he had to go and look at her. There was a tinge of colour in her cheeks already. He wanted to touch her, to kiss her, but did not want to risk waking her.

Victoria placed the baby in his cradle beside Nicole's bed, persuaded Charles to snatch some sleep in a spare room while all was quiet, and drove herself and the doctor home, exhausted. She might be 55, but there were still new experiences in life for her. Richard stirred as she slipped wearily into bed.

"Another little farmhand, dear," she murmured, and slept.

On Joseph's coming-of-age, in 1921, George had made him a partner in the family drapery business, just as his own father had done for him. George had celebrated his fifty-seventh birthday the same year, but he could not retire, for Joseph was not ready to take over the reins. Now, three years later, the boy was even more restless and George knew they must talk this over.

After dinner one evening he called Joseph into his study and broached the subject as casually as he could. Joseph revealed that he was not really sure what he wanted to do, but he was keen to travel abroad as a way to see what his future held.

"Have you any money for this travelling?"

"I have been saving for the past three years, Papa."

"And how long would you be away?"

"I don't know. Until I felt ready to settle down."

"That's a bit vague, isn't it? I can keep the shop going for a couple of years, but I'm not getting any younger, you know. If Edward were only here ..."

"Oh Pa, don't! Why don't you ask Bill to help? There would be room for us both and then you would know where he was, at least during the day. He *is* your son-in-law."

"More's the pity," muttered George. "But I thought you couldn't abide the man? You are right, though. For Sarah's sake I should take him on. A bit of responsibility might settle him down. I only hope it won't affect business."

"Can I book my passage then, Papa? I won't go until next year."

"Yes, I suppose so, if it is going to bring you down to earth in the end." George did not want his son to go, but it was not the same as Edward going to the War, he told himself. How hard it was to see himself as the head of the Hamilton family. He felt no older than Joseph in many ways, but he must seem ancient to the boy. He had never felt that yearning to travel, but Sam had, and Father had, too. He wondered who would be next.

Old Dr Macfarlane had often advised George to watch his weight. He had always been solidly built, and tall, too, and he knew he was overweight now. He so often forgot his age that it seldom occurred to him that he could suffer a heart attack at any time. He was sixty years old now and must heed the warning signs.

Following Joseph's suggestion, George approached his son-in-law and offered him a position in the family business. Bill accepted readily, although he knew next to nothing about the drapery business. Accustomed to selling books and stationery, he would need some training. George anticipated difficulties. Sarah's gratitude helped George to keep his patience when dealing with Bill. Teaching him the difference between chintz and crepe proved impossible and George soon resolved that Bill must be a store man before he could have contact with customers in the shop. Retirement was no closer, and the strain had actually increased.

It was no surprise to the family when George was found slumped over his desk one evening. Joseph had bounded into the study to show his father his ticket for the passage to London.

"I have got it, Papa. Pa? Oh no! Mother, Mother!" Rushing out he almost knocked her over. "I'll ring the doctor, Mother. It's Pa."

George was lucky. It was a mild attack, but a severe warning, as the doctor told him. He was exhausted, and he must have a complete rest – no worrying, no business – for at least a month.

Catherine telephoned Sam and Mary in Dunedin. Yes, of course, they would love to have George to stay. Rudi would not disturb him too much? Good, then they would expect him on the train tomorrow afternoon.

Persuading George to go was a formidable task, but Catherine was firm. She had no intention of becoming a widow yet if she had any say at all. *She* would take care of the business, with Joseph's assistance, of course. And between them they would handle Bill's training.

George was bundled on to the daily express, farewelled, and sent off to Dunedin. As he sat back, listening to the regular clack of the wheels on the rails, he thought back (how often he thought back now and how seldom ahead) to the time when his mother had made the same journey. It was when one of his children was born. It must have been Edward, for it was Sarah who needed to be cared for. Then it must be twenty-four years ago. Dear Mother – she had not wanted to leave Father, torn between two loves, two duties, but she had come, and then returned to find Father dying. Such an unselfish and giving person. It was hard to believe she had been gone for twenty years already. It was so much easier to let memories come flooding back than to plan ahead. He did not dare to think ahead in his business now, his instructions being to forget all about it. But he *was* anxious about having Bill there. Arriving at work smelling of spirits was a possibility, and if the customers found out, they would complain or, worse, go elsewhere. Poor Sarah, how had she let herself marry such a cad? That boy she had known before the War was worth ten of him. What was his name? Mark something. Jones? Wilson? Yes, that was it! He would have been a better husband.

He enjoyed his day of unaccustomed leisure. He couldn't remember when he had had time to muse about the family. It was good to see his brother Sam there to meet him at the station too. He would try to forget about all his worries while he was here with them.

It proved less difficult than George had imagined. Sam and Mary's, and thus Rudi's, world was oriented towards books, study, and discussion on the state of the world, rather than commerce. Young Rudi was fourteen now, a thoughtful, bespectacled boy, with a twinkle in his eye. He was now a pupil at his father's school, where his father was proud of his achievements.

Dunedin was not the place to be in winter, but sitting in front of a cheery log fire on a frosty night, talking with Sam and Mary, George barely noticed the weather. His month had passed quickly, and he felt stronger. He had done little in the month: a visit to Sam's school, where he had made a short speech to a group of senior students; accompanying Mary on a shopping expedition last week, just to prove to himself that he could climb the hill on the way home, but most of the time he had sat reading Sam's books or the "Daily Times", or just dozing in a comfortable armchair. Tomorrow evening he would be home again, ready, he hoped, to tackle the affairs of Hamilton&Son. Although he made resolutions not to work so hard, he knew that Catherine would soon be scolding him.

Joseph was at the station to meet him the next day. When he reached home, he found that Catherine had seen to it that he would *not* be overworked. She had hired an accountant. Shocked at first, George realised that it would be a relief to have that load taken from his shoulders. Now his evenings would be more leisurely with time to sit and talk with Catherine, and with Joseph until the boy left in a couple of months. He wanted their life to be more like Sam and Mary's. Catherine had been wise. Why had *he* not thought of that?

Nicole made such steady progress that the doctor decided not to send her to hospital. It was always such an upheaval in a household with small children, when their mother left them. Charles pampered her, and Victoria took over the house for a time. She felt like a queen. Her new son, John did not treat her as a queen, though. He was a demanding baby, always hungry, gulping from her and then suffering from colic. Nicole was glad she could devote time to him, without having to cook meals and care for the older children. Old Richard came to the homestead for his meals these days and Victoria went home with him in the evenings. Nicole tried to thank them both, but they were embarrassed by her gratitude. Richard muttered, "Our grandson . . . only one who can give us these now . . . have to look after yourself."

Victoria was more articulate. "You are our daughter now. You have no other parents and we have no other daughter. We love you as our own, dear, and we want to be of help to you."

"You are too good to me. Aren't they, Charles?" Charles could only nod. He had been deeply moved at how his parents had taken his foreign bride to their hearts, with never a murmur about marrying a girl from home.

Early in 1925 Joseph left for England, still unable to tell his father when he would return. George, however, was not concerned. He was content to work in the shop, with Bill doing the heavy work and the accountant seeing to the financial matters. He had built up the clientele, and he had always enjoyed the contact with customers. He knew he could never completely retire. He knew his limitations now, and lived within them. In the afternoons, while he dozed for an hour or so, Catherine attended to the shop. They would manage without Joseph, but would welcome him home when he returned.

CHAPTER 7

Travel Planning

Joseph's new life was exhilarating. He could remember how his grandmother used to tell stories about the Tower of London, Big Ben and Westminster Abbey. They had been only names to him, for he was just a little boy when she died. He had comfortable lodgings in Hammersmith, near the big stone arch. Nothing luxurious, but they kept the damp cold at bay. He knew no-one, but Charles had given him the names of some British soldiers, and if he felt lonely he would look one up. At present he was caught up in the richness of London's culture and history. He had been here for six months, and had scarcely spared a thought for home. He was lucky his parents had been understanding. They had never felt this *wanderlust,* but they recognised it as real in their son, something which could not be smothered. He knew they had not wanted him to leave, how precious he had become to them since the death of Edward. Yet they had agreed to his going for his peace of mind and happiness.

On a cool October afternoon Joseph sat in the bay window of his living room, planning to write to his mother and father. With winter imminent, he was visualising late spring in New Zealand. His mother's daffodils would be over by now, but that mauve cluster of flowers with the pleasant smell would be in full bloom. There were two bushes of it, one each side of the front gate at home. Not lavender ... no, it was lilac!

Surprised to catch himself reminiscing about home, Joseph put pen to paper, describing London in depth, recounting the shows and plays he had been to, and assuring his parents that all was well with him, as he hoped it was at home. In a postscript he added that he could almost smell the lilac as he wrote.

Catherine read the letter avidly, but the P.S. told her more than all the news. Waiting till George had read it too, she said, "You see, George, he is beginning to miss home."

"Now where did you find that in his letter, my dear? He's not one to say so, even if he were dreadfully lonely. It seems to me he is leading the life of a gay young bachelor, and good luck to him!"

"He will stay for the sake of his pride, and he probably doesn't realise the glow is wearing off, but I think he will be home before Christmas next year."

"I hope you are right, Catherine," said George wearily. "We could do with his help. Employing Bill might have helped Sarah, but it has done no good for our business."

"Oh George, do be patient! He's not a Hamilton, and he can't help that. Try to see some good in him. By the way, Sarah told me yesterday that she is expecting another child in June."

"Well, I hope it is not another set of twins. Those two have certainly kept her busy until now."

Catherine smiled. "I must remember to tell Joseph when I reply to his letter."

With the prospect of a lonely, cold Christmas looming through the persistent London fog, Joseph plucked up the courage to telephone one of the people on Charles's list. However, the friend had moved – gone to live in Scotland, the present owner thought. Sorry, no exact address, a little place called Lairg, he thought.

I must try the next one immediately, Joseph said to himself, or I'll never go back to the task again. Better luck this time. Yes, of course he remembered Charles Davis! How was he? Did he marry that pretty French nurse after all? Joseph was relieved. With someone like this he need only answer questions, and not have to say very much. He was shy, but an extrovert like this Henry Cahill put him at ease. Before he hung up, Joseph had been invited to spend Christmas with the Cahills. Henry warned, "It will be an early start – the kids hardly sleep that night!" It proved to be an unmissable experience.

A lively welcome awaited him as he stepped off the train at Coventry. Henry and three of the children, James, six years old, Frankie, four, and Joan, two, had come to meet him, as well as Stumpy, their Old English sheepdog. Joseph was glad he had only one bag, as there was little room to spare once all were in the car. The three children sat in the back, Stumpy in the open boot with the suitcase, and Joseph in the front with Henry. The children were shy at first, but by the time they had travelled the twenty miles to the farm, they were including Joseph in their chatter.

As they turned in through the imposing stone gateway, Joseph caught a glimpse of the name "Branlea" etched in wrought iron, one syllable on each of the open gates. The long driveway snaked through an avenue of bare trees and around to the front door, where Henry's wife, Jean, stood with the baby in her arms. Christened Elizabeth Mary only six months ago, she was already known to the family as Libby. A bundle of good nature, she put out her arms to Joseph, to the surprise of her mother and Joseph alike. The only babies he had held in his arms before this had been Sarah's twins, who had come willingly enough, but then he was no stranger to them.

It was Christmas Eve, the children were dispatched to bed and told to go straight to sleep or Santa would not come. The adults sat around the enormous log fire, sipping brandy and talking. Joseph was glad he didn't have to make idle conversation. He was contented after a good meal, warmed by the fire and the brandy, and rather sleepy, although the train journey had been neither long nor arduous. Musing on it, he decided it was the solving of the problem of where to spend Christmas that had brought on this lethargy.

With the knowledge that the morning would come very early, Henry got to his feet on the stroke of ten and suggested bed for all three. Jean and Joseph agreed readily.

It was a large house and Joseph's room was some distance from the children's bedrooms, but every corner echoed to the squeals of delight next morning, as parcels were discovered in crevices and behind doors. Henry, remembering his own staid upbringing, had set up a treasure hunt for their gifts, with clues to match the age of each child. When all the presents had been found, they were carried in triumph to Henry and Jean's room to be aired and approved. There was one gift for Joseph, to be unwrapped when he appeared. He passed Henry and Jean's room, and was called in to admire new clothes and toys. With these excited children clustering around him his one overriding thought was that it was children who gave Christmas its meaning.

Henry came to his rescue as he was in danger of crumbling under the weight of the children and their presents. Calling Joseph over to the bed, Henry handed him a small parcel.

"This is a small gift for you, to help you remember your stay with us. We want you to stay longer, of course, but this is the time for gifts."

"What is it, Joseph? Open it! Shall I help you?" volunteered the children, all at once.

"I think I can manage, thank you," replied Joseph, feeling dazed. It looked like a small book in shape, and he was curious to know what this friend of his cousin had chosen for him. He was deeply moved to find an ink sketch of Branlea, with the signature "J. Cahill" in the bottom right corner. It was obviously an original, and framed too. When he looked up from the picture to Jean, she smiled and said,

"I never tire of sketching it, from various angles. We always have one for guests if we think they would like to remember their stay. Henry had hoped your cousin Charles could have visited, but it was never possible."

"I will make sure that he sees this, Jean," said Joseph, with a lump in his throat. He was glad that he had brought something for this family who were treating him so kindly. He asked James to bring in the parcel on the hallstand. It was a large box of chocolates, bought when these people were merely names in his address book, and it seemed inadequate now, but Jean and Henry were delighted. He would send them individual presents when he returned to London.

In the days between Christmas and New Year Joseph spent time playing with the children. They taught him how to toboggan, using trays, slats and a sled, anything that was flat and smooth. It had snowed on Boxing Day, to everyone's great delight, and Joseph joined in their fun readily, never having seen such thick powdery snow. If it snowed in Christchurch it soon turned to slush, but this snow stayed fluffy like white marshmallows all day. How strange it must have been for his grandparents to go from this to a sunny, summer Christmas Day.

A snowball plopping against his jacket brought him back to the moment, and the fight was on. Little Joan took his side, while the boys bombarded them mercilessly. Joseph forgot he was twenty years older than these children, and kept up the barrage until everyone flopped down into the snow, exhausted. Frankie rolled over and set off down the hill, gaining momentum and snow as he went. Next went James, calling to Joseph to do the same. Carrying Joan halfway down the hill, he put her down, rolling over and over till he too reached the bottom. The boys were waiting for him, two cylinders of snow with heads and boots protruding. Amid much laughter they dusted themselves and each other off, before James trudged back up to carry his toddler sister down the hill. Near the bottom he gave in to her demands of "Me too!" and rolled her down the last few yards, to where Joseph was waiting to scoop her up. He could not remember when he had had so much fun.

It was not long after New Year when Joseph left Branlea. He would have liked to stay longer, and the Cahills urged him to do so, but he said he would return another time to see how the children had grown, to see the old house in a different season, and recount his own new experiences. So the farewells were exchanged and the trip made back to the station, this time with the whole family squeezed into the little car, and Libby on Joseph's knee.

"Now remember we are not far from London, and would love to see you any time," were Jean's last words as the train pulled away from the station. Henry's handshake had been warm, in spite of the bitter chill in the air. Joseph leaned back in his seat, enjoying the warmth of friendship as he thought of the Cahills most of the way to London.

At home on the floor in the entrance hall he found several letters, and immediately tore open the one from his mother. There was always the worry about his father, and he could never enjoy the letter until he read that both parents were well. At that point he refolded the letter, to be read later at leisure, and let himself into his rooms.

Catherine enjoyed writing to her son, especially when there were no sad tidings. The business was going well, or so the accountant assured her. George was still not happy with Bill, but had resigned himself to the fact that he would not change. In fact, his drinking was worse, and Sarah was showing the effects of living with two small children (and another due soon), as well as a husband who came home often in a querulous mood. If she questioned him he snapped back; if she did not, he complained that she ignored him. Catherine had no intention of burdening Joseph with this news. She just wrote, "Sarah is expecting another child in the new year, soon after the twins have their fourth birthday."

This reminded her to pass on the news of Charles and Nicole's new daughter also. They were calling the baby Marie, Nicole said, "after cousin Mary who has always been so kind to me". Catherine said that Nicole had been advised against more children after the premature birth of John two years ago, but she wanted a large family and this time there were no complications.

Catherine rambled on for several pages about the spring giving way to summer, about visits and visitors, family and friends, and Joseph read these details with real interest. Although there was still much he wanted to do and see, he resolved to plan his travels with a view to reaching home by next Christmas.

As the winter dragged on Joseph followed with some concern the newspaper articles dealing with the economic state of England. The threat of a General Strike was looming, and although the Government declared with quiet confidence that it was prepared for this eventuality, one could not help feeling uneasy. Joseph had not yet travelled to the north of England, but he knew that things there were not good. In a letter to his parents in March he tried to clear his own thoughts as well as informing them of the situation: "... 1926 promises to go down in the history books as one of upheaval. The Government has just released a report agreeing that conditions for the miners are poor, that their families should receive allowances, and that new ways of using coal need to be found, but the miners are not happy with this, they want the coal industry nationalised. Naturally enough they are not willing to accept a cut in wages – who would be? They cannot live on what they receive now, if their stories are to be believed. So it looks like trouble. They are looking to the other unions for support, and if they get it, there will be a serious strike."

Afraid that he might have alarmed them, he went on to say that he planned to cross to France at the beginning of summer, buy a bicycle, and see as much of Europe as he could. Henry Cahill had said his younger brother might be interested, and Joseph would be especially glad of his company, since Jack Cahill was a linguist. The situation in France was not much better, but there was no need to tell them that the franc was almost worthless, and that there were moves afoot to bring back Raymond Poincaré as the only one who could stabilise the franc. Anyway, Joseph would not be there long.

At the end of March Joseph returned to Branlea, where Henry introduced him to his brother Jack, a young man of twenty-four, taller than Joseph and with startling blue eyes under a mass of blond curls that fell down over his forehead as fast as he flicked them back. They took an instant liking to each other and before the evening was over they had their heads together over a map of Europe, planning their routes. Joseph was pleased to hear that Jack had visited Europe several times with fellow students during summer holidays, so was familiar with many places. Jack was well aware that Joseph was not accustomed to outdoor exercise, and hill climbs *he* found easy would tire him rapidly. By the time he returned to London four days later, Joseph was equipped with a list of requirements, the main one of which was a bicycle. He had decided to buy one in England to do some training. Their departure date was set for May 2nd. It was best to leave soon after the end of April, if this strike was to take place.

CHAPTER 8

Totara Ridge

As the service car departed, Vicki came running up the drive to the house with several letters in her left hand and one in her other hand.

"Look, Mamie," she said, "Look at the pretty stamp with that man's head on it. Where is the rest of him hiding?"

"That is a stamp from England. That man is King George V, but just a picture of him. He really lives in Buckingham Palace in London."

"That's where cousin Joseph is, Daddy says. Is this letter from him?"

"Let me see, chérie. Yes, it is. We will leave it for Daddy to open. It is the first time that we have heard from cousin Joseph since he is gone away."

When Charles came in for his midday meal, Nicole handed him the letter.

"Hmm, what would Joseph be writing to me about?"

'Well, open it and see, my love, we left it for you."

Charles read part of the letter to himself, and then called to his wife in the kitchen. "You remember Henry Cahill, Nicole? That fellow with the leg wound. Well, Joseph followed up the address I gave him and it seems they're firm friends. Listen to this!"

By now Nicole had brought the meals to the table and Richard had rounded up Vicki, John and Marie. Ignoring his meal, Charles read aloud: "I spent Christmas and New Year with your comrade Henry Cahill and his family, and am very glad you gave me his address. Christmas alone, and in the dead of winter, was too dreary a prospect, but with them I was absorbed into the family. Henry is such a jovial chap – not really my type, but we get along well nonetheless. He has a lovely wife, Jean, and four lively children."

Charles continued: "Did you meet Henry's younger brother, Jack? He's a couple of years younger than me, and we are planning a bicycle tour of Europe together for the summer. In fact, by the time this letter reaches you, we shall probably be struggling up some impossible incline, wondering why we did not plan a train trip instead."

Nicole interrupted, "Charles, your dinner will be cold! It is a very interesting letter, but perhaps later, non?"

"Of course, I am sorry. Such a rare treat to hear from someone so far away."

With an afternoon's work to do, but nothing so urgent that it could not wait a few minutes, Charles moved to an armchair and settled back to finish the letter after lunch. Nicole could read the rest once he had gone back to work. She would enjoy recalling the fun that had always surrounded Henry at the villa. He had played tricks on the nurses, told more jokes than anyone else, and seemed always to be cheerful, even though his wound had been a festering mess when he had been brought in. Having left before Charles, he had not known the outcome of the romance he had witnessed there.

It was a long letter. Joseph explained that he wrote letters so seldom that it was worth a proper effort when he did put pen to paper. England was in such a state at present, he added, that Charles might be interested to hear about it. It looked as though there would be complete anarchy before long. In less than two years there had been three general elections, but now Baldwin had brought some stability, with his rustic image of tweeds and soft hat … if you did not take too much notice of the miners' problems. With coal sales falling the owners had been forced to cut costs, so wages were being lowered and working hours lengthened, at the very time when the Miners' Federation was demanding a 30% wage increase and a 6-hour day. The largest union was not going to swallow that sort of pill, but they had backed down in 1921 when the other unions would not support them. In 1924 things had looked better once the French had got out of the Ruhr, but last year when competition threatened wages there was a further call for a general strike and this time both the Railways and Transport unions were in support. Baldwin had stalled them by fixing wages till the end of April 1926. And *that*, added Joseph, was now only a month away. Now the Government was sitting tight, stockpiling food and enlisting volunteers for distribution and transport, should the strike eventuate.

Charles was greatly interested in this letter as it provided the background to the newspaper headlines carried in The Press several weeks ago, proclaiming the general strike. It was good to have this unofficial view from someone on the spot. It helped to explain the recent article stating that when the cost of the strike had been counted after those nine chaotic days, the supporting unions were one and a half million pounds in debt, while Britain had lost one hundred and fifty million pounds in exports. Worst of all, the miners had had to face the fact that the coal industry was dying and that they must accept longer hours with less pay. If that were to happen in New Zealand the country would be ruined, Charles thought.

The remainder of the letter was about France, which Joseph said he had not yet visited, but there the political situation seemed to be even more disorganised. Two years ago Poincaré had been ousted and with him had gone the stability of the franc. From seventy to the pound it had sunk to the depths of two hundred and fifty before Poincaré had been called back to revalue and settle it. It would be interesting to see what their pounds would fetch on the French market. Joseph and Jack planned to take the paquebot to France on May 2nd, if the English ports were not strike-bound by then.

Charles finished the letter and thought back to the date the strike had actually broken out. Perhaps Joseph had been stranded in London? No, the strike was on May 3rd, was it not? He thought about the letter off and on throughout the afternoon. Strange that his young cousin should write to him in that way. Probably thought he should write about the Cahills – good that he had located old Henry, too – and then just passed on local news. Joseph would have known they would be interested in the French part of the story, and it seemed the French and English situations were connected. A pity there was no return address, even though he was no correspondent. Aunt Catherine would know it.

While life was difficult in England and France, it was no bed of roses in New Zealand either. However, for the Davises, and others who had kept their farms at a time when many had sold, some of the rough edges were being whittled away.

When they took over the farm at Totara Ridge the emphasis had been on sheep and crop, with only two cows for domestic use. But Charles had foreseen, along with many others that dairy products would be more lucrative for the farmer, and now he was running a herd of fifty cattle. This meant milking twice a day, but he had installed a new milking machine last year. It was petrol driven and he used almost as much energy to crank it into life as he did to milk the cows by hand. Still he was pleased with it and he saw the day when all the cows could be milked by machine, six or eight at a time, rather than just one. He had to remain nearby to check when the milk had stopped flowing. Touching the cup to his cheek, he knew that if the cup was warm the cow was still giving milk, if cold she had stopped.

Charles liked to think of himself as a modern man. He had welcomed the first herd-testing programmes and had joined those farmers who were top dressing their land with the new fertilisers to improve the quality of the soil. Better grass and crops meant better sheep and cattle, bringing higher prices at stock sales.

Nicole had been delighted at the advent of electricity to the farm. How much safer those globes were than the spirit lamps and candles, so easily tipped over by the children. She had heard from Sarah that there were soon to be electric ovens, but the thought made her nervous. She liked the coal range in the kitchen, and could not imagine how electricity could cook food.

Last year they had bought a car, which the children loved. Richard had at first asked where the horses were, but the others were too little to remember when all vehicles were horse drawn. On their first drive in the car Vicki had squealed with delight as they whizzed along at fifteen miles per hour. John's eyes were popping out and Richard held his mother's hand tightly. Nicole recalled her arrival at Totara Ridge, when Charles had driven her there in his father's car. Then, her nervousness had not been caused by the motor car, but now she felt uncomfortable. They had left Marie with her grandparents, and Nicole hoped that the children would continue to sit still. She tried not to imagine one of them falling through the gap between canopy and door. It was a beautiful car, but she would be relieved to arrive home safely.

She had to laugh at herself now, a year later, for she was learning how to drive. Charles was enthusiastic but still it was difficult for Nicole to imagine herself driving into town to visit Sarah or Aunt Catherine, or to go shopping. However she would not always be able to rely on her mother-in-law. Dear Mama would soon want to be the passenger. At 58 she was still an active person, but no doubt she would slow as time went on.

Richard and Victoria paid their regular Friday visit to Charles and Nicole that evening. They came each week for the evening meal, to enjoy time with their grandchildren. Then, after dinner, when the dishes were done and the children off to bed, the adults had a leisurely chat.

It was at this time that Charles brought out Joseph's letter. Victoria was also surprised that Joseph would write in this way to him. They had never been particularly close friends, probably because of the thirteen-year gap between them, but she was shrewd enough to see that it meant one of two things: either Joseph was so concerned about the situation in England that he felt he could not draw a true picture of it for his parents, and he had intended writing to Charles at just this time anyway, or it meant that the boy was homesick and needed someone familiar to talk to. In the latter case, Catherine would be delighted to know about the letter; in the former, the less said the better. Charles decided not to ask his aunt for Joseph's forwarding address.

Poor Catherine had enough to worry her at present, Victoria added. With Bill and Sarah's new daughter not more than a month old and the twins barely four, Catherine had telephoned just this morning to say that Bill had thrown in everything, all his responsibilities, and left them all. Sarah had no idea where he was, but she was sure he would not be back.

Nicole was aghast. Imagine trying to bring up three little children with no father! She would never manage without the love and support of her Charles, she exclaimed.

'But," Victoria pointed out , "Sarah had neither love nor support anyway. She is better rid of him, and George will see that she wants for nothing."

At ten o'clock Richard stood up to go home. A creature of habit, he had always risen early and retired early to bed. Victoria knew this was his limit and acceded silently. As they departed Nicole embraced Charles.

The only time they were to hear of Bill Houghton again was to read in the newspaper, some six months later, of his untimely death.

George and Catherine had invited Sarah and her children to live with them in the family home, but Sarah had preferred to stay on in the home she and Bill had shared. It was not through sentimentality. The past year, in particular, had hardened her, and she was glad it was all over. She had been a fool to think she could exert any influence over Bill, and her only sense of failure was in having married him at all. More and more frequently in these past six years she had thought of Mark and how different their life together would have been. Why on earth had she let herself think she had fallen for Bill? Like Emily, she had really died with her soldier. The rest had all been sham, and she admired her cousin's courage in doing what she believed was the only right thing.

She would never voice this thought, however, for Emily's death had broken her parents' hearts. Sarah couldn't have done that to her parents. Perhaps that was why I never thought about it, she pondered. Her desire to stay in the house she and Bill had bought was partly a wish for independence and partly because this was the home her children knew. No sense in creating more upheaval than necessary in their young lives. Besides, Mother spoilt the twins and they should not be given the chance to wheedle and cajole things from her too often. If Father was willing to help them financially this would be enough. She did not want to be obliged to work, especially at a time when too many men could not find a job, and the thought of leaving her children all day upset her. She would accept an allowance from her father, who, she knew, was glad to be rid of her shiftless husband from his shop. His sympathy was directed towards his daughter and her family.

George's quandary now, in the middle of 1926, was what sort of person to employ in Bill's place, having no clue of when Joseph planned to return home. Should he hire a permanent hand, which would give him a better quality of applicant, or take on a young man who could shoulder merchandise but had little brain? Catherine was adamant that that their son would reappear by the end of the year, but this was only intuition and he could not put any real trust in it. He decided, after much deliberation, to look for a lad who wanted temporary work, but who looked promising enough to stay on another year if Joseph did not come home for Christmas.

Mary, like Nicole, was shocked to hear that her niece Sarah now had the task of raising her three children single-handed. Nicole's letter made the husband appear a real layabout – a lazy, uncouth, drunken cad, she had called him. Nicole had certainly increased her vocabulary in the past few years, she thought with a chuckle. Sam and Mary had rarely met Bill, apart from at the wedding and on a few other family occasions since. They had found it hard to see how Sarah, such a gentle, good-natured girl, could have loved him. So here she was, at 33, with quite a burden to carry. At that age, Mary recalled, she and Sam were rejoicing in the birth of Rudolph, which cemented their love, while in Sarah and Bill's case the new baby was the last straw.

The thought of Rudolph brought a soft smile to Mary's face. The boy had always given them much pleasure. He was intelligent enough to see how much their love focussed on him. He had told her when he was about seven years old that he would like a brother or sister, but even then he had understood the look of sadness on her face, and he had never mentioned the subject again. His parents had encouraged him to bring friends home to play, or to stay overnight, and these days they often had several young men in the house.

Rudolph was still at school and, at sixteen, was now a senior student, with every chance of being dux of the school this year. Sam would be proud to see his son's name on the honours board in the main foyer as he entered each morning. If Rudi returned to school next year, as he certainly would, he would probably double the honour.

"He's a far better pupil than I ever was at school!" stated Sam. Mary had heard many of the hair-raising tales of Sam's schooldays from Henrietta just before they were married, and had hoped that any children she might have would inherit the steadier temperament of the Daniells family. Perhaps Sam was such a good teacher because he understood those less willing pupils better than others did? He certainly seemed to have great patience with the troublesome boys and, although he was now Master of Discipline, he rarely used corporal punishment. When he did, he felt he had failed.

Mary felt that life had been kind to her. There had been disappointments, of course, like not having more children after Rudi, but still she considered herself fortunate. She had married a man she loved deeply, and he still complimented her on her fine figure and her beautiful hair, in spite of the strands of grey appearing among the amber. Sam still loved to sit with her on the settee before the fire, taking the pins out of her hair and running his fingers slowly through her long curls. She sometimes wondered if it would suit her better short, but how could she deprive him of this pleasurable pastime?

The telephone jerked her out of her reverie. She stood up to answer it, and Nicole's letter fell from her lap. It was her father, telling her that her mother had just passed away peacefully. They had been waiting for months for this to happen. She had been in constant pain for almost a year, and the most they could hope for was that she would die in her sleep. Still it was a shock, and she knew poor Father was dazed. Putting on her coat and leaving a note on the table for Sam and Rudi, she drove to her father's home. At 76 he could not live alone. She would invite him to come and live with them. They had a spare bedroom downstairs, and she would enjoy his company through the day. Although involved in various charitable organisations, Mary found that time hung heavily sometimes. She was too reserved to have a large circle of her own friends, although she and Sam mixed with his colleagues frequently.

Mr. Daniells welcomed his daughter warmly, and Mary felt sorry for him. Her parents had done everything together, especially since Mary, their only child, had married, and he looked lost in the house by himself. He had wondered what would happen to him when Mother died, and had hoped Mary would take him into her home, so he was relieved when she proposed it. He put up some resistance, but both knew it was the best arrangement for him. In less than an hour they had placed everything he needed in the car, and were back at Mary and Sam's. Mary would return after the funeral to clear the rest of the house. It seemed wrong to take her mother's things from the house before she was even in her grave.

CHAPTER 9

En Route

Jack Cahill and Joseph Hamilton crossed on the ferry from Dover to Calais on May 2nd, beating the strike by only one day, and headed for Paris. Jack had insisted, "We must start and finish in Paris." He had not elaborated and Joseph had not asked questions.

They had worked out their cycling itinerary together before leaving London, but it was Jack who knew what they could achieve in ten weeks. He had drawn a rough circle on their map to represent the limits at which they must consider turning back. Joseph had an idea of some of the things he wanted to do and see, and most of them fell within the circle Jack had drawn. Visiting Greece and Turkey would have to be sacrificed for now. They aimed for about eighty miles per day, but the first few days would give them a better indication than any theoretical calculations.

Paris enthralled Joseph. Totally different from any place he had seen, and definitely unlike Britain, it had so much of its own character that he was caught up in its rhythm, and he could understand why it was called "The City of Light". They cycled the maze of paths through the Bois de Boulogne, rode on cobbled streets, along the Champs Elysées, around the Place de l'Etoile with so many avenues to choose, over the Pont Neuf and along to the Champs de Mars.

"Now," said Jack, "we continue *à pied*. First we lock our bicycles together and pass the chain around the lamppost, and then it's up the Eiffel Tower." Joseph knew "à pied" from his schoolboy French and he assisted with securing the cycles. With Jack as his able guide, providing details of the tower's construction from 1887 to 1889, they had soon attracted several followers, glad of an English commentary. "Monsieur Eiffel," he said, "had to fight opposition from large numbers of influential people, who thought his precious tower would be a blot on the horizon because it was made of material used for railway tracks." The view from the top was superb, and Jack pointed out the landmarks they would visit soon. "Away there on the rise is the Sacré Coeur basilica. It is quite new, built not long before the War, and definitely worth a visit. We'll take the Métro to get there. But we'll walk to see the Arc de Triomphe up close, with its Tomb of the Unknown Soldier, as well as the Louvre and Notre Dame cathedral. We probably won't see them all today, so we will start this side of the river, with the Invalides, where they buried Napoleon, and the Sorbonne University, and then we'll cross to the island to visit Notre Dame. Magnificent architecture, especially when you think of it being built in the twelfth century."

Joseph had learnt at school that the fleet of Maori canoes had reached New Zealand in 1350. It was hard to envisage men of that era constructing such elegant, lasting monuments of stone and mortar. Jack broke into his thoughts, "After that we'd better find ourselves lodgings for the night. We can't camp in the city."

After retrieving their bicycles and finding a modest place to stay, they retired early. Joseph was tired, sinking into the large bed provided for them both at the boarding house. Jack inspected the bed and announced triumphantly, "*Pas de puces*! No fleas!" before flopping into it. Joseph had not shared a bed since he and Edward were small boys, and he expected to be wakened every time Jack moved, but he was too weary even to notice Jack's snoring. Jack had said nothing about the nightlife of the city, apart from mentioning visiting Pigalle and the Moulin Rouge on their return to Paris. Joseph lay awake for a while, thinking how the nightspots would be a fitting finale to their months of camaraderie and hard work together before they parted in England. Jack's research could not wait for ever, he mused, as sleep overtook him.

In the morning, after a bowl of coffee and two brioches each, they were on their way, having been granted permission to leave their bicycles behind the *pension* for the day. Jack's plan was to see as many of the landmarks as possible by about two o'clock, return for the cycles, and be clear of Paris before having to find a campsite for the night.

Joseph found the pace exhausting, and his head was swimming with the stories Jack told. But it was all so interesting. The old crones sitting knitting while the guillotine did its horrible work during the Revolution; the Obelisk of Luxor, brought from Egypt, and the other one, made from melted-down cannons won from the Austrians by Napoleon. This was history alive! He had never really enjoyed History at school; it had seemed pointless to keep delving into things that had happened hundreds of years ago, but here you could see the results of those deeds, in the monuments, and in the people too. He wished that he had been more attentive at school.

They had hoped to reach Italy by the end of May. Since leaving Paris they had ridden over the Pyrenees into Spain, on to Madrid and Granada then followed the ruggedly beautiful east coast back into France near Perpignan. Now, at the end of the month, they were only two days behind their schedule. Jack had had a puncture near Nîmes, causing a delay of half a day. This gave Joseph a chance to visit the Roman arena, the oldest building he had ever seen, and in such marvellous condition for 2000 years. How *could* men so long ago have known exactly how to cut stone so that it made rounded arches, with no mortar to hold them in place? Each block of stone had been angled just enough to keep it steady. Jack told him about the Pont du Gard aqueduct, built at about the same time and still standing, near Nîmes, but they had to resist the temptation to make side trips or they would never finish their tour.

A month later they had been to Rome, where Joseph stood agape at the ruins, and back north through Bologna, with its wonderful colonnades, the busy canals of Venice, and then west towards Switzerland. The pristine grandeur of the scenery made up for the hard slog of the hill climbs, but each time they made a decision to stay in the circle drawn on their map, Joseph realised how much more there was in Europe that would have to wait for another time. In Germany it was Joseph's turn for a puncture, giving time for a look at the town of Mannheim, with its pink-tinged stone buildings in the town square.

On June 30th, having followed the Rhine valley, they crossed the border into Holland, with the relief of knowing there would be few hills for several days. They were still behind their schedule, but now felt they were on the downhill road to Paris and the ferry back to England. Neither man wanted to forgo the night in Paris, which Jack had mentioned again just before their steepest climb, in the Swiss Alps. It had kept them going when they were tempted to give up; when the rain had driven in their faces and dripped down their necks; when they had had to walk up longer climbs; when the sun had been as merciless as the rain and wind.

In a week they saw parts of Holland, which Joseph would remember for its magnificent windmills, wonderful flat roads, and threatening sea water. Belgium seemed more formal, with the ancient castles of Ghent and Bruges forming the nucleus of growing towns. He would remember churches, canals and bumpy cobbled streets. They paused to read the plaque at the monument where Napoleon was vanquished at Waterloo – what a waste of so many lives! – before Jack insisted on a detour to pass through the tiny country of Luxembourg. Here dignified buildings and a huge retaining wall gave a glimpse of a world in miniature. It reminded Joseph of Andorra, in the Pyrenees. They had pressed on, at Joseph's request, to Verdun, in the north-east of France, where Joseph located the grave of Frank Williams, his cousin Emily's husband, whose death had led to Emily's also. He found the name of his brother Edward, too. His young body had been blown to bits in 1916, not far from Verdun. Although it gave him no joy to see either, he would be glad to tell his mother and Aunt Catherine that he had taken the trouble. He photographed both names, as a tangible memento for them. It was hard to believe that was his own brother's name on the wall, along with so many others of the same age, in the long building they called the "ossuary". The word made him shudder; he had learnt enough Latin to know it came from the word for bones. Joseph turned hurriedly away, to rejoin Jack, who had waited outside. This was no time for joviality, and he respected Joseph's unspoken wish for silence as they rode about, steeping themselves in the all-too-recent history of this depressing place.

Joseph would have ridden all night to get away, to reach Paris and gaiety again, but Jack called a halt at Epernay, which meant fifty or sixty miles the next day.

"Two such different experiences in one day, old chap, too much! You'd crack up. Tomorrow will be soon enough for Paris."

"You're right. It's hard to picture your only brother in there. He was only nineteen, you know. So keen to go – I used to envy him and wish I was old enough."

"Could just as well have been *my* brother who didn't come back. Henry always was a madcap fool, into everything, with me tagging along."

This was their last night of camping together, and both men felt the closeness to each other that imminent parting brings. Tomorrow Paris, and then they would take their trusty bicycles on the train to Calais to board the ferry the following day. Joseph's experience today had created a bond between them too. It would be hard to imagine living alone again. As if reading his thoughts, Jack asked, "What will you do when we get back?"

"Now that I am so fit, and while it is still summer, I think I'll take the bike and have a look at Britain, if you'll sell me your half of the tent."

"Sell it? Great Scott, man, what would I want with it? It's yours! I have all sorts of friends you can visit if you care to. But you'll have to wait till we get home – I left my address book at Henry's."

Joseph had given up his lodgings in London before he left for Europe. There was no sense in paying three months' rent just to store his luggage. He had left his few possessions with the Cahills, and Jean had insisted that they both return to Branlea when they reached English shores.

They arrived in Paris from the north-east next afternoon, found the same "pension" and booked the same room. This time Joseph didn't want to walk during the day, saving his energy for the evening, so they went by Métro to see the Sacré Coeur. From the alleys of Montmartre they had to climb the hill behind the basilica, and later descend hundreds of steps in front of it, but it was worth the effort. Joseph had never seen the Taj Mahal, but he was reminded of the pictures he had seen as he stood before this gem of architecture. The Sacré Coeur's lines were so smooth and its stone still so white. He liked the Gothic buildings too, but to him they lacked the ebullience and warmth of this amazing building.

That evening Jack and Joseph ate in a restaurant in the Place du Tertre at the top of the steps, down a narrow cobbled street to the left of the basilica and Jack ordered all the French delicacies they must taste before they left France. After all, tomorrow night they would be at Henry and Jean's. Joseph duly ate onion soup, escargots and frogs' legs, along with an endless succession of more recognisable foods, until he gave up counting the courses, loosened his belt and looked appealingly at Jack. "Only coffee, cheese and fruit to come," Jack said.

It was dark by the time they emerged and clattered down all the steps of the Butte to the streets of Montmartre. Jack led the way as usual. Joseph had been the follower on this whole trip. Without Jack he would have missed many of the less obvious sights, and he would never have had the courage to stroll into the theatre, with "Folies Bergère" in huge letters over the entrance, as they were doing now.

This was another world for Joseph. As the show went on and the women appeared more scantily dressed, with plumes and sequins replacing clothes, he realised what a sheltered life he had led. He had never even seen his sister wearing as little as this! He dared not look at Jack, afraid to give away his naivety and terror. Some of the women went into the audience and sat on men's laps. Joseph dreaded that one of these creatures might come and sit on his lap. At the interval Jack, jumping to his feet, said,

"If we hurry we'll be just in time for the can-can at the Moulin Rouge. Come on!"

Only too happy to comply, and estimating that whatever the can-can was it could not be much more revealing than the Folies Bergère, Joseph hurried out behind him. It was not far to the Moulin Rouge and before long they were watching a respectably-clad group of young ladies doing a happy dance. He began to relax. Suddenly the tempo of the music increased, up shot the dancers' legs to reveal layer upon layer of frilly petticoats, even garters, and undergarments! The next moment one of the dancers cartwheeled about the stage while the others picked up their skirts and swirled them around to the beat of the music. Joseph looked about him. Everyone else was enraptured, clapping and calling out encouragement to the girls. He was stunned, but he could feel a change taking place in him. In his head a voice was saying, "This is what you returned to Paris for, so don't be such a prude! You'll never see this in Christchurch and no-one but Jack knows you here. Enjoy it with everyone!" Before he knew it both he and Jack had dancers on their laps, stroking their hair and kissing their cheeks. Joseph shot a glance at Jack, but he was too occupied to acknowledge it. Soon the frilly skirts and tantalising perfume were gone, and Joseph now found himself following *his* dancer with greater interest. It was really remarkable what those girls could do – they were acrobats as well as dancers, and very pretty too!

When the show was over the two men walked back to their pension. They had drunk a good measure of wine each and the cool breeze was a shock. By the time they reached their room it had sobered them up enough to know that they would sleep without their heads spinning one way and their stomachs the other.

"Well Joseph, was the evening a success, lad? You had me worried early on – I thought you were going to dash for the door!" remarked Jack.

"I can't hide much from you, Jack. Yes, I wondered what I had struck at that first show – didn't know where to look – but it grows on you, with the help of the wine. I could have stayed longer!"

"I thought of going round to the stage door afterwards to see those two girls, but you can't really bring them back to a place like this, can you?"

"Bring them back? What do you mean? Have girls in our room?'

Jack just laughed. "You've learnt a lot tonight, but you still have a long way to go, my boy. You're not exactly a man of the world, are you?"

Joseph was hurt at the Jack's tone of derision. They had never quarrelled in all their eleven weeks together, and he would not start an argument now, so he forced a laugh and just said, "No, I'm not."

"Sorry, Joseph. We're so different. I think that's exactly why we get along so well. You are unspoilt, I like you that way."

They shook hands before undressing and falling into bed. It would be hard to go their separate ways after Branlea. Joseph fell asleep immediately, dreaming of big flamingos that fluttered just out of his reach. He caught one, which turned out to be the girl who had sat on his lap, but she slithered out of his grasp and began to pluck her feathers out until she stood clad in only a sequined triangle cloth across her thighs.

"Hey, hey, what's the matter, Joseph? You're thrashing about all over the bed, man!" Joseph muttered something about not being able to catch her, whereupon Jack chuckled and they both fell asleep again.

The next morning was overcast for their cycle ride to the station, and they saw little from the train windows with rain trickling down them. A fitting farewell from Paris and they both felt a little sad. There was not much to say, even Jack silent much of the way to Calais. A choppy crossing on the ferry added to the feelings of anticlimax.

Once at Dover, however, their spirits lifted. For Jack England meant home, always great to get back safely, no matter how wonderful the holiday. His natural ebullience reasserted itself, so he soon cheered Joseph up. It was inevitable that all things must end, and they had stored up unforgettable memories.

After a train ride to Coventry they climbed back onto their trusty bicycles for the two-hour ride to Branlea, but such was their enthusiasm they arrived in an hour and a half. Their postcard a few days ago had said just "Friday" for arrival and the children had been waiting since morning for them. What a welcome! It was as if they had been gone a year, with the children clambering all over both the men and the bicycles.

The noise brought Jean to the door, wiping her hands on her apron. Her face lit up with pleasure. Henry would be in soon and they would celebrate the return of the prodigals. It *was* good to be back among friends, thought Joseph. It was time to enjoy the present and reminisce this evening about the past.

Over a tankard of brown ale they recounted some of the highlights of their travels. Henry and Jean were fascinated to hear about the places they had visited and, after dinner, they talked on well into the night.

Joseph would stay a few days but tomorrow his friend must return to Oxford, to apply himself again to the research he was conducting for his botany degree.

As he packed up his things next morning Jack handed several items to Joseph, including the tent. "No use to me now and it's half yours anyway. You won't know where you are with all that room to yourself. There's only one condition to your having this tent."

"And what would that be?"

"You must call on me on your way back to London."

"Did you think I wouldn't? It will be another farewell though, Jack, because I want to be on the boat for home by the end of August. It will be hard to leave all of you, knowing it's for the last time."

"Not as final as your brother's departure. Don't be morbid, Joseph. Who knows? I may look you up in your shop in Christchurch some day. If you can make the trip here then I can do the same to New Zealand."

This was good news for it left open the chance that they might meet again. There was nothing sweet about the sorrow of parting from a friend for ever, but the faintest chance of a reunion added a dusting of sweetener.

After Jack had left, Joseph realised how tired he was, and he lay about for days in the sun, sleeping if he was alone even for a few minutes. It was almost a week before he could romp with the children and swim with them in the stream. Libby was tottering about now and loved the water, no swimming without her. Jean came with them too, as three of the children could not swim. Frankie had been learning to swim at school, but it was holidays now and he still had to be watched. Joan, now three, was not so sure about cold water on her warm legs and hung back, until she saw what fun the others were having.

Later Joseph went out on the farm with Henry and his workers. In another month they would be busy harvesting, but there was always plenty to do while the weather was good. They were working on fences today. Many were dry stone walls or hedgerows but Henry used wooden fences in places and these needed repairs. Joseph enjoyed the work and the camaraderie. He could have stayed on at Branlea. It was always difficult to tear himself away from this family, but he wanted to explore at least some of the UK before heading home.

His plans were vague. He would simply head north for half of the time he had left, then turn and make the journey to London by different roads, detouring only twice: once to bid the Cahills adieu, and again for a night with Jack.

Before setting out he settled everything for the voyage home at the travel office in Coventry. Then he headed north on August 3rd. His sailing date was August 31st, which gave him just under four weeks. He would follow the map northwards until August 14th or 15th, and then, wherever he was, he would turn back and make his way south to arrive at Branlea on the 28th, spend the 29th with Jack and arrive in London on the 30th. He would give his bicycle to the Cahills – the older children would reach the pedals soon – and collect his trunk, before continuing by train.

His pace was slower without Jack to spur him on, but he still averaged fifty miles a day, and thus was able to reach the Highlands (he even found himself in Lairg, but had lost the name of the man he had tried to contact), before turning south. He had really had enough, and his heart was not in this trip, but he still enjoyed the beauty of the lochs, glens and heather clad hills. The lochs were at their best, he was sure, and at many of the beauty spots he met groups of tourists exclaiming with delight, but he was beginning to think of home now, especially at night as he lay alone in the tent. He wanted to belong somewhere. The Cahills had made him feel at home, and without them his time in England would have been barren, but he did not belong with them. His place was back in his father's shop, so that his father could enjoy a well-earned rest, and at 26 he should be doing something useful. He would never regret the decision to travel, giving him a chance to stand back, look at himself and his life, put them in perspective, and enjoy many different experiences. There might be no value in this for his business life – he had not noticed what European ladies were wearing as he travelled – but he knew it had enriched him as a person. He was sure his parents would see that he had matured. By arriving in early December he would be in time to help with the rush before Christmas.

Joseph returned to Branlea on August 27th, and rearranged his luggage there. The tent, the bicycle, the pots and pans were for Jack's family, and he planned to send them a gift from New Zealand, to say thank you for their kindness.

He was glad when it was time to leave, with everyone becoming a bit tongue-tied. It would be the same with Jack, he knew. One night in Oxford and he would take the early train into London, check his trunk onto the boat, and do some shopping for his family – small gifts for Mother and Father, Sarah and the children.

It was a long time since he had had any news from home, possibly before he left for Europe. He had not given them an address and his return date to England had been indefinite too. They would wonder at his silence from now. Perhaps he should post a letter just before catching the boat? He need not put a return address on it. Pleased with this idea he bustled through the next two days. It was on board the boat it dawned on him that he was actually heading home.

He had seen Jack, he had written and posted his short letter home, and now there was a telegram under his cabin door. His heart skipped a beat.

"GOD SPEED AND GOOD LUCK.

YOUR FRIENDS ALWAYS.

THE CAHILLS."

PART III

SAM AND RUDOLPH

1926-1968

A NEW GENERATION

CHAPTER 1

New Beginnings

Catherine smiled as she sat in the sun, darning Joseph's socks. Compared with what he had brought home with him, these were almost new. As her needle wove in and out her thoughts went back to his arrival. She had never credited herself with a sixth sense, but she was convinced on that December day six months ago she would see her son walk up the path. She had said nothing to George, not wishing to raise his hopes on such a lack of evidence, but she smiled knowingly when Joseph appeared as she was taking a cup of tea to George on the verandah.

George, at 63, had aged in the two years that Joseph had been away. In fact the doctor was convinced he had had a mild stroke, which had left him weak down the left side. He had refused to leave the shop, but was persuaded to hire a young lady to assist him. Having told Joseph he could manage until he returned, then that's what he would do. How his face had lit up when Joseph, more confident and mature now, strode up the steps and clasped his father's hand firmly. Catherine, still mobile for her 66 years, had slipped inside and filled the waiting cup, emerging into the sunlight in time to hear Joseph saying, "Now where did that mother of mine go?"

It had been a great relief to them both to have him home. Within days George had had a document drawn up, altering the name of the business to "J.D. Hamilton Ltd." This was his way of saying so many things: "Welcome home"; "Now I can retire and rest"; "I have complete faith in you" and other things that did not need to be voiced. Catherine, too, was happy to see her son safely home. His youth and strength were an advantage, not only in the business but also at home. There were small but heavy or skilled jobs that George could no longer do and it was frustrating to have to call in a tradesman for the want of an able-bodied son.

Joseph rejoiced in the glow of contentment that permeated the house. He would never exclude his father from the shop, but he knew George's appearances would be increasingly rare. The old chair on the verandah was a favourite spot where, even in winter, he could be found when his advice was wanted.

It was easy to settle back into a routine, albeit a different routine. There were times when he would think, "Did I ever really meet Jack and the Cahill family? Did we really cycle around Europe for over two months?" Recalling incidents or mishaps would soon remind him of the reality. But there was little time for reminiscing, since he had planned his arrival to manage the big increase in business at Christmas. Joseph was glad his father had hired two young assistants. He didn't know how much his mother had influenced this.

The young woman, Frances Brown, was very efficient. Tall and slender, she had an air of elegance which gave customers confidence when she advised them on a fabric or a style of garment. Always well dressed, she admitted readily that she made most of her own clothes, seeing no point in paying someone to do something she enjoyed, just for the sake of wearing a certain label, which could not be seen anyway. Part of her elegance came from her ability to choose clothes which complemented the unusual colour of her hair. Joseph had never seen hair of that colour before. Not like Aunt Mary's rich copper colour, Miss Brown's hair defied any adjective, being somewhere between gold and auburn, thick and wavy, and toning with her freckles. Her horn-rimmed spectacles added a primness to her pretty face. An intelligent young lady, she worked well on her own initiative, but appreciated Joseph's occasional words of praise.

George had also hired a new storeman while Joseph was away, a man called Donald Watson. Two years younger than Joseph, he was a giant of a man, good-natured and strong, but with a gentle manner. He was able to lift anything in the storeroom, and could help in the shop at busy times, which made him doubly useful. Joseph warmed to this young man, appreciating that beneath his joviality lay a sincerity and seriousness. In the year he had been at Hamilton's Donald had gradually formed an attachment to Miss Brown, but he had never dared tell her how he felt, for he was a humble man who thought her too good for him.

They were busy days before Christmas, as always. In the shop Catherine lent a hand, as did George from time to time. Miss Brown soothed impatient customers, then sent them away satisfied with their purchases and feeling the waiting had been worthwhile. Donald lifted and shifted new bolts of material on request, helped arrange displays in the shop, and admired Miss Brown from a distance.

Catherine decided Christmas this year must be celebrated at their home, because Joseph had not yet had an opportunity to see all the family since his return. She wrote to Sam and Mary and was delighted that they and Rudolph would come for a few days. Victoria replied to her invitation that she would come for the day with Charles, Nicole and the four little ones. Sarah and her three children would also come for the day, so it would be quite a reunion. Along with helping in the shop Catherine prepared for this gathering of about twenty people.

Christmas for the Hamiltons had always been a time for a big family celebration. Not deeply religious, they still liked the children to understand that it was more than Father Christmas and presents, and so each year they set up a large nativity scene in the corner of the main room. This was an integral part of the occasion for the children, each of whom brought their dolls and toys to be a part of the tableau. Selecting one to be Baby Jesus was always difficult, with someone having to remember whose doll had had the honour the previous year, but everything seemed to work out. Charles brought the hay, and Catherine unpacked the traditional donkey, several sheep and an ox from their wrappings, the same ones each year since she had joined the Hamilton family, and they all enjoyed watching the scene take shape. Only when it was finished and admired attention shifted to the tall Christmas tree in another corner of the long room. Underneath it a great pile of parcels was added to as each family arrived, and some of the smaller gifts sat in the forks of the branches. It was a dazzling sight, which the children had to enjoy untouched through dinner, because presents were given only after the plum pudding was finished and the grown ups were having their coffee.

Joseph thought back to last Christmas with the Cahills at Branlea. There had been warmth and they had wrapped him in their friendship, but looking around this room he knew he was a part of this large family and did not need to wonder whether he belonged. He knew that he belonged. There was young Rudolph, sixteen already, no longer the little cousin, but a fair headed, studious young man, his long legs stretched out as he sat on the floor to help his young cousin John unwrap a bulky present. A kind-hearted boy, Rudi, he always enjoyed being with his cousins and their children. As an only child he had been lonely, but he made friends easily and was well liked at school.

Next to Rudi sat Sarah, and Joseph had been saddened at how she had changed. Although seven years older, Sarah had always seemed closer to him than that, especially after Edward had died. Now she had lost that open look she had shared with her mother. Her face wore a clouded expression, which lifted in conversation, especially when one of her children brought a gift to be opened or just seen, but which settled over her features again when she was alone. She looked closer to Mary in age than to him, Joseph reflected. Joseph was not left to muse for long, Uncle Sam calling him over for a chat.

"Let's hear something of where you've been, boy!"

At fifty-three Sam's rusty curls were beginning to show threads of grey, but he was otherwise unchanged. Joseph had always admired this uncle, who never seemed to age. They talked about England, comparing notes, and Sam was interested to hear of the changes in the thirty years since he had been there.

"You know, you and I have something in common, Joseph. We were both bitten by the same bug that got my father. Why else would he have come all this way to see the other side of the world? Sure glad he did, though. It's a good place to live."

"I think I appreciate it more now. We need to be able to make comparisons before we understand what we have here in New Zealand."

"Well spoken, Joseph."

They were interrupted by Charles and Nicole's tiny daughter, Marie, who lurched about the room, having walked for only a few weeks, then tripped over Joseph's legs and fell flat on the floor. In the ensuing din their conversation was drowned out. Under the Christmas tree Joseph found a parcel with Marie's name on it pacify the little girl.

The time passed quickly, with afternoon tea punctuating the children's games and the parents' reminiscences. The evening meal, a cold one, was made up of contributions from each family. It was a day of continuous eating. George sat back contentedly, savouring his role as patriarch of this large brood. He recalled how his own father had gazed beneficently over his flock on such occasions too. It was good they were such a close-knit group, especially since he could not remember the names of all of his cousins in England, having left them at the age of four to travel to New Zealand.

As the children became weary, Charles and Nicole prepared to leave. It was a long drive to the farm. Victoria knew she would have at least two asleep against her before they arrived. Joseph took Sarah and her children home in his father's car. Bill and Sarah had intended buying a car, but their savings were minimal, with Bill spending most of their money on liquor. Sarah, like Joseph, had felt the warmth of the gathering, but for different reasons. For the first time she was managing by herself, but amongst this loving family she was never alone. Now she could look to the future and sort herself out. It was a milestone, but not as definitive as the one she would face the following evening.

For Sarah Boxing Day was spent with her children. It was a glorious day and they took a picnic lunch to the park. The twins, Bertie and Alex, were four now, full of energy and pranks. They were growing fast, but Alexandra could never catch her brother in height. Both were blonde and alike. Sarah had had blonde hair as a child, but it had darkened to a golden brown as she grew up. According to her mother the twins were very much like Sarah and Edward at the same age. Marjorie, on the other hand, had a mop of dark hair, which was still growing upwards. How ironic that she should be so like Bill, when she was the last straw, that had sent him away. Sarah did not think about him often, but as she sat in the sun watching the twins play and gently rocking Marjorie, who dozed in her pram, her thoughts turned to him. What sort of Christmas could he have had? Where was he living? Did he have any money, or had it all gone over the bar? She felt only pity for him, and regret that she had ever been foolish enough to think she loved him. She should never have married. It was Mark Wilson she had loved, and he had been one of the many war casualties. She smiled as she reflected on their secret love affair. There had been no need for secrecy, except from the curiosity of young brothers, but it was a game they had played, seeing how long it would be before the families discovered their love for each other. The game was interrupted by the War and Sarah didn't think either family ever knew the depth of their feelings. In fact, Sarah's mother had guessed the truth, especially when news arrived of Mark's death.

The children were hungry. Bertie was delving into the basket, while Alex spread the cloth on the grass. Sarah roused herself, leaving Marjorie to sleep while they shared their picnic. She had made sandwiches, but also cooked eggs and sausages, knowing how the twins loved to eat these in their fingers. There was Christmas cake, crackers to pull, and rosy apples to clean their teeth.

The bang of the crackers had woken the baby, who howled lustily until Alex sat her up and she saw her mother. The twins ran off to play again, munching their apples, and Sarah heated Marjorie's bottle with water from the Thermos flask. She would enjoy these outings more when Marjorie could romp with the others and there would be no more bottles and napkins to bring.

By the time they had dawdled home, stopping for an ice cream on the way, it was after four o'clock. The twins were tired and dusty and the baby had fallen asleep again. Sarah lit the range to heat the bath water, while the children settled down, one drawing a picture of playing at the park while the other built a castle of blocks. By seven o'clock all three had been bathed, had eaten their dinner and were tucked into bed. Sarah was finishing the dishes when there was a knock at the front door. Still wiping her hands on her apron, she opened the door to a policeman.

"Good evening. Are you Mrs. Houghton? Mrs. William Houghton?"

"Yes, I am."

"Were you expecting your husband home soon, Mrs. Houghton?"

"No, officer, he has not been home in the last six months."

Relief crossed the constable's face. "Then my task is not quite so difficult, ma'am. I have to tell you that William Houghton was accidentally killed by a tram at 6.30 this evening, outside the Boar's Head hotel."

"Poor Bill, what an end," said Sarah slowly. "But how did you know to contact me?"

"Your photo was still in his wallet and this is his only known address, Mrs. Houghton. He must have had lodgings, but we have no record of them. I'm sorry, we must have formal identification . . ."

"Of course, but I have three children – his children – asleep, so I can't go out. If I telephoned my brother, would it be all right if he went?"

"He knew the deceased, I presume?"

"Oh yes, he did. I'll ring him now."

While the constable waited, Sarah rang her parents' number. It was Catherine who answered. When Sarah told her what had happened, she asked, "What does this mean to you, Sarah?"

"I don't know yet, Mother. But there is no pain, if that's what you mean."

Catherine arranged for Joseph to identify Bill. She came to spend the evening with Sarah, and Joseph accompanied the policeman to the mortuary. Catherine had never forgotten what had happened ten years before when Emily, Sarah's cousin, had heard of her husband's death. Catherine had found her lifeless on the bed, with the telegram and his photo beside her, and although these circumstances were different, she was taking no chances.

They found it easy to talk about Bill, and about the accident. For Sarah it was good to let out the feelings she had bottled up so long. She had no tears for him; those had all gone in the stormy arguments before he had left her. Now she could tell her mother how the separation had come about, how unreasonable he had been, jealous of the children, demanding her attention for himself, more of a child than they were. Now she could think and speak of him in a more detached way. Catherine listened patiently, aware that her role as a mother had not ended when her family grew up. The only advice Sarah asked of her mother was should the children be told.

In Catherine's opinion it was better not to tell them at this stage. The twins had occasionally asked where their father was, but he had never done much to earn their affection and they were gradually forgetting him.

On the morning of the funeral Catherine delivered Albert, Alexandra and Marjorie out to the farm, where Nicole would add them to her brood for the day. Only Sarah, her parents and Joseph attended the service, where they met Bill's parents for the first time in several years. Sarah pitied them, as Bill had been their only child. They had never seen their grandchildren – Bill would not allow it – so Sarah offered to bring the children to meet Mr. and Mrs. Houghton one afternoon. They agreed with her that it would be better if the twins did not know they were their father's parents. The day was set and Sarah felt that she had helped to alleviate the grief of these fine people, whose son had caused everyone so much heartbreak.

It was two years since Bill had died, and Sarah's life had settled into a new pattern. She was happier now. Last year the twins had started school and Sarah had met several of the teachers, taking a liking to a jovial Irishman called Jim O'Sullivan, who taught the older children at the school. Jim was a good-natured man, kind and friendly, helpful too. Before long he was a regular guest to dinner, helping with firewood and repair jobs. Sarah realised she was beginning to rely upon him, to feel dependent again, but now it felt right.

One evening, as she held up a shelf while Jim screwed the brackets into place for it, he dropped the screwdriver on Sarah's foot, and although it barely hurt he was so contrite that they both realised their feelings had deepened. When the shelf was in place, he took her hands and led her to the sofa, sat her down and then knelt on the floor at her feet. A huge man, he had the look of a child in spite of his black hair and thick beard. He gently grasped her hands and told her how much she and the children had come to mean to him. Each time he went home he looked forward to the next time they would be together. Then, suddenly, he asked her to marry him.

Sarah was taken aback. She had not really analysed her feelings for Jim; she had just drifted with them, allowing the warmth of his presence to carry her along until he visited again. Now she was amazed to hear herself accepting his proposal. Lifting her as he stood up, he held her like a doll, at arm's length, then he clasped her to him in a tight embrace and kissed her. She had imagined his bushy beard would scratch, but it was soft and gentle like him.

They decided on a quiet wedding, in the registry office, with only Sarah's family there. The twins were page boy and flower girl. Jim and Sarah dispensed with a honeymoon. Jim wanted the children to share in their happiness. So they settled into a happy routine, the children adoring Jim and he, in turn, enjoying being a father to two six-year-olds and a two-year-old. A new contentment seeped into Sarah, her family was quick to notice. She looked younger and Joseph, in particular, was delighted to see his sister come alive again.

For Joseph the past two years had been busy. Apart from running the business, which he thoroughly enjoyed now, he became entangled in a triangle with Frances Brown and Donald Watson. Joseph, busy with the day-to-day running of affairs, considered Miss Brown a real asset to the business. Her work was meticulous, her manner with customers courteous, and she always stayed after the shop closed, if Joseph needed to discuss anything with her. He walked her home one night after they had worked late at stocktaking. Glancing over his shoulder as he turned the corner after leaving her at her gate, he was surprised to see her standing under the streetlight, watching him depart.

His mind full of plans for tomorrow, he gave it little thought. In the morning he would have Donald bring down the bolts from the storeroom and work with Miss Brown measuring and cataloguing them. Donald would be glad of the change in routine, and the chance to work with Miss Brown. Joseph had noticed his devotion to her, but he had no idea how Miss Brown felt towards Donald. He was to find out the next evening.

Catherine had offered to help in the shop during stocktaking, and Sarah, who visited her parents often with Marjorie while Jim and the twins were at school, kept her father company. She would have helped in the shop too, but was short of breath as she was expecting Jim's child, to the delight of them both. It was early days yet, but Jim had made her promise not to do anything too vigorous and she was touched at his concern. They had been amazed at her immediate conception – they had been married only three months now – especially since Sarah was thirty-five years old. For Sarah the child would set the seal on this marriage and end any association with Bill's memory.

While Catherine helped Joseph, Sarah made her father a cup of tea and looked on fondly as Marjorie snuggled in George's arms. George was happy to read her stories, or tell his own. It was thus that Catherine found them when she came through from the shop at lunchtime. She and Joseph staggered their breaks, with Frances coming into the shop over the lunch period.

Business was slack today, giving Joseph time to ask about the morning's stocktaking. He was shocked at the abruptness of Miss Brown's reply. She was always so composed and in complete command of herself.

"But Miss Brown . . ."

"Oh, for goodness sake, Mr. Hamilton, must you always be so formal?"

Joseph could not believe his ears. Was this the Miss Brown he thought he knew? "I'm sorry, I don't understand," he said, rather coolly.

"Oh, I'm sorry, Mr Hamilton, I should never have spoken to you in that way. Please forgive me. It's just that . . ." Her eyes filled with tears.

"Do go on. What is troubling you, Miss – er, did you want me to call you Frances?"

"Would you, please?" Her eyes pleaded with him. He doubted this was ethical, but her smile dispelled his doubts. "Well then, Frances, what's the tale you have to tell?"

"It doesn't seem important now, Mr. Hamilton. We should have the inventory finished by this evening."

Puzzled by their conversation, Joseph let it rest. When his mother heard him address the girl as Frances that afternoon, and caught the glance she gave him in return, she grasped some of the situation. Catherine had to go up to the storeroom a little later and overheard the way Donald spoke to Frances, enabling her to solve the equation. She made a mental note to speak to the girl before the end of the day. When Frances was discovered by Joseph later in the day, sobbing quietly in one of the aisles of the storeroom, Catherine could help a bewildered Joseph understand the whole affair.

Joseph had asked whatever was the matter and she had jumped up from the stool, flung her arms around his neck and murmured, "Joseph, Joseph. He thought: "I did not say she could call me Joseph. How strangely she is behaving!" Calming her as best he could, he sought out his mother, to make sense of this. When he told her Catherine shook her head. "I think you walk around with your eyes shut, young man."

It was only when they were together at home that evening that Catherine divulged her conversation with Frances.

"You mean she . . . oh Mother, what did you tell her? I have never really thought of her as a person."

"That is what I told her. I said that you admired and respected her efficiency in her job and I also told her that Donald worships the ground she walks on."

"Does he? I suspected he might be rather keen on her. I'm not completely blind, Mother!"

"Only when it concerns you, Joseph. The girl is obviously in love with you, and you haven't even noticed it."

Joseph thought back to the night he had walked Frances home. "Well, what am I going to do about this? I admire her, but I am not really the marrying kind. Not yet, anyway."

"Since you are asking my advice I will give it to you. You can't send the girl away for loving you. That would be unfair. So just carry on, but don't do anything to encourage her. Be strictly businesslike, including going back to calling her Miss Brown. In addition, do everything you can to turn her affections towards Donald. I don't mean pushing them together, like today. He was just too much for her, longing as she was for some attention from you."

"However did I get myself into this tangle? I don't think I ever encouraged her."

"Love lives on hope, Joseph. You need to snuff out the flame gradually."

For Sarah these were happy months. Catherine took her and Marjorie to see Nicole and little Bernadette several times during the winter and Sarah was surprised how much this beautiful baby made her long for her own. She had never felt like this when expecting Bill's children, for all that she loved them now. Marjorie and Marie became good playmates, one aged two and the other three, and it was lovely watching them play, while sitting on the verandah enjoying the winter sun.

At 35 Nicole had not changed much, in spite of having five children, two of whom had been born after she had been warned not to have more. Her English was fluent now – as she said, when you have four children bombarding you with talk how could you help learning – but she would never lose her slight French accent. Charles was glad of this as it was a souvenir of the fairy-tale way they had met.

At the end of the mild, wet winter Prudence Catherine was born. Jim was a devoted father, who never ceased to wonder that this beautiful baby was his, although there was no doubt in anyone's mind when they saw the plump, contented baby with thick black curls. The older children shared in the joy she brought to the family. Jim had accepted Sarah's children as his own so they could not understand just how special this child was to her parents. For Sarah Prudence would always have her own corner in her mother's heart.

In their family life there was no cloud, but Jim was spending more time poring over the newspaper, and he did not seem happy with what he read. When she asked what was troubling him, he forced a bright smile and replied that it was nothing for her to worry her pretty head about. After he had left for school, taking the twins with him in the new car he had bought when Prudence was born, Sarah picked up the paper and thumbed through it. She had no understanding of stocks and shares, omitting that page to read all the news articles carefully. Nowhere could she find anything to make Jim so strangely serious. At this point the baby woke up and she forgot the matter.

CHAPTER 2
Depression and War Again

They had been hard years for all. Since the Wall Street collapse in 1929 the state of the country had deteriorated steadily. Prices plummeted in Britain for New Zealand butter and mutton, so fewer imports could be afforded. The ports stood idle at times, the carrying business shouldered a large part of the burden, and shopkeepers were unable to supply the imported goods on which their reputation was based.

For the farmer, matters were much more serious. His income was halved, but his mortgage payments were not. After the build-up of meat and dairy exports in the last decade, he was suddenly facing bankruptcy. Tens of thousands were in the same predicament, through no fault of their own, but many were saved by the Government's moratorium placed on farm debts. There was still little enough to live on, but the pressure had been removed.

As many as a hundred thousand were out of work in a land of only one and a half million people. It was a chain reaction, with collapse in one area affecting those involved in the next. Fewer imports meant fewer goods, less labour needed to move or process them, less income to those who sold them and so less money to buy goods.

For Charles and Nicole they were anxious times, but they rode out the storm, having taken over an almost freehold farm and paid off much of the mortgage. It was the farmer who had bought during the boom period that they pitied, the one who had not consolidated before the crash. There were two families not far from Totara Ridge who were in a desperate plight. Nicole watched their children becoming ragged and miserable until she could stand it no longer. She collected up some of her own children's outgrown clothes, a quantity of milk, two dozen eggs, some of her freshly baked bread and two bowls of homemade butter and set off one day, while the children were at school, to visit the mothers of these hungry youngsters.

While the tearful mothers tried to thank her she brushed aside all their protestations with the single remark, "I am sure you would do the same for me", insisting that it was not through Charles's and her superior management that they were not in the same situation. At both homes she was appalled at the poverty. Half of the furniture had been sold, no doubt for a pittance, to pay for food. Much of the stock had gone from the fields too, and that which remained gave them meat but no money. Nicole took note of the shortages at each house, and observed the gleam of pleasure in the young women's eyes at the sight of the bread and eggs, storing this away for future visits. Within days she saw the change in the children as they waited for the school bus with her own. These visits became regular outings for her, and a close bond grew up between her and the women, knowing as they all did that she could well have been in their plight. Jim and Sarah had difficulties too. Because the Government's income from tax was much reduced by unemployment it created further unemployment by economising on its spending. Fewer teachers were allocated to each school, and among those whose jobs vanished was Jim. He had offered to step down in favour of a colleague who had eight children to support. Although his family numbered five now, with the birth of Jamie in 1931, Jim felt they could survive on their savings if this terrible slump did not last too long. With school classes of up to sixty-five children to manage he did not feel a martyr. During the winter of 1933 he had been part of a scheme where married men were obliged to leave their families and go into a camp to do labouring work in remote areas for thirty-five shillings per week. This had brought real strain for Sarah, left with five children and no beloved husband to lean on. George and Catherine stepped in, and Jim was persuaded to accept a similar amount from them if he would ease their daughter's burden. They had seen her suffer enough in the past. Jim had also seen enough suffering in recent months to make him realise how much Sarah had brought into his life. He now spent a part of each day at the relief supply depot, doing what he could to help some of the ten thousand who came each week.

Now, in 1934, they could see light at the end of the tunnel. The worst was over, and Mr. Coates's government was straightening things out. Prices were rising again overseas in some sectors. It was time to be cautiously optimistic.

For Sam and Mary the Depression had brought no personal hardship, and Rudi, living at home with them, felt little effect from it either. With a degree in civil engineering behind him and a bright future ahead, according to his professor and lecturers, he was enjoying his work in the town. But as top student in his honours class he was still studying in the evenings, not for any further qualifications but because he was stimulated by the books he read. Rudi's leisure reading always related in some way to engineering. It was not only his job but his hobby and passion. He was not interested in girls, to his mother's consternation and his father's amusement.

"When he's ready, Mary, don't worry," Sam would say cheerily.

"But he's twenty-four, Sam; it's not as though he's seventeen. He should be thinking of marriage!"

"Were we married at his age, Mary?"

"Well, no, but . . ."

"Then let's leave him to run his own life. He has too much on his mind to worry about women. Besides, I think he will be like his father, a one-girl man."

Mary had to agree. Rudi was the envy of all his friends: tall, athletic, good-looking and gentlemanly. Several of his friends were women, who would have leapt at the chance to be more than a friend, but Rudi was unaware of this. He was a provincial representative in both athletics and rugby, and Sam and Mary were very proud of his accomplishments.

Sam, at 61, had been principal of the high school for five years now. He was respected by pupils and community, who marvelled at his understanding of the miscreants' behaviour. Sam had not forgotten his many visits to the headmaster's study as a boy, when his high spirits had led him beyond the acceptable limits. His son had never caused them the same anxiety, having more of his mother's placid nature.

For Mary life had always been interesting. She liked people and enjoyed mixing with them in many spheres. As they became better known in Dunedin she involved herself in more clubs, societies and committees, filling several posts as president or patroness. Her gentle but firm manner and decision making were appreciated in the running of meetings, and she was admired. A striking woman, she was as tall and slender as ever, but her copper curls were threaded with silver now. This did not worry her. She knew she was 57 years old and could not look like a young woman for ever. She and Sam were both getting older, and she was thankful for their many happy years together.

Richard and Victoria's life had slowed to a gentle walking pace. They were not so old – only ten years older than Mary, Victoria mused – but there was little for them to do and they had worked hard all their lives. Now was the time to enjoy watching their grandchildren grow up. Young Richard and Vicki were already at high school, the daily bus trip not bringing them home until five o'clock. At the weekend, however, they would always find time to pop in and taste some of their grandmother's scones or loaf.

John was the quiet one in Charles and Nicole's brood, preferring to curl up with a book rather than play with the others in the family. Already, at the age of eleven, he was passionate about farming, his ambition being to study agriculture at Lincoln College. While Richard was out driving the tractor for his father, John would be thumbing through books on land types or breeds of sheep. Charles encouraged the boy, seeing in this interest a good future for the farm, if his sons would run it together. The boys got along well, each respecting their differences.

The two little girls, Marie and Bernadette, were the ones Victoria and Richard saw most often. They would persuade the school bus driver to let them off at their grandparents' cottage and then inveigle Victoria into telephoning their mother to ask if they might stay an hour or so. Nicole indulged them in these whims; who knew how long one would have grandparents, and she was so fond of Richard and Victoria herself that she was glad for her children to spend time with them. Marie never lacked initiative, and of course little Bernadette followed along. Richard would drive them home around five o'clock. It was hard to say who derived the more pleasure from these clandestine visits, the girls or the grandparents. Nicole was relieved that her family was so far from Europe now that there were rumblings of unrest there again. They made her uneasy.

Charles was also glad to be safely across the world from this new German phenomenon, with headlines in the newspapers. It seemed impossible that Germany would let herself be taken over by a dictator, yet the people, particularly the youth of the country, were flocking to this Hitler. What was he offering that was so appealing? He was certainly emphasising the creation of a national identity, and there was nothing bad about that, provided he was not too extremist. But there were more sinister undercurrents, thought Charles as he put down his teacup to turn the page of his paper, like this burning of books last year and statements about Jews, which signalled danger. He didn't like it, not at all. As long as Hitler was kept within limits, he decided, he could harm only his own country.

There were others who felt the same concern and for all of them there was no relief in sight, except to know that they were well away from a new dreaded spectre on the horizon. The dark clouds were gathering. It would be only a matter of time before the storm broke.

No-one could have been surprised. The build-up had gone on for months, although at times a peaceful settlement had seemed possible, especially when Chamberlain had worked hard for the treaty with France, Poland and Russia. That would have confined Hitler, but the Poles were none too sure they trusted Russia either. Unbeknown to Chamberlain and the world, Hitler was also courting the Soviet Union, trying to isolate Poland and ensure that the war he wanted would not be fought on two fronts. The announcement, last month, that Russia and Germany had signed a non-aggression pact had tolled the knell of doom. For Hitler it meant that Poland was his for the taking, without fear of Russian intervention; for Russia it meant freedom to move westwards.

No surprise then when the newspapers carried the banner headline that Hitler had invaded Poland, without any formal declaration of war. A week before, on August 25th , Great Britain had signed a formal pact of assistance with Poland, making inevitable today's headline that Chamberlain had declared war on Germany. France fulfilled her obligations by joining in the declaration.

For Charles memories came flooding back as he read The Press newspaper. Where was the enthusiasm he had felt when the First World War began – the Great War, the War to End All Wars? He had rushed off to avenge the deaths of Frank and Emily, and of Edward. He paused to reflect, that was twenty-three years ago. He realised that his son Richard was old enough to enlist. After all these years, he understood how his parents must have felt then. At fifty-two he was helpless to do anything that would avoid a repercussion of the slaughter of a generation of young men. His parents too, at the same age, must have felt powerless, especially after the tragedy of Emily's death. They must have wondered if they would lose their whole family.

Charles shook off these morose thoughts, but as he ploughed the hilly paddock away behind the house he chewed over how the creeping disease of war had wormed its way into his and everyone else's life again. The noise of the tractorshut him off from the outside world, so his thoughts could run free.

Five years ago he had been suspicious of Hitler's motives, from the time the propaganda had started. If his actions needed so much explaining and interpreting to the people, there must have been something to hide. But there was a hypnotic quality about the man: was it his own frenetic devotion to his cause? By now, of course, he was seen as a monster, but in those early days, destroying all the existing framework of government so that he could replace it with his own, there had been such fervour that many were carried along with it, not realising that there would be no barrage gates to check the flood when it reached danger level.

From the time that Hitler took over as President on the death of Hindenburg in August 1934 there had been a change from party politics to a personal rise in power. Any means, including murder, became legitimate. Charles could read between the lines, as the propaganda had camouflaged the stark reality.

But no propaganda could cover over the terrible treatment of the Jews. Again it had crept up on the German people and then it was too late. Charles shuddered at the inhumanity of it. By now there were concentration camps for anyone who did not see eye to eye with the Fuhrer.

Sam, too, was mulling over what it meant to be at war. If Britain was at war, then New Zealand would be alongside her. And his son was twenty-nine years old. Anyone less suited to being a soldier Sam could not imagine, but he would have to talk to Rudi, find out his thoughts about conscription. Mary would be dead against him volunteering, but Rudi was a grown man. Hadn't Mary said recently that he should be looking for a wife?

Rudi had also been thinking. Conscription would come eventually, and that would give him no choice of how he could serve his country. Perhaps it would be better to enlist in the medical corps, which should keep him away from the frontline, as well as allowing him to help his fellow soldiers. Inclined as he was towards pacifism, this seemed the best option. He would talk it over with his parents.

Mary sat wringing her hands as she read the Otago Daily Times. Her precious only child was in the firing line. Her thoughts spread to the wider family: Sarah's Bertie, Charles and Nicole's two boys, and even Joseph, all at risk. How could the actions of a fanatical man in Europe have an impact on young men a world away, in a safe part of the world?

That night Rudi and his parents tossed their thoughts together. None of them felt action was needed at the moment. Perhaps this threat of war was a flash in the pan, and it would be resolved by Christmas. The idea of the medical corps appealed to Mary and Sam, who recalled images of the First World War, where thousands were mown down in horrific battle scenes. They could not bear the thought of their only son being involved in combat.

Sarah and Jim sat talking after dinner, glad their children were too young to go to war, at least for now. But next year Bertie would be eighteen, and he could enlist if he chose to do so. If the war dragged on, as the last one had done, more men would be needed to swell the ranks, to replace those who would not be returning home. How many young lives would this war cut off? It was millions in the Great War, and then the Spanish flu had claimed tens of thousands more. Sarah couldn't imagine shy, sensitive Bertie coping in wartime conditions. Jim made the point that he would be as ready as many others signing up to face the Germans.

For George and Catherine there was a heavy feeling of *déjà vu*. They had already sacrificed a son to the relentless war machine, and nothing had ever filled the void left by Edward's loss. They were frightened that Joseph, their only remaining son, was old enough to be called up. They dared not even discuss the possibility, for fear of upsetting each other. They listened to news bulletins on the radio and read everything they could in The Press, as well as talking with friends and family. The general feeling was that New Zealand would probably not be affected by this ruckus between Britain and Europe.

It was 9.30 p.m. on September 3rd, 1939 and the Prime Minister was about to address the nation. Families clustered around the radio in their living rooms to hear the news they expected.

"We range ourselves without fear beside Britain. Where she goes, we go; where she stands we stand . . . a band of brothers". Mothers were not without fear for their sons, but all agreed that it was the country's collective duty to support the motherland.

Three days later a call was made for 6,600 volunteers. Within a month 15,000 had enlisted. Among them was Richard Davis, elder son of Charles and Nicole. Charles could understand the boy's enthusiasm, for he had felt the same way in 1914. There was no point in trying to dissuade him. His brother John was just as keen, but at seventeen he would have to wait a year or two.

In January, 1940 the first troops, having trained for three months, sailed for Egypt, under the protection of a British battleship. There they would undertake further training, in desert conditions. Richard was excited at the prospect. His parents hid their misgivings.

Rudi had reconsidered his ideas about the medical corps. Having made enquiries at the War Office in the city he was relieved to find that, with his engineering qualifications, there were opportunities in non-combat roles alongside New Zealand troops. He kept this information to himself, not wanting to upset his parents until it was necessary, but enlisted soon after Richard's departure.

Both young men had been moved by the passing of George Hamilton, the family patriarch, in November, 1939. In his later years George had led a quiet life, leaving business matters to his son Joseph, and social matters to his wife Catherine. He was always present at the family gatherings, and his dry sense of humour would be missed. The latest Christmas event was not the same without him.

As if he had known that time was running out, George had rounded up the family earlier in the year, leading them all out to the garden behind the family home, built for his parents in 1868 and modified over the years. There he patted the trunk of the sturdy oak tree that took pride of place on the verdant lawn, asking the children where this tree had come from.

"From the garden shop!" cried one little voice.

"It just grew!" said another.

"From the boat!" called a third.

"That's right, James!" said George. "Has your mama told you the story?" At that James was overcome with shyness, so George recounted the tale of the acorns that his parents, Joseph and Henrietta, had collected from their garden in England and brought with them on the Cressida in 1868 when they started their new life in New Zealand.

"So how old is this big tree?" he asked. One of the older children, little Bernadette, chimed in, "Seventy-one years, Uncle George."

"That's right. And I want all of you to remember this tree, because it is part of our family. It will still be here when you are old, like me." The children were wide eyed, trying to imagine themselves ever being as old as that.

Rudi's call-up letter arrived in March, 1940. He was to report for training in two weeks, and would be attached, as an engineer, to the third echelon, heading for North Africa. Now it was time to tell his parents.

This went better than he had expected, his parents having had time to realise that all the young men in the family were in a similar situation. However, he was sure his mother was holding back her emotions, for which he was grateful. His father, more pragmatic, pointed out to her the advantages of being an engineer over being a foot-soldier. Both said they were proud of him, and they would support him.

"Anzac biscuits," was his husky reply.

Rudolph Hamilton sailed with the third echelon of New Zealand troops in August, 1940, bound for North Africa. He trained with the troops in desert warfare, never knowing when the skills might be needed.

The following year New Zealand troops were engaged against Rommel's Afrika Korps, in an operation that lasted two years and spanned 1500 miles of desert. Rudi's role was repairing roads and bridges to maintain access for the troops.

In late 1941, New Zealand forces joined the British army in the battle of Sidi Rezedh, later described as "hell and fury". Although safe behind friendly lines, Rudi became thoroughly disenchanted. His letters home made difficult reading, lightened only by his frequent mention of a nurse he admired. Nola Greenaway, nine years his junior, was attached to the Canadian Armed Forces. With hospitals also behind the front lines they were able to spend brief spells together when there was a lull in the fighting.

While Rudi was in North Africa, Richard's echelon had been moved to Greece, to forestall a German invasion. However, the Greek forces collapsed and the supporting New Zealand troops had to be withdrawn. Losses were heavy, but Charles and Nicole were happy to hear from Richard that he was unscathed. He had been evacuated to Crete, where the Germans invaded, killing or wounding over a thousand and taking a further two thousand captive. It had been close, but he was safe back in Egypt.

On the home front Joseph received a letter from the Cahills, with condolences on the death of his father. They described a desperate situation in Britain, especially in the south of England. They were glad to be far from London, and had taken in several children evacuated to the countryside. Joseph could imagine the fun they would be having at Branlea. They were worried about Jack, who was working in some war-related employment in or near London. Joseph hoped his fun-loving friend would be safe. He felt some guilt that he was not involved in the war effort. When he had made enquiries, however, he had been assured that he was needed by his family, especially his mother, and business interests had to be kept afloat. At the same time he was too young to join the Home Guard, which was building defences on vulnerable beaches and watching, in shifts, for enemy activity.

Following the death of George, Catherine found her life quite empty. Victoria and Richard tried to include her in their social circle, which was kind, she knew, but sometimes she did not want to make the effort. Sarah and Jim were sensitive with regard to when she wanted to be with the grandchildren. Alexandra had a special bond with her grandmother, and often called in for a chat in her free time. At eighteen she had turned into a sensible, no-nonsense young woman, and Catherine treasured their times together. As the anniversary of George's death came and went, however, she fell into a state of lethargy, from which she had no desire to emerge. Joseph and Sarah worried about their beloved mother, but what could they do?

As the winter came in mid-year Catherine succumbed to pneumonia. It was Alexandra who found her, and she who perhaps best understood that her grandmother was finally where she felt most at peace, with her dearly-loved George.

Joseph, finding himself alone now in the family home, was forced to reflect on where he was in life. His parents were dead, his brother was dead. His sister was happily married now, with a family of five, two grown up and three still to be raised. What did he have? A family business and a house far too large for him. And no prospects of marriage, for this had never been a priority. He was forty years old. Was it too late?

At one of the New Zealand camps in the desert Rudi decided that he would try to locate his cousin Charles's son, Richard. Mary told him in her latest letter that Richard had had a close shave in both Greece and Crete, and was now back in Egypt. It proved easy enough to track him down, and they enjoyed a leave day together, exchanging family news. Richard had heard that the military were exploring the possibility of building a highway into Alaska, piquing Rudi's interest. He was sick of this war and the desert, in fact everything except Nola. He poured his heart out to Richard who simply suggested he marry the girl.

"Oh, but I haven't met her parents."

"Well, how does she feel?"

"I haven't asked her."

"Rudi, if you don't do something about this, someone else will. You do realise this, don't you?"

"I don't know much about these things, Richard."

"Well, when are you seeing her next?"

"Tomorrow."

"Then I suggest you tell her you love her – because you obviously do – and ask how she feels about you. If she loves you, then propose to her!"

Rudi shook his head trying to clear his thoughts. This was new territory for him, and things were moving too fast. He would have to think it through. Richard's final comment, as they parted company, was, "Just forget you are an engineer, Rudi. Sometimes you have to go with feelings, not logic!"

Next morning Rudi made enquiries about the projected highway. Because it was to be built by military forces, there was a chance he could be transferred to that unit.

He had acquitted himself well in Egypt, and could feel a plan hatching in his head. He needed to talk to Nola.

At the end of a long, tiring day Nola was leaving the infirmary when Rudi materialised beside her. Her face lit up as he fell into step beside her. Although not as tall as Rudi she was able to match strides. He said nothing, drinking in her beauty. To him she was the most beautiful girl in the world, with her dark brown hair a little tousled from a day's work and her blue-green eyes the colour of the Pacific Ocean near his home.

Perturbed by his silence she asked, "Is everything all right, Rudi?" It snapped him out of his dream. Now he had to follow Richard's guidelines. As he blushed and stammered like a schoolboy, she took his hand in hers. A shock coursed through him and he took her in his arms, telling her he loved her and wanted to marry her. She stepped back and gazed at him. His heart stopped. Then she said one word, "Really?"

Desperate to know what that single word signified, he waited, forgetting to breathe. Nola realised that this was not the organised, methodical engineer she loved, but a young man drowning in his emotions before her eyes. She had to do something, now. "Rudi, this is the dream I have had every night for a month. I can't believe it is really happening."

A sigh of relief escaped him. "Does that mean …?"

"Yes, Rudi, it means I am in love with you, and if that was a proposal, then the answer is yes!"

A long embrace followed, and they decided that on their next leave day they would go in search of a ring. For now they would have dinner together and make plans about telling their parents their wonderful news. Nola was twenty-one years old and so, technically, they did not need her father's consent, but Rudi would ask for it anyway.

As the war ground on into its third year, John Davis, Richard's younger brother, enlisted in 1942. Following several months of training, his division was sent to Italy. They arrived in winter, when the rivers were swollen and conditions were miserable. After crossing the Sangro River they were met by the enemy in the battle of Cassino, which involved hand-to-hand fighting. All of their training, which had seemed boring and mechanical, proved worthwhile. Casualties were high and conditions difficult, as the monastery, atop Monte Cassino overlooking the town, was occupied by the Germans. The New Zealand soldiers' acts of bravery would go down in history, with Monte Cassino forever associated with those troops.

Standing in the way of the Allies' advance to Rome, Cassino needed to be captured. In repeated battles it was battered beyond recognition. Although finally taken in May, 1944 it was at great cost, with almost five hundred New Zealanders killed and eighteen hundred wounded. Among the latter was John Davis who, at twenty-one, wrote home to his parents that he had lost a leg and was coming home a cripple.

All the while, more young people were being encouraged to join the war effort in New Zealand. When Sarah's Bertie enlisted in 1942, his twin sister joined the Women's Auxiliary Army Corps. They had always been together, and Alex saw no reason why that should change now.

Vicki, whose two brothers were fighting overseas, was co-opted into the "essential services". She was given a choice of assembly-line work, or being a railway porter, a tram conductor or a "postie". Although she chose postal deliveries, she would later regret this, seeing the distress some mail caused its recipients.

For those at home, waiting for news of loved ones, the practical problems of rationing were a constant thorn in the side. Tea and sugar, meat and butter were all in short supply, with coupons the only way to ensure a fair distribution. Those who complained were told that things were worse in Britain, where as much as possible was being sent from New Zealand, and this was a tangible way for ordinary citizens to make a sacrifice.

CHAPTER 3

A New Family

Like a dog with a bone, Rudi latched on to the idea of taking part in the building of the Alaska Highway. The quality of his work as an engineer meant that his superiors bowed to his repeated requests for a transfer/discharge so that he could be in Canada for the beginning of the project. While other New Zealand soldiers headed home on furlough, he was on a ship bound for Vancouver.

The one unachievable part of his carefully laid plan was obtaining a release for Nola. She would have to remain in Egypt for another year to serve out her contract.

While both were sad about this they accepted that Rudi would be away in the Interior for much of the construction period. They would maintain a long-distance engagement by mail, which would give them a chance to think about where they wanted to settle once married. Maybe in New Zealand, maybe in Canada.

As the outline of the coast came into sight Rudi found a spot on the deck of the troopship. Passing under the new Lion's Gate suspension bridge, completed just before the war, he took in the harbour, with mountains rising just behind the city. It was a sunny day, with a stiff, cool breeze, and he liked what he saw. He imagined how his grandparents must have felt as they approached Lyttelton port in 1868, after months at sea. There was a strange sensation in his stomach: a mixture of nervousness and excitement. This was because he would soon meet his future in-laws for the first time. The Greenaways had agreed to their daughter's request that they accommodate Rudi until he was transferred to Dawson Creek, where the actual construction would begin. They would meet him at the dock in just a few minutes. Would they like him? Would he like them?

He need not have worried. Mr. and Mrs. Greenaway had heard nothing but good about him, although they were determined to form their own opinions. They greeted him warmly, once he had spotted their sign bearing his name. Soon they were heading north, over the Lion's Gate, which he could admire from a different vantage, to their home in North Vancouver.

"The bridge must have made a great difference to the city. It looks quite new," he said as they crossed the harbour entrance.

Mr. Greenaway replied, "A huge difference. Before, it was a ferry ride to town, now it's only a few minutes by car. But of course that means the city has spread over here too. There are new homes everywhere."

"I am not surprised. It is beautiful."

"We sure like it here. This is where Nola grew up and went to school," added Mrs. Greenaway.

Rudi's thoughts turned to his lovely fiancée. "I am a lucky man," he murmured.

"Maybe she is lucky too," remarked her father.

The following Monday morning Rudi fronted up at the Canadian Armed Forces headquarters in downtown Vancouver. To get there he had taken a bus, which crossed the suspension bridge. It really was an amazing piece of engineering: he doubted he would ever tire of looking at it. Below it, on the south side, there appeared to be a large park. He must ask the Greenaways about that later.

Rudi would spend three to four weeks at the headquarters, before moving north to the construction zone. When he asked his hosts if he could stay with them for so long they were quite relaxed about it.

"Just one thing, though," insisted Mr. Greenaway. We don't want to be Mr. and Mrs. Please call us Dennis and Marianne."

"Are you sure, sir? I was raised to show respect to my elders. . ."

"We'll accept your respect, boy, but that doesn't mean formality. In this country we are pretty laid back." Rudi had never heard this expression. He had a lot to learn in his new country.

At the weekend Dennis and Marianne drove him to Stanley Park, the huge park under the bridge. In fact the great cables that held up one end of it were anchored in the park. It was such a large reserve that one visit could not do it justice. He was intrigued at the Indian totems and art installations, the swimming areas, the magnificent trees. He was falling under Vancouver's spell.

Rudi's letters to Nola were making her homesick. She longed to be sharing Rudi's discovery of her home city. But duty called for now and the months would eventually tick by. She was glad he was beginning to love Vancouver.

Following the bombing of Pearl Harbor by the Japanese in December 1941, New Zealand joined the war in the Pacific. Islands that were usually thought of as holiday destinations became the sites of jungle warfare.

In 1942 Bertie's unit was sent to New Caledonia. Alexandra, who had excelled at French while at school, begged to be allowed to go as an interpreter. As her family knew, Alex had a way of getting what she wanted.

They were based at Bourail, which was more central than Nouméa, in the south of the island. Bertie saw some action, but most of his deployment was spent waiting around. He was glad to have Alex nearby, and she taught him some French, which he was able to use with the locals.

By 1944 it was decided to withdraw the New Zealand troops from the Pacific. Those who remained lay at rest in the military cemetery at Bourail, and Bertie farewelled several of those friends before heading home. Some of his fellow soldiers were sailing for Italy, but he and Alex were returning to Christchurch, where they hoped to make themselves useful in one of the "essential services".

Rudi had never seen an engineering operation like it. Manpower had not been an issue. There seemed to be an endless supply of troops available for the unskilled work and the road took shape rapidly. Dawson Creek was dubbed "Mile Zero" and the unpaved, narrow road marched north-west towards Whitehorse in the Yukon Territory. After some months, when it reached Tok Junction in Alaska, Rudi knew this was where his contract ended. The Americans would take over from here. He also realised it was near where his father had found gold in 1899. Could he get to Dawson City? He would love to share that with his father. He asked around, and discovered that some heavy trucks were going through that way in a few days. He used his Kiwi charm and accent to thumb a ride. His father had raised him on tales from the Far North, Jack London's "Call of the Wild" and Robert Service's poems. The words of one ran through his head:

> *'There's a race of men that don't fit in,*
> *A race that can't sit still;*
> *So they break the hearts of kith and kin,*
> *And they roam the world at will.'*

His father had been such a man. He recited it to his colleagues, who could now understand why he wanted to make this sentimental journey. Unbeknown to him they talked to one of their superiors, who grumbled, "Take this greenhorn with you. He has worked darned hard for us."

As they drove along the Top of the World highway Rudi was in awe of the treeless hills, the tundra and the green valleys. It was early October, and soon there would be snow, closing the road for the long winter. His companions made sure he knew that just inches below the grassy surface there was permafrost. They stopped once and dug down, just to see his surprise when they struck ice.

Back on the gravel road his driver, ever alert for wildlife, pumped the brakes several times and brought the truck to a halt. Rudi, in the passenger seat, looked at him for an explanation. The driver pointed to the side of the road, and there was a big black bear emerging from spindly shrubs and preparing to cross the road. "Keep looking," said the driver. The bear marched across the road, followed by two half-grown cubs. Mother Bear then led them back the way they had come, and Rudi muttered, "Make up your mind!" After a moment she turned and started across the road again, this time with three cubs in tow.

"They know we will wait," said Don, the driver. "It's when they sit in the middle of the road that we honk at them."

Rudi had been busy with his camera. How lucky he was to have captured this bear family on film!

Not far from their destination Don remarked, "Got that camera ready?" as he pointed to Rudi's side of the road. There was a huge bull moose, with a full set of broad-bladed antlers, watching the truck, before crashing away into the undergrowth, too quick for Rudi.

At Dawson City the men went about their business while Rudi strolled along the bank of the Yukon River. He felt close to his father, and was aware that he had not written home for some time. He bought some postcards and an envelope, and was told he was near the confluence with Bonanza Creek. Excited now, he recalled the stories his father had told him. He bought a book of Robert Service poems to read later. What an atmosphere in this little town! And to think this was where his father and his partners had found their fortune.

By the time he met up with the truck crew he was glowing.

"We need to make tracks, to get back to Tok tonight. All aboard!" cried his driver.

Rudi was quiet on the return, grateful that he had had this chance to peek into his father's early life. It drew him closer to his father and he knew this day would stay with him for the rest of his life.

Back in Vancouver, his part in the road construction completed, Rudi spent Christmas with Dennis and Marianne. Their son Paul arrived with his wife, Christine and their two children. Rudi thought ruefully that the only one missing was Nola. It left him with a hollow feeling, but thoughts of family Christmas celebrations at home chased away the sadness. With his Uncle George and Aunt Catherine gone now it would fall to Uncle Richard and Aunt Victoria to fill the roles of patriarch and matriarch. But how many of the young ones would be there for this Christmas in 1942? Joseph, no doubt; John was in camp; Richard might be there; Bertie and Alex were still in New Caledonia, and he was here in Canada.

His reverie was broken by the call to the dinner table, where a huge feast awaited the family. There was turkey and ham, magnificently decorated, one at each end of the table, surrounded by a profusion of vegetables and even a salad, in winter. Christmas decorations filled every space on the table. Paul was asked to carve the turkey, while Dennis attacked the ham, removing cherries, pineapple and decorative leaves first. There was a lot of noise as food was passed back and forth, but then, after grace, with a special mention of Nola, there was silence while everyone started eating.

Rudi had managed to place a call to his parents late on the previous evening, knowing that they would have returned from the family gathering in Christchurch. They were tired after the drive to Dunedin, but were energised on hearing Rudi's voice. Could they come to his wedding in about six months? No, not unless the war in the Pacific had ended, but they promised to visit once the war was over.

On his return to Vancouver Rudi had found a job easily with an engineering company in the city. He was glad that he and Nola could be near her parents: they had missed her, and he knew he was a poor substitute, although they obviously liked him.

All three were delighted to receive news of the date when Nola would be returning. She would travel in a contingent of Canadian medical staff, on the same troop ship that had carried Rudi to Vancouver, arriving on June 15th, 1943. Rudi was all for getting married the next day, but Marianne put a quick stop to that.

"I have one daughter and I have looked forward to this occasion since she was in her teens. It will be done properly!" Rudi was about to learn, as his father had, that weddings were the province of the ladies. The date was set for mid-July. Because both parties had served in the Armed Forces they were entitled to be married in the Canadian Memorial United Church. Dennis and Marianne drove Rudi to see it. Situated in the suburbs, on West 16th Avenue, it was a gem. Built of stone, it looked solid, but inside the stained-glass windows let in a filtered light of many colours. The windows themselves depicted battle scenes, dedicated to those who had fallen in the Great War, as well as scenes from the Bible. Although not a religious person, Rudi felt it was perfect. Marianne made a booking for July 15th. That would give Nola exactly a month to prepare for the big day. Whilst inwardly groaning Rudi knew that this was the sensible decision.

Once the winter was over, Rudi bought a car. He worked hard learning to drive on the other side of the road, soon feeling confident, provided there was nothing unexpected to distract him.

On the day before Nola's arrival Dennis announced that he and Marianne had a commitment the following day, and could Rudi possibly go to the dock to meet Nola? Not fooled for a moment, and deeply grateful, Rudi accepted.

He left hours before her arrival time, knowing that parking his car would be a problem. However, all went well and he checked his watch many times before he saw the familiar outline of the ship glide under the Lion's Gate. In a whirl of excitement he scanned the faces of the disembarking passengers – there she was, waving to him. They were drawn towards each other, and oh, it felt good to have her in his arms again. She managed to gasp, "Where are Mom and Dad?"

"Too busy," he mumbled into her hair. She pulled back, but at his grin she understood.

After collecting her luggage, which included a bolt of Egyptian material for her wedding dress, they headed for the car. "Whose is this?" she asked.

"Ours," he replied proudly.

On the trip back to North Vancouver she admired his driving, but when her hand reached across to rest on his knee he was reminded about distractions, and gave all his attention to the driving.

It was some hours later that Nola's parents arrived home, thrilled to see their daughter looking so happy. Rudi excused himself – it was their turn – and took Nola's bags up to the room she would use until her wedding day. Although Marianne had insisted on this she had prepared the room right next door to Rudi's.

The month flew by. Between dress fittings, arranging attendants, deciding on a honeymoon itinerary and just revelling in being together, the wedding day soon appeared on the horizon. Rudi's dilemma over a best man was solved when Paul offered to fill the role. Rudi liked his brother-in-law-to-be. Never having had a brother he was enjoying the developing friendship.

The day dawned to a cloudless sky. The wedding was to take place at one o'clock, which would give the newly-married couple plenty of time to reach their first honeymoon destination, aptly named Hope, for the night. Nola was radiant. She had grown her dark hair, and wore it loose down her back, as brides did in earlier times. Her bridesmaid, a school friend, wore a dress of salmon silk, material brought home by Nola with her Egyptian cream silk. Both ladies wore a band of fresh flowers in their hair.

They entered the beautiful little church and processed down the aisle, Dennis proudly guiding his daughter towards her future. Rudi was amazed at how lucky he was. He had never shown any interest in girls in his youth, yet here he was, waiting at the altar for the one girl who had captured his heart.

Following the wedding and reception the newly-weds set off for Hope. They had some four hours of driving ahead over challenging parts of the highway. They had allowed ten days for their travels in the Interior, including the Rockies, and Rudi soon learned that British Columbia was huge. He knew that it was several times larger than New Zealand, but the reality of that had not struck him until now.

As they climbed towards the Rockies he was in awe of the scenery. It reminded him of the Southern Alps at home, but the scale was much larger. Around every corner was a new panorama to take his breath away. Nola was delighted at his reaction. She had suggested most of the points in their itinerary, and so far it had been rewarding. Lake Louise, Banff, the highway to Jasper – and perfect summer weather – had turned Rudi into a photo-snapping tourist. At the Radium Hot Springs, as they sat in the warm water surrounded by mountain scenery, they thought it was heaven. The days rolled by and soon it was time to head back to the real world.

They would stay with Dennis and Marianne until they found a suitable place to rent. Rudi had not wanted to arrange this before Nola came home, feeling that their marriage was a partnership. He loved her dearly but he also had a deep respect for her, just as his father had always shown for his mother. It was a pity that his parents had not been able to attend the wedding, but he remembered they had promised to visit, and meet their new daughter when the war was over.

The war raged on in Europe, and in the Pacific. Rudi and Nola settled into married life, welcoming baby Samuel a year after their wedding. They had found a house to rent in West Vancouver, not much further from the city than Dennis and Marianne. After the traumas of nursing in war zones, Nola was serenely happy with marriage and motherhood. Rudi was saving hard to buy their own home, but that would take some time.

It was soon 1945, a year of hope for an end to hostilities. In May surrender papers were signed, and May 8th became known as VE Day, signalling victory in Europe.

However, the horrors of two atomic bombs, dropped from American planes on Japanese civilians, still lay ahead. Following the devastation caused by these bombs, the inevitable VJ Day, on August 15th, brought an end to the conflict that had torn the world apart for almost six years. For many it left a feeling of guilt at the level of man's inhumanity to man.

Life returned to some sort of normality. Sam and Mary made plans for their visit to Canada. Now they had not only a daughter-in-law to meet, but also their first grandson, named for his grandfather.

In late September their ship docked in Vancouver, and Rudi was waiting to greet them. The five years since they had seen him melted away, but they could see changes in him. He showed a quiet confidence and maturity. As he spotted his parents he saw changes in them, too. They were getting old. His father's hair was white, and his mother stooped as she walked. How old were they now? He quickly calculated that his father was seventy-two and his mother sixty-eight.

All of that was forgotten amidst lingering hugs. On the drive to his home they caught up with details that letters cannot cover. Samuel clung to his mother's skirt as she greeted Rudi's parents. He tried to walk to his father but sat down suddenly and started crawling. As Rudi scooped him up the little fellow chortled with glee. Sam and Mary were captivated, and enslaved.

Their three-week stay passed quickly, but in that time they were convinced that Nola was exactly the right wife for their son. They saw a side of Rudi they had never known. He was a devoted husband and father, and they left feeling that they had gained a wonderful daughter, who made their son happy.

No one could see ahead to the changes the next year would bring to their family.

CHAPTER 4

Births, Deaths and Marriages

In the years following the war families came to terms with the changes. Those who did not return were mourned; those who came home wounded made the best of their situation; those who had escaped physically unhurt came to terms with the inner demons that no one could see. Many men talked little about the war, wanting to put it behind them.

The Hamilton family continued their get-togethers, and was glad to welcome back the twins, Bertie and Alex, as well as their cousin Richard, who was physically sound but bore some inner scars from his war experiences. His brother John called himself a "cripple", after losing a leg in Italy. He hoped to be able to have an artificial limb fitted in order to work on the family farm.

The only one missing was Rudi, but the family was pleased to know he was settling down in Canada, with a wife and baby son. Following their visit to Vancouver Sam and Mary could pass on Rudi's news and describe his happiness to the family.

Christmas 1945 brought another change. Richard Davis (senior) had died in the previous month, leaving Victoria to step up as matriarch of the family. Sam was well aware that the ranks were thinning, and that he would be the next to pick up the baton.

Vicki had married her soldier, Bruce Hunter, earlier in the year and settled in Christchurch. Alex and Bertie shared a house nearby. Neither felt any inclination to marry, being content with each other's company.

The following year, 1946, brought the marriage of Richard Davis (junior) and Maria Johnston, after a long courtship, interrupted by the war. Maria was a country girl, only too happy to settle at Totara Ridge with her new husband and his brother.

Later in the year Mary took ill and by the time Rudi received his father's letter the situation was dire. Rudi was able to send news of his second son's birth, as well as his expressions of love for his mother, but his father's next letter told of Mary's death. Rudi had never known such a feeling of devastation. He was thirty-six, and his mother had always been there, caring for him, encouraging him, praising him, but never forcing her opinions on him. How would his father cope? They had been married since 1904. Like himself his father had been a one-woman man. He had told Rudi that he had never been interested in women until Mary crossed his path. What would he do now?

Joseph had been the anchor for the family in Christchurch, continuing and expanding the family business, which now resembled a small department store. He had offered his sister Sarah the family home, situated behind the shop, during the war. She had gratefully accepted the offer, since she and Jim had never quite recovered from the setbacks and years of unemployment during the Depression, and the war years had been hard too. Living rent free was a great help.

Joseph had found a small house nearby, enabling him to walk to the shop each day. He was happy with his lot, resigned to remaining a bachelor, until a young widow called Edna McIntosh caught his attention. Tall and slender, with brown hair worn in a bun, Edna had been a regular customer through the war years, buying fabrics and notions for herself and her two children, while her husband was on active duty in North Africa. For some time she did not come to the shop, and he thought of her once or twice, wondering what this meant.

Then one day she came in, dressed in black and looking ill. She had received the dreaded telegram informing her that her beloved David had been killed at El Alamein. She had begun to take in sewing to make ends meet, to try to provide for her son and daughter.

Joseph's heart was stirred. A part of the feeling was pity, but he also felt moved to help the family. He had met the children, and had found them both well mannered and personable. Was this his chance to do something for someone else? He wanted to protect them.

As Edna worked through her grief, she confided more openly in Joseph, especially her concerns for her son, left fatherless at the age of twelve. They talked about Boys' Scouts and Boys' Brigade, and Joseph smiled to himself when he reflected on some of these conversations – a confirmed bachelor advising a young mother about activities for her son.

By the time the war was over they had formed a strong friendship, with Joseph invited to share a family dinner each Sunday. "Only if I can contribute to the meal," he stipulated. Having lived alone for many years, he had learned to cook, and so it was agreed he would take a surprise item to Edna's home in the suburbs. This caused some hilarity at times, when his contribution did not match the meal, but it was invariably devoured by two growing children, Edwin, fourteen, and Anne, twelve.

After much thought and a thorough discussion with Nola, Rudi wrote to his father, inviting him to come and live with his family. As an only child Rudi felt it was his duty, but he also knew the love his father felt for Canada, a love he now shared and understood. At 74 his father could manage the travel, and it would allow him to share in the upbringing of his grandchildren – the future of his family. With his brother, his sister-in-law and his dear wife all gone now, it seemed logical for Sam to join his branch of the family. However, the decision would be his. Rudi waited patiently for the reply.

When the letter from Rudi arrived Sam telephoned Victoria, asking if he might visit her. He would not explain, but his sister detected a note of lightness in his tone, for the first time since Mary's death last year.

The front door stood open. He was barely across the threshold when he exclaimed, "Well, I thought nothing could surprise me any more, but I was wrong. This has blown my socks off!" Seeing the look on his face Victoria could tell the news was good.

"Well, come on, share the news! I've already put the kettle on, but I can't wait to hear this. It has obviously got you excited." Sam passed over Rudi's letter, and watched her changing expressions as she read it. Turning to make a pot of tea, she said nothing. He waited patiently, accepted his tea, chose a scone and then just had to ask, "Well, what do you think?"

"I think that you have a wonderful son, but we both knew that already. You must have an equally amazing daughter-in-law, since she has obviously approved this idea."

"But should I do it, Sis? It's a big step, and I won't be coming back."

"What do you have to come back to, Sam? There are only the two of us left, and I won't last much longer. The future of your family is in Canada, and you have great memories of your adventures there in your prime."

They discussed the subject for a while. Victoria realised Sam really wanted to do this, but he needed her seal of approval. When she gave it, his decision was made.

Nola and Rudi knew they would need a bigger house if Sam accepted their offer. They began the search on hearing he would come. It was not urgent because it would be several months before he arrived. Rudi's recent promotion at work gave them the means to look in a higher rent-bracket, and they eventually found what they wanted. It was a four-bedroom home on three levels, overlooking Horseshoe Bay, in West

Vancouver. One of the rooms was set apart from the rest of the house – a perfect Grandpa flat. The owners were travelling overseas for eighteen months, so there would be another move when they returned. Rudi hoped he would be able to buy a home for his family by then.

With the help of Nola's family they moved in during the summer, and had everything ready for the arrival of Grandpa Sam in September. The children were taught that going into Grandpa's room was by invitation only, and that he would want to be by himself sometimes.

Sam arrived with the autumn colours, and felt a warm glow to be so accepted by his family. This was where he should be. He played games with Sammy and minded the children while Nola went grocery shopping.

Little Peter was a frail child with a chesty cough. Yet he loved life, and tottered about chasing a ball or the family cat. Rudi and Nola worried about him, wondering what the future held. Sam was determined that the child should make the most of whatever time was allotted to him. He would hoist Peter onto his shoulders, loving the throaty chuckles this brought, and gallop through the house, thankful for the high doorways. As soon as they came to a stop Peter would cry, "More horsey!" and they would be off again. Sam was glad of his healthy constitution, but Nola was usually the one to call a halt to the game. "Horsey tired," she would say, and Peter would reply, "Poor horsey. Rest."

Now that his father was living with him Rudi tried to keep in contact with Joseph in Christchurch, so that he did not lose touch with his New Zealand family. He would always be a Kiwi, and since leaving the land of his birth he felt more patriotic than ever.

He had been surprised to receive Joseph's news that he had married last year. In his excitement of relocating Sam had forgotten to pass this on. The whole family had been convinced that Joseph would be a bachelor for life. In his late forties now, Joseph had gained an instant family, which had enriched his life. As a devoted father himself Rudi could understand that.

Early in 1948 a cold, damp winter brought Peter his worst-ever chest infection. All the love and prayers of his family, as well as the medical expertise of the hospital staff, could not bring him back from the precipice, and in February they lost him. Gloom settled over the normally happy household, and Sam felt it keenly. He would have given his own life to save his little horse-rider, but that was not to be.

"It should have been me," he said to Rudi.

"No, Dad, it was Peter's turn."

At the funeral Rudi carried the tiny white coffin to the grave site, followed by Grandpa Sam, Nola and little Sammy, aged four, holding each other's hands. There were no tears, their pain going deeper than tears. Losing such a lively little character, who had brought them all so much joy, plunged them into deep despair.

Sammy struggled to understand what had happened to Peter. He visited the grave with his parents, and managed to read "Peter Joseph Hamilton" on the headstone, but was Peter in the box Daddy had carried? Why was he put in the ground? Wouldn't he be cold? His distraught parents made every effort to explain the meaning of death to their remaining son.

Joseph's acknowledgment of Rudi's tragic news contained further sad tidings. Just before her eightieth birthday Victoria had passed away peacefully in her sleep. Charles had said his mother was resisting any attempts to celebrate the milestone: having been a hard-working woman all her life she could not abide the thought of being eighty years old.

The main item in the letter, however, was a long and vivid description of a tragedy in which cousin Marie was involved. Joseph had been deeply affected by the incident, and wanted to bring Rudi up to date with its details. He provided some background on how Marie had come to be there.

When John Davis had returned home as an amputee in 1944, he received a letter from a school friend, Len Collins, who lived in Southland with his parents. Len had not gone to the war, being counted as an "essential worker" on the family farm. Feeling that he had not "done his bit" he offered to help on the Davis farm in Canterbury, at least until Richard returned from the war. Len's father was not happy but could understand his son's feelings, and the boy promised to return when he could. No-one knew how much longer the war would go on.

John and his father, Charles, were grateful for the offer and Len was welcomed to Totara Ridge at New Year in 1945. Marie and Bernadette enjoyed the company of someone other than brothers and it was a happy household. A romance gradually blossomed between Len and Marie, and at Christmas 1946 she accepted his proposal of marriage. In view of Marie's age – she was just 21 – her parents insisted they wait till 1948 to be married.

Early in 1947 Nicole, Marie's mother, asked cousin Joseph if her daughter might spend some time in Hamilton's Drapery, to see if that was the sort of work she would like. Not needing more staff, Joseph agreed that she could stay with him and his new wife for a month or two and attend the shop each day, but he could not pay her. Marie loved the shop environment. Joseph agreed to contact Mr. Kenneth Ballantyne, owner of a much larger drapery store in the city, to see if Marie could work as a trainee there. On Joseph's recommendation she began work there in March.

Rudi sighed and rubbed his eyes. It was taking a long time to get to the incident, but he understood that Joseph wanted to give the background first. Picking up the letter again, he read on.

Joseph gave details of the annual Agricultural and Pastoral Show, held that year from November 13th to 15th. Len had worked there for the Thursday and Friday, but was given Saturday as a free day, when he and Marie enjoyed the entertainment and animal events. Charles Davis had said to him, "Take a few days in the city and do your Christmas shopping for your family," since Len was due to go home for Christmas.

It was Tuesday, November 18th. Len had been into Ballantyne's, where Marie had helped him find a gift for his mother. They agreed to meet at five o'clock, when she would finish work. He went on his way, browsing along Colombo Street.

Marie was sent on an errand to the accounts office on the second floor. On the way she met staff returning there from their tea break. Someone commented that they saw smoke on the stairs, but there were people standing around unconcerned, so Marie continued to the office with them. Having completed her errand she had just stepped out of the office when all the lights went out. Should she try to go back to the office? She could see in the gloom it was full of smoke, and now flames were coming up through the floor. There was nowhere to go! Grabbing the arm of a work friend she shouted, "We have to jump!" The other girl hesitated. Marie pushed her out onto a stone ledge under a window and the girl launched herself downwards, followed by Marie. Screaming, they crashed into a firemen's ladder and landed, unconscious, on a verandah below, one floor above the street.

Len had seen the dense black cloud of smoke from further along the street. As he ran towards the building it suddenly blazed from end to end. He could hear the screams of the women and girls trapped inside. Did he imagine it or could he hear his name? He looked up in time to see Marie jump from a window. With no recollection of what happened next he helped firemen rescue the two injured girls from the verandah. They were two of the lucky ones, with only broken bones and bumps on their heads.

Joseph reported that the fire was so fierce there was nothing left of the building. Detritus lay three feet deep and it was impossible to identify all of the bodies. The death toll was established at 41, a civic funeral was held, they were placed in a common grave, and the building was demolished.

Perhaps Joseph felt some guilt that he had sent Marie to work at Ballantyne's; or did he empathise with Kenneth Ballantyne because they worked in the same industry? Rudi could sense that this event had a great impact on his cousin. He must write to Marie and Joseph.

In other family news, Vicki and Bruce had moved to the North Island, where Bruce had been offered a good job. Marie and Marjorie were planning a double wedding for later in the year. Charles and Nicole were preparing to move into Victoria's cottage on the farm; Richard and Maria were expecting their first child; and, news of all news, Joseph was about to become a father – at forty-eight!

When Rudi showed the letter to his father, Sam's eyes misted up at the news that his only sister had passed on. He thought of her saying she would not last long. Who would host the family gatherings now? Sarah and Jim were in the old house in the city, whilst Charles and Nicole would be in the cottage, and he was on the other side of the world. Time was moving on, changes were inevitable.

Later in the year the double wedding took place – Marie and Leonard Collins and Marjorie and Bernard James. Jim gave his step-daughter away, while Richard did the honours for his sister Marie. The social columns of the newspaper made much of the two beautiful brides, noting how fortunate Marie Davis had been in the catastrophic fire of the previous November. Following the reception the couples went their separate ways, with the Collinses moving to the family farm in Southland whilst the Jameses headed north to Auckland. Rudi mused that if he ever returned to New Zealand he would have to travel the full length of the country to see his relatives. Family gatherings would be few and far between from now on.

The year turned. Nola presented Rudi with a beautiful daughter early in 1949. They named her Adrienne and both Rudi and Sam were touched when Nola gave her the second name of Mary. She was born with dark hair, but there was also a hint of Mary's auburn.

From Christchurch Joseph reported the safe arrival of a precious daughter, whom they named Catherine Edna. Now he could plan for the future of his business, as well as delighting in being a besotted father.

When Bernadette married Thomas Dixon later that year, they too left the city, settling on the beautiful, untamed West Coast of the South Island.

At about that time, as the eighteen-month deadline for Rudi and Nola's rental approached, they received a letter from the Robinsons, who owned the house. Their travels had been part-business, and they had decided to set up their own enterprise in Brazil. They therefore needed to sell their house in Vancouver, but before they listed it, they wondered if Rudi and Nola were in a position to buy it? Once Sam was brought into the discussion it was a *fait accompli*. They all loved the house, and it would make things easier for the Robinsons.

The germ of an idea grew in Rudi until he could not keep it from Nola any longer. Commercial aviation was becoming more advanced by the month, offering a mode of travel better than lengthy sea voyaging. One evening, as they sat after dinner, he suddenly said,

"How would you feel about visiting New Zealand, Nola? It's nearly ten years since I left and I would love to see some of my cousins, now that they are grown up and married."

Startled, Nola responded, "But it takes weeks to get there, Rudi. How could you get enough leave from work?"

"It doesn't take long if you fly. Maybe four or five days each way, and two weeks to visit while there.

"Fly? Good heavens, is it safe? With a baby? What about your father?"

Sam, who had been pretending he could not hear the conversation, muttered, "You won't get me in one of those contraptions. If we were meant to fly we would have wings."

A glare from Rudi went unnoticed. He gave his attention to persuading Nola that airlines would not move large numbers of people if it was not safe. Having sown the seed, he left it to germinate, and continued formulating his plans in his own mind.

Chipping away at the resistance over several weeks, Rudi brought home brochures and timetables, putting together an itinerary for the next year. He suggested to Nola that maybe they should leave Adrienne behind with her grandfather, adding, before she could reply, "We could ask your parents to come and stay." Adrienne would be almost a year old, and Marianne would be well able to care for her. Sammy would be almost starting school, but if they went in January they would be back in time for that, and he would love the aeroplanes.

Nola's resistance was wearing down, and she realised Rudi was putting a lot of thought into this. She actually began to look forward to the adventure, once the obstacles were overcome. Her parents had readily agreed to move in for a month to help out. Sam got along well with them, especially with Dennis, and Marianne would be delighted to have her granddaughter to herself.

In the pit of her stomach Nola felt a real fear about flying. It was such an unknown. She would have to try to keep it to herself, and concentrate on looking forward to becoming acquainted with Rudi's country and relations. He had given up a lot so that she could be near her family. She would not spoil his visit home, even if it meant knots of fear in her stomach with each flight. It couldn't be worse than some of her wartime experiences, surely?

CHAPTER 5

Visit

The big day had arrived. Sammy was so excited he was hopping from one foot to the other, clutching his favourite bear, as he waited for his grandparents to arrive. Dennis and Marianne were to take Rudi, Nola and Sammy to the airport, before returning to stay with Grandpa Sam.Nola was less excited, as it meant handing over her baby daughter for a month. She hoped there would be enough happening to keep her mind busy, and she was determined to do everything to help her husband enjoy this visit to his birth country. He was almost as excited as his son. They had waited until Christmas and New Year had passed. It was now the beginning of January, deep into winter. They were all looking forward to the extra helping of summer ahead.

There were tears at the airport, as expected. Adrienne was hugged tightly, before being handed to Marianne, and they were off on their adventure. Sammy was overwhelmed at the size of the aeroplane, but the crew made him feel special and soon he was drawing pictures while they waited for takeoff. By the time they had landed in and left Honolulu, Tahiti and Fiji, all hot places, he was a seasoned traveller, and his parents could relax.

On the fourth day, when the plane touched down in Auckland, Rudi scanned the faces of the waiting crowd for Marjorie. The last time he had seen her was Christmas, 1939, and all he could remember was her dark hair. She must be twenty-four by now. Suddenly a dark-haired young woman was waving to them, and squeezing past others at the barrier. "Rudi!" she called. What a relief!

Rudi had planned an itinerary to visit as many relatives as possible. In age he fell between his much older cousins, and his second cousins, who were over ten years younger. He was happy to be "Uncle Rudi" to their children, but just "Rudi" to them. Marjorie and Bernard had not yet started a family, so the problem did not arise on this part of their trip.

Having arrived at the weekend, they had all day Sunday to be shown the sights. Auckland was a beautiful city, which Rudi had never visited. It reminded him of Vancouver. Nola agreed, the water everywhere reminding her of her home city.

Nola had travelled better than expected. She became accustomed to the constant drone of the plane, finding it quite soothing, and Sammy had slept much of the time. Rudi had been wonderful with him, aware that Nola was on edge about leaving Adrienne.

They had arranged to hire a car for their travels in the North Island, which would last for a week. Rudi wanted to leave most of their time for Christchurch, their final destination.

It felt strange to be driving on the other side of the road again, but Rudi soon adapted. Nola was reluctant to take the wheel, especially as some of the roads were narrow andwinding. She was keeping Sammy amused and enjoying the surprising changes in scenery. In Canada it did not change for hundreds of miles, but now she was seeing rolling green hills and valleys give way to lakeside vistas, bush-clad expanses, with beautiful tree ferns rising over bracken, providing elegant parasol-like shade. In turn this became harsh, dry land and wind-sculpted rocks.

On the second day Rudi pulled over, feigning tiredness, and asked her to drive for a while. She was nervous but agreed to help out. Rudi had chosen an automatic car, more expensive but with her driving in mind. She set off, whispering, "Keep left, keep left" as she drove. Rudi smiled and closed his eyes to show confidence in her. After an hour or so a squeal of brakes forced his eyes open. "Everything OK?" he asked.

"It was a rabbit!" Nola replied.

"Well, there are millions of those here, one less won't matter."

"Did you squish it, Mommy?" asked Sammy. "Can I see?"

"No Sammy, I didn't hit it."

Rudi resumed the driving, and Nola could admire the three majestic volcanoes rising from the flat land to their right. Even in summer they wore kerchiefs of snow. She could only imagine how breathtaking they must look in winter. One was a perfect cone, rising between two sprawling massifs. Rudi told her that they were all active volcanoes, and that this was known as the Desert Road. Soon she saw why. Having left the mountains behind they were now driving between tussock-covered, dry hills. It was an ever-changing panorama.

They arrived at Vicki and Bruce's in the late afternoon to a warm welcome. Nola felt completely accepted by Rudi's family, just as he had by hers. New Zealanders were a lot like Canadians, she mused. Was it the similar colonial history? Perhaps it was something to do with the Commonwealth? Whatever it was, it made her feel very much at home.

Vicki had a little son, Charles, nearly three years old. Sammy was warned not to be rough with him. He surprised his mother by replying, "I know, Mommy, like Peter." Nola fought back tears as she hugged him. "Yes dear, like Peter." The boys played ball and shared Charles's toys. Sammy was the perfect playmate, to his parents' relief.

Vicki had been doing some work on the family's history and was glad to pick Rudi's brain about his branch. She had not known about his father's Klondike experiences, and was especially interested to hear that Rudi had gone there recently. They put their heads together for several hours, both gaining from the shared knowledge. Rudi had always considered Joseph the guardian of the family's history, but it was good to know that someone from the next generation was also keen to record the details. Would Sammy and Adrienne be interested, too, as they grew older? They might if he could provide the spark.

After three nights it was time to move on. They had to hand back the car in Wellington and would spend two nights there before crossing on the weekly ferry to the South Island.

Although it had been good to stay with Rudi's family, Nola was pleased to have Rudi to herself again. They ate out, and wandered back to their hotel for Sammy's bedtime, before relaxing with a coffee in their room. Rudi put his arm around Nola, drawing her close to him. "You know, I have been so proud of you since we arrived here, my love. I know you were not as keen as I was to make this trip, and I know you are missing Adrienne, but you have made a wonderful effort to get to know my family. Thank you for that."

"It has been good to see you in your own environment, Rudi. You settled into my family, so it's only fair that I get to know yours, but I am glad to have you to myself for these two nights."

"Is that an invitation?"

"It could be."

"Well, we need an early night, don't we?"

The ferry trip to the South Island was magical. It was a sunny day, with only a light wind. The first part of the voyage was sheltered as the ship rode the channel out to the open sea. Gulls crowded overhead, screaming for scraps of food from the passengers. When someone threw them food there were squawks of indignation from the birds which missed out.

Out on the open spaces of Cook Strait the waves were a little higher, but the ferry pushed through them steadily. Sammy was thrilled spotting dolphins playing in the bow wave and racing the ship, but taking the time to leap and twist in the air, to the passengers' delight.

The third part of the voyage was through the hilly-sided fiords with turquoise water and little bays with tiny jetties. Although it reminded Nola of the trip to Vancouver Island, she thought these sounds were prettier, with their tree ferns and shaded bush.

The ferry docked at Picton, where they would spend the night before taking the train to Christchurch. There were not many trains in New Zealand, but Rudi and Nola had resolved to travel on as many as possible, in part so that their active little five-year-old could use up some of his boundless energy, but also so that they could both admire the landscapes without the stress of driving.

Picton was a charming place, with steep, bush-clad hills surrounding the harbour. On the beach, close to the ferry port, was a children's playground, and their motel was just walking distance away. They persuaded Sammy to go there and leave their bags first, before visiting the park, but Edward Bear would have to come, too. He would like the swings.

After a restful night Rudi, Nola, and Sammy with Edward Bear, who seemed to have become more treasured as the holiday progressed, strolled down to the waterfront late next morning, where Sammy gave Edward a swing and played in the sandpit. Rudi took several photos, which he knew would impress friends and family back in Canada, for it was truly a postcard scene. Large Canary Island palms framed his photos, adding a tropical air. Soon it was time to head to the train station nearby. Rudi was glad he had reserved their seats, since this was the tourist season, and also the summer school holidays. There were people everywhere, many of them families with excited young children. Sammy was scared of the big black engine, which was already puffing out white smoke into the blue sky.

On the train Rudi took charge of his son, laying down the rules and limits of where he could go alone. Then he took his hand and led him through to the open viewing car, where the wind rushed through their hair. Rudi wanted to take some photos, but did not dare take his eyes or hands off Sammy. Finally he decided to return the child to his mother's care. With all the excitement and upheaval Sammy was tired, and he soon fell asleep with Edward.

Nola found the journey relaxing. It was a blend of coastal scenery, farmlands, even some grape-growing areas, with occasional rivers which had huge, wide riverbeds, but the water chose its own path, hardly ever touching the banks. She learned later that they were, appropriately, called "braided rivers".

It was seven o'clock when the train pulled in to the Christchurch station. In the hurly-burly of hundreds of people disembarking, Rudi craned his neck to find Joseph, who had agreed to meet them. There he was, looking much the same as always. A few grey hairs, but a happier face than before. The two men shook hands, and Joseph kissed Nola on the cheek when he was introduced to her. Ruffling Sammy's hair, he remarked, "Good to see the next generation looking so healthy."

Edna had agreed for the visitors to stay with them in their large house. They would be able to come and go as it suited them. Nola and Edna became friends instantly. They had something in common, both having married into the Hamilton family, and they were both mothers of Hamilton children. Catherine was adorable, and Nola had to conquer the pangs gripping her as she thought of Adrienne in Canada. She knew it was the sensible thing to do, leaving her behind, and her mother's letters reassured her, even with news about a tooth safely through. They would be home in two weeks, she told herself. Meanwhile, she would enjoy getting to know this lovely child, who had brought such joy to her father, and indeed to her whole family,

Sarah and Jim arranged a get-together at the old homestead, to welcome Rudi and his family. The twins, Alex and Bertie, would be there; Prue and James still lived at home. Richard, Maria and their little boy, Jonathon would come in from the farm, bringing John with them. Charles and Nicole were also coming. Rudi was looking forward to it. He hoped it would not be too overwhelming for Nola. He had no such concerns for Sammy, who made friends easily.

It was cloudy in the morning, but by lunchtime the sun had come out. Sarah and Jim had taken the gamble – it was January, after all – of setting up trestle tables under the old oak tree, with seats and rugs scattered to offer each family a place for a picnic-style lunch. Each family had brought food to share, and it was a veritable feast.

Once the families were fed and the children were off playing, supervised by Prue and James, the adults were able to draw their seats together and catch up on each other's news. There were childhood anecdotes – Nola loved those – also war stories and tales of what it had been like at home during the war. John Davis even pulled up his trouser leg to show off his "fancy new leg", the prosthetic that had allowed him to throw away his crutches. With her nursing experience Nola was particularly interested.

It was a wonderful afternoon, bringing back many childhood memories for Rudi, and with the long summer evening still light, it was after eight o'clock when they went their separate ways to put tired children to bed and reflect on a successful reunion.

The rest of the holiday sped by, with day-trips to favourite places of Rudi's and two memorable train journeys. The first was through the mountains to Greymouth, on the West Coast – a breathtaking outing with glorious scenery that reminded Nola of the Canadian Rockies. It was raining and windy when they arrived, but the welcome from Bernadette and Tom was warm. They stayed a night and returned on the train the next afternoon.

The second train trip was a sentimental journey for Rudi, to Dunedin. Here he showed Nola the house in which he grew up until he left home to join the army engineers. They knocked on the door to explain to the owner why they were lurking about. He generously invited them inside and they were able to look in Rudi's old room as well as wander through the whole house. For Rudi it was an emotional experience: he saw his mother everywhere. Nola thanked the owner and led Rudi out of the house, where he wiped his tears away. He had taken some photos for his father, but wondered if these might have a similar effect on him.

It was not possible to see Marie and Len, who lived well south of Dunedin. They had hoped to drive up, but a fire on land adjoining their farm kept all the men on call.

Sammy enjoyed the train journey back to Christchurch. It was hilly for the first part with lots of exciting tunnels. He tried to hold his breath, but some were too long and he would have to gasp for air before the train emerged. The second part, after Timaru, was flat, and here he held races between the train and the cars on the nearby road. The train won every time. "We won! We won!" he would exclaim. Other children in the carriage would join in.

Rudi was happier than Nola had ever seen him. Would he be suggesting that they move to New Zealand? But what about her family? It was an unsettling thought, but the subject was never raised. Now that Rudi's father was living with them, they would probably stay in Canada.

The date of their departure was set for February 5th. The following day was a national holiday, so Rudi had avoided that date. They would fly to Auckland, spend the final night with Marjorie and Bernard, and then begin the series of flights that would take them back to Vancouver. This time they would stop over in Samoa and Honolulu.

The farewells in Christchurch were bitter-sweet for Rudi. Would he see his cousins Sarah, Joseph and Charles again? They were a few years older than him, and none was likely to visit Vancouver. Still, it had been a wonderful holiday, and he had no regrets.

Nola was unwell on all of the flights. She could not get comfortable, and had little sleep. Was it excitement, or something else? She had been feeling nauseous the previous few days, but blamed it on the upheaval of packing and sleeping in different beds.

Arriving at Vancouver airport, she forgot all her discomfort when she sighted Adrienne in her grandmother's arms. "Mama, Dada," the little one chirped. Sammy smothered her with hugs. Rudi shook his father-in-law's hand, with a look that said, "At least we have our feet on the ground." His father had not come, in order to leave room in the car, but he was fine and looking forward to hearing all the stories.

CHAPTER 6

Life, Death and Changes

There was an unexpected memento of their travels for Rudi and Nola when, in October, they became parents again. Conceived in New Zealand, and especially treasured because of that, the baby had to be called Rudolph. They added Dennis in honour of Nola's father.

Baby Rudolph was blond, as his father had been, and Grandpa Sam took an immediate liking to him. Whilst he loved all his grandchildren, he felt that this one was his. He resolved that he would imbue this child with a love for New Zealand: he would be a little Kiwi. Nola was amazed to hear him telling the baby stories long before the child could understand them.

On the other side of the world the family was growing, too. Richard and Maria had a daughter Clarissa, as did Marie and Len, who named her Alison Victoria. The following year Vicki and Bruce welcomed John, while Bernadette and Tom had a son called Paul. Rudi decided he would create a family wall chart, to keep track of all these new relatives.

Later in the year Marjorie and Bernard became the proud parents of golden-haired twin girls, Pamela and Amelia. Their joy turned to concern, for Amelia did not thrive. They hoped she would catch up to her sister as time went by. However, it became apparent that the child had some disability, and Marjorie worried for her future. Little Pamela was a joy, chattering to her sister in her own language, reaching out and hugging her. It broke Marjorie's heart to see that Amelia made little response. Something was wrong. She confided her fears to the Plunket nurse on her next visit, and from there she was referred to a paediatrician in Auckland city. One appointment followed another as the gap widened in the twins' development.

Late in 1953, when the girls were two and a half years old, Marjorie was told of the upcoming visit of an American paediatric specialist to be based in Wellington for a number of weeks. Marjorie and Bernard decided that she should take the girls there, travelling on the train. It would be a long journey, but they could break it by staying with Vicki and Bruce along the way. Bernard delivered his little family to the train on December 17th. They would spend three nights with the cousins, and then continue to Wellington on Sunday, December 20th, to be ready for the appointment next morning. On the return they would stay again and be home on Christmas Day.

It was a long day on the train, but Marjorie was able to take the girls for walks. Pamela pulled her along, while Amelia sat in her arms. It would be good to have a diagnosis and, hopefully, a course of treatment for her beautiful baby. Vicki met them at Palmerston North late in the afternoon. She had brought Charles and John with her, so it was a noisy ride to their home half an hour away, with three active children. She hid her consternation at the state of Amelia's health. Over the next two days the women talked about it, and Marjorie was able to share her concerns. Vicki looked forward to seeing her after the appointment, with answers to her questions and a way forward for Amelia.

On the train on Sunday afternoon, Marjorie concentrated on the shorter journey to Wellington, and then a taxi to their hotel near the hospital. The girls settled well and they were all well rested when they walked along the road to the hospital next morning.

Dr Gundersen, the paediatric specialist from the United States of America, was warm and friendly towards the little girls. Amelia sat on the floor while he interacted with Pamela. When it came to her turn she looked fearfully at her mother, but before Marjorie could respond he had picked the child up and placed her on his knee. He produced a colourful wand with all sorts of things hanging from it. While she reached for these he went about his examination. He explained to Marjorie that it was not uncommon for a second-born twin to show the symptoms he saw in Amelia. He asked if Amelia was the second -born. Was there quite a time space between the two? Marjorie's replies were noted and he proceeded with his work in silence.

Not wanting to interrupt, but on the edge of her seat, Marjorie waited. Pamela distracted her with a book and a toy, sensing that her mother was not happy. Marjorie gave her a hug. "Melia?" said the child. "Soon, dear," replied her mother.

Handing Amelia back to Marjorie, and removing his spectacles as he leaned back in his chair, Dr Gundersen cleared his throat.

"Thank you for bringing these charming young ladies to see me, Mrs. James. As I hinted to you, I have seen many cases that are similar to Amelia's. Sometimes when twins are born there is a delay before the second child is delivered. This can cause a lack of oxygen to the second baby, causing a condition known as cerebral palsy. I believe this is what has happened in your case."

Although glad to have a diagnosis, Marjorie felt overwhelmed. Had she done something wrong, had she caused this for Amelia? What did it mean for the future? She asked the doctor if Amelia would walk. Would she improve? Would she reach adulthood? She wished Bernard were here to help her absorb all this new information. The doctor was kind, answering all her questions and providing pages of details about the condition. When he ushered her out of his office, a nurse took her arm and steered her into a small room where she made a cup of tea for Marjorie and entertained the twins with some toys. Marjorie gradually composed herself, thanking the nurse for her kindness.

Since the train was not due to leave till 6.30 p.m. Marjorie stored their luggage at the station and they caught a bus to the beach. Here the girls splashed in the water – Amelia loved water – and Marjorie thought about the life ahead of the child. She and Bernard would do their best to give her a happy life.

Vicki was there to meet them again. She had put the boys to bed. Bruce was reading them a story. The twins fell asleep on the way back to the house, allowing Marjorie and Vicki to talk. The tears fell as Marjorie recounted the diagnosis, and Vicki reached out a comforting hand to her cousin. She felt almost guilty for having two boisterous and healthy boys.

By the time they left to catch the night train on Christmas Eve, Marjorie had come to terms with Amelia's disability. She knew it would be a shock for Bernard, who adored his girls, and that she would have to be strong. Dr Gundersen had made it clear that they were in no way the cause of the problem, a great relief.

The northbound Auckland Express pulled in to Palmerston North on time. Vicki helped Marjorie get her bags, and her girls, on board. Their reservation was for the second carriage, which, being second-class, had wooden slatted seats, far from ideal for sleeping. However, the girls were sleepy, and Marjorie was glad she had hired pillows for them all. The children were asleep before the train had rounded the first bend.

Marjorie did not expect to sleep, with her mind full of the details of Amelia's diagnosis, and what it would mean for Bernard and her. She dozed as the train hurtled into the night.

Waking for no apparent reason she looked out and saw a small light swaying back and forth in the inky darkness. What could that mean? She knew that they were near the mountains and there was a bridge nearby. A shiver ran down her spine. Something was wrong, the light was a warning. What Marjorie did not know – nobody on the train could know – was that a torrent of water twenty feet deep, rushing down from Mount Ruapehu, carrying ice, volcanic ash and boulders, had washed away the concrete bridge supports, and their train was approaching the bridge. It was chaos. The locomotive plunged into the icy river, dragging with it the first five carriages. The sixth teetered on the track before tumbling into the raging Whangaehu River.

There was a mad scramble to get out as the bitterly cold water filled their carriage. Marjorie grabbed her daughters, now awake and screaming. It was hard to carry them both, and she was glad when a strong young man offered to take Amelia. With Pamela in her arms she kept their heads above water and waded towards the bank. Helpers were there, the news having spread even before the train had reached the bridge. There had been no way to alert the train driver in time, although a man had run along the track swinging a lantern.

Passing Pamela to a man waiting with blankets, Marjorie turned back to search for the man who had taken Amelia from her. In the dark she couldn't see much, although people had parked cars with their lights facing the river. She could see the outline of smashed carriages, with rescuers delving into them. There were bodies in the water, which was flowing swiftly over the broken bridge. Someone took her arm and guided her to the bank. Cars were ferrying the wet, cold, shocked passengers to a community hall where the local people had assembled camp beds, blankets, jackets and towels, and brewed some hot soup. Those who were seriously injured were taken to hospital, and the dead were stored away from the rescue base.

Marjorie was frantic about Amelia. Had she handed the child to her death? As time went by, and she checked all the incoming wounded, her heart told her that her little Amelia was gone.

Bernard awoke on Christmas morning, looking forward to being reunited with his family. He had missed them. The train was due in at seven o'clock. He turned the radio on at six o'clock as he made toast for breakfast. The news was full of a train disaster. As he poured his tea he listened more carefully.

"Last night at 10.21 p.m. the northbound Auckland Express, carrying 285 passengers, plummeted into the Whangaehu River at Tangiwai, with the loss of 151 lives. It is the worst rail accident in New Zealand history," intoned the newsreader. Bernard froze. "Marjorie," he whispered, "and my angels." What should he do? He needed to know if they were alive. In agony he waited for the six-thirty news. Concentrating on details of whom to contact if family were on the train and desperate to do something he dressed, washed, shaved and decided to go to the central police station. He found a family photo to take with him.

Somehow the night had passed, and Marjorie thought ruefully that it was a unique Christmas morning. Rescuers had found sixty bodies downstream, among them that of a young man still clutching a golden-haired child. Although it broke her heart, Marjorie was grateful they had been found, and that Amelia would have felt safe in his arms till the end. He may have looked strong, but the raging river had the final say. In identifying her child she asked for the identity of the young man. She would write to his family to express her gratitude for his bravery.

Bernard and Marjorie were reunited that night, with Pamela still asking for Amelia. Her mother had tried to explain about the river but to a two-year-old it didn't make sense. The funeral would be difficult, but they owed it to Pamela to answer her questions about her sister.

Details of the Tangiwai Disaster, as the train tragedy became known, were released daily in the newspapers. The list of names looked like war casualty lists. Marjorie felt compelled to read every article, to understand how she lost Amelia. She read that the flash-flood from the mountain, only minutes before the train reached the bridge, was eighteen feet deep. She couldn't imagine the force of it! No wonder the bridge supports were smashed, because it was carrying boulders and ice with it. Four carriages had been completely destroyed, but many passengers who had survived the crash were drowned in the swollen river, like the brave young man who had tried to save Amelia. There had been only twenty-eight survivors from the first five carriages, and fifteen of those were from Marjorie's carriage. She was indeed fortunate. She felt for the families of the twenty never identified.

This disaster took place during the visit of the new queen, Elizabeth, and her consort, Prince Philip. In a much-appreciated gesture the Prince attended a ceremony where the unidentified were placed in a mass grave.

Following Marjorie's heart-rending phone call, Sarah and Alex made plans to fly to Auckland as soon as possible. They tried to understand the state that Marjorie must be in, her loss and feelings of guilt. Bernard was arranging the funeral. He too must be in disbelief.

Vicki and Bruce left their boys with friends and drove to Auckland for the service. Vicki was numb at the thought that this had occurred only a couple of hours after she had helped settle the little ones on the train. How could this have happened?

Rudi and Nola sent a heartfelt message. They knew what it was like to lose a loved child, and they gently advised Marjorie and Bernard to give Pamela a brother or sister as soon as possible. There would be a right time for it.

The funeral was heart-wrenching for the family. Bernard and Marjorie had agonised over whether Pamela should attend the service, finally deciding that she should sit with her grandmother and aunt, rather than with her distraught parents. Although too young to remember the event, she would perhaps retain an inkling of its meaning. She had stopped asking for Amelia, and Marjorie had sought some counselling for her, which was already beginning to show results.

After Sarah and Alex had left for Christchurch, Marjorie set about looking ahead. She and Bernard finally talked about the future Dr. Gundersen had laid out for Amelia. It was bleak. Whilst they would always grieve for her, they felt that possibly she had been saved from a lot of pain and embarrassment.

Late in 1954 Pamela was ecstatic to welcome a baby brother – "her" baby. He was named Edward, which was a family name but also the name of the young man who had tried to save Amelia. His birth seemed to inspire some of the cousins, with Marie and Len producing a third child, Alice Marie, in 1955, and Bernadette and Tom adding Victoria to their family in the same year and Sally in 1956, sisters for Paul and Thomas. Prue, who had married Tony Albright in 1953, gave birth to twin boys, Matthew and David, in 1955.

Rudi and Nola tried to keep up with the family population explosion in New Zealand. The wall chart in Rudi's office needed extensions! Their own children were growing rapidly, with Sammy turning eleven in 1955, Adrienne starting school, and little Rudolph thinking he should. Rudi's father Sam had his eighty-second birthday, and kept excellent health. He spent as much time as the children would allow telling them stories – of New Zealand, of the Klondike, of his imagination – and they were enthralled. He wanted them to love both countries, as he did. Rudolph seemed especially intrigued with Sam's tales of New Zealand: his eyes would light up and he would hang on every word.

It was 1958, a year of family anniversaries and significant birthdays. Grandpa Sam celebrated his eighty-fifth birthday in March by taking his family out to dinner. He included Dennis and Marianne in the invitation, since they had become good friends over the ten years since he had moved to Vancouver. There were messages galore from his New Zealand friends and relatives, who had not forgotten him.

Unbeknown to Sam there were other plans afoot. Sarah and Jim were marking their thirtieth anniversary, as well as Jim's seventieth birthday. Charles and Nicole were celebrating forty years of marriage. At the functions they held, a plan was hatched to go and visit Sam in the winter (the northern summer). Why not? They were all retired, and well enough to travel. It was decided to make it a surprise for Sam.

When Rudi received the letter from his cousins, he raised an eyebrow. How could they accommodate four people? He talked it over with Nola, and, true to form, she came up with an ingenious solution.

Young Sam (who no longer liked to be called Sammy) had progressed through Cubs and into Boy Scouts. This meant going camping, which he loved. He was constantly asking his father to buy a tent, so that they could camp. Why not buy a large tent, that they could all sleep in, and give the cousins the use of the bedrooms in the house? It would be summer, so the weather would be warm. They would tell the children that this was a practice, to see if they were ready for real camping. Any more information would certainly get back to Grandpa.

As the weather warmed the family made a trip to the Army and Navy supplies store, returning with a large tent. Rudi and young Sam pitched it on the back lawn and the children crawled in and out all afternoon. Being the only one who had a sleeping bag, Sam was given the honour of sleeping in it that night. Next morning he reported hearing all sorts of snuffling noises, but nothing had shared the tent with him.

By July the family had invested in sleeping bags, lanterns and a camp stove, as well as inflatable beds. If they went off camping anywhere further than their own back lawn they would need a trailer to carry everything!

It was worth all the effort, to see Sam's face when Charles and Nicole, Sarah and Jim walked into the house. Tears rolled down his creased face at the thought that they had done this for him. They all talked late into the night, long after the three children had been put to bed in the tent. Rudi and Nola joined them after midnight, having reminded their guests that not everything had to be said on the first night. Next morning the stories began again, and Rudi realised there would never be silence in his house while his cousins were there. His father was a new man: always humble, he still could not believe that his niece and nephew had come all this way, and brought their spouses, to see him. He was glowing.

To ration his energy the visitors were sent off on several excursions. They took the ferry from Horseshoe Bay to Nanaimo, spent two nights on Vancouver Island, and returned full of new tales of bald eagles, of whales and sea otters. Charles, a keen photographer, put his films in to be developed, and a few days later they all enjoyed sharing the pictures.

On another day they rode the buses downtown, the ladies going shopping, the men visiting Gastown. This latter was a dubious environment, but Rudi had told them that the city had plans to rebuild much of it to create a historic precinct. Charles and Jim could see the promise in this idea since this was the site of the original city. On the return trip they stopped to explore Stanley Park, about which Rudi had enthused. They could see why. What a magnificent asset for a burgeoning city! When Rudi came to collect them after work they were all exclaiming about its wonders.

The one reservation the visitors had made for their stay was the train into the Rockies. They were all looking forward to staying in Banff, being tourists in a tourist town. They were not disappointed. Charles was busy with his camera, catching the breathtaking views. They took a tour to Lake Louise, with its mountain backdrop rising from the clear lake and the impressive hotel hunched behind it. They gasped as their coach took them along the road to Maligne Canyon, where many magical peaks vied for attention, and the glacial water of the lake was a milky turquoise. Returning to Banff late in the afternoon they watched the sun move across the surface of Mount Rundle, highlighting its slope before bringing the shadows of evening.

The following day brought more beautiful weather, and they headed north to Jasper for the day. Around every corner a new vista appeared, with snowy peaks and hanging glaciers contrasting with summer flowers, grasses and trees.

When they returned to the family they were full of a newfound appreciation for this land that their cousin Sam and Rudi had adopted. It was easy to understand what had kept them here, especially with the emotional ties.

Young Sam was enjoying renewing the acquaintance of these relatives he had met eight years ago. He had forgotten how they talked, and was impressed – again – at how happy they all were. There was a lot of laughter, and it was good to see Grandpa with his own family. He had given up much to come and live with the Greenaway side of the family.

Everyone was sad when it came time to part. They all knew that nothing like this would happen again, not for the older ones anyway. But Young Sam, at fourteen, was beginning to feel that sense of adventure which he knew ran through the Hamilton family. His great-grandpa had pulled up his roots and set off for the other side of the world ninety years ago, when conditions must have been far more primitive. He made a mental note to ask his grandpa what it was like in New Zealand back in those days.

CHAPTER 7

The Growing-up Years

After the New Zealand relatives had left, Rudi kept his promise of taking the children camping, at the same time exploring with them this large province they called home. He drew up a list of places he wanted to see, and Nola added some she had visited as a child. They noted those that would require a holiday weekend, and decided to start, on a normal weekend, with Fort Langley. It was not far from home and was full of history. Although it was school holidays Rudi was still working, so they would leave on Friday and have two nights camping before returning on Sunday afternoon. Dennis and Marianne would look in on Grandpa Sam to make sure both he and the cat were fed.

As he expected Rudi had to buy an open trailer to carry the tent and all the other camping gear. With five in the car there would be little room for luggage. Sam, now 14, was put in charge of preparations and by six o'clock they were ready to set off on the 40-mile journey to Langley. Nola navigated them through the city to New Westminster, over the Patullo Bridge, and then along the Fraser Highway to Langley.

On arrival the first priority was food. Fortunately they found a take-out shop, which pleased the children and ensured their co-operation in pitching the tent on the site they had reserved in the campground. Adrienne and Rudolph were nervous – this was not the same as camping on their lawn a couple of months ago, and being able to go inside when they wanted to – but their parents assured them they would stay close by, and the children drifted off to sleep to the sound of their family's voices.

The fort was only a short drive north of the campground and it opened at 10.00 a.m. That gave the family time to tidy their site after breakfast next morning and be ready to explore the national historic park, which included the fort. To keep them focussed Nola, who remembered visiting the fort as a child, had prepared a sheet of questions for the two younger children, with a reward if they completed it.

When they arrived they discovered that there had been recent reconstruction work on several buildings, including the trading store and the palisade. Nola was delighted because it looked much more interesting than she remembered.

The fort had been established in 1827 by the Hudson Bay Company, to serve as a base for the British fur trade. It was located at this spot on the Fraser River because this was the furthest point that ocean-going vessels could navigate. Its heyday came in the 1850s, when 10,000 prospectors waited there for canoes to take them upriver to the goldfields. Once the gold rush was over, the fur trade wound down, and other ways found to reach the interior of British Columbia, the importance of Fort Langley faded, so it was abandoned and fell into ruins.

Rudi was fascinated by the story; he saw parallels with the 1861 gold rush in Otago, just hours from his childhood home. He also thought of his father's journey to the Yukon goldfields. Gold had always caused a kind of fever in men, making them act in strange ways. Some died from the fever, some returned to normal life, and others never regained their sanity.

Absorbed in his own thoughts Rudi lost track of the family. He found them buying unusual articles in the trading store. Nola was telling the children to choose a small item because they had completed their quiz sheets. Rudi rolled his eyes, but remembered his parents doing the same thing.

The remainder of the day was spent exploring the park around the fort. There were places to play hide-and-seek, information panels to read, and bench seats for relaxing or meditating. That night Rudi and Sam cooked a barbecue meal and Nola brought out the salad she had prepared at home. Sam introduced his siblings to damper, a thick batter that could be squeezed on to a stick and cooked over a fire. They loved it, and Nola's large marshmallows, similarly cooked, completed a real feast.

Sunday was a lazy day. They had nothing planned, and each of them did exactly what they wanted to do. Nola read, and Rudi kicked a ball around with Rudolph and Adrienne, while Sam stretched out in the sun. With some reluctance they packed up at about four o'clock and headed north for home. Grandpa Sam was pleased to see them, and to hear all about their first "away-from-home" camping adventure, as well as all the details about Fort Langley. The weekend had been a success and they were determined to go camping again, before winter.

The family managed one more camping expedition before the weather became too inclement. They decided to head for Vancouver Island for the Labour Day weekend, just before school started for the year. They would have three nights away, time to see a lot of the island, they thought.

Driving the car and trailer on to the ferry at Horseshoe Bay was an easy start to the weekend – the terminus was only minutes from their home. Grandpa Sam had wanted to go with the family, but they all felt that, at 85, he shouldn't. Rudi promised that he and his father would travel to Victoria together in the near future, in greater comfort.

The ferry sailed into the twilight, docking in Nanaimo just before dark. The Hamiltons, glad that they had eaten on the ship, scrambled to pitch their tent at the nearby campground, wanting to take in the fiery sunset. Their plan was to drive across to the west coast of the island the next day and they looked forward to a Pacific Ocean sunset there.

It was a winding, hilly road, which seemed endless to Adrienne, who suffered from car sickness. After their lunch stop at Port Alberni, situated at the head of a long inlet which almost bisected the island, Nola gave up her front seat and joined the boys in the back for the remainder of the journey. At the coast they turned south to explore the beautiful Ucluelet inlet, where dolphins glided among tethered canoes and kayaks, while other craft, already hired, were dotted about on the jade-green bay.

Returning to the car they drove back to the turn-off and continued along the coast, soon arriving at Long Beach, their destination for the night. Rudi felt emotional, knowing that these Pacific waters also washed onto the beaches of New Zealand. With a lump in his throat, he walked silently to the water's edge and splashed water on his face.

Once they had set up camp, Nola decided to take the short drive to Tofino, to show the children (and Rudi) where the road began that would traverse the huge country of Canada. Parts of the highway were still being constructed but in about three years it would be a 5,000-mile road called the Trans-Canada Highway. Rudi photographed the information panel for future reference, and wondered if he would ever see the other terminus.

They were treated to another glorious sunset after supper. Rudi was quiet and Nola left him to his thoughts, knowing he was thinking of his family thousands of miles across the Pacific Ocean.

Sunday was a driving day. Both Sam and Rudolph were restless, and several stops were needed for them to burn off energy. They returned to Nanaimo in time for lunch and a play in the park. Then it was south to a campground not far from Victoria, which lay right at the southern tip of Vancouver Island, where the Canada / United States border veered south to accommodate the island. A game of soccer, once the tent was up, kept everyone busy, while Nola assembled their meal. A cloudy night meant no sunset.

Nola wanted to visit the Butchart Gardens. She had heard about them from friends. They were formed to hide a pit from which limestone had been extracted for many years, and they were said to be amazing. Adrienne chose to go with her mother. The gardens were some way from town, so next morning Nola would drop Rudi and the boys at the Museum of Natural and Human History, while she and Adrienne would go on to the gardens. They arranged to meet again at two o'clock in order to reach the ferry departure point on time.

It was a good arrangement and time passed quickly. Rudi and the boys discovered all kinds of exhibits in the museum, including a display of the proposed route of the Trans-Canada Highway, showing the western terminus at Victoria. Confused, they asked an attendant about it, and discovered that the government thought connecting major towns was a more important project than including a small settlement like Tofino, even though it was further west. They were glad they had seen the "real" Mile Zero.

Meanwhile Nola and Adrienne were enthralled by the floral displays and early tinges of autumn foliage at the gardens. Nola bought a Japanese maple and a flowering shrub to take home. It was hard to imagine that this place had been a quarry.

There was a lot of chatter in the car on the way back to Nanaimo, as they exchanged stories about their day. Soon they were heading for Horseshoe Bay and Grandpa Sam. Although they had covered some considerable distance Rudi found, on looking at his map, that they had not really seen much of the island at all. Canada was much bigger than he realised.

On their return to New Zealand the four travellers settled back into their routines. The newspapers were showing pictures of the almost-completed bridge over the harbour in Auckland. Charles and Jim had caught a brief glimpse of it – like a huge coat-hanger – before landing in Auckland, but had not paid much attention, being more concerned with finding out how to reach the connecting flight to Christchurch

Marjorie and Bernard took their children, Pamela, nine and Edward, five to the special day when people could walk across the new bridge. It was May 29th, 1959, and Bernard emphasised that they would never again be able to do this, for tomorrow there would be hundreds of cars making the crossing. This was history in the making, he told them. History or no, it was a long way, and Edward, at the age of five, completed it on his father's shoulders.

At the same time as Edward was riding on his father's shoulders, the Canadian Hamiltons were planning a camping excursion into the interior of their province. It was early summer and Nola had read about a provincial park recently established

within the Kootenay National Park. She wanted to take the family there and base themselves at Lillooet, making a loop trip, perhaps on the Canada Day weekend. With the holiday falling on a Wednesday Rudi could apply for leave on the Thursday and Friday. The children would already be on vacation.

Rudi liked the sound of it. Apart from his Alaska Highway experience and his honeymoon journey to the Rockies, he hadn't explored inland. He would put in his leave application so they could make a July trip, adding in the following Monday, so they could return at leisure.

As school finished for the year in June, Sam, Adrienne and Rudolph looked forward to the summer vacation. Sam had moved up to Venturer Scouts, while Adrienne had recently graduated from Brownies to Girl Guides. Rudolph was in his final year as a Cub. All three were eager to work towards new badges during the holidays.

On July 1st they celebrated Canada Day with their neighbours at a concert and fireworks display in the local park The anthem reminded Rudi of his childhood when he proudly sang a different one.

Next morning it was all hands on deck, to make ready for their longest camping trip. Nola had done the itinerary planning, as well as the food arrangements. She and Adrienne packed the stores in the trailer, while Rudi and the boys sorted the tent, bedding and furniture. By lunchtime everything was ready. It was an unusual lunch, as they ate everything they weren't taking.

Rudi was glad he and his father had visited Victoria, on the Island, in the spring. They had stayed at the beautiful creeper-clad Empress hotel on the waterfront for two nights and wandered about the city as much as Sam was able. Rudi knew his father was past the age for camping. He would share the house with Nola's parents, Dennis and Marianne, while the family slept on narrow camp-beds for four nights.

After lunch they headed north, as the heat of the day filled the car. Windows were rolled down and papers secured as the breeze gave them some relief. As they neared Squamish, huge masses of rock appeared to their right, forming a ridge in contrast to the land that sloped away towards the inlet on their left. They stopped and changed drivers before heading on to Whistler. The road was not sealed, so Rudi swapped seats with Adrienne. The scenery was impressive, with steep-sided mountains towering over the settlement, but the dusty, narrow, winding road meant no windows could be opened more than a slit. Nola's home-made lemonade, shared out from the cooler bag, was a welcome reviver. They had been on the road six hours, with still some way to go.

Rudi drove on and Nola sat in the back with the boys, who just wanted to arrive and set up camp. Maybe this trip wasn't such a good idea.

Another hour brought them to the campground at Pemberton. Fortunately there was plenty of space and the team got to work, setting up the tent and preparing dinner. Spirits rose after dinner, the rigours of the journey receding.

Next day the family could take their time. There was no hurry to leave. They packed up, left the car off-site, and went hiking along a trail. The younger children could both qualify for a forest walk badge if they covered all the criteria. Nola and Rudi made sure that everything was done correctly and signed off. Sam remembered the excitement of gaining badges and handing them proudly to his mother to sew onto his uniform. In Venturers there were some badges, but most of the awards required long-term commitment to a project.

After lunch at a picnic site it was on the road to Lillooet. The road was rough and narrow, with signs stating it was to be used in summer only. It was not difficult to see why. Whilst it was dry and dusty now, it would be different in winter. They were 300 feet up, so there would be snow, and how would you know where the road was?

As the afternoon warmed to 34 degrees Celsius the sight of their destination rose like a mirage. Seton Lake lay, serene and welcoming, begging them to come for a swim. The tent could wait another hour. Claiming a campsite the family changed and headed for the water. *This* was why they had come so far on those awful roads!

Refreshed by the swim and a walk by the lake everyone was ready for the work detail. Later, in the cool of the evening, they played soccer with some neighbouring campers, before heading for bed as darkness fell.

The plan for Sunday was to explore the Marble Canyon provincial park, which lay between Lillooet and Cache Creek. It was only a short drive, but they left early to beat the heat. Magnificent lakes broke up the dryness of the scrubby vegetation. The park was nestled in the rugged Pavilion Mountain range.

Parking the car Rudi and Nola made sure everyone had hats, insect repellent, food and water before they set off for Marble Canyon. Unlike the granite mountains closer to the coast, this gulch was made up of limestone rock, with white chalk-faced slopes. The canyon floor was covered in vegetation, punctuated by patches of scree where the rocks had crumbled and fallen down the steep slopes. Clinging to these inclines the plants of the Indian paintbrush were showing their first spiky orange flowers, breaking up the green below.

Further along the trail Pavilion Lake glistened in the sun, perfect for Rudi taking photos as his family trekked on. By the time he caught up with them, they were looking for a shady place to stop for lunch, hoping to gain access to the lake.

Soon they found their spot, enjoyed a paddle in the lake to cool tired feet, and ate their packed lunch. Rudi wanted to go on far enough to see Chimney Rock, but the others wanted to relax before the return walk. He was about to set off alone when Adrienne offered to join him. Touched at her loyalty he asked, "Are you sure?" to which she replied, "We already left you behind once, and I was worried about you." The two went off hand-in-hand, and soon found Chimney Rock on the lake shore.

"It looks like all that's left of a fairy castle, Daddy."

"It does indeed. Shall I take a photo of my fairy princess in front of it?"

Giggling shyly Adrienne posed for the photo, before they returned to the others.

When the family got back to the campground, the young folk went for a swim in Seton Lake. There were some broken branches in the water, which the boys skirted around, swimming to the deeper water. A cry from Adrienne alerted Sam to her plight. She had caught her foot in a branch, and her head was almost under water as she tried to untangle herself. Sam sent Rudolph running for their parents, while he held his sister's head up. Rudolph arrived, eyes wide, stammering something about Adrienne. "Stuck … head in water … Sam, come!" His parents sprinted to the lake, with Rudolph gasping as he tried to keep up with them. Rudi rushed straight into the water. Once he was there to hold Adrienne's head up Sam could dive below the water and pull the leafy branches away from her foot. It took several attempts, but before long they had her back on shore, rubbing her painful ankle. Rudi piggy-backed the child to their camp-site, where Sam bandaged her ankle. They all agreed she was a lucky girl.

Next morning they made an early start to their journey south. The first 35 miles was an unsealed road, which followed the Fraser River, and then they would join the main road as far as their destination of Hope. They would spend the day chasing the river as it grew in force, fed by tributaries along the way. This was the beginning of their way home.

Rudi was pleased to have taken the extra day's leave, in order to pace the drive back. He was learning to respect the size of this country he now called home, and it had been a good idea to put Nola in charge of the planning.

On Monday they arrived late in the afternoon, with so many tales to tell Grandpa Sam that he had to give them appointments to speak to him.

The arrival of the Sixties seemed to usher in a time to cast off the post-war blues. Babies born at the end of the war were now teenagers, who had not known the strictures of the Depression, or the rationing of the war years, and did not want to. They were ready to have fun. The hippie movement in the United States had many admirers around the world. Those who were less daring opted for mini-skirts, back-combed hair and flared pants. Parents wrung their hands.

In 1960 Auckland was the first city in New Zealand to sell television sets, soon followed by Wellington and Christchurch. The programmes were American Westerns and the occasional comedy show. Those who owned a TV set suddenly found they had new friends.

Marjorie and Bernard were in two minds about buying a set. Would the children become addicted to it? Not if they set strict rules, they decided. Marjorie was more concerned that Bernard would be the one to become "hooked", as he would want to see it as a good investment. They waited for a few months, to let any teething troubles be resolved, and then Bernard arrived home with a carton one evening. Behind him came a van. Not trusting himself to set it up, he had paid for a service man. Marjorie smiled. She knew that once the children saw the TV set they would expect it to work.

Rudi smiled when he read Marjorie's letter about the television set. His children had grown up with TV, and were now discerning about which programmes to watch. Not so Grandpa Sam – he would watch anything, fascinated by the whole idea of radio with pictures. Rudi had installed a set in his father's room. These days Sam had less energy, often falling asleep in the afternoons and waking later in the mornings. He still loved short visits from the children. When Rudolph told him that he was keen to visit New Zealand, Sam knew he had succeeded in his mission. He suggested that 1968 would be a good time, because it would be one hundred years since his, Sam's, parents had emigrated from England. Although it was years away Rudolph set his sights on that year, when he would be eighteen.

In 1964, when Young Sam was twenty, Adrienne fifteen and Rudolph fourteen, their beloved grandfather took ill. He had never been sick before, and they all knew this was the end. He wanted to go to the hospital, not wanting to die in their home, but the family would not hear of it. They insisted that this was his home. They all took turns sitting with him, and a nurse came in for the nights. Sad that they were losing their inspirational Grandpa, so much loved by them all, they concentrated on making his final days as comfortable as they could. Did he really know how much they loved him? Adrienne stuck hearts all over his walls, decorated with "I love you" or "We love you". Sam whittled a kiwi from a block of wood, and Rudolph wrote out an itinerary for his future trip to New Zealand. Rudi spent as much time as he could with his ailing father. They did not talk a lot – they never had – but the bond was close. Rudi would miss him; he had always been nearby, except during the war years. Their final chat was brief: Rudi asked if they had done the right thing in uprooting him to bring him to Canada. Sam replied, "You did not uproot me, I chose to come, and I have never regretted it for a moment."

"And nor have we, Dad. Our children have been so privileged to have had you in their lives." They were quiet for a while, each with his own thoughts. Rudi thought his father had dozed off, and rose to leave, when Sam sighed and murmured, "Mary." He stared at Sam. His father was gone, his dying thought for his dear wife.

News reached the family in New Zealand just as the Beatles arrived for a tour. Mayhem reigned wherever the four young men went, but for Samuel Hamilton's family there were other things to think about. Those who had visited him in 1958 arranged a memorial service for him, and many of the widespread family gathered to remember this man who was the last of his generation, and the first New Zealand-born Hamilton. Sarah, Joseph and Charles realised that they were now the "older generation" and Rudi too, even though he was younger. Time was relentlessly marching on.

With ten teenagers in the family, however, the Beatles could not be ignored. When they arrived at Christchurch airport Clarissa was there, with her cousins Charles and John charged with keeping her safe. Her own brother would not have a bar of such duties. It was chaos! But they did all arrive home safely, and little detail was given. Later in the same year Rudi took Adrienne and Rudolph to the airport in Vancouver, mostly out of curiosity. What a lot of screaming girls, beside themselves! Thank goodness Adrienne showed more self-control.

A major event took place in New Zealand in July, 1967, the change from sterling to decimal currency. For children and young adults this was not a problem, but for the elderly it was an obstacle some never overcame. For middle-aged business people it was a lingering headache. To make matters worse weights and measures changed to metric at the same time. Conversion charts became a necessity.

For Joseph, now aged sixty-seven, it was complicated. Yards became metres (but were not equal), and then the customer's bill was in dollars, which sounded huge, because one pound was two dollars. Fortunately his daughter Catherine, on leaving school, had joined her father in the business, as he had always hoped she would, and now her ability to grasp all these changes was invaluable. Joseph could not retire yet: Catherine was too young to run the business, but in two or three years the time would be right. He found himself relying more and more on her, as well as her mother. Edna seldom worked in the shop now, but she helped as needed. She worried about Joseph working so hard, and hoped he could find time for more leisure. She would try to persuade him to hire a manager, to reduce his stress.

CHAPTER 8
Full Circle

It was 1968 and two young men were ready to spread their wings. Now twenty-four Sam Hamilton had never settled to any career. Strong and muscular, he was good at ice hockey, but not good enough to be a professional player. He enjoyed outdoor work, but it did not satisfy him, he was too restless. His father recognised his wanderlust. "We chose the right name for you – at your age your grandpa set off for the Yukon goldfields. Perhaps you need to see the world." Sam had worked and saved with this in mind.

His brother Rudolph had left school last year with the clear idea of fulfilling his pledge to Grandpa Sam. He had taken whatever work he could find, squirreling away his pay to save for his travels.

Now the plans were in place. Rudi and Nola had no idea when their sons would return, but were glad they would be together. It was ironic that Adrienne, whom they had left at home as a baby, would be their only child still with them now. She was hardly a child, at nineteen, but she was happy to live at home. She commuted daily to her nursing course at Vancouver General Hospital. Nola had not encouraged her to go nursing, but it was in her genes. She fervently hoped her daughter would never be involved in wartime nursing,

It was March when Sam and Rudolph left for New Zealand. Flights were less arduous now but Sam remembered with nostalgia "the big adventure" when he was five years old. They arrived in early autumn and decided to head south before the cooler weather. They found labouring work, and were able to meet Marie, Len and their family, Alison, Joseph and Alice. Marie was their second cousin, so her teenaged children were third cousins. It was becoming complicated, but the main thing was they were family.

In their work they made friends with Hemi, a happy, hearty Maori man who taught them a lot about his culture. One of the first words he taught them was "whanau", and they realised this was the very word they needed. It meant more than just "family", covering all the third cousins too. Hemi took them to the "marae", the meeting ground and house, where they ate "hangi" food cooked in pits in the ground. At the marae they met Hemi's parents and his sister Pania, along with the rest of the whanau. Sam had eyes only for Pania, with her flawless skin, her beautiful long dark hair and brown eyes. He had never seen anyone so captivating. Rudolph had to remind him they were being introduced to others.

Pania told them that she and her friend Moana were going to make a trip to Wellington for Easter. Moana had whanau there.

"But aren't you too young to go alone?' asked Sam.

"We are both twenty-one!" retorted Pania. Hemi joined the group, and asked when Sam and Rudolph were planning to go north.

"That would be a good time," said Sam, without consulting Rudolph. "When is Easter, anyway?"

"We're booked on the night ferry on April 9th, arriving in Wellington on Wednesday 10th."

Back at work Hemi confessed he was worried about Pania. She seemed so confident but she had never been away from home before.

"Can you go on that ship and look after her, Sam?" Little did he know what he was asking.

Sam promised to keep in contact with Hemi, who gave him the family's address. Rudolph and Sam moved up to Richard and John's farm, out of Christchurch. There they worked for several weeks, helping with harvesting. At the weekends they socialised with whanau, such a convenient word.

April came around, and the big centennial celebration of Joseph and Henrietta Hamilton's arrival in Christchurch was about to take place. Sam and Rudolph planned to climb "Great-Grandpa's tree" and have Charles take a photo for their parents. What a pity they would be absent, and Adrienne too. Everyone else would be there. Bernadette and Tom and their four children were coming across from the West Coast; Vicki and Bruce, with their two, were coming from the North Island; Marie and Len, and their three children, were coming by train from Southland. Even Marjorie and Bernard, with their two, were flying down from Auckland. All the local cousins would be there, of course. It was going to be a huge celebration. Sarah had pinned up all the family charts on the walls in the old house. The boys decided if they were going to represent Grandpa Sam's branch of the family they would give it one hundred per cent.

Meanwhile, Rudi made a snap decision – they had to be there. If he and Adrienne took a week's leave and added Easter to it, then the three of them could fly over and walk in on the party. They would have to return by April 15th, though.

Not a word was said to the family, and no-one noticed when a taxi pulled up at Sarah and Jim's house. With forty people present, no-one was aware of three more joining them, until the three strode up to Sam and Rudolph. Suddenly there was an eruption of shouts and back-slapping, and a few tears, as everyone realised the Canadian branch of the whanau had arrived. They were complete.

Adrienne was overwhelmed by the love and acceptance of this family she had never met, apart from the four who had visited Grandpa Sam. She began to understand why her father had decided they all had to come. Nola renewed friendships made in 1950, revelling in the warmth around her. But it was Rudi who was the star of the show – he was everywhere! First he greeted his cousins, Sarah and Charles, along with their spouses. Then he set about assigning everyone else to their correct branch of the family. This was no mean feat, as most of them were mere names on his wall chart at home. The task took him most of the afternoon, but finally he achieved it. Sarah realised she should have made name tags, but as they had not expected Rudi and his family, it had not occurred to her.

Vicki and Bruce invited Sam and Rudolph to join them after Easter. There was work they could help with on their new lifestyle block. The boys would spend Easter in Wellington and then take the train north.

Following the family party Sam and Rudolph joined their parents and sister at their hotel in the city, where they talked late into the night. Tiredness evaporated for a time, but eventually jetlag caught up with the new arrivals. It had been an amazing, memorable day, and Grandpa Sam would have been very proud of them all. One hundred years of Hamiltons in New Zealand – someone should be writing a record of this. Maybe Joseph would do it.

The weather forecast was for a tropical cyclone, but there was little concern as it was scheduled to veer away from the coast. The ferry would sail as usual, leaving Lyttelton, the port of Christchurch, at eight o'clock in the evening on April 9th.

Hemi had written to Sam, repeating his request that he and his brother take care of his sister Pania and her friend Moana. The girls were upbeat.

"How can we be worried? The ship is called 'Wahine' [wa-hee-nay], which means woman and 'Moana' means the sea. We have everything in our favour," said Pania.

The four spent the evening in one of the lounges. They parted company at about eleven o'clock, agreeing to meet just before seven in the morning, when the ferry was due to berth in Wellington harbour. Bedding down in their bunks, none of them was aware that they were about to endure one of the most severe storms in New Zealand history.

All was well as they hugged the coast of the South Island, but when they reached the open waters of Cook Strait they were buffeted by winds of one hundred miles per hour. Visibility was reduced and the captain knew they were in trouble. In the wind the ship rolled violently, crockery was heard crashing to the floor, and passengers were clinging to each other.

Fighting to keep control, the captain tried to enter the long harbour that would give his ship some shelter. But she lost her starboard propeller when she scraped against submerged rocks, and then the port engine failed. At the same time the winds increased to one hundred and fifteen miles per hour, making the ship list to starboard and take on water. Visibility was now zero and the Wahine was moving backwards. It was 6.30 a.m.

On board there was chaos. The crew were attempting to calm frantic passengers, and Sam was hearing Hemi's words, "Take care of Pania", but he had no idea where the girls' cabin was. It had not seemed proper to ask last night. The boys dressed, grabbed their passports and wallets and headed up on deck. What they saw stopped them in their tracks. They could just make out hills on both sides, so they must be in the harbour. The crunch they had felt minutes ago was apparently the ship striking a reef in the harbour, and now water was gushing into the vehicle deck below them.

They had to find the girls. They split up, arranging a place to meet, and set off in different directions. It was Sam who came upon them, huddled in the corner of one of the lounges with their bags. All the bravado of the night before was gone. Sam gave each of them a bear hug. They staggered back to the arranged meeting place.

Although the ship was anchored it was not safe. Calming announcements were broadcast at regular intervals, but everyone knew that, at some time, they were going to have to abandon ship.

Hours went by and conditions worsened. The cyclone had changed course and the gales had gained in intensity, barrelling down the harbour. As the ship listed it became obvious that most of the lifeboats would be inaccessible, some maybe even under water. Still there was no "Abandon Ship!" call. How could they possibly send people into that maelstrom? There were seven hundred and thirty-four people on board, from babies to grandparents. How would they survive?

Finally the mournful signal sounded, six long hours after the Wahine hit the reef. Only four lifeboats could be used, but thirty inflatable rafts were launched as well. Many of these were flipped by the huge waves. Passengers leapt into the sea and swam for shore, while others were blown to the rocky beach on the other side of the harbour.

Sam and Rudolph stayed to help, and the girls, Pania and Moana, assisted older passengers into rafts. A violent wave sent Pania skidding across the deck. She had to let go of her elderly charge, who fell into the raging sea, and she would have gone too but for Sam's quick reaction. He grabbed her foot and dragged her back to him, lifting her and holding her to him as she wept for the unknown person lost to the sea.

It was time to go. All four had lifejackets, and had attached their identities to their jackets. They leapt into the waves and struck out for the nearer shore. They were swimming into the wind, but with the boys helping they eventually felt stones beneath their feet and hands reaching out to them, placing dry blankets over them and guiding them to a first aid station.

In Christchurch Rudi, Nola and Adrienne listened in horror to the news flashes. Nola could only think, "Thank goodness they are strong swimmers." There was no way to contact her boys – she would have to wait for them to call her – and there were reports of fatalities. The weather in Christchurch was wild, with trees toppling and electricity wires causing power cuts. Schools were closed and the wind seemed to be increasing in its fury. If it was like this here, what must it have been like on that ferry?

When the telephone rang in their room, all three jumped up and reached for it. It was reception with an outside call for them. Rudi took control, but all three shared the joy of hearing Sam and Rudolph's voices. They were shaken but unhurt, and the girls were safe too. All four had lost possessions but had their lives, unlike the fifty-one known to have perished.

Rudi was able to bring their flight to Wellington forward a day, to enable them to be with their boys. Nola desperately needed to hug them. They were able to spend three days together, hearing all about the tragedy and the acts of heroism, before flying to Auckland to prepare for their return home to Canada. Rudi was carrying with him a copy of both "The Press" and "The Dominion". What a story to tell his workmates on Tuesday! Both he and Nola it was all unreal, in spite of the time with their sons.

Sam was anxious about Pania. She had given him the address of Moana's family, where the girls would be staying, insisting as they parted, "Keep in touch." Once they had seen their parents and Adrienne off at the airport, they took a train to visit the girls. They were given a heroes' welcome by Moana's family, much to their embarrassment. No doubt the part they had played had been exaggerated. It was good to see Pania back to her vivacious self, Sam thought. He strolled out into the yard, hoping that she would follow. Moana's aunty gave her a nod, and she was there in a flash. It was the first time they had been together without Rudolph and Moana, and Sam felt flustered at first, not knowing what to say. Pania linked her arm through his as they wandered through the garden, and Sam relaxed.

He told her that he and Rudolph were going to stay with their cousins out of Palmerston North for a couple of weeks, to help on their farm, and that they were due to fly home to Canada after that. He felt pressure on his arm as he said this, but she said nothing. Taking a deep breath, he asked if he could visit next weekend. If he came down on the Friday afternoon train he could stay two nights at the backpackers' near the station, and see her on Saturday and Sunday. Pania's smile told him all he needed to know.

Aunty gave a knowing look when they returned to the group inside. She sensed love in the air. Would Pania's parents approve? What would protective brother Hemi have to say? These boys would be returning to Canada in a week or two, and time would tell if the spark would stay alight. In the meantime she would give them her support.

The ensuing week was long for Sam. Vicki and Bruce made them very welcome and paid them for their work. Charles had left home and John was in his final year at boarding school, which meant they were glad of helping hands. Although it was a small block of land, Bruce had planted crops, and workers were needed to harvest them.

Rudolph enjoyed the work, but Sam was restless. Usually happy-go-lucky, he was battling with something. Rudolph had never seen him like this. On the Friday Sam went off to Wellington on the train, seeming more energised than he had all week. He had not mentioned Pania's name all week, but Rudolph was making his own assumptions about the purpose of the visit.

It was not what they had arranged, but Pania could not wait till Saturday morning, when she knew he was arriving on Friday night. Aunty had encouraged her to meet the southbound train, giving her some worldly advice as well. A girl should not throw herself at a man, but there was no harm in being there, and no, Moana did not need to go with her – that would send the wrong message.

As the train came to a halt Sam gathered his things. There was no hurry; plenty of others wanted to be on their way ahead of him. He sauntered along the platform towards the red brick station building, thinking how convenient it was that the backpackers' building was so close.

There was a movement to his right. He stared. It was Pania! Without a thought he wrapped her in his arms, just as he had on the ship. Then it had been from relief that she was safe, now it was the delight of seeing her. Whatever the reason, it felt good as she snuggled against him.

They walked together to his accommodation and checked him in. Pania knew a good place to eat, where they could sit and talk. This time the words came easily and Sam poured out the conflict he was feeling. He knew he had found his "one woman", but he was due to fly away in ten days. What should he do? He felt at home in New Zealand, but he could not stay on without thinking things through, and changing his visa conditions. Nor could he expect Pania to leave her whanau and relocate to Canada.

Arranging to meet the next morning, they parted at the station. They both had a lot to think about, but wanted to enjoy each other's company in the meantime. Lying on his bed that night Sam thought about his parents. One from New Zealand, one from Canada, they had met in Egypt. How did they decide which country would be their home? Did it have something to do with women wanting to stay close to their parents? Could he settle in New Zealand? What would he do to provide for a family? It was well after midnight before he fell asleep.

There was a fair in town, with rides and stalls along the waterfront. Sam and Pania rode everything, ate candyfloss, and even visited the fortune teller, although both were nervous about this. She told them she saw happiness and three small people in their future. They laughed and wandered on, stopping at a booth to have their photo taken. They bought a copy for each of them.

It was so much fun that they went back the next day to enjoy the rides again. Both were exhausted by the time they caught the train together on Sunday evening. Promising to write to each other, and knowing there was a long separation ahead, they parted at Pania's stop with a lingering kiss.

Back at the farm Sam tried to get his thoughts together. He wrote to Hemi, confessing that he had fallen in love with Pania. He said he knew there would be obstacles, but he was prepared to deal with them. He was delighted to receive a reply, in which Hemi said he couldn't think of anyone he would rather have as a new brother. That was Hemi, short and to the point.

Sam suggested to Rudolph that, rather than take the long train ride to Auckland ahead of their flights, they go back to Wellington and fly from there. Rudolph knew this was to give Sam a chance to farewell Pania. He could see there was a real attachment between them, and that Sam was struggling with his emotions.

Seeing his older brother's distress at the airport, as he farewelled the girl he loved, Rudolph reflected on the complexity of human beings. Sam had always been his rough-and-tumble big brother, yet here he was, brought to tears as he tore himself away from the love of his life for who knew how long.

Rudolph was looking forward to being at home with his family. He had fulfilled his promise to Grandpa Sam and had climbed Great-Grandpa's tree. Although events since that day had eclipsed the family centenary, that tree would always be, for him, the highlight of their journey to New Zealand. They had completed the circle begun by Joseph and Henrietta in 1868.

Epilogue

Sam and Pania held a long-distance courtship, with frequent letters back and forth. Sam was undertaking an adventure tourism course, which he loved, and Pania was working in a department store, while living at home. There were no immediate plans to be reunited, eighteen months on from Sam's departure.

Suddenly the letters from Pania ceased. A month went by. Something was wrong. Another month dragged by. None of Sam's increasingly desperate letters was answered. He decided to write to Hemi.

After a long delay (Hemi did nothing fast, especially writing a letter) Hemi passed on news which almost broke Sam's heart. At a family party Pania had been raped by a cousin who was drunk, and had become pregnant. Although she had had an abortion, Pania still felt soiled, and not good enough for Sam. She could not bring herself to tell Sam, but had given Hemi permission to pass on the explanation for her lack of letters. She would not be writing any more.

Angry at what had happened Sam talked with his parents. Their advice was, "If you love this girl, now is the time to show it."

A quick letter to Hemi followed. "Don't tell her, but I'm coming." In a week or so he was there, but Pania did not seem happy to see him. She was emotionally battered, and could not meet his gaze. Her mother took Sam aside and gently explained it was not that Pania did not love him: she simply did not love herself. They would have to be patient and work to build up her self-esteem.

It took time. Sam found a job with a rafting company, and threw himself into his work. The more tired he was the better he felt. On his days off he went to see Pania. Gradually she heard what he was saying, that he loved her even more than before.

After six months he silently passed her a small package one day.

"It's not my birthday, Sam."

"No, it's not."

"Then what . . .?"

"Do you remember the fortune-teller?"

Her eyes lit up, and she opened the parcel. Sam knelt at her feet, taking the box from her hands.

"Pania, will you please put me out of my misery and marry me?"

"Oh Sam, you really want me?"

"You are the other half of me. I am incomplete without you."

"Then yes, I will marry you."

Two months later they were married, and they went on to fulfil the fortune-teller's prophecy by having three children – three more Hamiltons for the family tree.

THE END

Sources

Modes of transport in 19th century – Museum of Transport and Technology, Auckland.

The Industrial Revolution, children in factories, Lord Shaftesbury, etc. –
M.E. Beggs Humphreys, *The Industrial Revolution*.

For details of 1888 earthquake damage in Christchurch – *The Press*, September 6,
1888 (Reprinted).

Yukon gold rush – Zaslow, "The Opening of the Canadian North", 1870–1914.

Causes of the First World War and Europe between the wars – M.L.R. Isaac, *A
History of Europe 1870–1950*;
New Zealand in the Twenties, R. Chapman and E.P. Malone;
Great Britain between the Wars, W.F. Mandle.

The Depression – W.B.Sutch, *Poverty and Progress in New Zealand*.

Nazism – Hermann Mau and Helmut Krausnick (translated by Andrew and Eva
Wilson), *German History 1933–45*.

N.Z. Troops in World War ll – Richard Wolfe, *On Active Service – N.Z. at War*.

Ballantyne's fire – Eugene C. Grayland, *New Zealand Disasters*.

Tangiwai Disaster – Richard Wolfe, *Looking Back*;
The Weekly News – Those Were the Days, the 1950s;
Lorain Day and Tim Plant, *On This Day*.

Wahine Sinking – *The Weekly News – Those Were the Days, the 1960s*;
Bob Brockie and Ada Woolf, *I Was There!*;
Lorain Day and Tim Plant, *On This Day*.

About the Author

Born as Diane Moyna at the end of World War II, I was raised and educated in Christchurch, New Zealand, graduating BA in Languages (French, German and Latin) two days before marrying Ian Ross in 1967.

From 1972 – 1974 I travelled with my husband and child in Canada, Europe and the UK, returning to settle in Masterton till 1996. Most of these years were spent teaching, adding English as a Second Language to my subjects.

For family reasons I returned to Christchurch, where my husband and I opened a Bed and Breakfast business, as well as teaching and working in the Visitor Information service.

After the destruction of our home and business by earthquakes in 2010 and 2011 we moved north again to be closer to family, and now reside on the Kapiti Coast, north of Wellington.